CHAIN
OF
EVENTS

CHAIN
OF
EVENTS

A NOVEL

FREDRIK T. OLSSON

Little, Brown and Company

New York • Boston • London

Copyright © 2014 by Fredrik T. Olsson
Translation copyright © 2014 by Dominic Hinde

Little, Brown and Company
Hachette Book Group
1290 Avenue of the Americas, New York, NY 10104
littlebrown.com

First North American Edition, November 2014
First published in the English language in Great Britian by Sphere, August 2014
Originally published in Sweden as *Slutet på kedjan* by Wahlström & Widstrand, March 2014

Little, Brown and Company is a division of Hachette Book Group, Inc. The Little, Brown name and logo are trademarks of Hachette Book Group, Inc.

The publisher is not responsible for websites (or their content) that are not owned by the publisher.

The Hachette Speakers Bureau provides a wide range of authors for speaking events. To find out more, go to hachettespeakersbureau.com or call (866) 376-6591.

ISBN 978-0-316-33500-3
LCCN 2014940683

10 9 8 7 6 5 4 3 2 1

RRD-C

Printed in the United States of America

PART 1

Base Four

Nothing would ever make me keep a diary.

Things happen. Time passes. Life begins and goes on and ends, and nothing in all the meaninglessness becomes better just because you write it down and look at it afterwards. One day, everything is going to be over, and if there's one thing I know it's that when the soil thuds on to the wooden lid above me there won't be a soul who wants to read what I did some Monday in March.

Nothing would make me keep a diary.
    Except for one thing.
    The realisation that soon there won't be anyone around to read it.

Tuesday 25 November.
    There's snow in the air.
    And fear in everyone's eyes.

1

The man they shot in the alley died too late.

He was a bit over thirty, dressed in jeans, shirt and a windcheater. Far too little for the time of year, but he was reasonably clean and reasonably well fed – that's what they had promised him and that's what he had got.

But nobody had told him what would happen next. And here he was.

He had come to a halt between the stone walls right behind the old post office, breathless, thin grey wisps appearing and dissipating in the darkness before him. A restrained panic over the metal gate that sealed the end of the side street – it had been a conscious gamble and now he stood there with nowhere to go and with the sound of the three men in reflective vests getting closer and closer behind him.

In actual fact, he had still been alive when the news reached the European newspapers a quarter of an hour earlier, buried in the stream of agency reports. Three short lines about a man found dead in the centre of Berlin, shortly after four o'clock on Thursday morning. They didn't explicitly say he was homeless and on drugs, but that was the impression you got between the lines and it was fully intentional. If you're going to lie you're better off telling the truth.

At best, the news might find its way into the morning papers in a side column with other bits of non-news. That would be more than enough – it was one of many safety measures and it probably wasn't even necessary. An explanation, just in case anyone saw them as they lifted the lifeless body in the darkness, carried it to the waiting ambulance, shut the back door with a smooth clunk and drove away into the fine freezing rain with the requisite spinning blue lights.

Not to a hospital.

Then again, there was nothing a hospital would have been able to do.

Inside the ambulance, three men sat in silence, hoping they had made it in time.

They hadn't.

2

It didn't take more than a few seconds for the police to force the elegant double doors to the stairwell, smash the lead-lined windows and unbolt the lock from the inside.

The real obstacle was the metal gate that came next. It was security-proofed, heavy and probably extremely expensive, it was closed and locked and the only thing that stopped them from coming to the aid of the middle-aged man who was reported to be in the apartment.

If he was even still alive.

The call had come in to the Norrmalm division in the early morning, and quite a bit of time had passed while the switchboard tried to establish that the woman making it was reliable, sober and that the call wasn't a hoax. Did she know the man? Yes, she did. Could he be somewhere else? No, that's impossible. When did she last see him? Not long ago, they'd spoken on the phone yesterday evening and he'd been mellow and calm and made small talk about this and that. And that scared her – when he complained, she knew where she was with him, but here he was putting on a brave face, trying to sound positive, and she just couldn't put her finger on why. And when she called him this morning and there was no answer, the realisation came as a stab from inside. This time, he'd gone through with it.

The woman had been articulate and precise, and when the switchboard operator eventually accepted her story, he alerted both the police and the ambulance service and went on to his next call.

As soon as the first patrol made it to the scene they knew the woman had been right.

The doors were locked. Inside, they could see the closed security door as a smudged pattern through the door's stained glass. And somewhere even further inside a radio was playing classical music, the sound mixing with the gurgling of water pouring into an over-full bathtub.

And that was an extremely bad sign.

Two steps further down in the elegant stairwell stood Christina Sandberg, staring straight through the black painted steel mesh ringing the lift shaft, eyes pinned to every movement over by the door to what had once been her own apartment.

Yellow, burning flakes of metal rained down from the locksmith's angle grinder as it ate through the security door, the one she had resisted installing for so long, until finally she was forced to accept it after the night when everything changed.

They put it in to protect them. And today he might die because of it. If she hadn't been so terribly, uneasily worried she would have been extremely, tremendously angry.

Behind the locksmith, four policemen were restlessly treading water waiting for something to do, and behind them stood two equally impatient paramedics. At first they'd been calling out to him – 'William,' they shouted, 'William Sandberg!' – but they didn't get any answer and eventually they gave up, slipped into silence and let the angle grinder do its job.

And all Christina could do was to watch.

She'd been the last one at the scene. She had thrown on a pair of jeans and a suede coat, tucked her discreet blonde curls into a ponytail and jumped into the car despite having found a perfect parking spot and despite having promised herself not to move it again until the weekend.

By then, she'd tried to call him several times, the first time as soon as she got up, then on her way to the shower, and then once more before she even had time to dry her hair. It was after that that she called the emergency services, and it had taken them ages to realise what she already knew. What, in fact, she had known deep inside from the moment she woke up, but had tried to push away the same way she did the guilty conscience that always came when they talked.

She hated herself for still keeping in contact with him. He had taken it much harder than her, not because her sorrow was any less but because he was the one who allowed himself to feel it, and despite two years of discussing and reasoning and going over the whys and the maybes and the what ifs, nothing ever seemed to change. She had been given the honour of bearing both their sorrows, plus an extra helping of guilt because she felt that the distribution wasn't fair.

But there you go. Life wasn't fair.

If it were, she wouldn't be standing here now.

Eventually, the security door gave way and the police and paramedics streamed into the apartment ahead of her.

And then, time ceased to function.

Their backs disappeared into the long hallway and the emptiness they left behind just went on and on and refused to end. After an unbearable length of seconds or minutes or years she could hear the music turned off, and then the water, and then everything was completely silent and that's how it remained.

Until, finally, they came back out.

They avoided looking into her eyes as they ducked around the tight corners, out of the hallway, through the small passageway past the lift. A sharp turn towards the spiral staircase without bumping into the expensive, frescoed walls, and then down, down, quickly but carefully, slowly but no time to waste.

Christina Sandberg pressed herself against the steel mesh to let the stretcher past, down towards the ambulance parked on the pavement outside.

Under the plastic oxygen mask lay the man she once called her husband.

∞◯∞

William Sandberg didn't really want to die.

Or to put it correctly: it wasn't his first choice.

He would rather live and be healthy, have a passable life, learn to forget, find a reason to wash his clothes and wake up every morning to put them on, and then to go out and do something that mattered to someone.

He didn't even need to have all of that. A couple of things would do. All he wished for was a reason to stop thinking about the things that hurt. And when he never got one, the next alternative on the list was to put an end to it all.

That obviously hadn't gone too well, either.

'How're you feeling?' asked the young nurse standing before him.

He was half-sitting in the crisp, over-washed bedclothes, made up in the classic way with the sheet folded over the edge of a yellow hospital blanket, as if the healthcare system still refused to accept the existence of the duvet.

He looked at her. Tried to not show how the pain from the poisons in his body still bothered him.

'Worse than you would like,' he said. 'Better than I had planned.'

It made her smile, and that surprised him. She probably wasn't any older than twenty-five, blonde and quite pretty. Or perhaps that was just the result of the soft light from the window behind her.

'Seems it wasn't your time after all,' she said. Her tone was matter-of-fact, almost conversational, and that surprised him too.

'There'll be plenty more chances,' he replied.

'Very good,' she said. 'Always be positive.'

Her smile was perfectly balanced: big enough to punctuate the irony, but sufficiently checked not to undermine the humour, and he suddenly found himself unable to come up with an answer. He was hit by an unpleasant feeling that the conversation was over and that she had won.

For several minutes he lay in silence and watched her work around the room. Efficient movements, a set schedule: drip to be changed, dosage to be regulated, details to be noted and checked against the patient record. A quiet efficiency. And he finally began to wonder if he'd misread her, and whether she had actually joked with him at all.

By then, her tasks were finished. She adjusted his sheets without making any discernible difference, and then stopped on her way out.

'Don't try anything stupid while I'm away,' she said. 'As long as you're in here, it is just going to mean a lot of extra work for both you and us.'

She winked a friendly goodbye, vanished out into the corridor and let the door close after her.

In his bed, William couldn't help feeling uncomfortable. Not because there was any reason to. All he knew was that he was uncomfortable. Why? Because she hadn't used the expected maternal tone, the one he'd already decided to be annoyed by? Or because her pithy comments were so unexpected that he'd allowed himself to feel challenged, almost amused?

No.

It took him a second, and then he knew.

He closed his eyes.

It was the tone. The tone was exactly the same.

Everything was exactly what *she* would have said.

Suddenly he wasn't bothered by the humming pain in his body any more – be it salt deficiency or dehydration or too much of some alien substance the pills had left in his tired, fifty-five-year-old body, all in vain and now destined to be broken down – nor by the searing wounds healing under the bandages they'd wrapped around his wrists. Instead, what tortured him was something else. It was that feeling again, the one that always, always came back to him, the one that attacked him with double strength if he ever managed to forget it, and that had finally made him go into the bathroom the evening before and finally decide to do it.

Just because he hadn't been able to see the signs.

There was no other way to express it, ironic as it was.

Him. Unable to interpret the signs.

The hell with it.

He should have asked her for something to calm him down when she was still here. A painkiller. Or diazepam. Or a bullet to his head if she could provide that, but she probably couldn't.

He was back in the same place as the previous evening: the endless fall through that dark passage, the destructive longing to hit the bottom and hopefully smash himself to death, getting rid of the thoughts that always managed to control him. Thoughts that deliberately seemed to allow him brief moments of hope, only to return with full force just to show him who's in charge.

He reached for the white cord hanging from the wall. Pulled it in, pressed the tube-shaped button to call for help. He hoped that it wouldn't be the same nurse coming back; it would be an irritating defeat to go from acerbic and articulate to having to ask her for sleeping pills. But then again, if she could help put him to sleep for a while, that was a price he'd be willing to pay.

So he pressed the button again.

To his surprise there wasn't any sound.

He pressed it again, longer this time.

Still nothing.

Not *that* strange, he told himself. After all, he wasn't calling for himself. As long as the buzzer went off somewhere else, wherever the doctors sat and did whatever doctors do, someone would notice and send a nurse to find out what he needed.

Then he saw the lamp. A red plastic casing on the wall just above where the alarm cord came out. Shouldn't it light up? Even if he couldn't hear it ring, surely the light should come on to show he'd pressed it?

He pressed the button again. And again. But nothing happened.

He was so occupied by the malfunctioning alarm that the sound of the opening door made him jump. He glanced towards it, tried to decide whether to choose defence or attack: complain about the broken lamp or apologise for pushing the button so hysterically?

But his thoughts didn't get any further before his eyes adjusted to the backlight from the window. And then, none of the options seemed valid.

The man standing at the end of his bed was neither a doctor nor a nurse.

He was wearing a suit, a shirt without a tie, and a pair of boots, disproportionately heavy compared to the rest of his attire. He was probably around thirty, but it was hard to tell with his head being shaved and his posture screaming of years of extensive physical training. Perhaps he was older than he looked. Or the other way around.

'Are those for me?' William said, for lack of anything better.

The man glanced at the flowers in his hand, almost as if he didn't know he was holding them. He didn't answer, dropped them in the washbasin. They had just been an excuse to help him blend in and navigate the corridors without standing out.

'William Sandberg?' he asked.

'Barely,' William replied. 'But yes.'

The man stood there; a long silence as they both looked at each other. Measured the other one with their gaze, even though William hardly would've been able to put up any resistance from his position. The entire situation was odd, and William could feel his senses brace themselves inside.

'We've been looking for you,' the man said at last.

Really? William tried to understand what he was talking about. He wasn't aware of anyone trying to contact him lately, but to be fair he probably wouldn't have noticed if someone had.

'I've been having a few problems of my own.'

'So we've gathered.'

We? What the hell was this?

William sat a little straighter, straining to give him a casual smile.

'I would love to offer you something, but they're not as generous with the morphine as you'd hope.'

'We're going to need your help.'

It came out of nowhere, almost too fast, and there was something in the voice that made William lower his guard for a moment. The young man looked at him, his gaze steady, but something hiding behind it. Urgency. Maybe even fear.

'Then I think you've got the wrong person,' William said, thrusting out his arms. Or rather, he tried to. IV lines and ECG cables limited his movements, but it all served to strengthen the point he was trying to make: William Sandberg was hardly in a state to help anyone with anything.

But the young, well-built man shook his head. 'We know who you are.'

'And who is "we"?'

'That's not important. The important thing is you. Your skills.'

The feeling that pierced William's body was familiar and unexpected at the same time. This was a conversation he would have anticipated twenty years ago. Perhaps even ten. Back then it wouldn't have surprised him. But now?

The man at the foot of the bed spoke impeccable Swedish, but somewhere below the surface there was an accent. Too polished to place. But definitely an accent.

'Where are you from?'

The man looked at him with feigned disappointment. As if

William should realise that he wouldn't be getting an answer, and as if even bothering to ask was undignified.

'SÄPO? Ministry of Defence? Foreign power?'

'I'm sorry. I can't say.'

'Okay,' said William. 'Then give them my best and thank them for the flowers.'

He said it with an air of finality: the conversation was over, and to stress his point he lifted the cord with the patient alarm again. Pressed the button with his thumb, gaze fixed on the young man as if to underline just how definitely over the conversation was. Again, nothing happened.

'If that'd been working the light would come on,' said the man.

Unexpected. William looked at him.

Another moment of sizing one another up, and then William let go of the cord, let it fall on to his stomach, draped across the yellow hospital blanket.

'I am fifty-five years old,' he said. 'I haven't been working for years. I am the Great Wall of China: I was important a long time ago but today I'm just crumbling away.'

'My superiors take a different view.'

'And who are your superiors?'

There was an edge in his voice. He was getting tired of the conversation; he just wanted to have his pills and float away, not to play Cold War games with an over-exercised puppy who'd arrived a decade too late.

But it was the young man who closed the conversation first.

'I'm sorry,' he said again. He sighed apologetically before turning on his heels.

He's leaving, William thought. A strange end to a strange conversation.

But when the man opened the door to the corridor there were two other men waiting to be let in.

∞◯∞

The clock showed ten past one in the afternoon as the medical team wandered through the cavernous corridors of the Karolinska University Hospital's intensive care unit to check on the progress of their charges.

They had completed half of their round without any great surprises, and their next patient was a man in his fifties who had attempted suicide: chemical overdose and lacerations to the arms. Hardly a case that would warrant a longer stay in intensive care. He'd been given a blood transfusion, both to compensate for what he'd lost from his wounds and to dilute his high dosage of prescription medicine, but his condition hadn't been life threatening when he arrived; either he'd made a mistake and taken too low a dosage or, quite possibly, he was just another case of someone trying to get the attention of people around him.

In any case, there was little doubt that he would soon cease to be their responsibility. Dr Erik Törnell stopped outside the patient's room, closed the medical record in his hand, and nodded at his colleagues: this would be a quick one.

The first thing they saw when they entered was the empty bed.

A bouquet of flowers lay head-down in the basin, a vase on the bedside table was turned over and smashed, the sheets were crumpled up on the floor and the IV line swung freely from the drip.

The bathroom was empty. The cupboard emptied of all the belongings the patient had arrived with. And the drawer in the small cabinet pulled out and overturned.

William Sandberg was gone.

After an hour's search it was concluded that he was nowhere in the vicinity of the hospital, and nobody had any idea why.

3

The ambulance that wasn't an ambulance stood parked in the middle of a large field of random, self-sown vegetation – wild plants stubbornly growing in the face of numerous unconscious attempts to wipe them out, time and time again growing back up from craters, nooks and blast holes. There was a slight irony in all the vitality, but it was an irony lost on anyone who knew that the place existed.

The men wearing reflective vests and paramedics' clothes were long gone, cleansed, rinsed and well on their way through the list of predefined security protocols.

Only the homeless man remained in the ambulance.

They had taken his life away from him, there was no doubt about it. But didn't they also give him a new one? A better one? Who knows if he didn't even get to live longer this way – perhaps the street would already have taken him if they'd let him stay where he was? They gave him food, clothes, somewhere to live. He had a purpose. He exercised. They even gave him an education of sorts.

But nobody had told him about the fear.

About the symptoms.

Who could have known it would go this far?

'It is what it is,' said the young, crew-cut helicopter pilot, as if every single one of Connors' thoughts had been printed out on a telex tape for him to read. He sat in his seat up front, headphones fighting to let them hear their own voices instead of the perpetual drone of the rotors above them.

Connors nodded back.

'Shall we?' the pilot asked him. Drummed his fingers against the throttle.

This time Connors paused before nodding, but they both knew that sooner or later he would. Without his binoculars the ambulance was just a shining dot far away in the early dawn, and yet he wouldn't take his eyes off of it.

As if he could avoid the inevitable.

As if he sat with the answers in one hand and an exam in the other, trying to come up with a different response, time after time, even though he knew what the correct one was.

Responsibility. An overrated thing to have.

But things were what they were.

He signalled his agreement with a move so slight that it could have been an involuntary shake from the turbulence, but the crew-cut young man registered it and did what he was supposed to. He already held the tiny box in his hand, and all he had to do was to press the button.

When the ambulance exploded in a fiery cloud the job was done.

And a new generation of grass and wild flowers were given a new crater to conquer.

4

When William Sandberg woke up for the second time on the day he originally planned not to wake up at all, he found himself several thousand feet up in the air.

The realisation immediately kicked him wide awake.

He was seated in a leather armchair, soft, warm and deep enough to fit right in in front of a home cinema in any suburban home. Outside the acrylic windows a low sun shone straight towards him, cutting through an inviting cotton landscape of tightly packed clouds.

He was on a plane. And he'd been dreaming.

As always, the dream lingered, without form but with a feeling of discomfort. For a second he considered doing what he had learned to do, to let the brain go on a journey back along the feeling in search of whatever it was that had caused it to begin with. More often than not it turned out to be the same thing. And more often than not it tortured him even more to go back and revive the images. But it was the only way he knew to get rid of them.

However, he let it be. He made himself focus on where he was, motionless in his chair as if the slightest movement would tell them he was awake and that it was time to come in and neutralise him.

Them? Who?

He didn't know.

The only thing he knew was that the last thing he remembered was three men in suits walking into his hospital room, that he had a persistent thirst in his mouth, and that he was currently in the custody of someone with a great deal of money.

It wasn't his first time aboard a private jet. But it was the most ostentatious one he had ever seen from the inside. His room – because it actually was a complete room; across from him there was another armchair, and between the seats a wall-mounted table hovered as a generous, common workspace – was divided from the rest of the plane by a sturdy panel wall. A door of imitation wood led to what was most likely a small corridor along the plane's port side. It was probably locked. Surely not very hard to force if you tried. But definitely locked.

Then again, he asked himself, why was that so certain?

There was nothing that suggested that he was a prisoner. The belt that someone had carefully tightened around his midriff was a normal seat belt, and when he pulled at the clasp it released as it should, and the only thing stopping him from standing up was his own decision to stay seated.

A stream of fresh air from a fan in the ceiling. Soft warmth from the sun outside. The day before, he had stuffed himself full of pills, and today he was sitting here. Wearing the hospital's shirt and shapeless trousers, slumped in an armchair that probably cost an average annual wage. If this was death, then death had a strange sense of humour.

It surprised him to be here. And it bothered him that it did. For a long period of his life he was perfectly prepared for things like this, or even for things that were considerably worse.

At the end of the 1980s, when William was in his thirties and the world was split between two superpowers in blue and red, he had been followed by vehicles through Stockholm on several occasions. He had parked his car and walked in complicated patterns through shopping centres and department stores, just as he had been taught to do, and every time he'd managed to lose his tail. He'd taken a taxi home and had a colleague collect his car a few days later, everything according to protocol. He had security cameras and alarm systems installed in his suburban house, almost invisible and outstandingly high-tech for the time, but that didn't stop the strange clicks in his home phone or the door-to-door salesmen who kept visiting his neighbours, then lingering in their cars trying to get a view of William's house. He was, quite simply, a highly interesting target, and it was all entirely because of his work.

But that was then. Back when he was active, young and promising – that blew over, as he used to say – and when his abilities were exceptional and in demand. Now he was discharged and surplus to requirements. Most of his work could probably be replaced by a few lines of code and a laptop from the high street.

He shook his head at himself. It was hardly the technological developments that made them transfer him. There were no external forces to blame; he'd made himself impossible to keep, to the point that they offered him retirement at barely fifty. He'd dug a hole for himself and he knew it, he'd jumped right into it and kept digging; and all the time he couldn't help enjoying it, taking an inexplicable pleasure in seeing everything he'd built up fall apart around him.

And now, here he was. With stiff muscles and a sandpaper tongue and two deep cuts in his wrists. On a very modern business jet. Spirited away by what couldn't possibly be anything but a foreign military power.

There was no logic to it whatsoever.

William Sandberg had been kidnapped.

But it had happened at least ten years too late.

∞◯∞

The young intern paid just as little attention to the piece of news as everybody else at the editorial desk had done that morning.

He was sitting at his large monitor, much too sleepy to concentrate on the article he was supposed to sketch out, and instead he'd turned to the long agency newsfeed, pretending to be responsible and up to date when all he really wanted was to avoid work for a minute without being too obvious.

He focused his gaze as best he could. Saw the constant stream of reports from news agencies around the world, short summaries in English of things that weren't important enough to merit their own newsflash.

It was unremittingly boring. But it was less boring than trying to summarise the debate about the rebuilding of central Stockholm for the thousandth day in a row. And even if ten out of ten messages would be dismissed by a click of the delete key, either because the news was too small or because it was geographically irrelevant for the paper, he was still able to claim that he was actually working. If anyone asked what he was up to he could say that he was checking the feeds. It sounded a lot better than saying he was too hungover to write.

And here he was with yet another uninteresting piece of news on the screen in front of him, his right ring finger hovering above Delete. A homeless man had been found dead in an alleyway in Berlin, and though the report didn't explicitly say so, it wasn't too hard to discern that he had taken an overdose or drunk too much and passed out before freezing to death. It was a local story, and scarcely that. One more of the hundreds of stories he would glance at without taking any action.

He fought against an oncoming yawn, but lost.

'Late one last night?'

It was a female voice. And it was close. And he still had his mouth wide open.

Damn.

He had consciously not removed his baseball hat when he came in, but just as effectively as it shielded his face from the eyes of others, it also made it impossible for him to see what was happening beyond the monitor without turning his whole head upward.

Which he hadn't. And now she was standing there, and for how long? Obviously at least long enough to see him air his throat to the rest of the newsroom.

'No. It was, what's it called, no,' he answered, removing his hat, trying to look as if that was what he'd planned all along.

The woman didn't say a word, just as he knew she wouldn't. And that made him even more insecure, just as he knew it would. Christina Sandberg was at least twenty years older than him, but she was attractive in an almost inexplicable way, beautiful, natural and irritatingly pleasant. Not irritating because her pleasantness was false or over the top, but because he really wouldn't mind her having some unforgivable shortcoming, something to stop his eyes from constantly wandering in her direction and losing the ability to construct full sentences as soon as he tried to talk to her.

'You've got, I sent, in your,' he said, hoping that a weak nod would complete what he failed to communicate himself.

It had become an implicitly understood task for him to take her messages when she was out, and she thanked him, and continued towards her office with a string of good mornings to the other staff.

It occurred to him that she looked somewhat more sombre than usual. But he forced himself to drop the thought. He didn't know her, and he knew only too well that nothing good would come of an unrequited love for an older, phenomenally successful newspaper editor.

He returned to his screen. The report on the dead homeless man in Berlin. And with a quick push of a button the three lines of text vanished into the computer's waste bin, and the tired young man turned his eyes to the next uninteresting piece of news.

Christina shut the door to her office, hung up her suede coat on the hook by the glass front wall and closed her eyes for a second. People could probably see her, but if they did, so be it. In a few minutes she'd be back on top again, quick-firing and full of initiative, and when the day was over nobody would even remember those couple of seconds anyway.

It had been a tough morning. And the morning had brought a close to a tough night. She'd seen her ex-husband on a stretcher, carried out into an ambulance, and perhaps it would have been more humane to climb into her car and drive after it. It would have been more humane to spend the morning on a plastic chair in a corridor, waiting for him to wake up, so that she might go and sit on another plastic chair next to his bed and talk and ask why and hear him say the same things over and over again.

But Christina had been humane for a long time. She'd been humane until she couldn't take it, and then she'd been humane for a little while longer, and then it was enough. William was like a car she should've got rid of a long time ago – those were his own words – one that you drown in money and attention but that is irredeemably beyond saving and breaks in three new places for every two you fix. He couldn't get better, because he didn't want to get better. He'd lost his belief or verve or whatever it is that makes people do things with their life, and he'd almost taken Christina with him, until that one day, two years earlier, when she couldn't take it any more and marched out of their apartment.

She hadn't been back until today. Yes, he'd kept calling her, and yes, it wore her down every time she answered, but she managed to keep him at a distance and slowly, very slowly, she'd become herself again. Not because the sorrow was gone, but because she let it be there, along with everything else.

And that was how she wanted to keep it. She couldn't afford to let him drag her into the darkness again. So instead of spending the day at the hospital, she'd called the paper and said that she wouldn't be at her desk until after lunch.

She stayed out in the city for almost four hours. She tried to wind down the way that she always did: she turned off her phone, went to the big bookshop on Mäster Samuelsgatan, and selected a huge pile of newspapers and magazines in the section with imported titles, even though most of them were available for free at the office. Then she sat in the bar at the Grand Hotel, ordered an improbably expensive breakfast despite having no appetite, and sat there until everything that happened in the world made her own problems seem like small, unimportant distractions. When she was finished she took a walk in the November chill, through the entire city, and ended up back at her office on Kungsholmen.

She knew she would pay for it now. There would be thousands of questions from the staff, calls waiting to be made, articles that should already have been written. But now she would be prepared to deal with them.

She turned on her mobile phone. Scrolled through the mailbox on her computer while the phone spluttered into life.

And then, the news hit her from all directions at once.

At the same instant that the phone beeped to inform her she had thirty missed calls, she saw the four emails from the intern telling her that the hospital wanted her to call.

Even if her colleagues had forgotten that Christina Sandberg began the day by closing her eyes, none of them would forget how she ended it four minutes later. Rushing through the office, heart in mouth and with her phone in her hand.

∞◯∞

William remained in his plane seat for at least ten minutes before he could bring himself to move for the first time. He listened for sounds, conversation, for the slightest sign or clue to help him work out where he was and in whose company.

But he didn't find anything.

The only thing he heard was the slow whine of the engines and the moans from the plane's joints as it collided with air pockets. No voices, no footsteps, no signs that there was anyone else on board but himself. Which, obviously, there had to be.

It occurred to him that he was getting hungry, and he tried to remember how long it had been since he last ate, but couldn't.

Firstly, he didn't know how long he'd been unconscious. Then there was the fact that he'd been on a drip at the hospital, which probably meant the sensation of hunger was delayed.

That was annoying in itself. It made it harder for him to tell what time it was, and if he knew that, he might have been able to work out where he was and where he was going.

He glanced up at the tiny panel above his seat. For a brief moment he considered pushing the little button with a stylised stewardess, but he decided it wouldn't be a good idea and refrained. Instead he stood up, his back slightly bent even though the cabin was big enough to let him stand straight with a good few centimetres to spare, and in two quick steps he was at the door.

Hesitated. Considered his options.

The acoustic comfort made the plane's background noise considerably lower than in a typical commercial aircraft, but it was still sufficient to drown the sound of his movements. If someone stood outside the door they probably wouldn't have heard him get up and move towards it. In theory he would have a significant advantage, merely by virtue of surprise.

In reality, though, the element of surprise would vanish before he had time to use it. He was still groggy from all the chemicals he'd been carrying inside for the past twenty-four hours, and he was hardly in his prime to begin with. What he could have done in the past would be futile to even attempt today.

But he couldn't just stand there.

He decided to open the door. Whatever was waiting outside it.

Put his hand on the handle. Felt the cold metal.

Turned it. Carefully. No resistance. It wasn't locked, and he slowly twisted it ninety degrees and then there was a click and the door swung open.

To his surprise, there was nobody there. No guns, no guards, nobody telling him to stay where he was until he was called for. Instead, he stepped over the threshold, paused, and looked around him. A narrow corridor ran along the port side of the plane's fuselage, just as he'd thought, lined by the same oval windows as in his own little room. The floor was fitted with a plush carpet that must have cost a fortune, and the walls were furnished in fireproof artificial leather. A few metres further along, the corridor opened out into a more conventional cabin with at least twenty more seats, each as luxurious as his own but organised in pairs on either side of the aisle.

If William had expected a dramatic reaction to his entrance, he had to accept that he wasn't getting one.

At the front of the cabin by the closed cockpit door, two men were seated. One of them had his back to William and made no attempt to turn around, while the one sitting opposite looked up, met William's eyes, and that was it.

William recognised him immediately. Suit, shaved head, a military gravity on a boyish face. He was one of the two who had been waiting outside his room at the hospital, the one who had been holding the expensive-looking fountain pen and forced it into William's neck with a crisp, mechanical click, and it hadn't been until that moment that William realised it wasn't in fact a pen. That had been his last thought before waking up here.

The injector man nodded his head briefly, a mute signal to William to tell him he'd been noticed, and then he turned his close-cropped head to William's right. Behind the corner of the panel wall between the main cabin and William's own sat the man who had spoken to him at the hospital. He put down his newspaper – German, William noted as he stuffed it into the seat pocket in front of him – and got up. Not threatening, but not very friendly either. A smile on his face, but it was more a mechanical process than a sign of human feelings.

'Awake?' he said.

William gave him a wry look back, as if to say that the answer should be pretty self-evident. If he couldn't beat them physically he could at least fight them with sarcasm.

The man moved out into the aisle, positioned himself in front of William, his muscular body slightly bent under the roof of the cabin – he was about two metres tall, William realised, an impressive bull neck fighting its way out of the loosely buttoned shirt – and William stood still, waiting for whatever would happen next. He was prepared for two things. Either the man would ask him to sit down with the others or they would order him back into his private cabin and tell him to keep quiet.

Neither happened.

'There are toiletries in the cabinet in your cabin,' the bull neck said. 'If you want to freshen up a bit.'

'For what?' William asked.

The man avoided the question as if he hadn't heard it. 'The bathroom is right at the back.'

Okay then. William nodded in thanks. The situation was not exactly hostile, but not too welcoming either.

'I take it that if I ask where we're going you're not going to answer that either, right?' he said.

'I'm very sorry.'

'So you keep saying. You should talk to someone about that.'

He said it with a smile, but the man in front of him showed no signs of being amused. Nor angry. Nor sorry, even though he said he was. His stare was fixed, summoning and quite dull.

'At the back?' William asked without really wondering. And the bull neck nodded in reply.

∞○∞

It took less than half an hour for Christina to travel from Kungsholmen back to Kaptensgatan, despite it being the middle of the afternoon rush. She had pressed the nervous cab driver into running at least two red lights, and under his own initiative he'd taken a shortcut across a pavement, and now she was back outside the door of her old apartment for the second time that day.

She had her phone in her hand, still warm from being pressed against her ear for the duration of the journey, sometimes shouting, sometimes lecturing as if the person she was talking to was a child and as if she herself was a parent with very limited patience.

'How on earth do you lose a grown man?' she'd said at one point, catching the driver's bemused eyes in the rear-view mirror. 'You lose things! Information! Sometimes kids! But you damn well don't lose a patient who's just tried to commit suicide!'

But that was exactly what they had done.

They had searched the whole hospital, gathered all the staff, tried to question witnesses. But nobody had any idea how, why or even when William Sandberg vanished from the Karolinska University Hospital. They were still going through footage from the few security cameras the hospital had been allowed to install, and so far William seemed to be as absent from the security team's hard disk as he was from the face of the Earth.

Christina's face was exasperatedly red by the time she turned off her phone, and for once it wasn't because of the heat from the battery. She was angry. The world was full of idiots. Her cab driver was one of them, but she still rounded up when she paid – risking your licence had to be worth something, she thought – and she ran up the stairs, convinced that he'd tried again. And convinced that this time he'd succeeded.

The first thing she noticed when she entered what once had been her own apartment was the facial expression of the middle-aged policeman who showed her in. He had hair growth that seemed unable to decide whether it was a beard or the product of sloppy shaving, and in the middle of the scrub his mouth kept gasping for air, or trying to find words, or perhaps both. But while his mouth searched for the right thing to say, his eyes already spoke to her. 'We're sorry,' they said. 'We're sorry, but there's bad news.'

'Is he dead?' she asked.

It came so abruptly that she surprised herself. Wouldn't it be more appropriate to ask how he was? Or at least 'Is he alive'? But deep down she was already so certain she couldn't imagine anything else.

Which made her all the more surprised when the policeman finally spoke.

'We don't know,' he said.

'Don't know?' she asked.

No answer.

'Is he here?'

Again, the policeman didn't answer. Instead he looked anxiously at his feet for a moment. Behind him, Christina could see his colleagues moving about the apartment, occasional camera flashes from a room out of sight.

The man hesitated. Didn't like asking his next question, but he had to.

'Have you had problems in your relationship?'

'We separated two years ago. I think that counts as a problem.'

The mouth inside the beard didn't know whether to smile at her sarcasm or to lament the situation, so it turned to what it knew best and gasped for air again.

'Where is he?' she repeated.

He took a step to the side. Nodded down the hallway. 'We believe he decided to run away.'

It took a second for her to grasp what he'd said. Run away?

With a few brisk steps she hurried in the direction he'd pointed. She passed through the long pantry, past the living room and the library, the exact same route she'd taken countless mornings in her previous life, wearing only a dressing gown or towel, sometimes not even that. Happily ignorant of the fact that one day she'd be rushing through the same corridors to explain to the police in William's study that a man with no desire to live wasn't very likely to just 'run away'.

But when she entered the room she stopped.

She met the gaze of two police officers – perhaps forensics, she didn't really know – both standing by William's desk. She looked around. She hadn't been in there since their divorce, but just like the police she was immediately aware that something was missing. Or, rather, *everything*.

Along the long wall to the right of the door ran a writing desk, placed in front of the deep windows with a view over the roofs and chimneys of Östermalm, its bay windows and its roof terraces and its outdoor furniture that probably wasn't worth a third of what they cost. To the right of the desk stood a cabinet, and inside it was a mounting rack for hard disks and devices, plugged in to a network router in the middle.

At least that's what should have been inside the cabinet.

Instead, it hung open, and the racks were empty, just like the desk. Yellowed patches showed where two giant flat-screen monitors had stood until recently, and on both sides of the window were the shelves where he'd kept his extensive library of books on codes and statistics and chaos and all of the other things she'd stopped asking him about ages ago. Now the shelves stared emptily back at her. Everything was gone.

She shook her head. A decisive shake. A no.

And the policemen looked at her, waiting for her to explain what she meant.

'It's a burglary,' she said.

The two from forensics didn't say anything. But they looked at each other as if they knew something she didn't.

'He hasn't run away,' she said. There was a touch of desperation in her voice, and she heard it herself, pausing for a second to emphasise how inconceivable it was that they hadn't reached the same conclusion. 'He has nowhere to go, he's got nothing for him anywhere, I know that, I spoke to him yesterday evening! Why in heaven's name would someone like that just run away?'

They still said nothing, merely looked sympathetically at her before moving their gaze to something behind her back. It was the policeman with the facial scrub. She hadn't heard him come in, but now he stood there and worked his mouth like a stranded fish while everyone waited for him to speak.

'*Why*, we do not know,' he said, as if the fact itself was irrefutable. And then he tilted his head to say, 'Come.'

She let him guide her through an apartment that she knew better than him, all the way into what had once been her and William's bedroom. Everything was the same, the smell of the walls and the floor and the fabrics, and before she could stop it she was overcome by memories she didn't know she even had. From when they sold their house in the suburbs. When they moved into the city, because that was where they liked to be. When they were finally going to have a life of their own again.

If only they'd known.

The bed was made and everything was tidy, and the man with the non-beard continued further into the room, throwing a glance behind him to make sure she was following. Stopped in front of what used to be their wardrobe. Pulled open the sliding doors and looked at her in a way that implied he didn't have to say anything more.

He didn't.

The wardrobe was empty.

All of William's jackets and suits, his well-ironed shirts, everything was gone. The shelves of underwear, the shoes. She had to admit it. It did appear as if they were right. It was just that she knew they weren't.

'Less than twenty-four hours ago my former husband tried to take his own life,' she said. 'And you seriously think he has suddenly decided to pack up the kitchen sink and run away?'

'According to the neighbour across the hall two men from a

removal company were here and carried out a couple of crates shortly after twelve.'

'Removal men, or men with shirts with a removal company logo?'

'What do you mean?'

She let the question go unanswered. If she didn't give him an answer he would have to work it out for himself, and it was always a better strategy to make people think rather than supply them with the solution. Especially since she didn't really have one.

Instead, she left him standing in silence, turned round and walked out of the bedroom.

She allowed herself a walk through the entire apartment. The kitchen, the dining room, the guest room – the damned guest room, she walked right past it without allowing herself to think back – and continued out into the living room. The place was well furnished, almost pedantically so, still bearing the hallmarks of the expensive taste they'd developed during their time together. Most of it looked exactly as it did before she moved out, and if she hadn't known him so well, she would have been surprised at his ability to keep his home in good condition despite his own decline.

But she knew that was simply the kind of person he was. Order from chaos. Patterns and logic. It was the only way for him to survive, and when everything else around him was in free fall, that was exactly what he would hold on to. You don't stop being pedantic when things fall apart. Quite the contrary.

Finally, she returned to William's study. The two policemen had gone to join the non-beard in some other part of the apartment, and now she stood here all by herself, looking at the things that weren't there.

The computers.

The literature.

The black expensive notebook, the one that he loved and hated and hadn't ever been able to bring himself to use, first because it represented a beautiful memory, and then because of the same thing but for a different reason.

As if it were the book's fault there were memories. As if he could have preserved all the good, just by keeping things the way they were. As if what happened after wouldn't have taken place, if only he didn't touch the memory.

She forced herself to think of something else.

They were lurking around the corner, and she knew it: the thoughts and the emotions and the paralysis that came with them if she let it. The way he had done, and the way she'd learned not to.

Instead, she focused on the situation.

It didn't make sense.

It just didn't make sense that he would leave, not like this, why would he?

She knew him. She knew that he had nowhere to go, no reason to leave the only place he still felt secure. And the computers? Why would he take them? Had he even used them since everything happened?

Something wasn't right. She'd felt it from the moment she entered the room. Something important was missing.

But she hadn't been able to put her finger on what, and she stood for a while, trying to work out what had given her the feeling in the first place, whether it was only because she hadn't been in there for over a year or whether she had actually, unconsciously, discovered some detail she wasn't aware of. Yet.

She closed her eyes. Tried to imagine the room as it used to look. The brim-full, meticulously arranged bookshelves, the files and the papers, the pens that he loved – he was the only person she knew who could spend hours in front of the pen racks at one stationer after another – everything arranged in straight lines and sorted thoroughly. And now everything was gone.

Everything. Was there more? What else was missing, that should have been there but that she couldn't remember?

She went to the desk. Looked out of the window. Turned round. Took in the room from the opposite angle.

And then she stopped.

There wasn't something missing.

There was something left that shouldn't be.

∞◯∞

The toiletries in the tiny cabinet surprised William more than he'd ever thought a set of toiletries could.

Not because they were particularly notable in themselves. But because they were his own.

The wash bag was the same black nylon one he always brought with him when he travelled, or at least used to bring when he still went places, and everything inside it came from his own bathroom, everything from razor to toothbrush to aftershave.

One of his jackets sat on a thin hanger, draped over one of his shirts and a pair of his jeans. On the floor were his brown shoes – not the ones he'd choose himself, but nonetheless his own – and beside them lay a pair of his rolled-up socks and a pile of neatly folded underwear.

They had been in his apartment. Instead of throwing him a standard wash kit and a generic outfit from a department store, they had broken into his home and collected his things.

That told him a lot.

It meant that wherever they were taking him, they were going to keep him there for a while.

But it also meant that they wanted him to feel comfortable. He was important to them. Regardless of why they'd spirited him away, they wanted him to feel at home, perhaps even to think of himself as their guest.

He could live with that, he thought. Not least because he didn't have much choice.

He looked at the thin, faceless version of his own body on the hanger in front of him. And then he pulled off his hospital tunic, put on his normal clothes and wandered barefoot through the corridor to the back of the plane.

The bathroom was fresh and clean and surprisingly roomy for being on board a plane. On the other hand, that didn't stop it from being unspeakably tiny, and it took quite some effort to go through the normal morning procedures.

William Sandberg took his time. He shaved, washed his whole upper body, dunked his hair into the unconvincing imitation-marble basin and shampooed it twice, just to feel the sensation of the cool water running in smooth streams over his head.

It felt good. Which came as a surprise. And he allowed himself a few seconds to enjoy the feeling, knowing that whatever awaited him when he was done, he wanted to be wide awake and clear-headed.

As he did, he felt both his ears pop at once.

Were they going down?

He held his nose between his thumb and forefinger, equalising the pressure in his head. The whine of the engines had started to change, too, their hum gradually shifting to a lower key, which could only mean one thing, and after a moment he realised he couldn't hear them any more and had to squeeze his nose again.

He waited a few moments. It could be just a change of course, a new altitude, and if it were they would soon level out again and everything would go back to the same monotonous silent tone as before.

But the plane kept descending. It turned, checked its direction. Levelled out for a moment and started to descend again, creating a vague sensation of displacement in William's stomach every time it did, playing with gravity for a second and making his body a fraction lighter against the floor below him. There was no doubt. They were preparing to land.

The question was where.

The sun had told him they were flying eastward when he woke up. Possibly slightly to the south-east, depending on what time it really was. But that was information that didn't help him much anyway; he couldn't know if they'd kept to the same course since they took off.

And it wasn't any easier to tell how far they had travelled, either. The sun had been high in the sky when he woke up in the hospital, perhaps eleven in the morning, maybe twelve. Then they'd sedated him and taken him to an airport – Bromma? Arlanda? There weren't any others still in use, but how could you load an unconscious man on board a plane without piquing the interest of the ground crew? – and if the plane had been ready and waiting and all the papers were in order, it meant they could probably have been in the air an hour later.

It was an extremely rough guess, but it gave him something to work with. The sun was still up. That meant they couldn't have been airborne for more than two or three hours. Perhaps less if they'd been flying eastward into the night, and more if they had been heading west, but the entire equation had such wide margins of error that they could be covered with asphalt and opened up to road traffic, and he decided that the difference was insignificant anyway.

Instead, he focused on the options. The way he saw it, there were two. Either they were somewhere above southern Europe or they were flying over Russia. Or, possibly, somewhere in between.

His thoughts stopped at one of the alternatives.

Russia?

It would have been the obvious answer, back then. But now?

Where was the logic in that? On the other hand, there was nothing logical about the situation. Why him? Why now? What value would he be, and to whom?

He let the thought pass. Zipped up his wash bag. He would find out soon enough.

One last look in the mirror.

After all, he looked okay for someone who should be dead.

And then he unlocked the bathroom door.

As he opened it, the suits were already waiting for him.

They stood in the corridor, just by his bathroom door, and outside the windows smoke-coloured clouds streamed past along the fuselage, leaving small vibrating droplets of mist on the acrylic glass.

'Guess I should go and strap myself in?' William said. Smiled politely, without the faintest hope that the little welcome committee would stop at that. And sure enough, the bull neck stepped aside, making way for his two colleagues.

'I'm sorry about this,' he said. 'It would have been easier for everyone if we didn't have to.'

William understood immediately.

And for the second time, he watched as the man with the shaved head took a step towards him, his signature fountain pen in hand. A moment later William Sandberg felt the synthetic tingling rush through his body, turning things off and shutting him down until the sound of the luxury jet vanished into a tunnel of black.

Christina Sandberg spoke briefly and to the point. She held up her phone in front of them, showing the pictures she'd just taken in his room, forced them to take her business card while she explained what she knew, not a trace of uncertainty in her voice. And before the policemen had found any time to argue, she hurried out of the apartment and left them with a report to file.

William Sandberg had been kidnapped. And given his personal history it was more than likely that his life was in danger.

As the echo of her heels died away in the large stairwell, down into the lobby and out through the heavy door to the street, their click against the floor marked the last time she would ever see the apartment on Kaptensgatan.

5

Janine Charlotta Haynes pressed herself against the stone wall, her heart beating so fast that she was scared someone would hear.

She closed her eyes. Focused on breathing as silently as possible, on not letting her feet make a sound, ensuring there was no rustling from the thick envelope stuffed into her waistband.

She couldn't hear the two men now. But she knew that they were only a few feet away.

There could be three of them, she wasn't sure: the moment she'd heard their voices echo up the staircase she stopped dead, looking for a way out, throwing herself into a tiny passage without knowing where it led. It didn't have any lights, and she pressed herself up against the wall as she heard them make it to her floor, stop just outside, only the stones lining the archway separating them from her.

They stood as still and silent as herself, and she could only hope that they hadn't heard her. It would be impossible to explain why she was there. Particularly in the middle of the night.

She had been running.

And now she was paying for it.

She had been running as fast as she could, barefoot so that her steps would make as little sound as possible in the hard stone corridors, terrified but fully aware that this might be her only chance. And now she stood there, her body crying out for oxygen, fighting to keep herself from breathing.

She couldn't let them hear her.

She stood perfectly still.

Listened to her beating heart.

Then, suddenly, one of them spoke.

His voice was so close that it felt as if he was speaking directly to her, and it was all she could do to stop herself gasping for air. She pushed her body even harder against the wall, composed herself, listened to their voices, tried to concentrate on what they were saying.

Single words jumped out. Security?

She wasn't sure. Her French was terrible. She had taken it for two terms in high school, priding herself on performing as badly as possible, and Janine's teacher had warned her that she would live to regret it. Now she was standing in a stone corridor, painfully aware that her teacher had been right.

Yes, there it was: *securité*. Were they talking about her?

She closed her eyes again, tried to assess the situation. The worst-case scenario was that someone had realised that the tiny piece of plastic she kept in her pocket was missing. That piece of plastic was her only opening, her only way out, and she clasped it as firmly as she could, as if holding it tighter would keep her safe.

She couldn't let them find her.

Nobody knew where she was. If they decided to kill her, there was nothing to stop them, and nobody would ever get to know. There probably wasn't anyone left out there still searching for her.

She pushed the thought away.

He wouldn't stop.

Would he?

She had to believe he wouldn't. The last six months had been chaotic, to say the least; she didn't know which side she was working for, or why, or if what she was doing was morally right or fundamentally wrong or somewhere in between.

The only thing she knew was that she had to tell someone.

That he was her only chance.

And that whatever happened, she couldn't let them hear her.

The men had been talking for an eternity lasting exactly four minutes, when one of them hushed the other.

The silence cut through her body, and she felt her own fear

vibrate inside her mouth with a taste of metal. Had they heard her? Had she relaxed, allowed herself to breathe? Did they know she was standing there?

She held her breath. Counted.

One. Two. Three.

Her lungs were on fire, but she mustn't.

Four. Five.

And then: a sound.

Somewhere, a helicopter was approaching.

She heard it as a weak, rumbling sound, but it was enough to give her an opportunity to let out her air, and just as she did one of the men began to speak again. Low voice, straight into the air in front of him. Short, confirmatory phrases. Someone had called him on the radio, and it was the person on the other end who did the talking.

Okay. D'accord. Bien.

And then, hell was over. The men started moving, a steady rhythm as their footsteps echoed down the corridor, fading away into silence.

They were gone. And they hadn't passed the archway where she stood.

Okay, she said to herself. Now or never.

She braced her feet against the wall behind her, pushed off into the corridor like a turning swimmer and let her bare feet carry her as fast as they could. A pounding ache seared her heels each time they made contact with the unforgiving stone floor, but she was running again, and the only way she would make it was if she was fast enough. She bit her lip, fighting to ignore the pain, kept going in the direction she had been before she heard them.

She passed the stairwell. Followed the corridor to the right. A new stairwell. Another corridor, more stairs. Heavy wooden doors blocked her way, but every time she ran into one she would take out the tiny piece of plastic from her pocket, hold it against the little box in the wall, listen to the faint buzz as the lock released and allowed her to move on. Every time waiting carefully for the silence to return, making certain that she was entirely alone before sprinting onward.

Down, further down, two more storeys. It was damper here, probably below ground. No windows or peepholes, nothing to suggest that there was a world outside. The feeling of being in a prison was even stronger.

It was only the third time that she had been this far down. But she'd forced herself to memorise the route by heart, and she saw every corner, door and staircase in front of her well before they appeared. And she sailed through the corridors, weak thuds of soft skin on hard stone, didn't slow down until she reached her destination.

The room on the other side of the locked door looked like a caretaker's office. Or rather: it looked like it used to be one. The walls were lined with wooden pigeonholes for letters, a large desk stood behind a glass partition, and a mountain of boxes lay stacked against one wall.

She could see subtle changes from the last time she was here. Stacks of paper were missing, new ones had arrived. Mugs with dried-up coffee dregs had been replaced by fresh ones. The room was in use. She hadn't dared to believe it, but it seemed to be true.

She went in. Pulled the thick envelope from her waistband. Pushed it into the middle of a pile of similar envelopes on the table. And then, as quietly as she arrived, she turned round and hurried back out, exactly the same way she had come.

Everything was a gamble. The envelope was addressed to a person who didn't exist. The contents, if someone opened it, would look like a love letter.

Except to one person.

The only thing she could do was to hope that he would get it.

It had taken her over six months to find a way to get a message out, and as she ran through the corridors in absolute silence, she squeezed her fingers and hoped she'd finally done it.

And that she wasn't already too late.

6

The moment he pulled the heavy curtains open, William Sandberg saw that his guesses were way off.

The room where he woke up was classical, with heavy furnishings, and extremely old. The floor was constructed from large, soft stones, worn down by feet passing back and forth across them over hundreds of years. Some of the slabs had been split by temperature changes or the ground settling, as had the walls with their hand-painted wall hangings, yellowed by time and damp air, but still impressive in their rich detail. Wooden panels separated them from the floor, and in the roof were huge beams, painted the same dark grey as the rest of the wood in the room.

If he hadn't been so painfully aware of what he'd experienced the last twenty-four hours, William could have led himself to believe he'd been brought to some upmarket castle weekend getaway.

All the elements were there. The heavy wooden bed where he'd slept, the wall hangings at its head, the fine fabrics draped over the intricately carved canopy. And the breakfast tray on its foldable holder, entirely out of place with criss-cross chrome legs but with an unbelievable spread of food: cheeses, jam, bread, all surrounded by exotic fruits whose names he didn't know but that obviously seemed to exist anyway. And of all the training he'd undergone in his working life – training to help him survive if imprisoned by a foreign power – not a single minute had prepared him for the risk of being served luxury breakfasts in castles.

But William got out of his bed and passed over the breakfast selection, even though his stomach cried out that eating was long overdue. He continued across the room to the curtains, a bright morning sun trying to sneak in around their edges.

When he pulled them open he stood motionless for several moments. All he could do was stare, partly from pure surprise: he'd been so certain they were taking him to Russia that it took him a couple of seconds to accept what he saw. But also because it was impossible not to be moved by the view that met him outside his high, multi-paned windows.

Several storeys down, large grassy meadows sloped dramatically towards barren cliffs, broken here and there by winding stone walls, steeply climbing downhill to a light blue mountain lake. Around it, and on the other side, more meadows and cliffs seemed to climb in and out of each other, forming a gigantic pothole of stillness and silence and the sensation of looking at a thousand-piece jigsaw puzzle on someone's coffee table.

They had been flying more south than east. The mountains were the Alps; they had taken him to somewhere between France to the west and Austria or Slovenia to the east, and for the life of him he couldn't understand why.

'Mr Sandberg.'

The voice was clear and articulate, sharp in the hard-walled room, and it made him spin around. Several steps into the room stood the man who'd just said his name, more as an observation than a question. William hadn't even heard him enter.

'Our apologies for putting you to bed in your shirt,' he said. 'You get a lot of questions if you try to take a man through Customs dressed in his pyjamas.'

He was about William's age, hair grey and neatly cut, and he had a friendly enough look in contrast to his starched, light-blue uniform shirt. He spoke with a perfect English accent, and even though William was far from certain he thought he could hear the traces of a working-class dialect in some of the vowels.

William nodded politely. Very well.

'And which Customs are we talking about?'

The man smiled back. Friendly, genuinely, but entirely without answering. Instead:

'The rest of your wardrobe is over there.'

'And you're sure that's a good idea? I shouldn't just keep this on until you decide I've slept enough?'

'You've reached your final destination,' he said.

'And at risk of repeating myself,' William said, raising his eyebrow to point out that the question still wasn't answered.

The man smiled again. He'd heard him the first time, but had no intention of telling him anything more.

'I suggest you eat something. You've been asleep for eighteen hours, and I understand you didn't eat much before that either.'

'I'll have some toast,' said William. He didn't move, but let his body language finish the sentence: when you're gone.

'Splendid,' the man said. 'I'll be back for you in half an hour. You'll get to know a bit more after that.'

He turned around, took a few steps towards the door and opened it. Unlocked, William noted. No visible security features, just like on the plane. Someone was going out of their way to make him feel welcome, and he couldn't stop wondering why. Or who. And what on earth they thought he could do for them.

'I'm sorry,' William said.

The man turned back towards him. Now what?

'William Sandberg. I didn't catch yours.'

He held his right hand out into the empty air between them, challenging, waiting for a handshake and a presentation. And the man looked back at him. Took William's hand, more of a firm grip than a shake, looked him directly in his eyes without the slightest hint of wanting to keep his name to himself.

'Of course,' he said. 'Forgive me.'

And then:

'Connors. General Connors.'

oo○oo

General Connors had a first name, but there were many things in his life that made him uncomfortable and his first name was one of them.

He grew up in a small town in north-west England, a working-class area where unemployment and petty criminality were everyday realities and went largely unquestioned. Right and wrong were flexible concepts and sometimes the difference was hard to see. The priority was getting food on the table and the rent paid on time; nobody could afford to ask how it was achieved.

For Connors it was the worst childhood possible. Early in life he realised two things: one, that finely honed social skills were one of the greatest assets a person could have, and two, that those skills were something he totally lacked.

Connors was always one step behind. He hated how things around him could change, how the king of the street one week could be overthrown the next, and how friends and allies could turn against you and change sides before you even grasped that there were sides to take. Even before he started school he began keeping to himself, doing everything to avoid friendship, gangs and peer pressure. For long periods he was bullied and labelled as gay, a significantly more serious crime than the petty theft to which his classmates dedicated their spare time.

An even greater crime was Connors' love of school. He was

good at maths, even when it got abstract and weird, and though he knew it didn't prove much, he quickly grew more skilled than any of his teachers. He loved rules and logical patterns and when one thing could be traced back to another. And every time he was beaten up in the playground for no reason it just made him love them more.

When he was first introduced to the army at the age of sixteen, he realised it was the perfect place to find the order he longed for. Not only did everyone have a clear rank and position, it was explicitly marked on everyone's uniforms, in as many places as possible to the point of being ridiculous. All changes were predictable, and almost exclusively involved moving upward – there was no risk of getting out of bed one morning only to learn that the major was the new colonel, and that the former colonel was having the shit kicked out of him for something his brother did.

Connors had found his home.

For the first time in his life he was able to wake up and feel good.

The army was the perfect place for Connors to develop what he was best at. He was a master in the art of applying patterns and rules, and soon enough he was making them his own, building on them and devising new ones. At the age of thirty he was no longer a working-class boy without a first name but one of the British military's foremost strategists. He was an expert at inventing scenarios of disorder and mayhem, and then setting the rules for how order and clarity should be restored. He supervised training, wrote manuals, and was the kind of person everyone wanted in the room when things got going. The government, the military, business and God knows who else – everyone wanted him on their side.

Connors had made it his craft to bring order from chaos. When things fell apart, he was the man to call.

And now he was confronted with a scenario nobody could possibly have imagined.

For the first time in years he was back to being a child.

In the depths of his heart he was scared as hell.

Connors pushed the key card against the reader on the wall and waited for the door to hiss open.

He walked along the wide corridors of steel and concrete,

towards the lobby and its low soundproofed roof and rigid chairs in impersonal dark blue. Turned through the double doors on one side of the room. Swiped his plastic key again, the lock releasing with a new whirr.

The room on the other side was circular. In the middle was a large conference table, mirroring the contours of the room, empty chairs everywhere, bottles of water lined up and ready for meetings that almost never took place any more, and when they did never filled up all the seats.

On the room's one straight wall hung an array of gigantic LED displays, glaringly bright to anyone who had just entered from the older part of the building. Connors peered at them as he walked towards them, saw the never-ending stream of numbers racing across them as they always did.

In front of the screens stood a man in a dark uniform. Didn't look up as Connors came in, didn't turn around as he strode across the needlefelt carpet, just stood there watching the numbers roll past. Until Connors stopped by his side.

'We know how he ended up in Berlin,' he said.

At last, Franquin looked up, met Connors' gaze, his eyes showing a lack of several days' sleep.

'He stole a truck from a petrol station. We found it drained just outside Innsbruck, it's been impounded and neutralised. Eyewitnesses say he hitched in a red Toyota RAV4.'

'And where is that now?'

The silence said it all. They had no idea.

'It's beginning,' Connors said. 'Isn't it?'

Franquin didn't answer.

And when he eventually spoke, his insecurity was gone, his anxiety masked behind layers of determination. There was only one way now, and it was forward.

'Is he here?' he said.

'He's in his room.'

'How is he?'

'He'll survive.'

Franquin gave a grunt. Good. If they still had a chance, Sandberg was the only one who could save them. And they had been minutes away from being too late. Again.

'What do we tell him?' Connors asked.

Franquin paused. And then: 'Exactly the same thing we've told her.'

He turned again, his back towards Connors.

And with that the meeting was over.

7

William got to spend forty minutes alone in his room before General Connors returned. It gave him enough time to eat, go through his morning routine and put on a tweed jacket and some trousers. No tie. It was a conscious decision: he didn't know what awaited him, and he wanted to look serious enough to appear on an equal footing and in control. What he didn't want was to look as if he was trying too hard. There was little doubt they had the upper hand, and he had no intention of making it worse by arriving dressed as a schoolboy. Plus, who the hell knew if their first move wouldn't be to stick a syringe in his neck again anyway.

The conversation started as soon as they were out of the door.

'I know you have questions,' Connors said. 'Ask away, and I'll do my best to answer.'

The offer wasn't entirely unexpected. There was no reason to give William the luxury of memorising his surroundings, to let him focus on which corridors led to which staircases, and a conversation was the perfect deception. Connors would still only answer the questions he wanted to, but he would take his time doing it, and William knew it. And Connors knew that William knew.

'You can begin by telling me where I am,' William said.

'Let's call it Liechtenstein,' Connors said.

'"Let's call it"?'

'I can't give you an exact address. But you're not going to be ordering pizza for the time being, anyway.'

He smiled wryly. An apologetic smile, designed to encourage

him to ask another question. And William played along. Put on a polite face. But behind it, he tried as best he could to observe and remember the twisting routes that Connors led him through the building.

'Can you tell me who's brought me here?'

'You'll get to know in due course.'

'Or why?'

'You'll get to know that too.'

'Okay. So can you tell me if there is any question that you'll actually be answering now?'

Connors smiled once again. An honest one, as if the absurdity of the situation was as clear to him as it was to William, as if the pointlessness of the conversation made him more uncomfortable than he would like.

William saw it, and gave him a nod of understanding. Very well, then. And with that, the question-and-answer session was over, and they kept walking in silence.

They passed along corridors, descended narrow staircases and ducked into yet more corridors. And all the while, William couldn't shake the feeling that they were walking through side passages and service rooms, as if the actual castle were somewhere else, inside of where they walked, with Connors leading him around it on purpose.

Everywhere the floor was made of stone slabs, worn down by countless feet over hundreds and hundreds of years. The walls were dark, sometimes with hangings or tapestries, bleached by the light and darkened by the damp until only a grey tone was left. It was impressive and beautiful and disconcerting and intimidating, all at the same time.

'Actually,' William said, 'I have one more question.'

Connors turned. They were halfway down yet another set of stairs, Connors first and William behind him, both stooping to avoid the ceiling.

'Should I be afraid?'

The question surprised Connors. He looked into William's eyes, unsure whether he was sincere or just playing games, and for a second Connors paused right there in the darkness, opened his mouth to speak. But he changed his mind. Turned round. And the conversation was left hanging in the air while they descended the last few steps to the next floor.

The room below the stairs was a hall. It wasn't very large, but the height of it was impressive, several small windows far up along the wall allowing in enough light for William to find himself squinting. At the other end of the hall was another, larger staircase, decidedly grander than the one they had taken, and in the inner wall was a gigantic, heavy double door of darkened wood.

Connors went up to it, stopped by the handle. Looked at William for a moment, as if he couldn't decide on an answer.

'There's no need to be afraid of me,' he said finally. 'Not of us.'

'But of what?'

For an instant, there seemed to be compassion in Connors' face. As if he lamented the situation, as if he didn't really want to do what he was doing, as if something larger forced him to kidnap people from hospitals and fly them unconscious to another corner of Europe.

But the expression vanished almost immediately. And Connors let the question slide.

'What we will be telling you today is incredibly sensitive and top secret,' he said. His voice was formal now, matter-of-fact and to the point. 'Certain things we won't be able to disclose at all. Others we will only reveal in part.'

'I'm in let's-call-it-Liechtenstein. You've taken my phone. Who are you afraid I might talk to?'

'There are certain things we know here that may never reach the world outside. Under any circumstances. Ever.'

'Does that mean you're going to let me go home again?'

Connors hesitated. And then, the honesty back in his voice: 'I hope with all my heart that there will come a day when *any* of us will be able to go home.'

∞○∞

The young intern standing in front of Christina Sandberg was awkward and shy and had trouble expressing himself, but right now he was the only person she could use. All she could do was to hope he was up to the task.

One moment he would avoid meeting her eyes, almost as if he were secretly in love with her despite being twenty years younger, and the next he would try to contribute to the conversation by spurting out parts of sentences in random order. She couldn't decide which of the two worried her most.

With strained patience she summarised everything one more time, to be sure. He was to contact the hospital, the neighbours in William's building and lastly the removal company, just to confirm what Christina already knew to be true: that there had been no pickup booked from William's address, and that his allegedly voluntary move was staged.

Leo Björk listened and noted it all down a second time, careful not to mention what they both already knew — that the job had nothing to do with the paper, but was entirely a matter of her personal concern for a missing loved one. Perhaps, both of them reasoned to themselves, perhaps William Sandberg's disappearance was the tip of a mysterious iceberg, a political scandal or an event in the shadows of a new, invisible cold war, and perhaps they would find something to write about that could retroactively justify what they were doing. A former military cryptologist, vanishing with all of his belongings and equipment — it did sound like a promising springboard for a series of articles about an international threat that nobody knew existed.

But as far as Leo was concerned, he didn't need any rationalisation.

He didn't have the slightest interest in questioning anything; the task already felt like a step up and the only thing he wanted now was to get started and show what an efficient and talented reporter he was. It would be an active, investigative job. It would give him the opportunity to think for himself, trace people to interview, find leads and locate sources. And not least, it would allow him to work closely with Christina Sandberg, and that made him disturbingly jittery in more ways than he cared to admit.

Eventually, Christina finished reiterating the tasks a second time, and Leo Björk closed his notepad and got up.

She stared after him through the glass partition of her office. She didn't have time to doubt him. Instead, she picked up her mobile and scanned the address book, searching for a name she hadn't even thought about for at least a year.

∞◯∞

The heavy doors opened up into a gigantic chamber, and William immediately found himself pinned to the spot in awe.

The room must have been twelve metres high. Thick stone pillars ran up the walls and met high up in a crown on the vaulted ceiling. Along one of the walls the sun shone in through uneven, stained-glass windows, filtering the light into coloured speckles, making the place seem dark and light at the same time. On the opposite end of the room, the few remaining sunrays that made it across landed in the glow of a large fireplace almost the size of a small room in William's apartment. In the centre of it all hung a huge iron chandelier, and under it stood a long table made of dark hardwood, full of grooves and furrows where generations of nobility had hosted lavish banquets.

The picture would have been complete with a skewered roast boar as a centrepiece, served on a tin tray with red wine in goblets. Instead, there was a solitary extension lead, from which a grey cable led to a laptop at the head of the table, a good nine metres from where William was standing. At the computer sat a man in dark uniform.

'Franquin?' said Connors.

The man who got up from the table was slightly older. His face seemed to have borne the brunt of every weather there is, and he moved slowly and laboriously, stopping a few metres away. No handshake. Introduced himself as General Maurice Franquin and bade William welcome. William couldn't decide whether to thank him or come out with some harsh remark, and decided to do neither.

'I could spend a lot of time apologising for bringing you here this way. But I won't.'

William didn't answer, waited while Franquin gestured to him to sit down.

'I don't know how much Connors has told you.'

'I think it's fair to say he's spent quite a lot of time not telling me anything.'

Franquin nodded. For a moment, traces of a smile seemed to

spread through his wrinkles. Either that, or some of them had just ended up pointing in the wrong direction.

'You'll be getting the short version,' he said.

'Any version will suffice for the time being.'

'We brought you here because we need your knowledge.'

'I got that much.'

'We know you possess a great expertise in your field. And right now we're facing a problem we can't solve by ourselves.'

'And who is we?'

'Let's just say it's an international partnership.'

'Between?'

'It varies. Mainly between twenty countries, occasionally more, from Europe to the United States and South America and Japan, and frankly it doesn't really matter. We act in the interests of all nations, but without their involvement. We are financed by special, ring-fenced funds; only a few people in the world know what those funds are used for.'

William looked at him. It could very well be true. It would explain the facility, the organisation, the ability to fly him out from Sweden without interference.

And at the same time, it didn't explain a thing.

'So what's the name of this partnership?'

'We don't exist, so we don't need a name.'

'Under the UN?'

'There are people inside the UN who know about us. Certain individuals, by which I mean two or three. But since we don't exist, we're not subject to anyone.' He made a pause, long enough to signal that what he just said was definitely a yes, and then a bit longer to signal that this was William's own interpretation and nothing else. 'We like to think of ourselves as an autonomous organisation, working for the safety and security of all nations in the world.'

William looked back and forth between them, tried to determine the level of truth in what they were saying. He still felt as if he was lagging behind. The things they were saying were, on the one hand, perfectly feasible. But on the other, the whole situation was so bizarre that he couldn't quite grasp it. The castle. How he'd arrived there. Everything.

What could be so dangerous and important and yet so secret that an entire organisation had been set up to deal with it, one that nobody could know existed?

'Security against what?' he asked.

Franquin raised an eyebrow in Connors' direction: your turn.

And Connors took a few steps across the room.

'We have . . . ' he began, but stopped almost immediately. A brief pause while he chose his words, carefully, looking for an explanation that would reveal enough but not too much at the same time.

There it was: 'We have intercepted a sequence of numbers.'

'Intercepted how?'

'How is unimportant. What matters is that inside that sequence, there's information. Well hidden, encrypted with an unprecedentedly complex key – or, to be exact: keys. Plural. Keys cross-referencing to previous keys, which in their turn are based on others, in ways that makes them almost impossible to break.'

William listened. Reluctantly felt his curiosity grow. This was his field, it was exactly what he'd once worked with, and precisely the type of challenge he relished. Finding the complex rules that always hid somewhere, regardless of how impossible or chaotic a code might appear at the outset. Testing and changing variables and testing again to see if it gave a result. It was maths and intuition in a combination he loved, few things in life made him more excited than finding a pattern in something that seemed to be nothing but a jumble of letters on a piece of paper, watching it reveal its face like a crossword where one single letter solves everything.

Part of William Sandberg felt like a child on Christmas morning.

The rest of him still felt very much like a fifty-five-year-old man who had just been abducted from a hospital against his will.

'What's the source?' he asked. He knew that it was just another variation on the question he'd already asked, but at the same time it was an extremely relevant one. Different codes take different forms, and if he was going to help them this was the kind of thing he would need to know sooner or later anyway.

'We can't tell you that,' said Connors.

'Is it written documents, is it radio signals, is it data from a file?'

'We can't tell you that either.'

'What can you tell me then? Can you tell me anything at all?' He realised he'd raised his voice. He regretted it immediately; he wasn't the one calling the shots here, and he compensated for his mistake with a dry smirk. 'I'm sorry. It's just that sometimes when people need help, it's much easier if you know what you're helping them with.'

Still a bit caustic. Be he didn't mind using a hint of sarcasm, as long as he had the situation under control and didn't let them break him down. He'd lost it for a moment but now he was back on top of his game, and he gave the two men a disparaging look. We're too old to be playing games, it seemed to say.

Okay then.

Franquin walked back to his place at the end of the table. Pulled over his laptop and pressed one of the keys with his index finger. 'This,' he said.

Above their heads four beams of light suddenly pierced the room, reaching out from the chandelier at its centre. Dust particles danced in the air like weightless circus artists, magically illuminated by the rays on their way to the walls around them.

What William hadn't noticed when he came in were the digital projectors mounted in the ceiling, resting on top of the heavy arrangement of iron and candles. They whirred into life in response to Franquin's finger, throwing their light at the pale wallpaper the last few metres under the roof where the sunlight didn't reach, and where everything had been shrouded in darkness.

A stream of projected information stretched across the entire hall, seamlessly transitioning from wall to wall, data rolling from one edge of the room to the other.

Numbers.

Endless rows of numbers.

They raced forth, row by row, feeding upward and replaced from below, and when a row reached the ceiling it was shifted one column sideways, into the realm of the adjacent projector, continuing upward and shifting sideways again, over and over until it vanished for good. At the same time, there were other things going on. Numbers were changing colours and were grouped together with other numbers, marked and moved to a new field to the side of the main stream.

William knew what he was looking at. Somewhere in the building there were more computers, significantly larger and more expensive than Franquin's aluminium-shelled laptop, and what he saw now was the result of the mainframe sifting through the code Franquin had talked about, hunting for patterns of logic and trying to pull out the key to the message that someone had hidden in the forest of numbers.

Judging by the amount of data it was quite a forest.

'How much code are we talking about?' William asked.

'This is a part of it.'

'And where did it come from?'

'You already asked us that.'

'And I'm still very curious.'

'I'm sorry.'

William sighed. They were back in the same absurd circle again.

'And what if I help you to work out what this means? Am I allowed to read what I write or would you like me to shoot myself when I find something?'

Judging by Franquin's expression, he didn't appreciate the sarcasm.

William changed his strategy.

'So,' he said, 'who is it that's in danger?'

'We can't say.'

'Can you say who's making the threat?'

'That's information you don't need to know.'

'So what the hell am I allowed to know?' There was anger in his voice now. 'You bring me here against my will. You ask me to play along but you won't explain what you're trying to achieve. Give me one reason to help you. Just one. Please.'

'Because you don't have a choice.'

William didn't want to raise his voice. And he had almost succeeded. Now he breathed slowly through his nose, bit his lip to calm himself. And started over, a silent, barely suppressed disdain beneath his words.

'Big difference,' he said. 'Work and work.'

No answer.

'You can force people to work for you. Of course you can. You can whip somebody into pulling a cart or crushing a rock or moving this whole damn building a few metres to the left – as long as you whip hard enough you can get anyone to do anything. Except for one thing. To think. It's going to be very, very hard to make me find a solution if I don't want to find it.' And then, closing the subject: 'So of course I have a choice. One always does.'

'Tell us about your suicide attempt,' Franquin said.

William turned sharply. That was totally unexpected. And more than a little disrespectful.

'You want some ideas?' he said. 'Because if it's advice you're after, you'd probably do better to ask someone else. I don't seem to be succeeding too well.'

'Tell us why,' Franquin said. Nothing more.

'If I want to go to therapy I'll pay for it, thank you very much.'

'I can send you an invoice if it makes you feel better.'

Okay. This conversation was going nowhere, and William threw his hands into the air to illustrate that he was done here. It was obviously nothing more than a charade, he wasn't in charge and he knew it, but at least it was a way to show what he felt. And he turned to Connors, gave him a confrontational look. It's time to leave.

'You couldn't live with the knowledge that you failed to save someone,' Franquin's voice said behind him.

It cut straight to his heart.

'You know nothing about me—'

'On the contrary,' Franquin said. 'I would say we probably know more about you than you do yourself.'

He got up. He moved restlessly; he didn't want to discuss Sandberg's past, they needed him to start working and every minute spent in this room was a minute spent doing the wrong thing.

'You virtually grew up with a soldering iron for a hand. You were the wunderkind in school, the maths genius slash oddball who threw together homemade electronics before most of your class-mates could even spell. You fixed your friends' radios and had three patents to your name before you left secondary school. You had companies throwing money at you for university scholarships, and you could have taken your talent and become stupidly rich. And you knew it.'

William shrugged. So?

'But you chose to stay in the military.'

'I was well paid.'

Franquin shook his head in disagreement. 'You'd have been paid a lot better as a civilian. But there was a cold war going on. You used your knowledge for a cause you believed in. You saved lives. That's what you did, that's why you stayed, and no matter how much you try to convince yourself that your passion is numbers and technology and patterns, there is no single thing more important to you than saving other people's lives.'

William looked away. It was the reflex denial of someone presented with the truth.

Sandberg did love the problem-solving and the structures and the maths, and his military work had given him the chance to do it every day. That was the reason he had chosen to stay. But Franquin was right. The payoff was the knowledge that he was doing something meaningful. William had decoded messages containing threats to Swedish interests and individuals, and more than once he'd found himself sprinting down linoleum-lined corridors with urgent information on plans for attacks and assassinations. It felt almost dreamlike thirty years later, but back then it was routine. And every time someone's travel plans were changed or someone's speech was cancelled because William had done his job, that's when he knew why he loved his work and why he kept doing it.

But even if Franquin was right, it didn't make much difference. William had no intention of helping an organisation whose aims he didn't know.

'I am terribly, terribly sorry,' he said in a voice that revealed he wasn't sorry at all, 'but I can't quite grasp what my daughter or my family or my career has to do with this.'

Franquin waited him out. 'We can't force you to work for us, Sandberg. If you refuse there's little we can do about it. *But . . .* ' He shrugged. 'You are not going to say no. Because if you do, you will be risking the lives of . . . ' He stopped for a moment, searched for the right word but couldn't find it.

A second of silence. Two.

And William couldn't keep himself from looking up at him. For the first time since the whole encounter started it was as if something broke through. A fear, somewhere deep behind the desert landscape that was Franquin's face. It could obviously be one more part of the act, a choreographed move in their efforts to persuade him, but William kept watching him and couldn't shake the feeling that Franquin himself was actually afraid.

'Of who?' William asked.

No answer.

'Whose lives would I be risking?'

Franquin's eyes exchanged a couple of unspoken words with Connors, before turning back to William. And then, he cleared his throat. 'The lives of an incomprehensibly large number of people.'

He sat down again.

William didn't know what to think. They were pressing all the right buttons, telling him just enough, catching his interest and curiosity in a way that annoyed him.

'What is going to happen to an incomprehensible large number of people?' he asked.

Silence.

'What is it you want me to do?'

Franquin was motionless for long enough to make William wonder if he had any intention of answering, but eventually he reached for the computer again, nodded back up at the wall. Look.

William's eyes followed his, and as he did, the images from the projectors began to change.

In the space of a few seconds most of the numbers faded away into the background, a handful remaining in focus before being grouped and sorted along the edge of the projection. At the same time the whole thing appeared to zoom out to a far larger scale, accommodating more and more numbers, smaller and smaller in size. And all time, numbers kept fading away as if they were discarded by an invisible hand, while others were picked out, paired and placed on the growing section in the corner until it spread to cover the whole of one side, gradually transformed into a binary series of ones and zeroes.

William realised he was holding his breath.

He could already see the patterns among the zeroes and ones, but not until every number was replaced by combinations of squares in black and white, lined up in a pattern of filled or empty pixels, not until then did the full picture become clear to him.

What William saw would have been at home in a museum.

Perhaps at a university or a research institute, anywhere but here. Not projected on to an ancient wall in a castle in let's-call-it-Liechtenstein, and definitely not in the presence of two serious men in military uniforms who said that this was an important message they had recently deciphered.

The projection that William Sandberg was staring at consisted of hundreds of rows of symbols and marks and outlines, neatly sorted and rendered in illegible vertical columns.

'Do you know what this is?' Franquin asked.

William nodded.

Cuneiform script. He'd only ever seen it in books. One of the world's oldest written languages, the kind you see scratched into clay tablets on archaeology documentaries on TV. Now the walls around him were covered with pixelated black-and-white versions of precisely that type of inscription, symbols racing over the room as if they were spelling out an urgent message that nobody could understand.

William stood transfixed, scouring the unreadable words. The two men let him take his time.

'I don't get it,' he said. 'You intercepted this – now?'

'It's a collection of material,' Connors said. 'We've had it for a while.'

'Do we know what it says?'

'*We* do. You don't need to.'

He threw Franquin a look, but he didn't have the energy to make anything of it. What William couldn't understand was far more fundamental.

'I think you've made a mistake. I think you've been misinformed about what I do. I work with numbers. I'm not an Egyptologist.'

'Sumerologist,' Connors corrected him. 'The symbols are Sumerian.' And then: 'We know very well what your field is. There are other people who translate the text for us.'

'So why am I here then? If you already deduced this message from those numbers, if you already cracked the code, what do you need me for?'

And at last, Franquin cleared his throat. He took his eyes off the wall, looked at William, firmly and unflinching. When he answered, there was a deep note of worry in his voice.

'Sandberg? We don't have very much time.'
And then:
'We need you to code a reply.'

8

As Christina entered the warm café on Rörstrandsgatan, her eyes searching for Palmgren, she found him standing up, his arms already stretched out to greet her.

He'd seen her through the window, hurrying across the street outside the thin, outdated curtains that covered the windows, the kind that he himself had discarded decades ago but that had travelled full circle around the fashion carousel and become state-of-the-art hipster decor. He knew she would come in wearing the same hard-set expression she'd had the last couple of times they'd met. But he also knew that she was still a tangle of emotions on the inside.

She let him hug her before even saying hello. Pulled back out of his arms just a little too fast, knowing that if she didn't she would end up crying, and she really didn't want that. She avoided his eyes, muttered a brief hello.

'You having anything?' he asked, mostly to give her the chance to talk about something else. To let her feelings subside before they got down to business.

She shook her head. Hung her suede coat across the back of the ragged armchair, sat down across from him. Waited for him to begin the conversation.

'You were right, of course. But you already know that.'

She nodded. Lars-Erik Palmgren had been a friend of the family for as long as she could remember, and after the separation he'd carried on as before – a neutral point of support for them both, the only one of their mutual friends who hadn't taken sides. Perhaps it was a learned behaviour, a part of the diplomacy picked up from all his years with Armed Forces Headquarters. Or perhaps it was simply the person he was. It obviously didn't matter – regardless of why, he'd been a sober voice of support for both her and William long after they had gone their separate ways. She still felt a sting of guilt for not keeping in touch with him. But she'd had to leave her old life behind to be able to move on, and she had a feeling that he understood, too. In many ways, he was the most sensible person she knew.

'Did you know he was planning to do it?' she asked after a long silence.

He shook his head. 'And neither did you,' he said. The tone was emphatic and serious, as if she'd implied that she should have. 'You have worried about it before, over and over again, and up until now you haven't been right once. Correct? Just because you're scared that something's going to happen, it doesn't mean it's your job to predict it if it actually does.'

She shrugged. Whatever Palmgren might say wouldn't help her, and he knew it as well as she did. Her guilt for not having been able to stop her former husband in time was very real, rational or not, and nobody would be able to talk it away.

'Whatever you think,' Palmgren said, as if trying to lead her from her thoughts, 'whatever you say, neither of you could have predicted – this.'

He held out his hands to illustrate what he meant by *this*: she'd explained it all over the phone, William's disappearance, the missing computers, the files and the notes and the reference books. And he'd instantly known that she was right.

William Sandberg wouldn't just follow up on an impulse to leave. William Sandberg wasn't the kind of man who had impulses, full stop.

'So what do you say?' she asked.

'I've thought about it,' said Palmgren. 'But I can't make sense of it.'

'Go on,' she said.

'First, let's bear in mind that there may be things I don't know about. I'm retired. If there's been some major development within the last few years I wouldn't know about it.'

'And you don't think the press would have found out?'

He smiled. 'With all due respect, you don't know everything.'

Fair enough. She smiled back, gestured for him to carry on.

'But no, I don't believe the security situation has changed very dramatically. I don't see who would have a reason – or even the resources – to kidnap a retired cryptologist. However big their needs might be. A state?' He shook his head in answer to his own question. 'That's not what today's political situation looks like. Nations work together. If a foreign power needed some Swedish cryptographic skills they'd simply call us and ask.'

'An organisation then?' she asked.

'Terrorists?' he asked back.

'For example.'

He considered it for a moment. 'What can I say? Maybe.'

'But why choose William? Why not someone who's active, someone still working? Someone who isn't so self-absorbed that they think the solution to all problems is to lie down in a bathtub and die?'

He gave her a sad look. She didn't mean that, and he knew it too.

'Because William is the best there is.'

'You know that, and I know that,' she said. 'But who else does? Unless they had inside knowledge from the Swedish military. And who would have, apart from another military organisation?'

They sat in silence. Avoided the looks from the dyed-haired waitress as she cleared the table next to them, casting lingering glances towards the empty table in front of Christina, trying to communicate that this was a café and not a public waiting room and that she was expected to order something.

When they were alone again Christina leaned forward.

'What sort of contacts do you have nowadays?'

'What are you getting at?' he asked.

'The things William did. Before he retired. Who's doing them now?'

'I don't know.'

'But someone is, right?'

'I assume so.'

Christina placed her hands on the table. Looked him straight in the eye.

'If there is somebody out there, a group, or an organisation, or – I don't know – a nation or a political fraction or a conspiracy theorist in a house in the woods. Whoever it may be. If there's anyone out there who'd be interested in William's skills . . . ?'

She let the rest of the sentence hang in the air between them. And Palmgren gazed back at her, already aware where she was going.

'If there is,' he said, nodding, 'then yes. William's replacement would know who.'

She said no more. Just waited. Waited for him to say the only thing left to say.

'Yes. I'll try to contact them.'

From out of nowhere, a flush of gratitude rushed through her body and made her turn her eyes away, swallow hard. She silently wished she'd bought a coffee after all. Something to focus on, to hold in her hands, anything to avoid having to look at Palmgren right now.

He pushed his hands across the café table. Took her palms in his. Leaned forward, as if trying to enter her field of vision even though she wanted to keep him out.

'Everything's going to be all right,' he said. 'I promise you.'

The warmth from his hands around hers broke the barrier. And as she felt the surface tension give way at the corner of her eye, she realised that this was the first time she'd allowed herself to cry since William had disappeared.

It took her a minute, and then she looked up. Smiled at him. A smile of gratitude.

And even if they both knew that he was in no position to promise anything, neither of them said it out loud.

∞◯∞

For the second time that day, William was led through the castle's seemingly endless corridors of neatly stacked stones. This time Connors didn't talk. He left William to his own thoughts, gave him space to digest what he'd learned, both of them knowing there was too much for him to process to be able to concentrate on the geography.

They kept walking in silence until they passed the room where he had woken up that same morning. Further down the narrow hallway there was another door, and Connors turned to open it —

no lock here either, William noted – and showed him into the room on the other side.

'Your office. Just tell me if you need anything.'

William looked around. As offices went, this wasn't bad. It ran along the same outer wall as his bedroom, and the view was equally breathtaking from there. Four large windows opened out on to the lake, along the side wall stood a long desk with monitors and computer towers and even a supply of stationery, and next to it all there was an office chair that actually looked as if it might bear sitting on.

It was like coming into a new office for the first day on the job.

And, to be honest, what an office.

'Feel at home?' Connors said.

Huh? The question was absurd, and William looked at him, only to see the shadow of a smile in Connors' face. And as the smile refused to go away, William slowly turned his focus back into the room again.

It took a moment before he realised he actually did feel at home.

And then another couple of seconds before he understood why.

The computers were his own.

They were set up and arranged in exactly the same configuration as in his apartment.

Monitors and processing units and modified machines with processors he'd once designed himself and ordered in utmost secrecy. And on a shelf above the monitors sat his own books, his files and everything else he'd had in his study back in Stockholm, and – very convenient – just about everything he would need to carry out his task here.

It wasn't until he let his gaze wander across the desk for the third time that he realised something was out of place. He took one step forward, closer to the table, up towards a thick steel box in a greyish green. It was almost cube-shaped, perched on the far edge of the desk, alongside all the other equipment.

It couldn't be what he thought it was. It was impossible.

He placed his hand on it. Felt the casing, ran his hands over the cold surface. Turned it over, exposing the maze of terminals and circuit breakers drilled and soldered on to the plain metal sheet at the back. It looked like a DIY job from the eighties.

'Where did you get this?' he said.

'We got hold of it.'

'"Got hold"?'

William looked at Connors. This wasn't an item anyone could just walk in and buy in a shop. It wasn't even something you could break in somewhere and steal. This was something you couldn't find at all, and if you did it would be surrounded by security measures, alarms and thick concrete walls that wouldn't be penetrated without endless amounts of official signatures on endless amounts of paper.

That much was a cast-iron certainty.

He should know: he was the one who built it.

He had started construction in the spring of 1992 and refined it in stages for almost two years. It was the key element in a top-secret research project, and it had seen seven years of use before it was mothballed and stowed away in a bunker as an extremely well-kept secret. And even though each individual component inside was probably more or less antiquated, the machine itself was designed for one single purpose, and probably still remained one of the world's most powerful tools for decoding encrypted information.

It was called Sara. Named after another Sara he knew.

'We know some people,' Connors said, answering his question.

'So I gather,' William replied. 'So I gather, for sure.'

He tried to bat away his emotions, but it was too late. They were just machines, he tried to tell himself, but he knew that on the other hand they were parts of his life. They were parts of a past he'd done his best to forget and shut off, or at least to look back on with disdain, and now they were here, reminding him of it all, unexpectedly and out of nowhere and with overpowering force.

He looked up at Connors with a nod.

Thank you, it said.

Doing its best not to reveal how deeply he meant it.

Connors stayed in the room for another couple of minutes, watched as William dived in behind the computers, checking sockets and connections and making certain everything was in place. Eventually, feeling superfluous to requirements, Connors decided to leave and turned towards the door.

'Connors?'

William was standing now, next to one of the computer towers, a gravity in his look that Connors hadn't seen before. And for the first time, Connors realised in full that he was standing across the room from a man who tried to take his own life only the day before.

The blunt scornfulness was gone from William's face. Instead, Connors looked straight into something else, a bottomless pit of humanity that he hadn't expected even though he probably should have, and for a short moment he had to fight the impulse to walk up to him, put his hand on William's shoulder and tell him that everything was going to be fine.

But if there was one thing Connors wasn't sure of, it was that. Instead, he signalled at him to ask away.

'I can see one single reason as to why the UN should establish a secret paramilitary organisation under its own direction.'

Very well. Connors waited for him to continue.

'If there was an actual, tangible, all-consuming threat, one that wasn't directed at any particular country. If something was about to happen that affected us all, and if there was a fear that it couldn't be avoided. If that were the case. And if there was a fear of what the consequences would be, should the public find out. Then. Then, perhaps.'

If there had been a warmth to Connors' face as he turned to listen to William, that warmth was gone now. He stood perfectly still, his eyes deeply serious, motionless and staring straight into William's.

He said nothing, and his answer couldn't have been clearer.

And then Connors turned angd left the room.

∞◯∞

The clock was showing long after midnight when Christina arrived back at the editorial desk. In her hand she had a scrunched 7–Eleven bag with colourless takeaway pasta in an equally colourless paper box, not because she was hungry but because she knew that she probably ought to be. She would reheat it in the office microwave, trying not to think about how many times this particular pasta had been reheated before, and then she would eat a few mouthfuls and let the rest sit on the desk until the cleaners arrived to remove it in the small hours along with her waste bin. Hopefully, she would be at home in bed by then.

Coming into the office at night always evoked a particular sensation. The tempo was lower, and those who were working did it in silence. The perpetual clamour of ringing phones that blended together into a disharmonious concert had rung out, replaced by the whizz and hum of fans, computers and fluorescent lights. For anyone who wanted to avoid going home and seeing themselves in the mirror, the office was a perfect retreat. You were not alone, but the only social interaction required would be to throw a tired nod at a passing colleague. And as far as Christina was concerned, that was exactly what she needed.

Or, at least, that's how things usually were.

But on the desk at the other side of her glass office wall, one of the lamps cast its warm glow over a turned-on computer and a baseball hat resting on a notepad beside it.

Leo was still there. And before she had even started to look for him, the sound of a toppling coffee mug from the kitchen interrupted the sleepy hum of the office and drew her attention in his direction.

He was standing by the long work surface in the middle of the kitchenette area, intently focused on spreading out a huge heap of paper tissue before the light-brown puddle of equal parts milk and coffee reached the edges of the bench and cascaded down on to the floor. She watched him silently as she walked towards the kitchen, unsure whether she should allow herself to smile or worry over the fact that this was the person she had to assist her at the moment.

'You're still here?' she asked.

Leo glanced up. He hadn't heard her approach. Held out his hands as a mute way of saying that yes, he was.

Lowering his arms again he toppled the coffee mug back on its side, swearing under his breath before returning to the tissue roll, pulling out a fresh ream and commencing a new attempt to prevent the trickles of fluid from reaching the precipice.

'Okay then,' she said after a short pause. 'Since we're both here anyway.'

She popped the carton of pasta from her desk into the microwave and set it whirring away. Then she leaned against the row of cabinets to give him a brief summary of her meeting with Palmgren, their mutual thoughts about who and why, and his promise to try to establish whether the army had any idea what was actually going on.

There wasn't all that much to say, and she was done long before the microwave pinged. She glanced at Leo, indicating that it was his turn to talk. But instead, he just nodded. Took a breath as if he was about to speak, but couldn't find the right words and turned to the coffee machine to refill his empty cup.

She realised she'd have to draw it out of him.

'So what did you find?'

'Not much,' he said. 'I spoke with the removal company, and no, they say they haven't even been near the place. Place, being, you know, William's. But the neighbours are one hundred per cent certain it was that removal company's name on the men's shirts.'

'What time were they there?'

'Nobody really wants to admit how closely they monitor their neighbours. First they don't know, then they try to be unspecific. But probably sometime around lunch.'

'And when did he disappear from the hospital?'

'The last time they saw him was at eleven. More than that, they can't say.' He paused for a second. 'The police have the files from the surveillance cameras. But nobody expects to find anything. You know. Hospitals. Integrity and all that. There aren't a whole lot of cameras up to begin with, and if you know where they are you can move just about anywhere without getting caught. On, you know. Tape.'

The thing he said next was not at all what she expected.

'I tried it myself. After a few rounds I knew exactly what routes to take. It wasn't even hard.'

'You were there?'

'You wanted me to speak to them, right?'

Of course she did. And it was perfectly reasonable to go there; she would probably have done the same thing herself – the phone was a great tool but nothing beat looking someone straight in the eye when you talked to them. But to be honest, she had expected him to take the easy way out and make a call. She was delighted to be wrong.

'I just didn't know you went there,' she said.

'Well. Since I was out anyway,' he said. 'I was down on Strandvägen and then the removals office is in Vasastan and then, I don't know, the hospital is almost on my way home.'

She couldn't stop herself from breaking into a smile. 'Which begs the question, why are you *here*?'

Leo looked up at her. There was a note of friendliness in her voice, a tone he hadn't heard before, and the realisation forced him to find something else to think about, quickly, before he started to blush.

'I – thought – that,' he answered, trying to look like he had just said an entire sentence. Obviously well aware that it made him sound like an idiot, but he still preferred that to looking like one, too.

A new silence.

'When was the last time you looked at your watch?' she said.

He shrugged. He knew it was late. But there had been a reason that he went back to the office, and for a moment he glanced over towards his desk and had a rapid negotiation with himself.

He could tell her. But he didn't want to say anything. Not yet. He might be wrong. Instead, he shrugged again, even though he knew exactly what time it was.

'Go home,' she said.

'I'd really rather stay a little longer,' he answered.

It was quite possible that this was the first sentence she'd ever heard him utter without getting tangled up in his own words and having to start over, and what's more he'd delivered it with a clarity and poise she didn't recognise. She was already smiling. Now it turned into a grin.

'What?' he asked.

'Nothing. I'm tired. And so are you.'

She was right, but he hadn't allowed himself to notice it.

'Take a cab,' she said. 'You can give me the receipt tomorrow.'

She leaned over and took the coffee from his hand. He was an awkward young man, but there was no doubt he was capable of more than she'd thought. And she didn't want him to burn out.

'You start at eight thirty tomorrow morning,' she said. 'And I don't want you yawning at your desk.'

With that, she grabbed her pasta from the microwave.

And turned back towards her glass-walled sanctum.

Leo had put on his jacket and hat when he approached Christina's room with cautious steps one final time before leaving. Stopped outside the door. Leaned forward on to the glass, his down jacket flattened against it like an exploded airbag on a windscreen.

She looked up, waiting for him to make enough connections in his head to be able to string a sentence together.

'How come you're so sure?' he said. 'I mean, about him not leaving, you know, voluntarily?'

It was a legitimate question. And even though she didn't know if it was a good idea to let him in on a past she'd rather forget herself, she couldn't come up with a good reason to keep him out of it.

'Everything was packed,' she said after a pause. 'He'd taken his computers. His clothes. Even his toothbrush. Everything.'

He looked at her. So?

And she picked up her phone, flicked through her photos until she found the right one. It was a picture of William's study, one of those she'd taken that morning, and she pinched her fingers to zoom in on one of the room's walls.

An arrangement of picture frames covered the entire side of the room, from the edge of the low cabinet up to the point where the wallpaper met the stucco on the ceiling. The frames were full of photos, all showing the same face. A young woman, in different situations: smiling at the camera, posing for a portrait, captured in action. In some of them she was younger, maybe fifteen, and in others she looked a few years older.

But nowhere was she more than twenty.

'Who is she?' he asked.

'Sara,' she answered. 'She was our daughter.'

He heard her tone. *Was.* Said nothing.

'If he'd done the packing himself, they wouldn't still be hanging there.'

She turned off her phone. Placed it on the table. A sad smile as she looked away from him.

'Leo? Seriously. Go home and get some sleep.'

He stood for a moment. Then he freed her window from the

weight of his jacket, and made his way to the lift on the far side of the open-plan office.

Christina sat where she was. Stared at the white-hot cardboard carton with the colourless pasta. And then she flung it into the waste bin without even opening it, turned on her computer and tried to focus on the job she was paid to do.

9

William Sandberg had stayed in his office until long after midnight, until eventually the guard outside had knocked on the door and politely but firmly suggested he get some sleep.

He'd asked for permission to bring a few printouts and pens to his room, and once there his bathroom mirror had become a makeshift whiteboard, and William had kept working in front of it until the clock showed well past two in the morning and all the fruit from the breakfast tray was gone.

When he woke up five hours later, his second morning in captivity, it was with an energy he couldn't remember the last time he'd felt.

Nobody had knocked on his door. There was no alarm clock, nobody telling him that it was time to get up, and yet he was fully awake almost exactly at the stroke of seven, sitting straight at the edge of the bed, his mind ready to begin where it left off the night before.

He let his thoughts wander for a few minutes on their own, and then he went into the bathroom and took a long, warm shower while his mind took care of itself.

When he was done, he surprised himself by lying down on the bathroom floor.

His hands behind his head. Knees bent, ankles crossed. And then he pulled his upper body upwards, doing his first sit-up in as long as he could remember.

It was a lot harder than he recalled.

He felt his skin fold in front of him, the creases significantly deeper than they used to be, and his stomach burned like fire for every second he tried to hold himself up. But as he fell down on to his back after what could almost count as twenty passable repetitions it wasn't without a sense of success. He was completely exhausted, and he wouldn't manage another one if his life depended on it, but it meant the muscles were still there and they knew what to do. That was a good thing. It was just a matter of doing it again.

Like so much else. Just doing it.

While William was still in the shower, someone had been in his room and left a new breakfast tray by the bed. It was as huge and exotic as the previous morning, but he settled for a cup of coffee and a single fruit, turning his attention to the newspapers that had accompanied the breakfast. Yesterday's date. Still, he couldn't help being impressed.

Both of them were Swedish.

He glanced swiftly over both front pages but nothing caught his interest. Instead, he picked one of them up, and flicked straight to the Stockholm section. Read each of the headlines. Carefully. Twice to make sure. Put it down again, changed to the other, did the same thing. Nothing there either. Fair enough.

He folded the newspapers back up. Put them on the tray again, with the front page facing out. There was no point in letting them know what he'd been looking for.

His disappearance wasn't mentioned in either paper, and even if he would have liked it to be, it didn't really surprise him. The only person who'd be missing him was Christina. But he was quite certain his captors would have taken precautions to create a scenario that people wouldn't question. Whatever Christina might think had happened to him, it wouldn't be anything that made the news.

All the more reason, he thought. All the more reason to do what he planned.

And when Connors knocked on his door at ten past eight to ask if William was ready to start the day's work, William had been dressed and prepared to go for quite some time.

He was looking forward to the day in front of him.

He had a plan.

And no intention of telling Connors what it was.

∞◯∞

Almost eighteen hours had passed since the first time Connors left him in his new workspace. At that time, William had been considerably less optimistic.

He had remained standing in the middle of the room, alone and motionless for ages, looking at the endless mass of unfathomable information on the walls around him. On one of the walls hung reams of paper with printed number sequences, enough to cover the space from floor to ceiling, and on the wall next to it there were printouts of the symbols, those that apparently were Sumerian cuneiform but didn't tell him anything, pinned to the walls as if someone had wallpapered the room with a black-and-white graphic pattern.

They were organised into groups, hundreds of pieces of paper side by side, the groups separated here and there by little gaps of wall to indicate a break in the sequence. As if to say that here and there, some of the information had been written off as unimportant, and some of the numbers and groups had been removed.

It was an overwhelming amount of data.

He had no idea where to begin.

And what worried him even more were the things that were only implied.

For one thing, he obviously wasn't the first person here. Someone had worked with the material before him, performed the initial task of deciphering the endless sequences of numbers hanging around him, cracked the key to how they should be transformed into other numbers that were then in turn transformed to the long pixelated images of Sumerian text.

What did that tell him?

Had someone else started his job, but stopped before they made it all the way? Why? And where was that person now?

The sequences around him had obviously once been decoded, but what they still lacked was a universal key that worked in both directions. They still didn't know how to re-encrypt new data, and what they needed was a general formula, or who knew, perhaps a *collection* of formulas, to allow them to encode a new message at any given moment.

The process could be immensely complicated. Perhaps the formulas were based on where in the sequence the encrypted text appeared, perhaps even on what *other* texts were already in it, or why just there, why not in completely different sequences that he couldn't even envisage?

He cursed out loud to himself. How the hell could he help them code an answer to a message he wasn't allowed to read? One that they weren't even prepared to tell him the origin of?

He needed to start over. Take it all in, get an overview, see what he could learn from what he saw.

He positioned himself facing the printouts. Then he started from the end.

The wall with the cuneiform.

It told him nothing, but then he didn't expect it to. It could just as well have been a wall full of children's drawings, pointless clumps of lines that didn't mean anything to anyone, except that obviously wasn't the case. Instead, someone had deemed them so meaningful and important that the nations of the world had assigned an entire organisation to take charge of them. And who was he to argue with that?

From a few steps back, the cuneiform texts appeared to go on and on in long, contiguous blocks, page after page. But on closer inspection he could see that every printed page was framed by a thin border, as if it were a discrete object in itself, a separate piece of the puzzle in the gigantic mosaic of A4 pages hanging from the walls.

Every A4 page was a matrix of tiny squares, each with its own pixelated part of the message, 23 pixels wide, 73 high. In total 1679 pixels, forming a row of Sumerian dashes and symbols, telling him absolutely nothing.

Okay. On to the next wall. The wall with all the number sequences.

On each page there were two sets of numbers. The upper half of the page was printed in black and the lower in red, side by side and without spacing. The letters C and P told him the difference between the two.

Cipher and *Plaintext*.

The black numbers were C. The encrypted code. The one they had intercepted. And the red was P. The decoded material. The numbers that in turn represented the countless groups of pixels that made up the cuneiform images on the adjacent wall.

So far so good. Nothing too much out of the ordinary. But what did strike him as odd was how the numeric sequences were made up of four numbers.

He hadn't registered it when they rushed past on the projected video wall in the large conference room, but as he thought more about it he realised he'd seen it back then, too.

Four.

Not two, like digital sequences of binary zeros and ones. Not ten, like the good old familiar numeric system everyone was taught from the day they stopped dribbling and could sit up straight. The sequences in front of him were made up of values from zero to three.

Base four.

Not that this was a revolutionary idea in itself. He'd seen it before, of course he had. But as far as he knew he'd never seen it used in any practical applications, not outside of anecdotal thought experiments, examples to show how arithmetic systems can build on any base you choose. Programmers use sixteen. The Babylonians sixty. But who on earth would decide to use four? And why?

It surprised him, not least because of what he was looking at. If something was going to be turned into pixels that were either black or white, then what was the point of storing them as values from zero to three?

Why put binary numbers in a quaternary code?

He shook his head. Why wasn't the point.

His job wasn't to turn the red, decrypted numbers into the Sumerian symbols on the next wall. Somebody else had already done that, and someone had translated that script into something modern and legible, and that wasn't the point either since nobody had any intention of telling him what it said.

His only task was to work out the connection, how the black numbers had been transformed into the red, and then how some new goddamn red ones should be transformed into new goddamn black, and he felt his frustration grow and the entire job overwhelm him and all he wanted to do was to give it all up and leave.

He glanced over at the desk. The binders. The computers.

He could, but he shouldn't.

In the binders he'd find his predecessor's calculations and notes, and he'd be able to use them as a shortcut into the material, and it was extremely tempting but a very bad idea.

If someone before him had figured out a cipher key that only worked in one direction, it meant it was incomplete or even plain wrong, and William didn't want to walk into the same trap himself. He didn't want to get stuck inside someone else's reasoning, accepting the conclusions that had already been made simply because they looked so good on paper.

He needed to start from the beginning. No prior knowledge. No help.

And no computers.

Because if he didn't know, the computers wouldn't either.

As long as he was fumbling the computers would fumble too, and before he knew it he would be further away from the answer than he already was. Right now there was only one way of getting into the material. Paper and pen. Sketching and counting by hand. Getting to feel the code inside him, like he used to do, back then.

But back then was a long time ago.

And he stood there, his gaze travelling back and forth across the numbers. Desperately trying to get close to them, but not knowing how. A sense of claustrophobia started to grow inside of him, it pressured him and made it hard to breathe, and gradually he felt it dawn on him, no, he knew it beyond doubt already, a realisation that made his shirt go moist and warm and stick to his back like a wet blanket.

He'd lost it.

He wasn't up to the job.

After hours of agony, William had thrown his pen and his papers away, pushed the files on to the floor in sheer desperation, opened the door and marched out into the corridor. He needed air. He needed to look at something else. To think afresh.

The first thing he saw was a guard in a light-grey uniform. It was an unfamiliar face, not someone from the plane, and he was firmly parked a few steps away from his door, the empty gaze of a museum attendant on an out-of-season weekday.

'Can I help you?' he said, though his voice made it perfectly clear that he had no interest whatsoever in helping. His sole purpose was to stop William from going anywhere he shouldn't.

William explained that he needed to stretch his legs.

'You can walk up and down right here,' the guard said.

'I can stop working, too,' said William. 'I need to walk to think, and thinking is what I'm here for. Your choice.'

They stared each other out for a couple of seconds. The guard obviously had his orders, probably to keep William in his room and to make sure he was reasonably content, and William could see him negotiate with himself which of the two was the highest priority.

Eventually the guard jerked his head in reply. His gaze remained stony, even if they both knew William had been the victor in their little battle.

'But don't you try anything,' he said.

William gave him a wry smile. For a moment, he considered asking him what there was to try when you're held captive behind massive stone walls, but he chose not to. Instead, he jerked his head back at him, leaving the guard to interpret whether it meant thank you or fuck off or something in between. And then he started to wander off down the corridor.

It wasn't much of a stroll.

The air had the same damp edge as in the room, and the walls were built from the same endless blocks of stone.

But if nothing else, it was a break from the numbers and the printouts. He let his eyes wander across the walls and the floor, counting the stones and looking for patterns in the masonry to clear his mind.

But his thoughts couldn't let go.

1679.

23 by 73.

What annoyed him most was that he recognised the combination, and he had an inkling that he should know where from. But no matter how he tried he couldn't figure it out, and it annoyed him to the point that he eventually had to tell himself to drop it.

At the end of the corridor the passage took a turn to the right, the same way that Connors had led him to the meeting with Franquin, and further down, there were other smaller passages running in different directions. He chose one he'd not been down before, and as he tramped along it he continued counting the stones, silently and calmly, but with a growing awareness inside of him.

The first thing that occurred to him was that he couldn't see any cameras. That was quite remarkable. Either it meant there weren't any, which didn't make any sense, or it meant they were so well hidden inside the thick stone walls that they couldn't be seen by the naked eye. Which would be even more remarkable. Cameras did their job best if they were clearly visible and worked as a deterrent.

He decided to assume they were everywhere.

The second thing that struck him was that he had been presented with an opportunity. The guard had let him wander off to reconnoitre by himself, probably without understanding that's what he was doing, which in turn was probably because William hadn't intended any such thing. He'd only wanted to stretch his legs. But now that he was here, it was too good an opportunity to waste.

And so he kept walking. Still the same, dawdling pace. But this was no longer a casual stroll. Rather, he concentrated on memorising the route, noting which passages went where and what they looked like, and silently decided that this little walk would be followed by many more, as often as he could until he had a clear mental map of as large a part of the castle as possible.

Eventually, his journey came to a halt. A large wooden door blocked the passage in front of him, and next to it on the wall was a box with what could only be a sensor for electronic key cards. A red diode glowed dimly at the top, telling him the door was locked and that it would remain so until the right card came along to open it.

William looked at it for a moment. And decided that he had been ambling around for long enough. That it was time to turn back before anyone began to worry about where he was.

On his way back to his own corridor, he declared two goals for himself.

The first was to see to it that he stayed ahead at all times.

Not by one step, or two, but by as many steps as possible.

To do everything he could to solve the structure and the logic of the cipher key, and to keep releasing his findings to Connors and Franquin, but at a pace he decided for himself. He would do enough that they were satisfied with his performance, but at the same time he would make sure he knew more than he told them. Not that he knew what to do with the information, but it was always better to hold more cards than them. Rather than the other way around.

But his second goal was the important one.

Whatever might happen, he promised himself, he would find a way out.

∞C∞

Consequently, when Connors left him alone in his office the following morning, it was with a new level of energy that William got to work.

The night's calculations on the bathroom mirror might not have helped him discover anything new, but they'd forced him to think. He had accessed parts of his mind that he hadn't visited for years, he'd forced himself to search for links and patterns, and even if it didn't lead to any immediate triumphs he knew that the work was necessary if he was to crack the code in the end.

For the second day in a row, William started moving about between the walls, back and forth between numbers and symbols, columns and rows, looking for connections, anything that stood out or repeated itself. He looked, moved to a new position, looked again. He scribbled on paper, stuck Post-it notes to the wall with different colours representing different links or thoughts or ideas, and slowly, slowly, he felt it coming. The feeling of being back. For a man who'd tried to commit suicide only two days earlier, euphoric was a strong word. But if someone had asked him to describe how he felt, that's exactly the word he would have used.

He worked for two hours before putting his pen down. By then, it was time for part two of his project.

His own part.

This time the guard was prepared for his question, and significantly more cooperative. William explained his need for a walk, received the obligatory admonitions, and strolled away.

Same tactics as yesterday. Slow stroll, casual steps. No obvious destination. And all the while, he registered everything he passed, tried to memorise each detail and add it to his mental map. He chose passages he hadn't been down, methodically and precisely checking them off in his mind to keep track of which ones remained to be covered. And after a while he was tired enough to decide to turn back to his office.

One more corridor, he thought.

Peeled off down a side passage.

One more corridor, then I'll go back.

Instead, he found himself confronted with a choice.

He saw it the moment he turned the corner.

The door at the end of passageway, some ten metres away, exactly like the one he'd encountered on his walk the day before. A big, heavy wooden door. Iron hinges. A metal box to one side.

But there was a difference.

The diode on the box was showing green.

Someone had just passed through it, the door had closed but the lock hadn't yet clicked back into place, and a faint whirring sound revealed that the bolt was still retracted and the door could be opened.

William stood transfixed. Should he? Should he not?

It was his chance. But it was a chance he didn't want, not now, not already, not yet.

He wanted to know more. He wanted to understand what he was working on, wanted to find more passages, perhaps be led to new meetings in parts of the castle he hadn't yet seen, all to further his chances of getting out of there, and to give him more to tell the world once he did.

But there was no time to think about it. It was a chance he might never get again. The lock in front of him was showing green, and that wouldn't last for ever.

He hesitated.

And then suddenly he didn't hesitate any longer.

It was more an instinct than a conscious decision: he charged forward, rushing down the corridor towards the door, and with each step he took his mind's eye saw the light switch back to red, but it never did. A few seconds later he was there, yanking the door open, gliding through it and letting it slide closed the instant he was on the other side, afraid that the alarm would be triggered if it wasn't back in place when the lock closed.

Behind him, it clicked back into its frame, immediately followed by the whirr of the bolt turning, as the green diode on the box returned to red.

Only then did his brain begin to work properly.

And he realised he'd been stupid beyond belief.

He stood perfectly still, breathing as quietly as possible. Somebody else must have passed through that very same door seconds before him, or else it wouldn't have been unlocked in the first place. If he'd only allowed himself a moment's thought, he would have realised that that person couldn't be very far away.

In front of William was a new passage. It was almost identical to the one he'd just come from, same stone floors, same masonry walls. In the distance he could see it come to an end in a small alcove with a tiny window, perhaps some stairs leading in different directions, he couldn't tell from where he stood.

And it was completely silent. Which made him uneasy.

He would have preferred the sound of footsteps, some sign of life that echoed away at a distance, fading and vanishing and giving him an idea where the person who'd used the door before him was currently at.

Because the alternative was that the person was still nearby. And that would give him some explaining to do.

He remained motionless for so long he lost the feeling of how many minutes he'd been standing there, and eventually he decided that he didn't have anything to lose. He had already entered a corridor he shouldn't be in. The only thing he could do was to continue forward, try to find out as much as he could before they found him, hope that he might discover something that he could use in the future. Quite possibly, they were already looking for him.

He started moving again. Didn't see any cameras here either, but continued to assume they were there, very well hidden. As before, he pretended to stroll casually, all the while scanning his surroundings and registering everything he saw.

He passed an archway. And another one. Beyond lay smaller passages, low ceilings and no lights, all of them ending in heavy wooden doors that he knew he wouldn't be able to force open if he tried. He added each detail to his mental map, kept walking towards the distant alcove. With a little luck perhaps it would be a landing, with stairs or passages leading further away, perhaps even to an entrance or an opening where he could get out.

He wandered. Soft, measured steps. Like running away in slow motion. But he had no other choice.

And then he stopped short.

Footsteps.

He looked around. The sound came echoing from somewhere in front of him, and it confirmed his suspicions. There was indeed a staircase. The bad news was that the footsteps were growing louder and louder.

Pulse at breaking point, he searched for an escape route.

His only line of retreat was blocked by a wooden door, guarded by a glowing red light. Perhaps he could jump into one of the side passages? Hope they'd pass without seeing him? On the other hand, if they caught him, he wouldn't be able to pretend he wasn't consciously trying to escape, and that was the last thing he needed. The alternative was to stay put and convince them that he'd simply got lost.

That didn't feel like a very tempting scenario either.

And ahead of him the footsteps came closer.

William wasn't given the opportunity to choose.

By the time he felt the rag against his face, it was already pressed firmly into his mouth. And he wanted to scream, but wasn't able to make a sound.

∞◯∞

The man who'd passed through the door after her had waited for so long that she began to wonder if he was still there.

Janine was pressed up against the stone wall in the dark side passage. Breathing silently, berating herself in her mind.

She hadn't noticed anyone following her. She had been careless. It had gone too well for too long; it had been too easy, and she'd let herself believe that she was smarter than anyone else. And this was her punishment. Someone had been behind her, and now he stood right outside the archway waiting for her.

Or did he? Then why couldn't she hear anything?

Maybe she was wrong. Maybe she'd been imagining things, and here she was hiding in a passage for no reason, maybe she was paranoid and nervous and needed to shape up and go back to her room. Perhaps that was all there was to it? She was just about to leave her spot when she heard the footsteps again.

Slow. Cautious. Looking for something?

A strange rhythm. Almost like strolling.

It didn't make any sense. There were two types of people around, one was the guards and military staff and the other one was herself, and the steps she heard sounded as if they belonged to a visitor or someone who was just out for a walk, and that was a type of person that simply didn't exist, not here.

It wasn't until the man walked past her opening that she realised he wasn't a guard. He passed her with slow, mooching steps, and for a moment she didn't understand what she was looking at. And the moment she did, it was too late.

She heard them first.

A split second later his ears picked them up too. He halted a few steps away from her, listened for the same sound as she did. Footsteps. Far away. Guards coming up the stairs.

And she hesitated; she could let them take him, it might even be her best chance. When they led him away, that might give her the chance to go on unnoticed.

Might.

But she couldn't afford to take chances.

This was what she'd been waiting for.

And she pulled off her T-shirt in one move.

She mustn't allow him to scream. It had to be quick and silent, and if she injured him he wouldn't be of any use.

Even without a T-shirt stuffed into his mouth, William Sandberg would have been too surprised to say anything.

The young woman who stood over him couldn't be any older than thirty. Her dark hair was swept back into a ponytail, she was barefoot and wore tight black leggings, and where her T-shirt had been until a few seconds before, a black top clung to her well-trained body as if someone had painted it there.

She gestured for him to hush, staring insistently into his eyes, and sandwiched him between herself and the wall as the guards continued on their way to the same door the two of them had just passed through. Heard them take out their key cards, and then, at last, the sound of the door thudding back into place as the guards disappeared on the other side.

She waited with bated breath for the whirr of the electronic bolt to stop.

When it finally did, she looked him in the eye again.

'You and I need to talk.'

10

The streets of Amsterdam had been covered with Japanese cherry blossom swirling in the breeze when Janine Charlotta Haynes first met the bull-necked man.

It was spring. Warm enough to take a stroll, no wind, but still with a wintry freshness in the air. It was going to be a perfect evening.

At least, that had been the plan. In reality, it was already ruined, and it was still only quarter past eight. She was dressed up, as much as her budget allowed, and waiting at the little restaurant even though the table wasn't booked until nine. She'd hoped there'd be time for them to have a glass of wine at the bar, to watch people around them and pretend to insult each other with their childish, intellectual word games, a practice which had grown into their own tongue-in-cheek mating ritual. They were so good at it that it had taken months for their colleagues to work out they were a couple; the more widespread belief was that they were liable to kill each other, given the chance.

The table was booked under the same name as always. And as always, she'd had to struggle not to smile as she talked to the maître d'.

'Name, please?' he'd asked.

'Emanuel Sphynx,' she'd answered. 'With a capital x.'

The waiter had looked at her. He'd heard the vibration in her voice as she swallowed the giggle, but he couldn't quite make out what she was laughing about. Perhaps she was poking fun at him. But he shrugged it off, smiled his featureless smile, and decided to let it lie.

'There's a message for you,' he said, leafing through the booking list in search of a note he knew should be there, scanning it quickly before looking at her:

'Mr Sphynx will be fifteen minutes late.'

He passed the note to her. A formal gesture, as if the note were something she might want to save in an album or hang on the wall. But disappointment had already taken the shine from her eyes. The smile he thought he'd heard was gone now, and she mumbled something about waiting in the bar before heading off into the dark restaurant.

And here she sat. Phone in her hand, thumbing listlessly to avoid looking lonely, a half-empty glass of wine in front of her. It might as well have been gravy. She couldn't taste it, anyway.

One year earlier, Emanuel Sphynx had come into the world. They had been laughing like children. Now it didn't seem the least bit amusing.

Janine and Albert had been sitting at the back of an unbelievably boring seminar, and over lunch they'd secretly downed a couple of glasses of wine, and that had made a considerable difference. The afternoon had been much more exciting.

And even if the only part of the seminar that had actually stuck was the two of them passing a notepad back and forth, giggling like school kids, every time with a new, made-up name or ridiculous acronym based on something the lecturer had just said, it still couldn't be considered anything but a rather fruitful day. She had followed him back to his place, and as far as she could remember they'd only spent four nights apart since.

That was one year ago to the day. This was Emanuel Sphynx's first birthday. Janine's and Albert's anniversary. And he was late. Fucking Europeans.

Fifteen minutes meant at least an hour. Having lost interest in the phone, she folded the napkin in front of her into a crumpled-up nothing, and when that was done there was little else to occupy her. She hated sitting alone in places made for company. Not that she had a problem with solitude, quite the contrary, but she very much preferred to be alone in private.

When the man in the suit sat down next to her, that didn't make things any better.

He was about her age, noticeably muscular under his heavy

tweed jacket, his white shirt casually unbuttoned around an impressive neck. And he seemed to want to chat, and she definitely didn't.

'I'm busy,' she said.

'I can see that,' he said, but didn't mean it. 'What is it? A swan?'

He indicated the crumpled napkin in front of her. It was a lot of things. But it definitely wasn't a swan.

'I'll make myself a little more clear,' she said. 'Had I been single, I would have preferred to stay that way.'

'Don't look at me, I wouldn't have stopped you.'

She heard his tone. Looked at him. Was he joking or was he being rude?

His face was serious, unmoving and firm, as if he meant exactly what he said. But there was a faint glimmer in his eyes, faint but obvious to a trained eye like hers, and that could only mean one thing. He'd enjoyed her sarcasm, and he had sent her a curveball to match her own. Now it was her turn.

'So that's why you sat down next to me,' she said. 'To tell me you weren't interested.'

'God no. I usually save that one for the second date.'

It came fast enough to stun her. She glanced up at him to make sure they were playing the same game, and as she did he was sitting there, ready to catch her eye. Damn. The same instant their eyes met, she realised she'd lost. She didn't have an answer. And that annoyed her. Almost as much as it annoyed her that it did.

'Roger,' he said, stretching out his hand towards her.

'Janine,' she replied, taking it. He had large, powerful hands and a British accent she couldn't place. It bothered her that she noticed that, too.

'No, that wasn't why,' he concluded. 'The main reason I came to sit here was that you were the only person I could hear speaking a language that wasn't just a lot of noise.'

'I wish I could say the same.'

His turn to fumble for an answer. And he grinned, reluctantly but widely, and she returned to her glass and mentally chalked up a point for herself, fully aware the match had only begun.

When forty-five minutes later she caught sight of herself in the mirror of the ladies', she was struck by an overwhelming feeling of guilt. She was smiling. She was smiling a relaxed, slightly inebriated smile and her cheeks were flushed and that was even worse. She was having a good time. No, she was having *fun*. Albert would be there in half an hour and here she was, giddy like an idiot and looking forward to going back out to a charming muscular man with a clipped English accent and what the hell was she doing?

She pulled out her phone and brought up Albert's number. New text message.

I love you, she wrote. *See you soon.*

It was embarrassingly transparent. The whole thing was dripping with guilt, and she deleted it and started over.

I'm two and a half glasses ahead. If you don't come in fifteen minutes I'm off with a strapping Englishman.

That was better. She sent it out. One last glance in the mirror, but she decided against fixing her hair – not now, not for the sake of the Englishman, perhaps later – and turned to go back into the restaurant.

To her surprise, he was waiting outside the door.

The cloakroom outside the toilets was unattended and empty, and a number of thoughts immediately flashed through her head. Perhaps he'd grown bored and wanted to leave, maybe he wanted her to come with him, or perhaps he wanted to try to pull her in among the jackets and coats in the hope of a quick cuddle.

The moment the situation changed from an adventure in her fantasy to a reality in a restaurant cloakroom it also changed from tempting to the opposite. Convinced as she was of his intentions, she was equally convinced that she wasn't interested; she dodged past him and set off along the rows of coats and jackets, but he took a step forward and laid a hand on her shoulder. Her intoxication was gone now, and she sent her brain off in search of a suitably sarcastic response, her entire body bracing for the worst.

And then she stopped dead.

He'd stuck something in her neck.

She looked straight at him. He wasn't smiling any more. And just as she found the words to say, her mouth stopped working.

*

Thirty-five minutes later the glass doors swung open, and a young man by the name of Albert van Dijk walked up to the maître d', asking if there was a woman waiting for Emanuel Sphynx.

By that time, neither Janine nor the bull-necked man were anywhere near Amsterdam.

ဆၚ

The muscular Englishman who'd once presented himself as Roger couldn't quite put his finger on what made him react. But something felt wrong, and he walked up to the heavy door to her room and knocked.

He'd already made up an apology in his head. Not that he needed to explain why he wanted to know what she was up to, he was head of security and she was under guard and none of it was a secret, but the orders clearly stated that the guests shouldn't have to feel like prisoners unless it was absolutely necessary.

Martin Rodriguez – that was his real name – understood exactly why. The Organisation relied on the guests' willingness to do what they should. If they weren't treated well they might refuse, or worse still, they might purposely deliver incorrect results, believing that the Organisation were the bad guys and that every attempt to go against them was an act of good.

Which was the reason he had an apology prepared. He'd thought he heard her screaming, and simply wanted to check if everything was all right.

He waited.

It had been seven months since he brought her here. Sometimes he tried to convince himself that the man she'd been waiting for was an idiot and a bastard, and that in fact he'd been doing her a favour. But that was a lie and he knew it. Some very thorough research had been done, and they knew exactly who she was. Her relationship was annoyingly good and the only bad guy was himself: he'd abducted her without explaining why, and whatever was happening to the world it wasn't fair that Janine Charlotta Haynes should pay.

But nothing was fair, he reminded himself.

And even though he was merely a cog in a giant machine, he knew that what he was doing was ultimately right.

*

When Martin Rodriguez opened the door to her room, his thoughts changed completely.

It was empty, even though he hadn't seen her leave.

Ten seconds later he alerted the others over the radio, and all hell broke loose, just as he knew it would.

∞◯∞

A few hundred metres away the evening air hit William's face, cool and refreshing as if he'd turned over his pillow on a hot night. It was later than he'd thought. Already dark. And he had no idea what awaited him.

He'd followed the young woman as she ran down winding staircases, along corridors and hallways, sometimes passing a passage he recognised from his walk with Connors, but for the most part he didn't know where they were and could only rely on the stranger in front of him. Her, and that blue piece of plastic that got them through the heavy locked doors, one after the other.

Eventually they'd begun running upwards again, and she'd led him up a staircase that climbed so steeply he thought it must be a tower, until the moment she opened a low door and ducked through it, out on to a vast stone terrace.

He was already aware that the castle was large, but only now did he get to see just how impressively huge it was. The outer walls continued in both directions, weaving in and out to form alcoves and bay windows, and the terrace followed them along the castle's entire length until it ran out of sight where the building came to an end. A stone banister was all that separated them from the landscape below, and from where they stood the drop to the ground and the alpine lake below seemed as good as endless.

It crossed his mind that if the woman wanted to kill him this was the perfect place. Physically he wouldn't offer any resistance, she was quick and in extremely good shape and William, quite frankly, was neither.

But he shook off the idea. From what he could see, she'd rescued him from being caught by the guards. There was no reason to suspect she was anything other than a fellow prisoner.

'I'm Janine,' she said when she stopped running. 'Janine Haynes.'

She was still short of breath, but her voice was focused, her clear gaze composed and alert.

'I'm not sure how much time we have. I don't know if they can hear us or see us; the only thing I'm certain of is that you and I aren't supposed to talk. And if they knew we were here, they'd . . .' She paused. 'I don't know what they'd do,' she said.

'Who are they?' asked William.

'I assume they've said the same things to you as they did to me. An organisation under the UN. Maybe it's true, maybe it's not. The important thing is they lied to me and they'll be lying to you as well. And we need to get out of here.'

'Lied about what?'

'You've seen the texts, right?'

'The old keys?' he said. 'You were the one who figured them out?'

It took her a second to understand what he meant. But she shook her head. 'I know nothing about codes. That wasn't me.'

'So who are you? What are you doing here?'

'Until the seventeenth of April I was a research student at the UvA. University of Amsterdam. PhD in Archaeology.'

Of course. 'The cuneiform script,' he said.

She nodded. 'They did their best to make sure I didn't understand,' she said. 'They gave them to me in the wrong order. I got texts that didn't belong. And nobody told me what it was. The whole thing wore me down, I couldn't think, I didn't know where I was or why or—'

She'd raised her voice, and she stopped as she heard it, listened for noises around them. Nothing but wind and water. She calmed down.

'How long have you been here?' he asked.

She paused. There wasn't much time, but she decided to give him the short version. The papers she'd published when she was an undergraduate in Seattle. The scholarships for her research on ancient written languages. The move to Europe to become a researcher, the wonderful life she'd had in Amsterdam with a cat and a cast-iron balcony and a view over a canal, and then everything went black and she woke up in the castle. That was seven months ago.

'And you?' she asked.

'Same thing,' he said. Except he didn't have a wonderful life, and he was allergic to cats. But it didn't seem relevant to the conversation.

'I heard you arrive,' she said. 'I heard the helicopter. I knew they were bringing in someone new.'

'New what?'

She tried to find the words. But it was too complicated; she didn't know where to begin or how much time they had. So she shook her head, tried to structure her thoughts. The conversation was starting to go in the wrong direction, and if she was going to tell him what she knew, she had to start in the right place.

But William interrupted her. Rephrased his question, asked her again. 'Why am I here?'

She looked into his eyes. That was an easier question to answer.

'Because the woman who was here before you is gone.'

∞○○∞

The guard who'd been half-asleep outside William's office was more awake than ever.

He sprinted through the corridors, faster and faster every time he reached the end of a blind passage without finding William there.

He just couldn't understand it. Only a few minutes had passed since he received the alarm that the girl was missing, the pretty American academic, and his first thought was that this time Rodriguez had screwed up big time and how the hell had he let it happen.

And here he was running around and understanding even less. Somehow, the old guy had vanished too. As if he'd managed to disappear through the locked doors, pass them without a key card and without setting off an alarm; it was categorically impossible and yet it had happened. And the guard cursed his way down the empty corridor, doubled back into passages he'd already checked, clinging on to an ebbing hope that he wouldn't have to report that his subject was gone, too.

When Franquin called over the radio asking him where Sandberg was, he knew his chances had run out.

∞○○∞

Several storeys below him, inside a musty underground room, Evelyn Keyes had already begun sifting through material in accordance with rules she had once reluctantly created herself.

A bank of monitors on the wall in front of her showed the fuzzy pictures from various surveillance cameras, and one by one she scrolled through the recorded material, swiping backwards and forwards over the timeline of the individual cameras in search of the tiniest movement that shouldn't be there.

She already knew she wouldn't find anything. They had too few cameras, and they sat in the wrong parts of the castle to be of any use. She was angry, and she had every right to be. What was the point in putting her in charge of a security system if it didn't work?

She'd pointed it out before, but nothing had been done. She had warned them to expect disaster, long before the first one happened, and they had failed to act. And now here they were again, everyone caught napping.

They hadn't fixed the holes.

The facility hadn't kept pace with the developments of the last couple of decades; the system wasn't designed to contain prisoners but to stop unauthorised personnel from gaining entry, and nobody had wanted to spend money on security. As if there was anything else to save money for.

'Tell me what you see,' Franquin said from behind her.

He said it so brusquely the words came out as a stream of consonants, his hands resting tightly on the back of her chair and his eyes anxiously hunting from screen to screen in the hope that Keyes had noticed some detail he hadn't.

But she didn't reply. Gave him a cold glance and indicated the monitors. He knew the problems as well as she did.

On the floors above them, guards ran down corridor after corridor checking that Haynes and Sandberg hadn't somehow magically appeared inside their sectors. But in spite of that, they only occasionally appeared on Keyes' monitors. They had thousands of square metres to cover and only a handful of cameras to do it. The chance they might spot something useful was slim to non-existent.

'Whatever happens, they'll never get out of here,' he said. Registering her expression, he added: 'We've made improvements since then.'

He saw how she made a conscious decision not to respond. She didn't have to. He knew she was right. They should have upgraded the security, but then again, when? They were already racing against time. How could they prioritise something that wouldn't tangibly advance the project?

Their only hope was that their two guests wouldn't unleash a disaster before the guards could catch them. They were somewhere in the castle, they had to be, because what he had just said was true. It would be impossible for them to get out.

Nonetheless, he heard his headset crackle as the guards called in, one after the other, reporting that their sector was empty. That none of their doors were open. But that, even so, their guests were nowhere to be found.

Franquin shut his eyes for a moment. He didn't want to be fatalistic. He knew everything pointed straight to hell, but he refused to accept it. There had to be some clue they'd missed, there must be some way of retrieving this situation. It wasn't pointless to fight. Even if it seemed so.

Because if he was wrong, everyone had already lost. And he just couldn't bear that thought.

'Franquin?'

He glanced up. Keyes sat in front of him, looking at him with an energy that startled him.

'Helena Watkins,' she said.

For a moment, he wondered what she was talking about. And then she nodded at her computer. At a long table of never-ending columns running down the screen: numbers and times and numbers again. He immediately knew what they were.

The logs. Which key cards opened which doors, and when.

'What about Helena Watkins?' he said, fearing that he already knew the answer.

'She's up and about.'

∞◯∞

All over the castle, guards on the various levels heard Evelyn Keyes' voice in their headsets. They slowed down, stopped where they were, listened. Waited to hear what Franquin would say next.

There was silence for a few seconds. And then for a few seconds more.

'What do you mean, up and about?' Franquin's voice asked. Calm. Measured. Definitely about to crack.

'She's gone through seven doors today alone.'

It was Keyes' voice. And standing in his corridor, Rodriguez immediately knew what had happened. Said nothing, waited for Franquin's voice to return, knew that it would.

'For Christ's sake,' it said after an eternity.

Rodriguez didn't need to hear more. He'd already raised his gun; as head of the guards it was time for him to take command. He pushed his radio button.

'Which door did she go through last?'

∞◯∞

Janine Charlotta Haynes had been inside the castle several weeks before she met Helena Watkins for the first time.

Those had been rough weeks, and Janine had broken down completely. She'd stopped eating, hadn't been able to work, and eventually the Organisation had decided to introduce Watkins to be her friend and offer moral support.

And it worked. Not immediately, but Helena Watkins was a good listener and had almost twenty more years of life experience, and she'd let Janine talk and talk and talk again. And even if Watkins couldn't give her any answers about why they were there or what they were doing, she gradually provided Janine with a new sense of purpose.

'It didn't take me long to understand that she was one of them,' she said.

William was in front of her. The large terrace around them.

'Helena wasn't a prisoner like me. She knew things she didn't want to talk about, or maybe wasn't *allowed* to talk about – what do I know? But I needed her. She gave me routines. And as time went by I started doing my thing and gave up asking questions when she told me to. We became friends. Not equal friends. But friends.'

'What happened?'

'She was afraid.' Janine paused. Searched for words. 'One night, in the middle of the night, she came to my room. Or rather, she stood outside. Said I mustn't let her in. And there we were, on opposite sides of the door, and she warned me, and . . . ' She shook her head. There was no point in telling him everything. Especially considering how little of it she understood herself. 'And then she vanished. That's more than a week ago.'

'So I'm here to replace her?'

'She was a mathematician. She specialised in ciphers.'

William felt the energy drain from him. She was right. Clearly he was there to replace Helena Watkins. He wondered whether they were standing by to replace him too as soon as he ceased to deliver the results they were looking for.

'What do they want?' he said.

'I don't know. At first all I knew about was the cuneiform script. And I thought that maybe it was some kind of historical discovery, an archaeological find so earth-shattering that it would turn our understanding of human history upside down and so revolutionary it was worth hiding away.' She shrugged. 'But they couldn't keep everything secret from me, not with Helena so close to me. And eventually, I was able to put two and two together. For all I know, maybe that's exactly what she wanted.'

'What? What did you learn?'

She paused. Stuffed her hand into her right pocket, pulled out a folded piece of paper. Opened it and passed it to him.

He looked at it. It was full of cuneiform script. 'I'm sorry,' he said. 'This doesn't tell me anything.'

She took a deep breath to explain.

But didn't get the time to talk.

Perhaps it was the darkness had made them feel safe. Or perhaps it was the comfort of speaking to someone, standing eye to eye with another human being who had the same questions and worries, and being able to vent all the thoughts that kept spinning and growing the way thoughts do when they're trapped inside.

Then again, perhaps it was just because the guards had been moving up the stone staircase in absolute silence, the sounds of their footsteps muted by the huge wooden door at the far end of the terrace.

William and Janine were standing in a narrow passageway, well out of sight of the door, when the unmistakable sound of its electronic lock broke the silence.

'Afraid of heights?' she asked, without waiting for an answer.

Before William had a chance to think, she took his arm again, this time pulling him along the terrace and away from the door, and he kept following, worried that the terrace might suddenly come to an end and that her question would start to make sense. Her bare feet hammered on the ground with an almost inaudible rhythm, and William tried to keep pace with her, as quietly as possible with his hard-heeled shoes, and below the banisters the dark abyss didn't become any less terrifying no matter how far they ran.

Then, without warning, she stopped. Looked at him, serious expression. 'Two floors down there's a window. Watch me, and do exactly as I do.'

The next moment, she swung herself out over the precipice.

William's immediate thought was that she was about to die.

But she didn't.

As he opened his eyes, he realised this wasn't the first time she'd gone down that way. Not once did she have to search for a hand- or foothold, she kept reaching out for holes and protruding stones, expertly using them to lower herself one storey down, on to a narrow ledge that ran along the wall. There she waited, halfway to the window she was aiming for.

Looked back up at him. Your turn.

It struck him that he hadn't answered her question, and he realised she probably wasn't too interested anyway. But if she were, he would have said yes. No matter how suicidal he was, he didn't like the thought of falling from a cliff.

Behind him, he could hear the guards' feet moving across the terrace.

And as he saw the first beams from their flashlights dance over the stone floor, he decided that heights probably weren't the biggest threat facing him right now.

11

When William climbed through the lead-lined window two floors down, he was so high from adrenalin that even if he had lost his grip and fallen he might not have noticed.

His body was perfectly ready to die.

He'd tried to memorise the few holds Janine used on her way down. It had all looked remarkably easy when she did it, but William hadn't seen an obstacle course in several years and trying to follow her lead didn't get any easier, especially with the steep mountain slope beneath him and the guards closing in on the terrace above. He lost his grip several times, fighting to cling on with slippery palms and with his wrists still stinging under the surgical tape, but at the last minute he managed to steady himself and hang on, until he finally lowered himself down on to the narrow shelf beside Janine.

Then came the hard part. Under the overhang, her climbing route continued beneath the ledge itself, and even if the good news was that it shielded them from view, the bad news was there was nothing there to break their fall, nothing but a sheer wall and a long, deep plunge.

But there hadn't been any time to think.

Janine had hauled herself over, signalling for him to follow, and he did as she instructed, trembling from fear while his fingers kept feeling for the cracks and crevices she pointed at. It was cold, but his shirt was soaking from sweat, and every time he let go of a grip, swung his body in a panicked arc until a hand or a foot made it to the next hold, every time he could hear himself promise all kinds of things to all kinds of higher powers if only he made it to the window in one piece.

When he finally caught sight of Janine's hand, he grabbed it and let her pull him in to the opening where she was crouching. Pressed himself in next to her, stock still and his back firmly against the small window behind them, aware that the tiniest movement might send him tumbling into the abyss.

She couldn't help smiling. 'And when I lived in Nevada I used to do a bit of competitive climbing. Did I mention that?'

'Just get me out of here.'

She put a reassuring hand on his shoulder. 'Still have the piece of paper I gave you?'

Hardly daring to move, he reached into his pocket to hand back the folded piece of paper with the cuneiform script. And she took it, slid it carefully between the sill and window, pushed up a latch on the inside.

He crawled through, heaved himself down from a deep recess, landed with his feet against the metal floor of a long hallway. And as Janine closed the window behind them, jumped down after him and pointed towards a fluorescent-lit walkway, his mind ran through all the promises he'd made on the way down and hoped they would be open to renegotiation.

As they hurried along the corridor, William could see it was different from the others.

He was completely lost now, it was impossible to determine whether he was above or below the floor with his office and bedroom. Either way, there was no doubt this part of the castle was used for a different purpose. Apart from the fluorescent lights in the ceiling and the sterile steel flooring, the hallway was lined with huge steel doors in faded olive-green; at a glance, it could have been anywhere in the world, in any building that had been insensitively renovated in the mid twentieth century.

But while William was lost, Janine had clearly been there before.

She walked with rapid, purposeful steps, and he couldn't help being impressed by how well she knew the place. Somehow she'd got hold of a key card – he told himself he had to ask her how – and she must have formed the same plan as William: to map out as much of the building as possible, to learn its weaknesses and shortcuts and security loopholes and then, eventually, try to escape.

A plan that had just hit a brick wall. Somehow, they had set off an alarm. The guards were looking for them. And whatever might happen if they were caught – *when* they were caught, he thought to himself – they wouldn't be getting another chance.

At the end of the corridor, cutting across the ancient stone passage, was a massive door in the same faded green steel as all the others, and with the usual electronic lock next to it.

But this time, the diode refused to turn green. As Janine held up her plastic card, the way she'd been doing at all the doors leading to the terrace, all she was met with was an obstinate click and a low tone informing her that something was wrong.

She tried again. Same response. And again.

She knew what it meant. And yet, she tried again. And once more.

Finally, her shoulders sank in desperation. And she turned to William.

'They've got us.'

∞○∞

Deep down in the heart of the mountain, Keyes was seconds away from missing the three red lines that slowly scrolled downwards on the monitor in front of her.

Minutes earlier, she'd instructed the program to warn her the instant Watkins' card was used in any of the readers. When Janine tried to open the door, the computer registered the time and location, exactly as it always did, but marking this entry in flashing red to stand out on the screen.

Keyes, however, was engaged in a heated argument with Franquin.

She hadn't managed to keep quiet. She had told him what everyone already knew: that their security system was a patchwork of upgrades that made it impossible to work with, and that their cameras were far too few and too poorly positioned. Eventually Franquin had snarled back at her that this was hardly the moment, and then they both snapped.

And all the while, Janine's flashing rows kept travelling down the screen.

Step by step, further and further down the list as other cards were swiped in other locks and squeezed in as new lines above hers.

It wasn't until they were about to scroll off the screen altogether that Keyes turned and saw the red rows at the bottom. And in that instant, the argument was over.

Her first move was to alert the guards.

Then, she realised which door they'd been trying to open.

As she lifted her radio for the second time, there was terror in her voice.

∞○∞

When the sound of running footsteps started to echo on the other side of the metal door, it was impossible to tell how far away they were. But they were undoubtedly the footsteps of more than one person, which meant William and Janine were only seconds away from meeting the very guards they'd just risked their lives escaping.

They were trapped in a sealed corridor. Around the corner in one direction were a couple of doors leading to small, windowless rooms, storage facilities or cells or service quarters or whatever they had originally been built for. Regardless, they were nothing but dead ends. Janine had been here before, and she knew all too well that none of them led out of there.

Behind them was the window leading back out to nothing. In front of them a metal door that refused to let them pass. There simply was no way out.

William looked round. Of three bad options, the only thing they could do was to choose the least worst.

'What's in the rooms?' he asked.

'Nothing.'

'Can they be locked from inside?'

She couldn't say.

He was clutching at straws, but they couldn't just stay here. As he grabbed her hand, pulled her away from the sealed door, back towards the row of doors down the corridor, he noticed that she offered no resistance.

She was terrified now, the sound of running feet coming ever closer, and she surrendered, allowing him to lead her away, her eyes fixed on the lock. Soon the diode would change, the guards would find them, and everything she'd done these last few months would be wasted.

She was almost apathetic when William opened the first door. Ushered her inside.

And the moment it slammed shut behind them, the red diode turned to green.

Later, when William would ask himself what he expected to find inside that room, he wouldn't have an answer. Probably because he hadn't expected to find anything at all. But also probably because whatever he might have expected would have been as nothing compared to the sight that confronted them.

Only the thick pane of acrylic glass prevented the woman from grabbing them.

Like an invisible obstacle, it stopped her hand in mid-flow, a rattling smack that made William and Janine spin around, meeting the woman's eyes on the other side of transparent, centimetre-thick walls.

She could have been fifty, maybe younger; it was impossible to tell, given the state she was in. Her blanched grey skin was bathed in sweat, her eyes half closed as if exhausted but desperately fighting to stay awake, her hair plastered across her scalp in moist, wispy strands.

She lay in a glass coffin, an adult-sized incubator in the middle of the windowless room illuminated by purple fluorescent lights, as if someone had laid her to rest in a reptile tank.

She let her hand stay glued to the plastic as she breathed raggedly, until gravity took control and pulled her emaciated fingers down to the mattress. Sliding red smears along the pane were the only trace of her attempt to make contact, a vertical roadmap of her hand's journey downwards, back to its place on the mattress where it came to a lifeless rest on a sweat-sodden, bloodstained sheet.

'Helena?'

It was Janine's voice. Though barely more than a whisper, it cut through the silence as sharply as the smack of the woman's hand had done against the plastic, and William turned, looked at her. Her eyes were fixed on the tank in front of them. She didn't speak. Merely shook her head, as if she refused to believe what she was seeing.

And the silence seemed to last for ever, until eventually the woman forced herself to turn her head. Lock her tired eyes on to Janine's.

'Run,' she said.

Her voice was barely a voice at all. It was a barely perceptible movement of her mouth, an exhalation of air and hardly even that.

'What have they done to you?'

The woman closed her eyes. She didn't have much time left.

'Run,' she said again, with unimaginable effort. 'Now.' She spoke without opening her eyes. Without moving. Without anything.

'Helena?' whispered Janine. No answer. 'Helena!'

But there was no response.

Not when Janine hammered on the acrylic glass, harder and harder, trying to make contact. Not when she bit her lip to stop her tears, or turned away because she couldn't bear to see.

And not even a second later, when the door to the corridor flew open, the massive frame bulging like foil where the bolt had been blown out of its socket. Six men surrounded them, maintaining a safe distance, disposable gloves clutching their automatic weapons, white masks over their faces. Shouting at them not to move.

The chase was over.

William and Janine did as they were told. They stood motionless at the centre of the floor, let the guards flood them with questions about where they'd been, which corridors they'd used, what they'd seen and what they'd touched. Their voices were strained, almost scared, and every time Janine or William moved, the guns rattled in their direction to remind them that the slightest show of resistance would have dire consequences.

Eventually, the guards backed out of the room, their sights still trained on the two prisoners. They kept their distance, gestured to William and Janine to follow them through the door that had previously blocked their way.

And they obeyed without a word. Left the room. Marched slowly down the corridor.

Behind them, the door slammed shut into its busted frame.

Inside her glass coffin, the woman whose name was Helena Watkins had already stopped breathing.

12

If Franquin had refocused his gaze, he would have seen his own face reflected in the glass pane in front of him. He'd have seen the concern in his eyes, the wrinkles around his mouth that always grew deeper when he was worried: cracks through an already bumpy landscape, spreading like caverns from the pursed line that was his lips.

But Franquin had more important things to worry about than his appearance. His eyes were focused on the other side of the safety glass, far away into the large, blindingly illuminated chamber.

The window was almost three centimetres thick. Then came a layer of absolute vacuum before the next centimetre-thick pane of the same tempered high-security glass as the first. It was designed to resist anything, made from the same kind of quartz glass as the space shuttle, and all entry and exit to and from the room was via an airlock that had been specially manufactured by another NASA subcontractor.

And yet, he thought to himself, they still hadn't managed to contain it.

His eyes passed over the long rows of hospital beds. Avoided counting the number of bodies in various sweaty stages of inexorable decline towards an agonising death. Avoided fixing his gaze on anyone in particular, avoided trying to determine who was still alive and who was still clinging on the brink.

After all, he had saved them. At least, that's what he tried to tell himself.

Most of them had been given significantly better lives; they didn't have to freeze or go hungry any more, and many of them would long since have been dead if they hadn't ended up here. What they were going through now was the price they had chosen to pay. Admittedly, they hadn't been aware of the consequences, not to the full extent, but nevertheless it had been their own choice. And as his eyes travelled from one bloodstained sheet to the next, Franquin shook off the uncomfortable feeling with the same determination as always. Or at least with the same effort to revive that determination, to make it drown out the nagging voice of his own conscience.

Sometimes you have to look at the bigger picture.

In order to save the world, you must sacrifice individuals.

That was his mantra, and he did what he always did, he kept repeating it inside his head until he believed it.

Eventually his eyes reached the wall at the end of the room. The woman slowly walking around inside, back and forth between the beds, sensed his gaze and looked up at him through her misty visor. She wore thick, airtight overalls in a white, rubbery plastic, the air pressure high inside them to ensure that any puncture would push the air out rather than drawing it in, giving her a chance to get out before it was too late. Her eyes were empty, devoid of emotion, but Franquin knew that the same was true of his own. It was the only way to cope.

She stopped at the foot of one of the beds. The sheets were

clean, and the man who lay under them, sedated and on his back, had a faint shade of stubble on his face. From a distance he looked perfectly healthy.

Franquin hoped he was. Not for the man's sake. And not for his own.

But for everyone else's.

The woman stayed by his bed. Ran though the same routine she'd followed with the other patients. Took readings from the machine by the bedside: heart rate, temperature, oxygen levels. Lifted the sheet and inspected his body. Felt his skin, looked for lesions, let her rubber gloves wander in search for anything that shouldn't be there. And Franquin waited. Allowed her to take her time.

Until, finally, she looked up at him again.

As soon as their eyes met, he felt his hope leave.

∞◯∞

The guards who took over at the other end of the corridor had respirators that covered their mouth and nose, overalls of rustling plastic, carefully sealed at every seam. They wore rubber gloves, yet they avoided contact, ushering Janine and William forward with orders and pointing hands.

They passed through an airlock, entered an ice-cold chamber. Fluorescent lights in the ceiling, walls and floor in shiny steel. It looked like a slaughterhouse, or a morgue: ducts in the flooring joined together in one corner, feeding into a drain. The room's only furnishings consisted of a sprinkler system of piping, branching out here and there to valves and taps mounted on the far wall.

William heard Janine breathing behind him, and he turned to look at her. Her eyes were fixed on the wall in front of them. Staring vacantly, overcome with emotion but fighting to keep it to herself.

It wasn't until that moment that he understood how afraid she was.

Unlike him, she'd never been trained for this. She hadn't been through detainee simulations or mock interrogations or long, gruelling disaster exercises. She had no idea what was going to happen to them.

He wanted to say something, but there was nothing he could say that would help. All they could do was to follow the guards' orders, avoid provoking them and wait and see what would happen next. So William followed Janine's example, and steeled himself.

They were instructed to stand in the middle of the room, and so they did.

Waited. Heard the men behind them take a few steps back. Then a voice ordered them to undress.

Beside him, Janine stood frozen to the spot. Hesitated. And William went first.

He unbuttoned his clothes, dropped them straight on to the floor, and eventually Janine followed suit until they were both naked, eyes fixed firmly on the wall in front of them to avoid making the situation any more uncomfortable than it already was.

They were instructed to stand against the wall, their palms spread on the metal, their backs to the guards. Behind them, there was the sound of a hose being drawn across the floor.

'Close your eyes and mouths and try to hold your breath,' some-one said. And then their backs exploded with pain.

The water that hit them was blisteringly hot, and the hose was so powerful that William had to struggle to stay upright. A stabbing pain inched over their bodies as the fluid smashed into them and ran down towards the ducts on the floor.

The fluid. Because it wasn't water. It smelled of alcohol and chlo-rine and maybe iodine and something else, and whatever it was it was concentrated and unbelievably strong. Only when the stream had worked its way down to his legs did William dare to breathe again, opening his eyes ever so slightly to see the disinfectant flow down his calves. It circled in burning swirls around his feet, ran past Janine's and on along the floor until it disappeared into a clump of acrid foam, compact and white and with edges brown from iodine, danc-ing on top of the drain like a large, burnt meringue.

Then, the guards instructed them to turn round. And as the hose worked its way back up and the pain surged across his chest, William closed his eyes so hard that he wondered if he'd ever be able to open them again.

The whole experience lasted a matter of minutes, and when it was over they were ordered into the next room.

They walked in a line, Janine first and William behind. And his eyes fell on her back, red raw from the disinfectant but her muscles as clearly defined as on an anatomy chart, before forcing himself to focus ahead of her instead, his gaze fixed on the room in front of them. It struck him that if she'd been here for seven months she must have been working out the whole time, and he couldn't help wondering if she'd been doing it secretly in her room or if it was something the nameless organisation wanted them to do.

The room they entered was no more welcoming than the one they'd just left. The walls were tiled, and along one of them pipes hung from the ceiling, each ending in a massive shower head. Around every shower was a tubular tent of thin, transparent plastic, with room enough for one, sealed with a zip at the front and with top and bottom welded shut with the same transparent material.

They were each shown into a tent. Told to wash themselves with cleaning gel from dispensers suspended inside. Every hair, every fold of their skin, parts of the body that had probably never met soap before, now they were to be scrubbed, washed, scrubbed again. The soft foam soothed slightly, but their skin was so scalded it would take several days for it to recover completely and every drop of water from the nozzle above seemed to fall like the tip of a newly sharpened pencil.

William washed away the last of the soap, stayed under the shower, let it keep pouring over him as if he couldn't trust that the danger was over.

The image of the woman in the glass box wouldn't leave him.

What had they been exposed to? Anthrax? Ebola?

And what was it Janine had been about to tell him when the guards arrived? Who was she, what did she know, what did it mean?

He let his eyes wander in her direction.

Only to connect with hers.

She was staring at him, and his instinctive reaction was to look away, point his eyes into the wall in front of him, innocently pretending to be far more interested in studying the tiles than the naked woman in the shower next to his own.

But there had been something in her look. She was trying to tell him something. The whole of her naked body was turned to the wall in front of her, but her eyes were glued to his, peering at him with an intense impatience that made him wonder how long she'd been doing it. And if perhaps she'd deliberately been trying to make him feel it, trying to make him look at her.

He looked at her again. Discreetly, without turning his head, as if he was still just showering.

Her eyes were still there. Her head was half-bent so the guards wouldn't see her face, but her eyes were doing their best to communicate with him.

The wall. That's what she seemed to be saying. The wall in front of her.

William stared at the tiles, but couldn't see what she meant. All he could see were tiles. Tiles and piping and nothing more.

He raised his eyebrow a minute fraction. *What do you mean?* She flicked her eyes towards the wall again. There. *Follow my eyes. There.*

He didn't understand. Looked again. What did she see that he couldn't?

Behind them one of the guards moved, and the sound of it made them both jump.

They looked straight ahead again, rinsing themselves in the warm water, waited to see if they'd been caught. Motionless in their showers as one of the guards came up to them, tapped on the plastic of Janine's shower, directing her to switch it off. He pulled at the zip, passed her a towel, ordered her to dry off completely before stepping out.

She did as she was told.

Threw William a final glance, but her eyes met a bent neck.

She had tried to tell him, but he hadn't understood, and now she didn't know what would happen to her.

Maybe it was all too late. Maybe she'd missed her chance.

Disaster was coming, and she hadn't been able to do anything about it.

And she left the shower with her message behind her.

It wasn't until the guards led Janine out of the room that William saw what she had been trying to show him.

In the steam inside her shower, her fingers had traced four letters. One short message, slowly vanishing as new mist started to cover the lines her skin had formed on the plastic wall.

AGCT. That was all it said.

He looked in her direction, but she had her back to him. They had wrapped her in thick towels and were whisking her out of the room, still without touching her, out through the door and into the corridor.

For a split second their eyes met. It was too brief to communicate, all he could see was the fear in her eyes as they led her out of sight. And then the heavy door swung closed. Only this time it wasn't the fear of what would happen to her. It was the fear that he hadn't seen her message.

But he had. He just didn't understand what she meant.

AGCT.

Adenine, guanine, cytosine, thymine.

But so what?

He closed his eyes, letting the warm water wash over his body. Tried to concentrate.

The nucleic acids in genetic code. The four building blocks of DNA. It couldn't mean anything else, but why had she written it there, why did she want him to see that?

He focused. Shook off the thoughts of whatever it might be they were infected with, pushed away the anxiety that came with what they'd seen.

A dying woman in quarantine.

DNA.

A virus? Was that what she was trying to tell him? Some genetic mutation? But if so, again: so what? What was he supposed to do with that information?

His thoughts didn't get any further before the guards returned. They stopped outside William's bubble, told him to turn off the water and dry himself, just as they had with Janine before him.

Their sober expressions scared him. They were genuinely afraid. And as they led him away again, clad in their protective masks and rubber gloves, it wasn't only the cool of the air in the long, dark corridor that made him shiver.

∞◯∞

The silence in the room continued unbroken as the door behind Franquin slid open and Connors entered. Franquin remained where he stood, didn't even look up. Partly because he could tell from the steps who it was, and partly because he wasn't confident he could maintain a neutral and composed expression. As if it was a secret that they all had feelings. As if uncomfortable – no, inhumane – decisions were to be carried out with a shrug and without looking back.

Connors stopped next to him. Peered through the safety glass in front of them. There they were, two silent men in uniform, doing nothing but listening to the hiss of the air conditioning. As if whatever remained unsaid would also not have happened.

Beyond the glass lay the rows of dying people, eerily motionless under their blankets, alone and unconscious and waiting to cease to exist. The nurse had long since finished her rounds, and Franquin had lost track of how many minutes he'd been standing there.

'Well?' he said after a while.

'I thought you should know. It's over.'

'Watkins?'

He already knew the answer. He kept his eyes fixed on the room in front of him, counted the people on the other side for the hundredth time. As if Watkins' death wouldn't be quite as pointless if he could remind himself it was part of something bigger, that it was one in a long series of unavoidable deaths that nobody could control. In reality, it wasn't that far from the truth.

'We've informed her family,' said Connors. 'She died following an accident in the lab.'

Franquin nodded. That wasn't really a lie, either. Not the whole truth, but definitely not a lie. 'And our friends?'

'We know what routes they've been taking. There's nothing to suggest they were exposed.'

'But we're testing them anyway?'

'Yes. We'll know for certain tomorrow.'

They stood for a few more minutes, staring at the rows of nameless beds, until eventually Connors felt he'd been there long enough and turned towards the door.

He was on the verge of stepping out into the corridor when he turned. There was still one issue remaining, one that neither of them had mentioned, and even if Connors knew that this was probably an answer in itself, he looked past Franquin, through the windows, at the man with the stubble.

He was sleeping soundly, no signs of sickness. On the outside. But inside him, an unstoppable war was raging, a war that he was about to lose.

'It would've been more of a surprise if she'd succeeded,' said Franquin.

'It's our job to hope,' replied Connors.

That was all they needed to say.

Connors waited a couple of moments, then left.

Watkins had been wrong. And the man under the sheet was the proof of that.

Their only hope now was William Sandberg.

Connors would have wanted better odds than that.

∞◯∞

Nicolai Richter sat in his red Toyota RAV4, climbing one of the highway exit ramps off the A9, deeply annoyed about two quite different things. For a start, the traffic was crawling, which forced him to manoeuvre from lane to lane, swerving in and out between other cars, braking and speeding up again, earning him extended middle-finger salutes from the drivers around him, in order to advance as fast as he had to. He was late, and he needed a minor miracle to make it on time.

That was the first thing.

The second thing was that his back was itching.

Not just slightly, not the kind of mild itch that you can relieve or at least silence temporarily with a rub against the car seat until you can get out and give it a proper scratch.

No, this itch was violent and persistent. In fact, the irritation was so intense that he couldn't decide whether it constituted an itch or a pain. As he zigzagged through the morning traffic, well in excess of the speed limit and with one hand on the wheel, he let his other hand dig down inside his collar. He made his nails march down across the skin, pulling his arm as far down as possible, desperate to reach the itch and stop it before it drove him mad.

It didn't help.

Each touch of his nails against the skin only made the feeling stronger. And as he scratched again, hard, harder, it felt as if the skin gave way and everything turned warm, and yet the itching wouldn't stop, just as he couldn't stop scratching.

Cars whizzed by on both sides as he threw his car from lane to lane, passing the slow bastards blocking his way.

He wasn't in a very good mood.

He hadn't been for days, and it was all Yvonne's fault. He'd known she wouldn't be his type, he'd known it even before they met, and as soon as they'd sat down at the restaurant in Innsbruck last Tuesday and begun to make small talk, he'd regretted ever having asked her out. If it hadn't been for her accusing him of being selfish and lacking empathy, he would never have picked up the homeless hitchhiker at the service station and given him a ride all the way to Berlin. And then the bastard wouldn't have sat there coughing next to him, over and over, mile after mile.

And now, here he was.

And he wasn't even supposed to be here.

The homeless guy had made him promise, and he hated himself for it, first for caving in and saying okay and then for fulfilling his promise even though he ought to be in The Hague by this time. He was taking a detour via Amsterdam to deliver a message to someone he didn't even know how to find – and that was obviously Yvonne's fault, too.

Nicolai Richter was as empathic as the next person. And this was the proof. And he would have been delighted to tell her so, if only she'd had the decency to answer her phone.

And here he was in Amsterdam, feeling a fever coming on, and of course it was the homeless guy's fault. The homeless guy's, and hence Yvonne's. And if only she'd answer when he called her, he'd love to tell her as much.

He'd just started the long turn across the bridge, eight lanes of motorway below him, when he noticed his shirt. The glimpse of fabric that poked out from under his jacket, between the waistband of his trousers and where the seat belt clicked into place. His white designer shirt – soaked in a deep red.

Blood. And lots of it.

He pulled his hand from under his collar, ripped his jacket open, and gasped for breath. He was bleeding so heavily that the inside of his jacket had turned dark, his shirt was red and clinging to his body all the way from his arm down to his waist and what the hell was going on?

The lapse in concentration lasted only a few seconds, but that was all it took.

The first thing he heard was the sound.

The sound of steel against steel, glass, tyres squealing, brakes screeching.

Then came the jolt as his car dropped from his own fifty miles per hour to the thirty that the car in front had travelled before he hit it.

Then the mental snapshot that he would never forget. The sight that would plague him for the twenty seconds he had left to live: the dented BMW in front of him, dancing around on the road, blurry to the point of invisibility beyond the hand he'd used to scratch his back. His fingers in front of him, dripping red. It wasn't just blood, it was skin, it was flesh, it was spongy and porous, it was his own back that had come off and now he had it on his hand as if he'd peeled a layer of cream off a birthday cake. And yet it didn't hurt, it just kept itching, violently and intensely, and even as he saw the BMW rotate from the impact and block the road ahead like a big, black barn door, all he could think about was scratching the itch, just a little bit more, just to get rid of it.

At the same time, Nicolai Richter's left hand reacted instinct-ively. It turned the wheel to the right as far as it could, making the car lurch, slide sideways towards the slanted BMW, the engine revving and the tyres skidding on the asphalt. There was chaos all around him as cars braked, swerved to avoid the spinning twister of steel in the middle of the road, rolling like a mechanical snowball, adding new layers of metal for every rotation.

And through his fingers Nicolai witnessed it all.

The glass shattering around him as the truck to his rear collided with his hatchback. The judder as his tyres struggled for purchase. Cars he hadn't been anywhere near braking and swerving so abruptly their front wheels folded, black smoke rising as their axles scraped the road.

And the itch. The itch that drowned out everything else.

The itch he had to get rid of.

Nicolai's car was at a ninety-degree angle to the road when the wheels found traction. The speed seemed to come out of nowhere, the car suddenly freeing itself from the screeching cluster of wreckage, racing out of the collision and straight towards the edge.

The barrier was made of concrete and girders, but it didn't stand a chance.

Nicolai Richter's Toyota lost none of its speed as it climbed the parapet, began a somersault from the edge of the bridge and sailed like a gigantic leaf towards the carriageway below, landing on its roof in the path of westbound traffic on the A9.

He didn't feel the itch any longer.

By the time Nicolai Richter was involved in his second car accident of the morning, pushed around across the asphalt and thrown under the wheels of the oncoming traffic, he was already dead from the fall.

The news networks spent the rest of day competing to provide the most comprehensive reports from the catastrophic accident outside Badhoevedorp, Amsterdam.

But not a single journalist reported the most gruesome detail of all.

The fact that Nicolai Richter's shattered body was rushed with blazing sirens and flashing lights to Slotervaart Hospital, five miles away. And that he was declared dead by a medical team who then went on to attend to other casualties.

13

William lay on top of his bed, staring up at the ceiling, wondering if he was about to die after all.

Wouldn't that be some turn of events.

Only a few days before, that had been exactly what he wanted. But as he'd found himself examined and subjected to test after test, helplessly bundled up in towels and surrounded by personnel in hazard suits, he'd gradually come to realise that he wasn't in as much of a hurry as he'd thought.

It was early morning. A weak light was pushing its way through the heavy curtains. And William Sandberg hadn't slept a wink.

His head was full of questions.

What would happen next?

What had he been exposed to?

And what did the dying woman have to do with his codes, how was his work supposed to help against a contagious disease, how the hell did everything he'd seen and been told fit together?

All he had to go on was what he'd learned from Janine.

That the material they'd given her was deliberately mixed up, intended to confuse her and make it impossible for her to work out what she was dealing with.

There was no way he would be able to solve the puzzle. Not with the pieces he had, not so far. Not until he knew what was true, and which pieces didn't belong.

There was nothing to be gained from fixating on matters beyond his control. He needed to focus, to do what he did best. To understand. To find patterns and logic and solve problems.

AGCT. Why would she write that?

In his mind he returned to his office, the room where he'd been sitting just hours earlier, and he tried to recall as much as he could. The cuneiform script on the walls. The number sequences, the rows of zeros and ones and twos and threes that had been translated and rearranged to form the countless pixels forming the symbols.

Where had they come from?

Why 23 by 73?

Every time he tried to get to grips with the numbers his thoughts seemed to be deflected, bouncing away as if to tell him that no explanation could be arrived at until he had the whole picture. Until he knew where they came from, where the sequences had appeared, through what medium.

Through what medium.

The feeling spread through his body as a warm tingle of satisfaction. He recognised it instantly. It was the rush of realisation.

The thought had no sooner hit him than he sat bolt upright on the bed, staring into space, his eyes searching the room without focusing on anything. Not looking for something that could be seen, but searching within himself. He felt adrenalin and endorphins dance in his veins as he raced through every detail he'd heard, over and over again, tried to hold on to his realisation, tried to make it stick, to see if it held water.

It did. It was the only possible explanation.

Base four.

∞○∞

Palmgren was already waiting at the table.

His coffee was untouched even though he'd been there for more than fifteen minutes, and he watched in silence as Christina wriggled out of her suede coat, pulled her handbag through one of its sleeves, and hung it on the chair before sitting down.

His eyes were worried.

'I contacted them,' he said when she was ready.

Christina nodded in reply. It was both a thank-you and a sign that she was listening despite apparently being occupied in ridding her newly purchased latte of its plastic lid without spilling the contents.

'William's job doesn't exist any more,' he said. 'Nobody has taken over his duties, at least not in the way that he performed them. But ... ' He unfurled a piece of paper to help his memory, though he knew it wouldn't make any difference. 'I got hold of a woman, Livia Eek. I think she's probably in her thirties now, maybe thirty-five. I met her back when I was still active, she was an assistant then but today she's responsible for many of the things William did.'

'Okay.'

'And when I say *many*, I mean *some*. Not everything. You have to remember that the stuff we did back then, the threats we were dealing with, they don't exist today.'

Christina wasn't sure what to say. Took a sip of her coffee instead.

'It was quite an awkward conversation,' he continued. 'The things I wanted to ask her are still classified, and she couldn't give me any details or straight answers. But she did express her regrets about what happened. She knew William too, and she wanted me to tell you how upset she was.'

Christina shrugged. It didn't help her very much to know that a thirty-five-year-old cryptographer was sitting in a bunker somewhere feeling upset.

'But essentially, she confirmed what I told you. She said it was inconceivable that an organisation would exist with the need, or the capacity, to do something like this. And as far as she could tell, there has been no web traffic or other communication that would imply matters are about to escalate.'

'And you're sure she would tell you? If she actually knew there was?'

Palmgren got her point. Of course he couldn't know. But he was sure enough to nod and continue:

'We talked for quite a while. She understood the situation you're in. And eventually she promised to ask around and get back to me, just in case someone else could come up with an explanation.'

'And?' said Christina.

Palmgren paused. It lasted for so long the atmosphere grew strained. His troubled eyes remained solemnly focused on hers.

'Did William ever tell you about a computer he built?'

'We never talked about work. Especially not his.'

'You're very loyal,' he said. There was a wry note in his voice, but it was warm and friendly and without hostility.

'Let me put it this way,' Christina said, 'we had people sneaking around in our garden. Our phones were tapped – or were they? Nobody could ever prove it – and at times there were vans parked in the street for days on end until the police came and parked next to them. I didn't *want* to talk about his job.'

Okay. Her point was made.

'William was in charge of a small, top-secret research group,' he said. 'Only a handful of people knew of its existence. He developed a machine for cracking extremely complicated ciphers; it was the best thing you could get at the time – at least as far as we knew – and for all I know it may still be one of the most advanced machines in its field. He called it the Scientific Assistant for Reconstructional Arithmetics.'

A second passed, and then she registered. As she broke into a smile, it took her by surprise. Not the smile so much as the lump in her throat.

'The son of a bitch,' she said, but with tenderness. 'He named it Sara.'

Palmgren leaned forward in his chair. 'As I said, nobody knew this computer existed. Nobody outside the research team, and obviously some people further up the chain of command who provided the finance or made the decisions. You know how it works.'

She did. 'And?'

'Livia never called me back. But three hours after we hung up – don't ask me who, don't ask me why – but three hours later, I got a call from a withheld number. It was a man. He wouldn't say who he was, but he told me he worked for the same unit. And the first thing he said was that he wouldn't be answering any questions, and that he would hang up as soon as he'd finished talking. Of course I immediately started looking for a tape recorder, but who the hell has a tape recorder lying around these days? All I could find was a pen and some paper. Then I listened to him for two minutes, and when he hung up, I realised I hadn't written a single word.'

'What did he say?' Christina heard herself ask. As if he weren't about to tell her.

'Sara's gone.'

'What do you mean?'

'The computer.'

'Stolen?'

'Not according to man on the phone.' He shifted in his seat. 'Two weeks ago Defence Headquarters got in touch with him, enquiring about an inventory check. They asked questions about equipment and material, as if they were conducting a routine survey of resources for the lack of anything better to do. And one of the things they asked about was Sara.'

Christina listened intently. Forgot about the coffee in front of her. Concentrated to hear his soft-spoken voice over the espresso machine.

Their asking about Sara had made the nameless caller suspicious. Sara wasn't mentioned in any official logs. Nobody could call and check if the machine was okay, because nobody knew it existed. And *if* you did, you knew what it was built to do. And that meant that, if you asked for Sara, it was a dead certainty that something was going on.

Three days later the man had decided to carry out a little inventory check of his own.

By then, Sara was no longer in the storage unit.

Somebody had taken Sara out through gates and iron doors and heavy underground lifts and without registering their entrance or exit. There were no records of visits to the facility, and yet, Sara had ceased to exist, in the same way she had never officially existed in the first place.

When Palmgren finished relating his story there was a moment of silence.

'Who?' she asked. 'Who took Sara?'

'I don't know. He never found out.'

'Defence Headquarters?'

'When things don't go through formal channels? Ten times out of ten, it's because they *can't*.'

'Which means they're wrong,' she said, 'aren't they? You are wrong and they are wrong: something is happening, and even if you have no idea what it is and William's replacement doesn't know, then someone in the Defence Headquarters does. Right? Something is going on, and the military wants to keep it secret.'

'I don't know.'

'But *somebody* does.'

He said nothing. And she started over.

'If you're saying that the Swedish Armed Forces in one way or another have allowed someone to buy or borrow or use William's computer, it's logical to suppose that that someone would also know who abducted William.'

Palmgren's silence was a yes.

'So who would be allowed to do that?'

Palmgren gave her a long look.

'Who would be allowed to borrow a top-secret military computer?'

Silence. And then came his answer:

'Nobody.'

Christina stayed sitting at the table long after Palmgren had left, going through what he had said and trying to understand exactly what it meant.

What worried her most was that he was afraid.

Two days earlier he'd been as eager as she was. But something had changed.

She'd ended their meeting by asking him to contact William's replacement a second time, but this time he'd refused. He'd told her he was unable to help, and politely warned her not to ask again.

This wasn't simply about a misplaced computer, it was something much bigger, and to Palmgren it was frightening enough to make him refuse to help a friend. That could only mean William's disappearance was tied up with a major classified operation, perhaps on an international scale.

Which meant this was no longer just a personal issue.

The combination of military secrets and an abduction, possibly with the approval of Sweden's top brass, from a journalistic standpoint reeked of headlines and copies sold. Christina knew she would have no trouble talking her bosses into letting her follow up on the case.

She reached for her phone. It had been on silent since the moment she entered the café at least an hour earlier, and as she looked at the screen there were four missed calls flashing back at her.

They were all from Leo.

She called him straight away. Listened to the ringtone as he no doubt fumbled around in his pockets for his phone. If his pockets were as well organised as his thoughts, she'd probably end up being switched to his voicemail and would have to call back.

But he answered on the third ring.

She could tell from the background noise that he was outdoors. He was short of breath, and spoke quickly.

'We need to meet,' he said. 'We need to meet now.'

∞◯∞

William stood in front of the handbasin, whiteboard pen in his hand. His breathing was ragged with excitement, his mind darting about, restless like a tracker dog that has cornered its prey and doesn't know what to do next.

As if his brain couldn't believe what it had just found out.

He looked at the bathroom mirror in front of him. It was covered with the number sequences he'd written up the night before last. On the left side was the coded version, next to a clutter of calculations and arrows, scribbled haphazardly in an attempt to link them to the decoded numbers on the right.

And beyond the pen strokes his own reflection stared straight back at him. His skin ruddy after the disinfection process. His hair left to dry in a haphazard mess. But what surprised him were his eyes. Focused, energetic, burning with an enthusiasm he hadn't experienced in years.

It was a bizarre situation, and he didn't like it one bit. He could very well be infected with a deadly virus. But looking at himself in the mirror he couldn't remember when he'd last felt this good.

He shook it off. He didn't want to lose track. Refocused, concentrated on the text on the mirror.

He needed to see it. Tangibly, written out in front of him.

And he took the lid off the pen, looked back and forth between the numbers. He erased all the zeros. Replaced them with As. Same thing with the ones, replaced them with Gs. The twos and the threes he replaced with Cs and with Ts, and eventually all the numbers were gone.

And there it was, in front of him.

It was as obvious as it was simple, but he'd had to see it laid out like this, visually and irrefutably, to be certain his mind hadn't got carried away and skipped across holes in the logic without seeing them.

In front of him on the mirror was a long chaotic row of As, Gs, Cs and Ts.

A DNA sequence.

That had to be it. That's what she'd been trying to tell him. The code he'd been given, the one they wanted him to crack, had arrived hidden in some form of DNA.

In a virus? So it seemed. A deadly, contagious virus.

Yet it felt far-fetched. Who would write a text in cuneiform script, turn it into pixels and store it in encrypted form inside a virus? And why? Why on earth would anyone do that?

It *was* far-fetched.

He reached for a towel and carefully wiped the mirror clean, ensuring that nothing stayed on the glass and that nobody would be able to see what he'd discovered. He threw the towel into the bathtub, pressed his forehead against the tiled wall, hoped that the coolness of the glazed ceramics would clear his head.

He needed to speak to Janine again. There were thousands of questions he hadn't known to ask when they stood out there on the terrace. It occurred to him that he didn't know where she was at this moment. Perhaps she was being kept in her room, just like him – assuming she had private quarters like his – and perhaps she was waiting, like him, to find out whether she'd been infected or not.

He had to concede, though, that they'd probably taken her somewhere else. Perhaps they were interrogating her, perhaps worse. Perhaps they were doing everything they could to find out what she'd told him, what she'd come up with that she shouldn't. Perhaps they were using methods that went against international law, but who would ever know, beyond these stone walls. Maybe the same fate awaited him, too. Maybe he knew too much now, and she knew even more; maybe that was the reason his predecessor had vanished. Maybe Janine would follow, and him too.

And who would know? Who misses someone who's already missing?

He pulled himself together. Rolled his forehead across the tiles, left, right, temple to temple, trying to cool his head.

The texts. That's what she'd said.

She'd been given cuneiform texts to translate, and they'd given her other texts that didn't fit, and she'd been given them in the wrong order to confuse her. But she'd guessed something. The question was what.

He started over from the beginning.

What did he know?

A text. Written in a language that had been extinct for thousands of years.

Okay.

That someone had then digitised into black-and-white matrices.

Very well.

Matrices that had been converted into quaternary code.

And which had then—

Wait.

His thoughts stopped short. It was that feeling again, for the second time the same morning. A realisation breaking over him like a wave; the overwhelming sense of discovering something that had been visible all the while, like that name of that actress who was married to the guy in that movie and whose name comes to you the minute you stop thinking about it. That exact feeling.

The matrices.

He stood absolutely still, his face flat against the tiles, eyes shut so as not to let his thoughts escape.

Suddenly it came to him. The structure of the pixelated images, where he'd seen it before. It was as absurd as it was obvious.

And just as suddenly, he realised that what he had been given to solve was far more improbable than he'd ever imagined.

'Congratulations.'

The voice made him spin around, unsure how long he'd been standing with his head against the tiles, and for how long someone had been able to watch him from behind without him noticing.

It was Connors. He was leaning casually against the inside of the open door, his fingers resting on the handle and his head cocked slightly against the frame. The pose was almost friendly, relaxed and informal, and even if that was unexpected in itself, it wasn't what made William stand straight. Something else had grabbed his attention.

Connors was wearing his uniform. That was all. No biohazard suit, no mask, no gloves. Just the uniform.

'You're not infected,' he said.

'I'm glad to hear it,' William replied. 'By what, exactly?'

Connors smiled. Dodged the question.

'How's the girl?'

'She's feeling very much like you. She's resting, but she's all right. We didn't intend for you to talk to each other.'

'We noticed.' A pause. 'So, what is it that we're not allowed to talk about?'

Connors stood in silence for a few seconds more. There was a minute furrowing of his eyebrows, as if he was giving himself one last chance to reconsider a decision he'd already made. And then:

'What experience do you have of handling classified information?'

'I think you know that already.'

Connors nodded. Of course he did. They knew everything there was to know about William's past. And it wasn't as if there were any real grounds for concern. Or there wouldn't have been, were it not for the magnitude of what they were up against. Because regardless of what kind of sensitive knowledge William Sandberg had been trusted with before, none of it had come close to what he was about to hear.

'Tell me,' said William.

But Connors shook his head. 'It's about time you met the others.'

And with that, he let go of the door, and gestured for William to follow.

14

William Sandberg was fifteen years old the first time he heard of the Arecibo message. That didn't stop him from having an opinion, and that opinion was that the entire thing was without doubt the most dim-witted project ever carried out by human hands in the name of science.

From the world's largest radio telescope, built by the same human hands in Arecibo, Puerto Rico, designed to scan the night skies and find out more about the universe's origins and physics and god-knows-what, from that telescope a message was sent into space on 16 November 1974, purely to inform any alien civilisations of our existence.

That in itself was enough to provoke an opinion.

Even as a teenager William had formed a dislike for his neighbours. Just because you happened to share a wall or to trim the same hedge from different sides, it didn't mean you were friends. Neighbours were people who got in the way, who wanted to make pointless conversation or who complained about things that weren't their business. And with that in mind, it was completely impossible to fathom why scientists wanted to get in touch with our interstellar neighbours when nobody had any way of knowing who they were or how they would react. Wouldn't it be more sensible to stay away and not bother one another?

William thought so. But this wasn't what annoyed the young William Sandberg the most. What really disturbed him was the message itself.

The first time he'd had the chance to study it in any detail was in one of the science magazines that lined his teenage bedroom, sorted by year and date and catalogued in a separate notebook to help him find any article he was looking for. And his first thought had been that the scientists must have been smoking something inappropriate.

The message humanity had fired into space was a picture. Or, to be more precise, it was a collection of incredibly low-resolution pixels in black and white, on or off, intended to show the recipient what humans looked like, what we were made of and where we could be found.

Intended to show them. Assuming they read it the right way.

Which was a lot to ask.

For a start, the alien at the receiving end would have to come up with the idea of rendering the pulses as a collection of dots and non-dots, turning them into the pixels we wanted them to see. They would then have to guess what the pictures represented, which would be far from obvious. Even in 1974 William had seen computer games with better graphics than that.

But the most ridiculous thing was how the scientists expected our new extraterrestrial friends to succeed in making the pixels into a picture.

There was only one way to do it.

By dividing the pixels into 73 rows.

Not 72. Not 74. Not 11 or a million or anything else, but 73. Only then would each row contain 23 pixels from left to right, and only then would the pixels arrange themselves into the images we wanted to convey. Any other arrangement and the rows of dots and spaces would make no sense.

But, hey. Surely it would be obvious to any carbon-based being in the universe that an unexpected message from an unknown planet should be grouped that way?

Clearly, the scientists thought so. They happily sent their hello into space, and sat back and waited for an answer. As far as William knew, they never got one.

This was what occupied William's mind as he wandered through the vast server room, an entire labyrinth of modern technology that had been installed far beneath the ancient castle.

Below the maze of stone passages, Connors had taken him to another network of rooms and corridors, much more recent than the castle above, with metal-clad walls and cast concrete floors. It gave him a new perspective on how incredibly huge the castle must be, and as he breathed the dry, cooled air that circulated to keep the servers' temperatures down, he hurried to keep up with Connors and the two guards on either side of him. All the while struggling to take in what his own brain was telling him.

He knew he'd recognised the pattern: 23 pixels wide. 73 pixels high.

The cuneiform script hidden in the codes he'd been given was arranged in exactly the same way as the message humanity beamed into space forty years ago.

∞O∞

On the other side of the server hall an automatic glass door slid aside, opening up into a control room, and beyond that a metal door took them to new corridor. They kept walking past endless rows of side doors, corners and staircases, everything in steel and aluminium and glass, and here and there the mountain protruded in over the floor as if someone had poured molten rock through the walls and allowed it to cool there.

Their walk seemed to go on for ever. And even if William couldn't say exactly why, he got the impression that everything he saw was decades old. The architecture was typically East European retro-futuristic, a Stasi-cold preparedness for a future that would soon arrive with flying cars and silver suits. He couldn't decide whether he found it terrifying or wonderfully naïve.

Nonetheless, it worked. It told him that the Organisation was vast and powerful, and that message came through loud and clear.

But it also prompted questions.

In spite of all the doors and control rooms and frosted windows to meeting rooms and offices, there was one thing missing. People. During their entire walk, since after leaving the last wooden door to the old castle behind and until now, he'd counted ten or twenty people at most. But the facilities they passed had been designed to accommodate at least twenty times that number, maybe more. So where were they?

William kept his questions to himself. They had reached an underground foyer, a huge windowless room with areas for waiting, with airport-like sofas and standing tables in parallel lines, designed for quick conversations between larger meetings. He was no doubt being escorted into an auditorium. Two steel double doors stood open on the far side of the foyer and they continued through without stopping.

If the meeting room where he first met Franquin had seemed impressively large, it was nothing compared to the one he entered now. At its centre was a huge circular table, surrounded by what must have been thirty or so chairs. Beyond the table a bank of LED screens were suspended in darkness, edge to edge, and the entire room was flanked with rows of fixed chairs, as if this was a room where the leaders staged huge plenary meetings and where lower-ranked officers and decision-makers could sit and follow along in discussions and reports.

It looked more like a parliament than a conference room, and William knew they had him where they wanted him. He was impressed and overwhelmed, and it was abundantly clear that they called the shots and he didn't.

He was escorted to the table. Ushered into one of the blue, upholstered seats, a cross between an office swivel chair and a recliner.

Around him sat at least a dozen men in uniform. The rest of the chairs in the auditorium were empty. The only face he recognised beside Connors' belonged to Franquin.

'Aren't you a bit old to be running around at night?' he said to William.

'I'm clearly not old enough for you to tell me the truth.'

Franquin didn't dispute this but replied: 'You have been in my position, haven't you?'

'I never kidnapped anyone and forced them to work for me, if that's what you're asking.'

'You've worked with classified material,' Franquin said, ignoring the sarcasm. 'You've worked with personnel who haven't been given the whole picture; you've assigned different people varying levels of access to information. There's no shame in that.'

'Two differences,' William countered. 'I never led any of my colleagues to believe that they were being given the whole truth.'

'We have been very clear that we haven't told you everything. You may not like it, but that doesn't mean we've misled you.'

He was right, of course he was, and William responded with an ambiguous move of his head.

'And the second difference?' Franquin said.

'I've always let my colleagues know everything they needed in order to do their jobs.'

Franquin shook his head again. Not unfriendly, but tolerant, as if he knew that William knew better but was reluctant to admit it.

'One of the most important tools you brought here, Sandberg? You know what that is, don't you?' No reply. 'A fresh pair of eyes.'

William snorted. 'I prefer to be trusted.'

'And we prefer not to take risks. You would have done the same, in our shoes. You'll be told exactly what you need to know, no more, no less.'

'So why are we sitting here?'

There was a brief pause before Franquin spoke. 'What did Miss Haynes tell you?'

Oh. So that's what this was about? Damage limitation. Were they here to find out what information she'd given him, and to ensure he didn't find out anything else?

'She didn't get too far. You came, we ran. You found us with the lady in the incubator, who didn't seem too well.'

He wasn't sure where it came from, but for a second he sensed that he had the upper hand. They didn't know what he knew. And he dwelled on the thought, trying to determine the best way to play it. In the end he decided to take the lead.

'Let's put the games aside for a moment, shall we? You have gone to great lengths to get me here. You seem determined to make me work for you. That's about the only thing I know.' He paused for effect, then carried on. 'That and the fact that what you've told me so far doesn't add up.'

'Is that so?' Franquin said. 'How did you come to that conclusion?'

William was acutely conscious that the hand he'd been dealt wasn't a strong one, and he didn't want to lose what leverage he had. But he also knew he wouldn't win if he didn't gamble.

'Arecibo,' he said.

There was utter silence in the room. William looked from face to face, but it was impossible to tell if their silence implied what he'd said was relevant.

'A city in Puerto Rico,' said Franquin. It was an invitation to continue.

'Yes. A city in Puerto Rico. A city with a radio telescope, which was used to broadcast a message into space forty years ago. A message consisting of sixteen hundred and seventy-nine pixels. Twenty-three times seventy-three. Exactly like the cuneiform texts you've given us.'

No response. But he had their attention, and that was a positive sign.

'And what do you construe from that?'

'I don't know. That we never learn?'

'I beg your pardon?'

William locked eyes with him. 'Call me narrow-minded, but wasn't it a touch presumptuous of us to sit there forty years ago and call out into space and think that whoever heard, whoever caught the message, would know how to read it?'

Franquin's eyes darted to Connors, and for a moment William thought he glimpsed a smile. There was a hint of one on Connors' face too, as if they toyed with him, as if they possessed one extra piece of the puzzle that William hadn't found.

'What makes you think we were the ones calling?' said Connors.

William didn't grasp what he meant.

And then he did. And understood even less.

'What are you saying?' he asked.

'We answered,' said Connors.

A chill passed through William's body when he realised Connors was serious. 'Bullshit,' he said. But he said it without conviction. It could well be true. Except for being completely absurd, it was a lot more logical than the other alternative.

There was no good reason why the astronomers had chosen to structure their message the way they had. No reason whatsoever, except, perhaps, one: that someone else had previously tried to contact us, in the same way.

He shook his head in disbelief. Was he really sitting in a room with a dozen stone-faced men telling him the code he was working on had been delivered from space? And that the message he was supposed to encrypt was an answer that humanity needed to send back?

It didn't add up. There was one key detail unaccounted for.

'In that case,' he wondered aloud, 'where does the virus come in?'

The men around the table looked at him. Not in surprise, but asking for more. Twelve pairs of eyes urging him to explain.

'The quarantine. The woman we saw, in the glass box. It is a virus, isn't it? And that's where the texts came from.'

'What makes you think that?' It was Franquin asking.

'Base four. Who would decide to store something in quaternary code?'

He heard the eagerness in his own voice, disappointed that he hadn't managed to suppress it. But the conversation was beginning to annoy him. In front of him sat a group of stiff uniforms who knew it all, but who seemed absolutely determined not give him any facts he couldn't reveal for himself.

'It's the only sensible answer,' he said. 'Nobody stores anything in base four. Not unless the medium requires it. And I can think of only one such medium.'

'DNA,' Franquin said. 'That's your conclusion?'

'I asked where the codes came from and you wouldn't tell me. This is the only thing that makes sense: that the texts have been pulled out of genetic material. Someone has contacted us, sent us a virus with a built-in message, and now it's our turn to send a reply. There's no other explanation. My only question is who.'

The advantage he'd enjoyed was gone. He was one step behind again, the conversation steering him instead of the other way around, leaving him no time to arrange his thoughts, forcing him to draw conclusions as he spoke.

And they were conclusions he didn't like.

Somewhere in the back of his mind a thought had started to emerge, and he struggled to ignore it. It couldn't be, he told himself. It was a dead end.

Connors watched him. As if he knew exactly what William was thinking.

'You already know the answer,' he said. 'Don't you?'

William shook his head.

'Where do you think the texts came from?'

He hesitated. Shook his head again. 'I'm sorry,' he said.

'Try.'

'No. I'm confused. Right now ...' The thought was still there. Fighting for attention from the back of his mind. 'Right now I can only come up with one way to explain it. The problem is, it's unthinkable.'

'Everything is, until you think it.'

William closed his eyes. Tried one last time to put all the pieces together, hoping they would suddenly start to land logic-side up. But no matter how hard he tried, he could only come to the same, impossible conclusion.

'Tell us.'

'Based on what I've heard,' he said, piecing it together in his mind, 'and going on what I've been able to deduce from what I've seen and from the conversation we're having right now, I can see no explanation other than ...' It was so ridiculous, he could hardly bring himself to say it out loud: '... no explanation other than that you have discovered a virus.'

He paused, waiting for objections. But nobody spoke.

'How, or where, I don't know. But somewhere, somehow, you've discovered this virus. And for whatever reason, you've concluded that...' He almost couldn't bring himself to say it. But he had to. 'You've concluded that this virus is not from our planet.'

He tried to read their faces. But none of them uttered a word. Nobody stopped him or mocked him for his outlandish theory. So he decided he might as well continue.

'Subsequently, as you studied that virus, you discovered that it had a message embedded in its DNA. And now, we – or rather, you – are trying to work out an encryption key that can be used to send them an answer. Them – whoever *they* are.'

He was finished, but the room remained cloaked in silence. He squirmed in his chair, feeling an urge to defend himself.

'It's preposterous, I know it is, but it's an explanation that takes all known factors into account. The Aricebo message could have been an early, unsuccessful attempt to answer them, formatted with the right matrix but without knowing how to encrypt it. And now we're all sitting here with a contagious virus and a message we need to answer, but no idea as to how.'

Silence again. The only sound was the murmur of the air conditioning, keeping the air in constant circulation.

'If it's all the same to you,' he said, assuming from the silence that he must have fallen woefully short of their expectations, 'I'd be grateful to hear the correct solution now.'

Connors cleared his throat. 'I'm afraid it isn't preposterous enough.'

William looked at him. Come again?

'Your conclusion is by no means ridiculous. But it *is* wrong.' Connors paused. 'There is a virus. That part is entirely correct. But we are the ones who created it.'

'We?'

'Yes.'

'Define we.'

'Not us, not the people in this room, but colleagues of ours. Scientists who are no longer alive.'

William breathed in. It wasn't too hard to guess why. Not after seeing the woman in the fish tank.

'Something went wrong?' he asked.

'Yes. Something went wrong. The virus didn't work as we'd hoped. Thirty years ago there were almost eight hundred people working here. Today we're down to fifty. None of us here are survivors from back then. We had to start over from scratch.'

He waited for William to process what he'd said.

'And so in this virus,' William said slowly, measuring his words one by one, 'in this virus, manufactured here, you placed an encoded text?'

Connors nodded, but it was a reluctant nod. 'Yes, we did.'

William sensed there was a *but* coming: 'And this text was written by you?'

'Yes,' said Connors. The same tone in his voice. *But.*

'Then I don't understand,' said William. 'If you came up with the code yourself, why do you need me to crack it?'

Connors cocked his head to one side. A friendly pantomime gesture to tell William he still wasn't asking the right questions.

'Because, Sandberg, we're talking about two different things here. It's not the code in the virus we need you to crack.'

'You're losing me,' said William.

The silence returned. There was a palpable uneasiness in Connors' eyes as he looked around the room, seeking clearance to take the next step. Nobody seemed to object, so he turned back to William.

'That sequence of code we gave you to work on, the one we want you to find the key for?'

'Yes?'

'It doesn't come from the virus.'

15

Christina's phone conversation with Leo lasted for less than a minute. He was extremely anxious, telling her it was vital they meet as soon as possible, pretty much ordering her to take a cab back to the office right away.

Him. Ordering her. She should probably be annoyed, but instead she couldn't help finding it amusing, and she hurried out of the café and hailed a cab. Not until she was sitting in the back seat, en route to the office, did Christina begin to worry that his findings wouldn't be as important as he believed, and that their meeting would turn out to be awkward and embarrassing.

Leo was waiting for her by his desk. He was still wearing his down jacket, which meant he had just arrived, and the moment she saw him she realised he should in fact be having the day off. Whatever he was about to show her, at least there was nothing wrong with his commitment.

He hunched over his computer, fingers hammering across the

keyboard while his eyes looked for the right words on the screen. He told her he'd been sitting at home, logged in to the news servers and reading agency newswires going back the last six months, convinced that there was something he'd seen but not registered at the time, something that could be critical for them now.

'I wasn't sure,' he said. He was breathless, more from excitement than from exertion, and looked at her in brief glances as if he was afraid to take his eyes off the monitor. 'I wasn't sure if I'd imagined it, or, see what I mean? You know how the mind works, when you combine things that weren't really like that?'

Christina stood behind him, coat still on, and concentrated on Leo's screen.

His fingers danced across the keyboard, browsing back to the date he was looking for. To that one newswire he knew would be waiting there.

'I knew I was right.' He looked at Christina. Turned the screen slightly, as if that would make it easier to read even though she was standing next to him. 'There.' He pointed at the screen.

He'd opened a newswire from Reuters, text in English, a short and to-the-point report of a meaningless event.

Amsterdam, 24 April. The headline: *No Trace of Missing Student.*

Christina scanned quickly through the article, jumping between keywords as years of practice had taught her, scanning it to get an overview and to tell if there was anything of value.

No trace – boyfriend worried – deliberate disappearance – police regard case as closed.

'See what I mean?' Leo said.

She didn't know what to say. In fact, she didn't have a clue what he meant.

She scanned the text a second time.

Okay, it was a disappearance. But how many people disappear every year? Plus the individuals involved were much younger, the story was seven months old and it had taken place in the Netherlands. Whatever parallels Leo had detected between this and William's disappearance were lost on her. Aside from the missing woman's partner being adamant that she hadn't disappeared of her own free will, Christina could find no similarities between the two.

Leo seemed to be reading her mind: 'Before you say anything, I did some googling.'

Oh? Christina looked at him.

'The missing student. Name: Janine Charlotta Haynes. Moved to Amsterdam four years ago on a scholarship – quite a prestigious one, as far as I can tell. Before that she studied in Seattle and everyone raved about how good she was.' He turned the monitor back towards himself. 'And then,' he said, 'her Master's thesis. Here.'

He closed the long list of newswires and switched over to his email client. At the top of his inbox was a message with himself as the sender. One attachment.

'Power of the Internets,' he said to fill the silence. And then he clicked to open the file.

Christina pulled out a chair, sat down in front of the computer.

She felt Leo's eyes on her, sensed his pride, and couldn't help thinking he was perfectly entitled to be pleased with himself. Every doubt she'd had was gone; his lack of social skills had nothing to do with his capacity as a journalist, and it annoyed her she hadn't been able to separate one from the other.

In front of her on the screen was a scanned document. Almost a hundred pages long according to the thumbnails on the side. And Leo scrolled until the front page filled the middle of the screen. The title in English, centred on the monitor. *The Eternal Search for Meaning: A Study of Codes And Hidden Messages in Prehistoric Manuscripts.*

'What was it he used to do, your husband?' Leo said. 'I mean, or, ex?'

She turned her head towards him. His gaze was steady, as if he and his job had become one and the same, as if suddenly he was forgetting to doubt himself. He was no longer an insecure young man, simply because he was too busy thinking of something else.

He hadn't asked the question to get an answer. He'd asked it to reinforce the fact that he was right. And she nodded: it was too similar for it to be a coincidence.

'You think we can find the boyfriend?' she said.

And Leo looked at her. His eyes confident, proud, as he nodded his yes. And passed her a note with a name and telephone number.

'I've already left him a message.'

∞◯∞

The pale yellow square of paper with the phone number of a Swedish newspaper scribbled on it was one of many that disappeared under the heavy file that Albert van Dijk dropped on to his desk.

He was tired.

No, he wasn't tired, he was shattered.

He sank down into his hard office chair, slid out on to the edge of the seat, collapsing until he could feel the armrests under his armpits. Rubbed his eyes and forehead with hands covered in smudges from whiteboard pens.

It drained him completely to give lectures. But he knew he had to do it, knew that the energy and the adrenalin he got from standing there, energising the room and balancing what he'd planned to say with his students' questions or his own improvisations, were the only things that kept him going. It drained him, but paradoxically it was also what spurred him on. Sometimes it even made him happy, or at least as close as he could get.

The problem was, his pain had doubled. It had been more than seven months now, and her memory was slowly starting to fade. That created a second layer of sorrow, on top of the loss.

She was out there somewhere. He knew she was. Somewhere Janine was waiting for him, and he didn't want to forget her, didn't want to get over it, not as long as there was anything he could do to be reunited with her.

As if he hadn't already exhausted every possibility.

He tried to bring himself back to the moment. Outside his window he could hear life carrying on, today as every day, students talking or making phone calls or hurrying across the echoing yard to places they should have been ten minutes ago. He used to love sitting here, listening to the sounds and letting his eyes wander across his bookshelves, pausing every now and then to settle on some book that had been left behind by one of his predecessors.

But the joy had gone. Life had retreated from him, everything took place through a colourless filter, and even if he saw that life around him was carrying on the way it always had done, at the same time it wasn't the same, not really. He wasn't present. No matter where he was.

That was probably one of the reasons he failed to notice the chubby young man in his doorway.

Albert drew himself up in his chair before realising that he had. Sat straight, as if he were the one to show respect for his secretary and not the other way around. And the result was a silence that was uncomfortable for both of them.

'I just thought I'd let you know I took a few calls while you were out,' the young man said when the silence had lasted long enough.

He pointed at Albert's desk, the heavy file on top of the Post-it notes. He was a little over twenty but looked like a teenager. And if it hadn't been for his job, he'd probably never have seen the inside of a university.

'I saw,' said Albert. 'I'll deal with them later.'

'I just wanted to be sure you'd seen.'

'Thank you. Was there anything else?'

There was. But the assistant hesitated, still uncomfortable, and decided that it could probably wait. He shook his head and left the room.

Albert closed his eyes again.

'Actually, there was one thing.'

The voice was just as close as before, and Albert looked up to find the irritating little man back in the same spot as ten seconds ago.

'Have we stopped knocking altogether now?'

'It was open,' said the assistant.

'Because you didn't close it.'

'I mean, not now. But before. You usually close it if you don't want to be disturbed.'

Albert searched for a response, but could find none. Waved his hand for the secretary to tell him whatever was on his mind.

'Do you know the people who worked in this office before you?' he asked.

What the hell kind of question was that?

The secretary held out a padded envelope, embarrassed now at having raised the subject, realising too late that this wasn't a matter for the head of the faculty. But he was still learning the routines and he had to ask someone, didn't he? And it wasn't his fault they'd given him a boss who was moody and depressed and refused to accept he'd been left by his girlfriend.

'It's just that it must've ended up in the wrong place,' he said. 'It's addressed to someone who doesn't work here. I didn't know what to do with it.'

'Okay,' said Albert. 'Take it to the porter's office. They'll either forward it to the right person or return it to whoever sent it. It's not our job to go looking for people who don't work here.'

The boy mumbled his thanks. Turned to leave for the second time.

Albert stayed in his chair, watching him as he went back outside. As he put the envelope on his desk. And kept existing. Shuffling around. Tending to things. Distracting him. Albert looked at his watch. It was too early for lunch, but it didn't matter. He needed to be alone. Where didn't make any difference, so long as it was somewhere nobody would bother him. And that letter was as good an excuse as any.

He got up and went out into the reception area.

'Tell you what, give it to me and I'll take it there myself.'

He saw the surprise in his secretary's face but didn't stop to explain himself. Just grabbed the letter from the boy's desk, dead set on finding a quiet corner in the cafeteria or one of the libraries or perhaps even outside if it wasn't too cold. And he walked out of the room and continued towards the stairs.

It wasn't until then that he saw the name of the addressee.

Seconds later, Albert sprinted past the porters' office. He still had the envelope in his hand, focusing only on getting through the large wooden doors and out into the cool winter air and the clear, bright sunlight to be able to see.

He stopped at the foot of the stairs. Ran his finger down the fold to open the envelope. He trembled from the tension, didn't even notice when the stiff, yellow paper cut into his skin and made him bleed.

The letter was stamped with a franking machine. No logo, no name, no return address. But the edge of the print had the word BERN on it. And it was dated the day before.

Addressed to the University of Amsterdam.

Attention: Emmanuel Sphynx.

Albert fought back the tears, tried to keep his voice from shaking as he punched the number to the police, waited for someone to answer.

'I need to speak to the Missing Persons Division.'

16

The conversation in the parliament carried on for another half hour without anything new being said. It ran down one dead end after another, and every question was met with evasive answers or new questions about what William and Ms Haynes had seen or talked about. Around him the dozen stone-faced men had remained silent aside from occasional brief contributions.

Eventually William lost his patience. The situation wasn't going anywhere, and there wasn't much to lose. Plus, he was getting hungry.

'You know what?' William said, loudly and with bite in his voice. It came from nowhere, butting in while someone was still talking. The room fell silent. He had everyone's attention.

'Here's how it is,' he said. 'I've told you everything I know. Which, I might add, isn't much. You don't have to believe it if you don't want to, you can keep asking me questions until I fall asleep or die or god knows what it is you're after. But we're not going to get much further than this. This is all I've got. And right now you're the ones who choose what we're going to waste our time on.'

'So what do you suggest?' It was Franquin. 'What do you think we should be wasting our time on?'

'I'd like to make a deal. Can we do that?'

No answer. Not that William expected one.

'I'll offer you my services. I'll promise to do my best. I can't promise you results, because you can't guarantee anything in this line of work, but I promise to do my utmost to find the cipher key you need. But I want one thing in return.' Again, the only sound was the whirring of the air conditioning. 'I want to know exactly what it is I'm working on.'

The silence held. But there was something else. Glances were being exchanged across the table, as if a collective decision was being made.

'Sandberg?'

The voice came from behind him, and he had to turn around to see.

Connors was standing up now, face and voice a notch lower, the entire tone frighteningly serious. He took a breath, held it to underline the significance of what he was about to say.

It wouldn't be the first time he'd told someone. There had been at least twenty people before William, many of them present in the room right now, and they all stared at him, all of them knowing that in a couple of minutes he would be having thoughts he'd never previously had, that this moment would for ever mark the end of *before*, and that the rest of his life would be *after*.

Before and after the moment he got to know.

'You're a programmer,' Connors began.

William shrugged. 'Passably.'

Connors gave him a sympathetic glance. It hadn't been intended as a question, only as a conversation opener; everyone in the room knew exactly what William's role had been in the Swedish military. No one doubted that William was a skilled programmer.

'So you know what a comment line is.'

William shrugged again. Of course he did. In common with anyone who'd ever tried to write a computer program. Comments were bits of the program code that were meant to be ignored by the computer. They had no significance to the functions the program actually performed, inserted merely as plaintext notes to be read by people rather than a computer. Sometimes they were there as reminders of what a certain part of the program was doing, sometimes to tell other programmers how a certain sequence was written. Or, not uncommonly, they were little in-jokes for fellow programmers to find. Quite simply, they were lines in the computer code that didn't add any value to the actual program. Incidental messages from the ones who wrote it.

'So?' he said.

Connors looked at him. 'What do you know about human genes?'

'Significantly less.'

Connors expected as much. He cleared his throat.

'In every single piece of scientific writing you can find today – every article or paper published in the modern era – there'll be one thing you'll read over and over again. So far, we have mapped out the purpose of slightly less than two per cent of the human genome.' He held up his thumb and forefinger, close enough to touch each other, to show just how small a percentage he was talking about. 'Two minuscule per cent, that's all we can point to and say *this*, this part we know what it's good for. But as for the remaining ninety-eight? Today, we simply don't know what it does.'

There was another pause, mostly to give William the chance to show he was following. He showed more than that.

'Junk DNA,' he said.

Connors raised an eyebrow. That was more than most people knew. On the other hand, it probably wasn't all that surprising, Sandberg read the right papers and kept up to date with the buzz from the science world. Or at least he used to, when he was still active.

'Some people call it that,' Connors confirmed. 'Even if I've learned to prefer *non-coding* DNA.'

William gave him an enquiring look.

'The truth,' Connors said, 'is that we've been wrong. Junk DNA isn't junk after all.'

It took a moment for William to register what Connors had said. When he did, he found himself sitting up straighter in his chair. The conversation was going in a direction he hadn't expected, and there was no way he could keep pretending he wasn't interested.

'This is obviously not something we shout about,' Connors continued. 'You won't be reading it in the newspapers or in magazines or in scientific studies. But just under fifty years ago, a group of scientists managed to interpret the remaining ninety-eight per cent too.'

He stopped. Looked at William, waited until he could see that William had understood and was ready to receive the last, crucial piece of information.

But William was already there. Connors had given him all the pieces he needed, there was only one way to put them together, and the only thing stopping William now was the thought that this could not be. It was unbelievable – worse, impossible. For a moment he glanced at Connors, hoping against hope that he'd misunderstood.

He hadn't.

William shook his head in disbelief, signalling to Connors that he must have come to the wrong conclusions and that Connors needed to help him get it right.

And Connors obliged. Carefully emphasising every syllable:

'What the scientists discovered was that the human DNA is full of comment lines.'

∞○∞

Once, about ten years earlier, William Sandberg had found himself on board a plane that almost crashed.

For three minutes of eternity the military jet had spun out of control, plummeting at an increasing speed, engines whining and pens, newspapers and coffee mugs hanging motionlessly in the air, hurtling towards the ground. Together with himself.

Terror had intertwined with the dizzying sensation of weightlessness, every last one of his organs had lifted from its socket, and throughout it all his panicking brain kept telling him: Now, now it's almost over, one more second and it stops, one more second and we'll regain control and the feeling of firm floor below will return.

But for each time that thought occurred, he was confronted with the fact it didn't happen. And his thoughts turned into an endless vortex of fear and terror, mixed with hopes for a relief that never came, and then double the terror when he realised that it was truly happening: This is *now*, we're crashing and we're not going to make it.

Three minutes.

Then he'd been pushed back into his seat as the plane righted itself, climbed again with its jets screaming in desperation as the pilot manoeuvred them up into the clouds once more. Outside the windows, red mountainsides whizzed by as a sign of how low they'd come and what an extremely close shave it had been.

Afterwards, he'd learned that they were seconds away from dying.

It took him weeks to be able to sleep again.

What stayed was the feeling of terror, and the constant spiral of hoping for a salvation that didn't come.

The emotions that William experienced as he stood up from his chair in the parliament and ran out of the room were identical to his minutes in the crashing plane.

Thoughts and reactions followed each other in that same terrifying spiral, a numbing combination of detachedness and absolute reality, swinging back and forth between disbelief and pure panic.

He leapt through the futuristic steel corridors, rushed up the centuries-old stone stairs, out to the disarmingly beautiful view on the terrace, the nameless mountains around him and the lake that rippled below. He needed air, or so he thought; he needed to see sky, but that didn't help either. He stood there, one moment perfectly still, catching his breath, trying to wrap his mind around what he'd heard. And the next moment he was racing along the banister, as if anything would change because he'd moved to a new location.

As if he could run away from what they'd told him.

Who.

That was the question that kept returning. Like a sweaty loop, always ending up in the same place. Like the nightmarish feeling of being about to wake up, not now, but soon, and every soon became now without anything changing, over and over until he couldn't stand still. And he moved to the next spot, then to the next, gazing out into the distance in the desperate hope that somewhere out there was an answer.

Who.

He'd been standing like that for quite a while when he noticed he wasn't alone.

Connors waited behind him, leaning against the heavy wooden doors, watching without saying a word. Again. What was it with that man and watching people?

He couldn't tell how long Connors had been there. In fact, it was hard for William to determine how long he'd been there himself. He was wet with mist, or maybe it was sweat. Everything around him had become a blur, as if someone had kicked down the foundation to his entire worldview, and now it was lying in ruins.

'I know,' said Connors. He didn't add *how you feel*, but that's what he meant. 'All I can say is that you get used to it.'

William stood silent. Rays of sunlight jutted at angles through the mountain peaks, a slow wind ruffled his hair and sought its way into the openings of his clothes, making his hairs stand on end in the chill.

But none of this penetrated William's consciousness.

'The codes we're working with ...?' he began.

He couldn't find the words to finish the sentence, but then again Connors didn't need them. He answered carefully, almost like a teacher explaining to a student.

'All the information you and Janine have been given has come from human DNA.' He waited for William's reaction. Already knowing what the next question would be.

'And who put it there?'

Connors shook his head. Looked William in the eye.

'That's the question we've been asking ourselves for fifty years.'

PART 2

Plague

People used to tell me I should live in the now.
I always laughed at them.

Now is just a precursor to then.
That's all it is and nothing more.
It's a transient phase that will come to an end, one that there's no reason to get attached to, because sooner or later that moment will pass anyway. And people can say whatever they want, but if you live in the now you're this close to living in the past. And only fools do that.

I have always lived in the then.
I've eaten breakfast thinking about lunch, I've loved thinking about my next; I've sat in sunsets with a beer in my hand knowing that when darkness comes we're going to have to go back to the house. Either that, or we run out of beer and then we'll have to go back anyway. Or someone will start to feel cold and it's always the same.
Sooner or later you always have to go back to the house.
So what's the point of living in the now?
Then will always come. You might as well be ready for it.

And then one day I decided I didn't want to be alive.
And the only thing I wanted was for then to come as quickly as possible.

Morning. Wednesday 26 November.
Today I'm not so sure.
Today I'm not sure there is a then.
Today, for the first time in my life, I wish I could live in the now.

17

In Connors' life, the border between before and after was marked by an impenetrable, leaden grey rain.

He'd had an excruciatingly slow afternoon. He'd been struggling through endless reams of folded phone-tap printouts – conversations between people exchanging nothing secret whatsoever, recorded on to rolls of magnetic tape and transferred into writing by hammering secretary fingers at green computer screens – and outside the draughty window to his room daylight had come and gone without anybody noticing.

It was October and it was cold and the world was a dangerous place. Washington was run by an actor and Moscow by a KGB chief. And on the giant table in Connors' office lay huge maps of London and England and the entire United Kingdom, ready to be covered in stiff sheets of transparent plastic to map out the hostile attacks that were always around the corner.

But it was neither politics nor weather that made the hours drag.

The afternoon was slow because Connors was waiting for the clock to strike six.

The memo in his pigeonhole that morning had been unusual, not extreme but unusual nonetheless. It was written on an electric typewriter, posted inside a brown standard envelope with his name on the outside, the edges of it still wrinkled after being fed through the typewriter cylinder.

But most of all, it didn't have a stamp. And that could only mean one thing. The letter had reached him via the internal mail, perhaps even from inside his own building, even if that felt less likely given the size of the place. No matter how secret the letter was, it would have been far simpler for someone to simply walk into his room, lower their voice and speak to him directly. All the same, he was certain that it came from within the organisation.

Truth be told, that excited him. The building he worked in was unknown even to most of MI6, and an internal memo consisting of one single sentence was enough to create a sense of thrill and urgency, a feeling he no doubt had expected to encounter more often when he was recruited to his position just six months before. At last, there was something happening, and he wasn't quite as spoiled with things happening around him as he would have wanted.

At four minutes to six he put on his coat.

He walked down the uneven, creaking staircase, out through the inconspicuous door and further down the street to the phone box outside the closed-down pub on the far side of Berkeley Square, entirely according to the instructions of the memo.

And there he stood. Waiting in the cold phone booth as drips of condensation slithered down the inside of the windows, drawing transparent stripes on the misty panes and racing the trickles of raindrops on the outside. The cold Bakelite handset in front of him. The damp slowly working its way up under his coat. The second hand on his watch plodding its way towards the hour. And past. Ten seconds past six. Twenty. Not a sound from the phone.

He started to feel uneasy. Had he misjudged the memo? Was it a trap, was he exposing himself? Someone could well have been watching him come out of the office, they could have stood in the dark without him seeing them, of course they could, and that bothered him. In fact, how could he be sure there wasn't somebody looking at him from the other side of the square right now, taking his picture with a telephoto lens, perhaps even preparing to follow him as soon as he left? Or worse?

He didn't have time to finish the thought before he sensed something moving outside.

He spun around. And stared right into a face on the other side of the glass.

The man outside the booth looked straight into Connors' eyes, his voice inaudible, drowned out by the rain and the wind and the hum of the city seeping in through the gaps under the door. But from the movements of his mouth, there was no doubt the man was saying his name.

Connors nodded back. And the man with the weathered face

opened the door. Gestured for Connors to step out into the cold autumn night.

It wasn't at all what Connors had expected. He felt the uneasiness grow inside him, but he did as he was told, walked out into the evening chill, the rain falling in white streaks across the headlamps of the waiting diplomatic car. It was as if someone had drawn his life in charcoal, everything was dark and blurred at the edges, and he hurried through the downpour, the stranger one step behind, across the street and over to the pavement and into the damp warmth of the rear passenger seat.

The man sat down beside him and closed the door. Introduced himself as Franquin.

He signalled for the chauffeur to start the engine and they swung out into the evening traffic and from that moment nothing would ever be the same again.

Afterwards, Connors' mind was in free fall for days.

What he'd heard couldn't be true.

And yet it was.

Why him, he kept asking himself? Why should he have to know?

His everyday life had consisted of theoretical conversations about hypothetical scenarios, a reality that wasn't his own, filtered through typewriters and telex machines. And even if he knew that somewhere on the outside there was a real world too, that somewhere beyond the wooden panelling and out-trays of the office his theoretical models were the reality for diplomats and defence staff and agents all around the globe, even if he knew that, he didn't have to be *there*. He could watch it from afar, and that kept him sharp and rational; it allowed him to find solutions that weren't affected by stress or rushes of adrenalin or the panic of what-the-hell-are-we-going-to-do.

And that was how he liked it. Connors was a theorist.

Even so, he'd found himself treated to an expensive dinner in a private room at the Ritz, of all places, with chandeliers and heavy curtains and wool carpets so thick that if he'd removed his shoes he wasn't sure he'd find them again. And there he sat with a starched white napkin on his knee, a dead pheasant on his plate, and a strange man across the table. Speaking in a low voice and telling Connors things he couldn't keep at a distance.

Messages. In human DNA.

At first all they'd found were patterns, Franquin told him, a recurring logic in a flow that should have been random, the same way you discover coded messages in a stream of noise. And this had triggered the alarm, which meant nobody was allowed to know outside the most trusted.

It had been at the height of the Cold War. A scientist had been the one to make the initial discovery, inside the body of what happened to be a deceased British ambassador. The immediate conclusion was that he'd discovered a way for enemy agents to send coded messages into England, and as outlandish as it seemed, it was entirely logical when they thought about it. What better way to get a message behind enemy lines than by hiding it in one of their own? What could be more secure than letting the enemy work as your unknowing carrier pigeon?

But it turned out that the guesses were wrong. The same sequences were found in other bodies. Bodies that didn't belong to ambassadors or agents, that had no connection whatsoever to global politics or to warfare. In every single blood test, in every single human being they secretly analysed, in every new sample of human DNA the same code appeared.

And while experts worked around the clock to crack the code and understand what it meant, it became more and more obvious that wherever they looked, the code was there. Any Briton, any European, any living person on the entire planet – no, even inside those who were no longer living, from the recently deceased in hospital mortuaries to medical specimens in preserving jars retrieved from dusty university archives all over the world.

Whoever had put the message inside the human DNA did it a long time ago. So long that it had been spread and copied and passed on, generation after generation.

And the scientists had started working their way backwards, convinced that the incidence would fade the further back in time they went. That the code could be backtracked as it branched out through generations, narrowed down to the time and the place where it was initially planted inside the human genome. But the incidence didn't fade.

No matter how far back they went, how many far-flung

graveyards they visited, how many ancient crypts they entered and pyramids they excavated under the pretext of archaeological missions. The results were always the same.

The code was a permanent part of the human DNA.

As long as people had existed, so had the code.

And there was no explanation as to how it got there.

∞◯∞

As Connors opened the door from the underground safe zone, breathed the stale air from the castle stairs as he had done every morning for almost thirty years, it was with a sense of sadness. Sadness at the time that had passed, and at the limited results they'd managed to achieve.

The big breakthroughs had been made before his time. They had cracked the codes. They'd interpreted them as cuneiform script. And then, they had translated the script, and realised what it meant and that the truth was worse than they'd imagined.

Desperately they'd searched for an answer.

They had called out into space but nobody had heard. Perhaps because they lacked the key to encode their signal, because what they sent out was in plaintext, with the ones as ones and the zeros as zeros. But what else was there to do when they didn't know?

Or perhaps, space was the wrong place to turn.

But if it was, then what else was there?

He took a deep breath, tried to shake off the questions even though he knew they would bounce right back, again and again and always without answers. And that filled him with a greater sadness than ever.

Sadness that nothing had changed, that this was his life. What had become of it.

He shook his head, didn't want to go down that route. He wasn't yet sixty. He had at least twenty years left, hopefully thirty, with a bit of luck maybe even forty.

But where would they come from?

What did he have to dream of?

He who knew the truth?

He heard his own steps echo up the stairwell.

They were shuffling. They never used to do that.

And he asked himself whether he'd made the right choice when Franquin had persuaded him to join them on that rainy October day.

Whether there still was any hope left that they'd succeed.

And whether it wouldn't have been better to let Sandberg know everything, now that they'd told him this much anyway.

18

The first morning William Sandberg woke up to a new understanding of the world, he stood at his window, gazing at the view for a long time, before he could bring himself to do anything else.

Everything was exactly the same but behind a layer of make-believe.

Everything he'd done before, everything that was standard and routine and nothing special, of all that he now performed and watched and tasted with a constant filter of detachment, as if everything that was true and real the day before had suddenly and in one single blow been transformed into something different.

He hadn't slept well. Yesterday's conversation had kept repeating, over and over in his head. He'd tried to analyse single words, the way they were said and how heads had been turned in the room, all in his hunt for some detail he might have heard but not grasped at the time. And in the space between sleep and consciousness he'd tried to form new questions, steer the conversation in new directions, only to realise that his subconscious couldn't reveal things he didn't know.

What they'd told him was nothing short of absurd. And no matter how much he grappled with the facts, how much he tried to understand, he always came back to the feeling that it wasn't true. Because, he thought, it simply couldn't be.

He stood inside the thin windows, watched the view bend through the uneven glass, as if the entire world around him wanted to join in and illustrate that nothing he took for granted could be relied on any more. Eventually he closed his eyes, let his mind wander freely.

He thought about the conversation. He thought about the woman with the American accent, Janine, who'd wanted to show him something on a piece of paper but who hadn't had the time.

And most of all he thought of Sara.

She was adopted, but from the moment they first saw her she was theirs. She was such a natural addition to their little family that William and Christina didn't give it a second thought, things were what they were and there was nothing remarkable about that, and not until the day they told her did it occur to them that for Sara, the whole world had been transformed completely because of one single piece of news.

One moment she was mature and ready to hear it. She was fifteen, sensible and grown-up enough to know the truth, fifteen and dressed-in-jeans and living-in-the-city and coffee and hidden cigarettes. And the next moment she was a child again, the same girl who used to crawl up to them at night when they still lived in the house, the same girl who'd proudly stood in her pyjamas ten years previously, that stupid damned morning when he turned thirty-seven and that would always be etched in his memory as a time when everything was good.

The same girl, that's who she was. Older, but then again not older at all. Mature, but not mature enough.

They'd told her right there across the dining table, and in an instant they were transformed into two strangers, a pair of liars seated in front of her, smiling and comforting her and claiming that they loved her, and behind them gaped a void of unknown reality, a void that had always existed but that they hadn't let her see until now.

The colour of Sara's eyes had changed before them. They used to be green and warm, but that morning they'd turned a black that would never go away, she got up from the table without a word, and that moment drew a thick line across their reality, a line that nobody could ever cross again.

Perhaps that had been when it all began. Perhaps that moment marked the start of everything that would happen, the snowball that was set in motion and that kept growing until William was lying there in the bathtub with a chemical drowsiness and a locked front door.

Perhaps.

He had never been able to understand why she'd reacted the way she did. He and Christina were her parents, and for them nothing changed. Their world was the same as the day before, or as last week or as any other day. But for Sarah everything crumbled.

And here, standing in front of his window, William suddenly understood.

It was as if somebody had just told him his life wasn't actually his. As if he'd just been told he'd been adopted by reality, as if in fact he'd come from somewhere else and now he didn't know where, or why, or whether anything around him was indeed what he thought it was.

The human DNA. Full of text.

His own DNA, and Christina's, and Sara's, even though she wasn't their biological child, and the bull-necked man and Connors and Franquin and the children in the park and the old lady at the supermarket and everyone else in human history, the same coded texts, and why?

He closed his eyes, turned away from the view, tried to clear his head. He wanted to stay sharp, sceptical, to keep asking.

How could he be certain it wasn't a lie, a smokescreen to stop him from understanding some other truth?

He couldn't be. And he sat down on the bed again. Tried to run through the previous day in his mind.

His biggest concern was the feeling they still weren't telling him everything. There remained too many unanswered questions.

He got up. Grabbed some fruit from the tray next to his bed, poured a fresh cup of coffee. There were holes in what they were telling him. And they were holes he couldn't fill himself. He needed to know what those messages said, what they meant and what everyone was so afraid of, and what they thought they'd solve by having William help them code an answer.

There were holes, and only one person could help him fill them.

He was almost certain they'd do all they could to stop him from seeing her.

William had showered and dressed in a white shirt, new pair of jeans and a thin, dark jacket when his appointed guard opened the door with timing too good to be purely a coincidence. He was probably under surveillance in his bedroom too.

'I'm coming,' William said, his tone brisk to signal that he was perfectly capable of managing his own schedule, and that he wouldn't need to be escorted between his room and his office for the rest of his life, or however long they planned to keep him there. 'I think I can find my own way.'

But the guard stood firm. 'Connors wants to speak to you.'

William stared at him for a second. Took a last swig of his coffee. Placed the mug on the table to show he was ready. He wanted very much to talk to Connors, too.

And so they exited into the stone corridor and disappeared into the cold maze that was the castle.

∞◯∞

Within a second of waking, Janine was hit by a crippling fatigue.

She recognised it all too well, and she fought the urge to turn over and go back to sleep, away from the castle, away from everything and back into her dreams and just stay there. She couldn't let herself break down again. Not now.

Instead, she made herself sit up on the edge of her bed. No lying down. Up, walk across the room, go into the bathroom. Small steps. Think ahead.

She got into the shower and turned on the water, first ice-cold to wake her up, then as hot as she could take for as long as possible, and then back to a normal, soothing temperature that allowed her body to recover from the shock.

She couldn't let it happen again.

Helena Watkins had pulled her out of her depression the last time. Without her she wouldn't have made it.

It was Helena who had let her see the codes, even though it was against protocol, it was she who'd told her about the mailroom in the cellars and who'd pushed the key card under her door that night, trying to warn her, rambling on about a plan B that was in fact called something else. Back then Janine hadn't understood anything of what was happening. Now she did. Only too well.

Helena Watkins had known too much. It couldn't be any other way. And now she was gone, and wouldn't be able to help if Janine fell apart.

So she couldn't. She had to stay alert and continue to fight.

They had kept interrogating her until two in the morning, and she suspected they weren't done even though they'd eventually called a halt to let her rest. But she also knew they hadn't beaten her. She had managed to remain composed and awake and sincere, and they wouldn't know what she'd found out as long as she didn't tell them.

And she hadn't told them.

Which gave her an advantage.

That was an advantage she was going to use, and then Albert was going to show up, and after that everything should be fine again.

It was the only option there was. Everything had to be fine again.

When she walked out of her bathroom ten minutes later, her tiredness was gone.

Small steps.

The first thing she had to do was talk to William Sandberg.

It turned out to be quite a long walk.

The guard led William through the stone corridors, the same routes he'd tried to explore himself the previous day, and then on and down the large official staircase that he'd seen at a distance but never made it up to before someone put a T-shirt in his mouth and made him shut up.

After that, new passages appeared, wide and with arched ceilings and with iron chandeliers hanging at regular intervals, and when at last they came to a huge pair of wooden doors, he once again reassessed his impression of the castle's size.

The chamber inside was a chapel, large enough to accommodate a congregation of a hundred or more. The bricked, vaulted ceiling peaked in sharp angles high in the air above him, hand-painted frescoes covered the walls, from the back of the rows of weathered pews and all the way to the altar, bathed in the light flooding in through the huge stained-glass windows behind it.

The guard waved him forward. Remained by the entrance, waiting until William was halfway up the aisle before he withdrew, closing the heavy door behind him with an echo that never seemed to end.

On the front pew sat Connors. His eyes fixed on the stained glass, with only a brief glance at William as he sat down beside him.

It was a strange place to meet. And yet, William thought he knew why Connors had chosen it.

'I'm not a believer,' William said.

'Neither am I,' said Connors.

They sat for a moment. Silent, listening as their words echoed like staccato whispers along the ceiling before they faded out and disappeared.

'How was your night?'

'It's a very comfortable bed to not sleep in.'

Connors smiled. Good answer. Looked back into the tinted light. 'No,' he said. 'I'm not a believer. I'm a thinker.'

William remained silent.

'There's something soothing about sitting here. The first time I came here I was exactly where you are now. As if someone had taken everything I believed in and shaken it like a large ... what are they called? Those souvenirs you shake to make it snow on Big Ben or the Taj Mahal or whichever airport you happened to buy the thing at. All your thoughts fly around just like that, and you can't keep hold of any of them, or follow them with your eyes, the only thing you can do is to wait until they land, until things calm down and you can start to make out what it is you're looking at.'

He turned to William for a response. And William nodded. That was exactly where he was.

'It used to help me, sitting here. The stillness. The silence. The light. The feeling that people have always been looking for answers. We aren't the first who don't understand.'

We. William registered the choice of words, but didn't say anything. We, as if they were a team now, as if they were facing a common problem and had the same starting point and the same knowledge and it was obviously complete bullshit, but he didn't say so. Instead, he looked at Connors:

'I'm the first person to see the usefulness of a useful idiot.'

Connors turned his head, surprised.

'You're right, of course,' William continued. 'I've been exactly where you are. I've had people working for me without letting them know everything. I've seen to it that they've understood their part of the job, separate tasks for separate people, and then it was my job to put the pieces together.'

There was a *but* in the air, and Connors waited for it.

'I wonder if I wouldn't be more useful an idiot if you let me know the reason I'm here.'

Connors looked ahead again. Let the seconds pass, either to allow him time to work out what to say, or possibly to ensure that William didn't forget whose job it was to steer the conversation. Eventually, he decided that he'd been silent for long enough. He reached into his breast pocket, pulled out an envelope, handed it to William.

It was small and white, informal and standard-sized, one that could hold anything from a Christmas card to a wedding invitation. And William took it, quite sure that it wasn't either.

Its weight surprised him. It wasn't paper inside. It was an object, flat and significantly smaller than the envelope, and it seemed to slide from end to end as he turned it over, let his finger run under the flap to fold it open.

Let the contents fall into his hand.

A blue piece of plastic.

I'll be damned. A key card.

He looked up at Connors. This wasn't what he expected. And he tried to find words to express himself; he couldn't understand why they would give him this, how it changed his status and what they hoped to achieve by it. And it occurred to him that once again, they'd shaken his snow globe, and perhaps that was the entire point.

'Here's how we want it to be,' Connors said. 'We want you to feel that you have everything you need to help us. We want you to feel free to ask us questions. And we want to help you with answers as far as we possibly can.'

'And how far is that exactly?'

'There'll be limits. I don't want to put you under more stress than necessary. But when we say we're afraid of what's going to happen, we're not exaggerating. We need that code key. And we don't have much time.'

'Until what?'

'As I said. There will be limits.'

William watched him. He had thousands of questions. And yet, he couldn't find a single one to ask. Perhaps it was exhaustion, perhaps his subconscious was struggling to keep up, but whatever the reason he couldn't express what he was wondering. Which was the worst kind of uncertainty he could imagine.

'Is there anything you'd like to know right now?' Connors asked.

'I want to know when I can see Janine Haynes.'

The treble of William's voice echoed around the chapel, ebbing out into cool streaks of air between the Christian icons in the rafters, leaving behind that silence that Connors had talked about, the one that made time stand still.

As Connors had said. It was soothing.

'Soon,' was the reply.

And they sat for a few moments, until Connors was sure there wasn't anything else that needed not to be said, and he stood up, moved past William in his pew and set off down the aisle towards the exit.

'One more thing,' William said behind him.

Connors turned. Yes?

'Can I assume this thing here isn't going to let me go anywhere in the castle I'd like?'

Connors smiled. An amused smile, sincere and friendly in the midst of everything. 'You're not an idiot,' he said. 'Neither are we.'

And then he carried on towards the wooden door, leaving William alone with a worldview that wasn't ready to be understood, in the middle of a room that tried to impose its own.

∞◯∞

William was still sitting in the pew, a black silhouette in front of what should have been a multitude of colours but that shone like an overexposed white field on one of the monitors, as Connors entered the surveillance room a good twenty minutes later. He closed the steel door behind him, took his place on the floor next to Franquin.

Both of them hesitated to speak. As if William's presence on the screen meant he could hear them, as if every thoughtless word or raised voice would allow him to detect the conflict that lingered under the surface, constantly waiting to flare.

When Franquin finally spoke, he did it calmly and quietly. 'I only hope you know what you're doing,' he said.

'You know as well as I do,' said Connors.

Franquin waited for him to go on.

'I'm clutching at straws. That's what I'm doing.'

'Let's hope you've chosen the right straw, then.'

Franquin was frustrated. Not just at seeing the situation running away from them, but at the way Connors kept making his own choices and getting the others to accept them, even if they clashed with every protocol. It was wrong, and the timing was the worst possible.

'How much does she know?'

'They're still not sure about that,' Connors said.

'And if they are allowed to meet and compare? What happens then?'

Connors shrugged. 'We allowed her to meet Watkins.'

'Indeed. And look how well that turned out.'

Connors threw him a tired glance. Didn't want that fight, not again.

'Why are you so afraid of letting them know?' he said.

Franquin's expression changed. As if Connors needed to ask. He lowered his voice even further, did his best to hold his irritation back. 'Let's say Sandberg can do it. Let's say that his background still counts for something, in spite of all the things we know about him, and what he just tried to do to himself. Let's say that in spite of all that he can handle the confidentiality.' He locked eyes with Connors. 'Even if he's up to it, there's still Haynes to consider.'

'Quite. But that isn't what I'm asking, is it?' Connors shook his head, repeated himself, lowering his voice to match Franquin's: 'What are you *afraid* of?'

Franquin stood silent. It was a rhetorical question, it had to be. Connors knew damn well what the danger was.

'That she's going to talk? Is that it? That we're going to let her out and that she's going to tell the world what we know?'

Franquin didn't answer. Of course that's what he was afraid of. That and a long row of problems that would follow.

'Because if that's the case,' Connor said, 'I think you're afraid of the wrong thing. If we ever do let her go, it'll be because this is all over. And that isn't a scenario I'm afraid of. Quite the contrary.'

Franquin sighed.

'I'm afraid because our greatest enemy is panic. And if there's one thing I want to avoid—'

'Don't you think it's a bit late for that?'

'I'm not a fatalist, Connors. Are you?'

It was Connors' turn not to answer.

'Good,' said Franquin. 'Because if any of us are, they're in the wrong place to begin with.'

They stood there, watching Sandberg in the monitor. Watching him without a word.

They'd talked themselves into a dead end, one they'd been in before and where the only way out was silence, and they both kept staring in front of them until the moment was over and their positions weren't as entrenched.

'I gave him the key,' Connors said.

And Franquin knew what he meant. Knew that whatever happens now, happens.

'We can only hope, then, can't we? Hope they're not going to find out.'

'Perhaps,' said Connors.

Glanced back at Franquin.

Knew that he shouldn't, but couldn't help himself.

So he said it.

'Or perhaps that's the only hope we have left.'

19

The man who sat alone, staring blankly on the other side of the glass panes to the narrow meeting room, had lost a lot of weight since his last visit.

Back then, he'd been healthy, well built and with a body that clashed completely with expectations of what a professor in archaeology ought to look like. His eyes had been stressed and worried, naturally, but they had been awake, alert, full of energy.

Today, Albert van Dijk looked ten years older. Yet it had only been a matter of months since their last meeting. The humour he had displayed then, constantly ready to tackle his problems with an odd, wry wit, had been replaced with a weary sorrow, the restless energy that had kept him perched on the edge of his seat now reeking more of desperation than of hope.

Inspector Neijzen of Amsterdam's Central Police Division watched him from afar while the espresso machine spurted out two cups of polite pointlessness, a black goo that was neither coffee nor espresso but something in between that never made anyone happy.

His breathing was laboured. Not that this was unusual – Neijzen had stopped watching his scale at two hundred and twenty-six pounds, and judging by the protests from his knees and his heels his weight hadn't changed for the better, any more than his eating habits.

But today he was panting because he'd had to rush to get here. He'd been relaxing at his country home when his secretary called to tell him there was a young man in his office, and that the man refused to talk to anyone else but Neijzen.

So van Dijk had been waiting in there for almost fifteen hours. He'd slept on the same chair as he was sitting in now, the same one he'd been sitting in since showing up the previous afternoon, assuming he'd slept at all, which judging by his appearance wasn't a foregone conclusion.

Neijzen couldn't help feeling there were a million reasons to feel sorry for the guy. It wasn't his job to get personally involved, nobody would gain from having him pity them, but there was something about the way the young professor had dealt with the situation that made it hard to keep a distance. Screaming, panic-stricken victims who vented their fears, cursed the police and the authorities and some arbitrary divine power for not doing enough, those he could easily handle. Or the ones who cried and blamed themselves, or withdrew and sat there, catatonic, rocking back and forth as if they'd lost the will to live. Years of experience had taught him to maintain a distance from victims overwhelmed by grief and stress; it was a shame that they were suffering, of course it was, but that was life.

Albert van Dijk, however, remained composed. Measured and composed and maintaining a sober distance, and if there was such a thing as a capable victim of crime, Albert van Dijk was the epitome.

Which, of course, didn't change a thing.

His partner was gone. She had been gone for seven months.

And she wouldn't ever come back.

*

'Have you slept?' was Neijzen's first question as he squeezed himself into the tight space between his chair and his desk, breathing heavily as he placed one of two steaming cups of coffee in front of the young man. Hesitating for a moment; perhaps he'd better give him both.

'Since yesterday? Or since we last met?' Irony without a smile.

'I came as fast as I could,' Neijzen said without elaborating.

'I'm grateful for that,' said Albert. And repeated the words he'd been saying over and over since last night: 'I wanted to talk to you.'

Neijzen's secretary had made that perfectly clear. There'd been at least five others on duty who could have dealt with van Dijk considerably more promptly, but whatever it was the man had to say, he steadfastly refused to say it to anyone else.

'Please,' said Neijzen. 'Tell me.'

Albert cleared his throat. Explained that of course he understood that the police had closed the case long ago. And Neijzen was about to interrupt, but Albert cut him off, saying that he fully understood why, and there was sincerity in his eyes as he said it. How long could you keep looking when everything pointed to her disappearing of her own free will? Just because some sad boyfriend protested and refused to believe he'd been dumped?

He knew the police had helped as much as they were able. And he'd chosen to stay out of their way, didn't want to make a nuisance of himself, electing not to contact them again unless he had something useful to tell them.

'And now you do?' Neijzen asked.

Albert nodded. 'I've always said she was taken against her will.'

'And we've followed up on everything you've said. And it hasn't led anywhere. Whatever you might believe, there's no evidence to support it.'

'I know that,' said Albert. 'But now I can prove it.'

Prove it? He had actual proof? This made Neijzen sit up in his chair.

'And how can you do that?' the detective asked.

'Because I know where she is.'

Neijzen looked at him. Leaned across the desk. And the cup that was neither coffee nor espresso remained untouched in front of him until it was stone cold.

∞◯∞

Janine Charlotta Haynes looked at the blue piece of plastic in her palm.

And then at the man opposite her.

She hadn't expected to see it ever again, and now that she did, there was only one explanation she could come up with. It must be a test. What kind she couldn't decide, but she had no doubt whatsoever that it was.

'We really should stop meeting like this,' she said, not even a hint of a smile on her face.

The bull-necked man who'd once claimed his name was Roger and who now said it was Martin Rodriguez and who frankly could be called whatever he liked for all she cared, stared back at her. Steady, penetrating eyes. But behind them there was something else, something she couldn't quite make out. Pity?

Hardly, she told herself.

'I understand you had rather a long night,' he said.

'About average,' she replied. As if she were thirteen years old, as if the only weapon she possessed was to obstruct the conversation and as if she wanted him to see she was going to use it as much as she could.

'Can you stand a couple more questions?'

'That depends,' she said, 'whether it's going to be you or me asking them.'

'You're welcome to try,' he replied.

'What did you do to Helena?'

'Watkins?'

'Unless there are other Helenas around, then yes, probably her.'

He gave her a look. His face was as flat as their conversation, and it struck her that their tone hadn't changed much since the first time they met. The game was the same: their efforts to answer with a question rather than divulge anything.

Except now the playfulness was gone.

'She was careless,' said the bull neck.

'Is that a threat?'

'No. It's an observation.'

'Difference being?'

'Significant.'

A pause. It was her turn, but she didn't want to play now. She shook her head, waved at him to get on with it and tell her what he was there for.

'So,' he said. 'I'm here for two reasons. Firstly, to ask you to tell me everything you know.'

'You know what?' she said. 'I've been here for almost seven months. In that time I've done nothing but tell you things. And if you have even the slightest bit of understanding about what goes on here – and maybe I'm over-estimating you, maybe your remit is just to abduct people and keep them locked up here – but if you do have the bigger picture, then you must be aware that since I arrived here all I've done is read and interpret and translate and tell you. Everything I know, you know too. End of story.'

She leaned back, said no more. She'd raised her voice, she'd let her anger seep out, and now she sat in silence as if cursing herself for not controlling her temper.

But in actual fact, she had. Her temper was a deliberate diversionary tactic. She hadn't told them everything, there were things she was starting to put together, and she wanted to keep those things to herself.

Martin Rodriguez shook his head. She had misunderstood his question:

'You spoke to William Sandberg.'

'Not for long.'

'*How* long?'

'I think you probably know that better than me. Because I assume you know exactly which doors we passed through, and when.'

He couldn't deny that. Of course they knew.

'So. How long did we talk?'

'You were out on the terrace for a little under twelve minutes.'

'There you go. And how much do you think a person can say in that time?'

'That's exactly what I'm here to find out.'

She heaved a sigh. Letting him know the conversation was boring her. 'And the second part?' she said.

'What do you mean?'

'You're listing things. You're currently at *firstly*.'

She stared blankly at him, waiting for him to figure out for himself how highly she thought of people who got lost in a two-item list.

'Secondly,' he said, 'it's my job to make sure you have everything you need to do your job.'

Janine hesitated. What was this about? First the key card, now this. 'Such as?'

'That's my question to you. What do you need?'

'What are we talking about? Pens? Paper? Books? Internet?'

'Can't offer you Internet. Otherwise, just ask.'

'In that case,' she replied, 'tell me exactly what the texts I've been given are about.'

'You know I can't do that.'

'So when you say *everything*, what, in fact, does that include?'

It was his turn to sigh. 'I'm going to be perfectly honest with you. I'm not happy that we brought you here the way we did. *Nobody* here is, I can promise you that. But we are in the middle of . . . ' – he paused, looked for the right word – 'an extremely sensitive security situation. Because of that, some information isn't available to you.'

'So I'm supposed to solve a riddle without hearing the whole question?'

'We have given you as much as you need.'

'Apart from the context.'

'Which is of no interest.'

She stared at him. Stared for several seconds. And then she said:

'Two trains leave London for Brighton, one at two p.m. and one twenty minutes later. The first train travels at a hundred and twenty kilometres an hour, the other at a hundred and fifty. How large is the distance between the two trains at three o'clock?'

He studied her, expecting her to continue, but she was finished. And she waited, confident that sooner or later he'd ask the inevitable question.

'What's your point?'

'*Context*,' she said. 'Without context, what have you got?'

He looked for an answer, but she wasn't done yet.

'If I only give you abstract values, and if you don't know how they fit together, then you can't solve the problem, because you don't know *why* you're solving it. That's the reason every school textbook on the planet frames everything in little scenarios: *everything is important*. The solution comes from the whole picture.'

'I dare say it does. Nevertheless, that whole picture is something we can't—'

'In that case,' she interrupted him in a razor-edged voice, 'if you won't let me know the background, how can I *ever* solve your problem?'

He paused. Then, as if it was the most natural thing in the world, he said: 'One hundred and twenty times one, minus one hundred and fifty times forty divided by sixty.'

She looked at him. He was quicker than she'd anticipated.

That was the formula to solve the problem she'd given him. The numbers, but without context.

'I don't know where you're going with this,' he said, 'but it isn't any harder than that. The context makes no difference. It could be London to Brighton, Earth to the moon. For crying out loud, it could be two snails creeping across a lawn. It isn't your job to see the whole picture. We give you the relevant details, and your job is to help us deal with them. With all due respect.'

He gave her an almost apologetic look. 'Twenty,' he concluded his little speech. 'The answer to your problem is twenty.'

She raised an eyebrow. Just enough for him to notice. And that frustrated him; he didn't want to lecture her, but for fuck's sake. She'd forced him into it.

'It isn't your job to know if it's a train. It isn't your job to know if it's kilometres or miles, you don't even need to know it's a distance. Your job is to look at the texts we give you and translate each of them and get back to us with the result. Irrespective of the context.'

He held out his hands: Okay? Agreed? Can we let this go now?

By all means, her shoulders answered.

'So. I take it you don't need anything more at the moment?'

'Yes, I do,' she said. 'I want to speak to William Sandberg.'

He looked at her. Saw her face prepare for a no.

'What you use that key card for is entirely up to you.'

That took her by surprise. She tried to read his expression, didn't know how to interpret it. Was he kidding?

But all he did was get up and move to the door.

She let a second pass. One more. And then:

'The thing is,' she said.

He turned.

'The thing is that the answer is zero.'

Now what was she trying to do?

'From London to Brighton is ninety kilometres. By three o'clock both trains will have arrived, cleaners are walking around emptying waste bins and the passengers are already checking in at their hotels. The distance between the trains is zero.'

She looked at him, savouring his confusion.

'You see, that's how it works. If you don't look at the whole picture. If you focus on the details and don't consider the context. Then you'll end up shooting yourself in the foot. No matter how clever you think you are.'

Rodriguez was unable to come up with an answer.

'With all due respect,' she added.

She looked him in the eye. She might be their prisoner, but she didn't intend to let them think they were smarter. She was there because she had skills they didn't, and if nothing else she could at least keep reminding them of that. It was her only card, and it was a card she would play as often as she could.

It took a second. Two. And then, when Rodriguez eventually stopped staring at her, she saw him smile for the first time that day.

'He's in the chapel,' he said. 'I don't believe you need me to show you how to get there.'

∞◯∞

Inspector Neijzen's breathing was loud enough to drown out the whine of the photocopier in front of him, the humming sound as the light slid back and forth under the glass and scanned the letter squeezed under its lid, inch by illuminated inch.

His hands were shaking, and it wasn't from the coffee. His cup was sitting untouched on his desk, and hopefully van Dijk was still sitting right next to it – Neijzen had a long list of things to do and the last thing he needed was a worried victim hanging on his heels.

She'd sent him a letter.

The young professor had told him about it with agitated excitement in his tired eyes, and Neijzen had been filled with sympathy.

He'd known what he'd had to say. He had prepared his most mournful face, the one where he tipped his head to the side to say the same words he always said to others in the same situation.

'The world is full of sick people,' he'd say. 'We all know it is, it doesn't come as a surprise to anyone, but the *extent*,' he'd say, and he'd put emphasis on the word, 'the *extent* is worse than anyone can imagine. I couldn't imagine it myself, not until I came here.'

That's how he would start, and he would go on by recounting how many times in his career he'd been forced to crush the hopes of someone's relatives, all because some lunatic had read about their case in the paper and sent in a clue, or a made-up eyewitness account, or even claimed to be the person they were searching for.

He would say all of that, and then he'd explain that this was just another case of the same phenomenon.

But then Albert van Dijk had handled him the yellow envelope. And suddenly none of the things he'd rehearsed were applicable any more.

The first thing he noted was that the envelope was stamped with an electronic franking machine. And next to the thick letters showing the postage and the date there was the name of a city. Bern. Printed in a thin, simple typeface.

Neijzen took the letter, opened it, removed three sheets of paper covered in writing.

Feminine hand. Tightly spaced. And Albert nodded at him. *Read it.*

He did. And then he read it again. And again.

Albert said nothing, merely waited for Neijzen to finish.

And Neijzen read it through a third time. Even more carefully now.

'I don't understand,' he said when he was done.

Albert didn't expect him to say otherwise. At first he hadn't been able to work it out either, standing at the entrance to his building on campus, reading it over and over and with a growing disappointment.

There was no doubt it was written by her. She was the only person in the world who could address a letter to Emmanuel Sphynx. And the handwriting was her neat print, the same lettering he used to find scribbled on Post-it notes in unexpected places, often sarcastic and taking him by surprise and sometimes tucked away inside his lecture manuscripts, making him stand there and smile sheepishly in front of a packed auditorium. The entire letter contained references to things they'd experienced together, secret places they'd visited and things they'd seen and the food poisoning they both got from the dried ham at the corner deli, the one that had smelled of petrol, but that the old man had convinced them was supposed to smell that way.

And yet, it *contained* nothing. The letter said nothing about where she was, how he could find her, what she was doing. All it said was how much she missed him. And then, this long list of things they'd done together. Three pages of elegant handwriting, one single letter after seven months of silence. And no content, other than nostalgia?

Eventually, it had fallen into place. 'It's childishly simple,' he said to Neijzen.

He'd been standing in the university courtyard, reading the letter over and over, until finally he asked himself the right question. Why the rambling? Places and objects and food and things. And then suddenly he'd understood, there and then it had become clear to him and all he wanted to do was to hold her close and tell her how great she was. Which, obviously, he couldn't.

The seminar. *That* day. Their day.

They had sat beside each other, inventing names and acronyms, giggling like children. And it was Emanuel Sphynx that had stuck in their memory and become a part of their mutual past.

But – the acronyms. The absurd abbreviations of one phrase after the other, solemnly recounted by the speaker at the podium. It was them she wanted him to remember, that was why she'd lined up the words like that, and he'd sat down on the stone staircase, read the letter again, and this time it took on an entirely different content and he loved her more than ever.

Simple enough that he could work it out. Yet devious enough to make it under the radar in case someone found it before it reached him.

'I give up,' Neijzen said.

'Take all the nouns – names, places, things. Take the first letter in each word.'

'You're joking?'

Albert shrugged. And Neijzen read the letter through again. And for a moment he felt a chill travel through his three hundred and twenty-six pounds as if somebody had just opened his body like a refrigerator and replaced his internal organs with cold air.

As codes went, it was ridiculously simple. But he'd missed it all the same. And Albert hadn't, which meant it had done exactly the job it was intended to.

Neijzen spelled his way through the first page a couple of times to find out where he should separate the words and the sentences. They weren't very long, but they were succinct enough.

'What – I – See,' he mouthed.

Albert nodded to confirm.

'Castle. Alpine lake. High mountains. No snow.'

That was all he could make out from the first page. And Neijzen glanced over at Albert. As information went, it wasn't much to go on. 'That could be almost anywhere,' he said.

Albert disagreed. 'It could be many places. But not anywhere.'

Neijzen kept silent. Van Dijk was both right and wrong. There were probably hundreds upon hundreds of castles surrounded by alpine lakes, and even if you checked the weather, looking for mountains near castles that hadn't had any snow yet, there would still be far too many to mount a search.

Albert knew it too. But gestured to Neijzen to continue. 'There are two more pages.'

Okay. Neijzen turned to the next page, scanned the handwriting, once again stopping at every noun and pointing them out one by one with his finger. He could have marked them with a pen, but he didn't want to contaminate the original and he was too absorbed with the contents to walk out across the hallway and make a copy.

'Names – I've – Heard,' he mouthed.

Albert nodded again.

'Connors. Franquin. Helena Watkins.'

'We must be able to do a search on that,' said Albert. 'A Connors and a Franquin and a Helena Watkins. Maybe they have criminal records, or they're in the tax register, I don't know. That's your thing. But there must be a way, mustn't there?'

'We can definitely give it a try,' he said.

And Albert breathed a silent thank-you. Waited as Neijzen turned to the final page. And fell silent.

It was on the third page that things got strange.

'What – I – Know,' he said finally.

Albert confirmed with a nod.

And Neijzen read it. Then read it again. And one more time.

Albert said nothing. Waited. Aware what Neijzen must be thinking. And he could only agree: the whole thing seemed unreal. The words were unthinkable, they were words you couldn't expect in a letter sent from someone you knew – strike that, someone you loved and who shouldn't be gone, who should be at home and probably still in bed, and who'd refuse to get up even if you called and told her what time it was. That's where she should be, that's how everything ought to have been, but now everything was something else and no matter how you refused to believe it, that didn't stop it from being true.

Neijzen cleared his throat. Spoke in a low voice. And read the words, extremely slowly.

'Codes in Sumerian writing,' he said. And then: 'DNA.' And: 'A deadly virus.'

And then he stopped. Puzzled over the last couple of letters one more time.

Albert already knew what they said. There were tears in his eyes as Neijzen looked up from the letter.

And read the last sentence.

'Find me.'

Neijzen leaned towards Albert, folded his hands under his chin, and for a moment his fingers hung like tangled sausages in front of where his neck would have been, had he had one. He knew the pose wasn't flattering but right now he didn't care.

Everything he'd said until this moment had been true.

But he had one thing left to say, and it was going to be a lie.

'I am going to do everything within my power to find her,' he said. He looked sincerely at Albert, two compassionate eyes in a body that had given up and started to decay, perhaps because his body resented who he'd become and had chosen this way to punish him. 'I'll be back in a few minutes. I need to make a copy of this.'

He got up, walked to the photocopier, and stood there. Breathing heavily.

Damn his body, damn his physical condition, damn the doctor at the health service who was right, but more than everything else damn Janine Charlotta Haynes and the people of that blasted

Organisation, those anonymous figures who obviously hadn't been able to stop her from sending this. Now here he was with their problem in his lap.

He had a long list of things to do next. And he could only hope that Albert van Dijk didn't know what they were.

Because that would make his next step infinitely harder.

20

The phone call from Christina Sandberg had come shortly after five in the morning. Her voice had been clear and alert – either she'd already been up for a while or she hadn't slept – and Leo had fought against heavy eyelids as she'd informed him that she'd be picking him up at exactly ten minutes to six, told him what he needed to pack and then hung up. It wasn't until he was standing in the shower that he'd realised he was actually awake.

The obvious thing to do would have been to put on the same clothes as the day before. Instead, he'd grabbed a fresh pair of jeans and a plain long-sleeved T-shirt. And then he asked himself the question that made everything go awry.

What would a journalist wear? A journalist who's about to travel abroad?

The answer he came up with was a blazer.

Leo hesitated: was he really a journalist? Only if he allowed himself to feel like one. And so at ten to six he found himself in front of his building in his one wrinkled blazer, and the only thing he felt like was an idiot.

The moment he stepped out of the door he knew he'd made the wrong choice.

She would think he'd put it on because of her. Or, even if she didn't, he would think that she did, and that would be bad enough.

But there was no time to do anything about it.

The taxi pulled up at the kerb, a click as the door opened, Christina leaning across the back seat summoning him to get in. And as he took his place beside her, the cab turned down towards Folkungagatan, and then north through the empty dawn.

The only movements were occasional cabs and thousands of almost invisible flakes of early snow, floating in below the yellow streetlights for a few whirly moments before vanishing back into the darkness.

The sound of the tyres on the cold street. The windscreen wipers. The engine.

'Did you get hold of him?' asked Leo.

Christina shook her head. 'I've left a voicemail for his secretary. I'll try again before we take off.'

'So you don't know, then. That he's there. I mean, if.'

Christina closed her eyes. She had a headache that had kept her company since she got home from the office, and a single hour of sleep on the couch hadn't helped her much, any more than having her intern question her judgement. Especially having to decipher his half-finished sentences in order to work out that's what he was doing.

'What I do know is that we don't have much time,' she said. 'Your Dutch student has been off the radar for seven months now.'

He looked over at her. *Your* student? What was that about? Was she giving him credit for finding her, or was she trying to unburden herself of responsibility?

'I don't want William to have to wait that long.'

She stared out of the window, listening to the engine changing its pitch as they turned on to the Centralbron bridge. Saw Stockholm's lights reflect in the water beneath it, still too early in the year to ice up.

'Is it okay if I ask you something?' Leo asked.

She looked at him. As if I could stop it. She didn't say, but thought.

'You're not doing this for the paper, are you? You're doing it because you still believe in the two of you.'

It was unexpectedly direct and free of his usual mumblings. She glowered at him, her headache replaced by irritation. Irritation because he had opinions about her decisions, she told herself, not because he read her so annoyingly well.

'We're journalists,' she said. 'Journalists dig. We would be neglecting our duty if we didn't.'

Leo gave a smile that was far too grown-up.

'But what I don't think our duty dictates,' he said, 'is that you need to put on that thing, there. Especially as you haven't been wearing it for the last six months.'

She knew immediately what he was talking about. But she still followed his gaze. Down in her lap, to her left hand, resting there. Her wedding ring.

Yes, she had put it on. And yes, maybe the brat was right. But couldn't she please be allowed to make her own decisions without having him sticking his nose in?

'Journalism school,' she said. 'First year. My lecturer gave me some advice that I've carried with me ever since.'

He waited for her to go on.

'If you've got something important to say? Write it.' She paused. 'And don't talk so fucking much.'

She looked away, hid her left hand under her handbag, didn't utter another word for the rest of the journey to Arlanda airport.

And Leo turned back to his own window, watched the lines on the road whizzing by. Smiled, but did his best not to let her see. She had a sharp tongue. And he was finding the whole situation immensely entertaining.

On her side of the back seat, Christina Sandberg was doing the same thing. She was smiling too.

Leo was going to be a first-class journalist.

And she was perfectly happy about taking him with her to Amsterdam.

ooOoo

William Sandberg sat at the front of the chapel, almost as if he was waiting for her.

The sun had moved, painting the pews in a kaleidoscope of colours, William right in the centre like a lecturer in front of a badly focused PowerPoint presentation.

Maybe it was the room that made her come to a halt. Or maybe it was the knowledge that she was in a part of the castle where only days before she'd had to run, silently and cautiously and in the middle of the night. Whatever it was, Janine paused at the back of the chapel in silence, even though all she wanted was to start talking, eager to tell him what she knew and compare it with what they'd told him.

To understand why they were there. Or rather: how they could get out.

Finally, she moved down the aisle towards him. Sat down on the other side of it, facing him from the edge of the bench.

'They're telling me you're okay,' said William.

'In that case,' she said, 'who am I to disagree?'

He half-smiled at her in reply. He looked tired, but in all likelihood so did she.

'We need to sync what we know,' she said.

She wanted to move quickly but without undue stress. Somewhere on one of the many floors of stone above them William had his room. And there, if everything was the way she hoped, maybe she'd find the answers to the thoughts that jostled in her brain.

'What do you know?' he asked.

'I'm not sure I know anything.'

He leaned against the pew, looked over his shoulder at the huge wooden doors. As if he didn't feel safe. As if he expected the doors to burst open at any moment, guards to storm in with weapons at the ready, pull them out of there and lock them up and interrogate them about what the other one had said.

But it didn't happen.

Nothing happened. Only silence and the colours and neither of them knowing where to begin.

'AGCT,' William said eventually.

To his surprise he found her smiling.

'I didn't think you saw it,' she said.

'How long have you known?'

She hesitated. Since day one, the information she'd been given had been limited to the absolute minimum. What she'd said was true. She didn't *know* anything.

'You're a sumerologist, right?' he said. He knew perfectly well that she was, but he had to start the dialogue somewhere and why not there.

She made a quick calculation in her head. She wanted to give him as much as he needed to keep up, but without getting lost in details.

And then, she began from the beginning. The details she'd skipped during their twelve minutes on the castle terrace. How she'd woken that first morning in a luxurious bed, just like William's. How they'd escorted her to a huge hall, given her a brief overview of the Organisation and the codes and the cuneiform script. Told her that everything was urgent and pressing and thank you and goodbye.

And then they'd shown her to an office, and all of her possessions were there waiting for her: books and publications and computers and reference literature, arranged almost identically to the set-up she'd had at home, except now it was all suddenly here and nobody would tell her why.

They started by giving her brief excerpts. Single lines of cuneiform script, instructing her to interpret and translate them and come back with the result.

On a purely academic level, she'd been thrilled. The texts were older than anything she'd seen. There were signs and symbols she'd never come across, like a dialect or linguistic branch that hadn't been discovered until now, and to every scientist in the world that would have meant success and champagne and writing essays to tell the rest of academia about their breakthrough.

But this, nobody wanted to tell anyone about.

And that didn't make sense. Worse: it tortured her. The more she worked with it, the more apparent it became just how astonishing and pioneering it was, and the more it tore her apart to think that nobody outside those suffocatingly thick walls would ever find out.

Because it wasn't an unknown dialect. It wasn't a later evolution of the Sumerian language.

It was the opposite.

The symbols were precursors. The texts she'd been given were older than any text ever found, and the unknown symbols were prototypes, early versions that would develop and become simpli-fied, sometimes combined, sometimes divided through centuries of progress until they came to resemble the oldest examples of writing that science had found.

It appeared that someone had discovered an unknown ancient civilisation. One that predated any known society in human history.

And Janine had been overwhelmed – no, ecstatic. But when she asked the men around her where it had come from, and how, and why, they refused to answer.

William listened. And as soon as she was finished he started speaking.

'Your job was to tell them what it said?'

Janine nodded. But with a reservation. A yes leading to a no.

'That's what I thought. At first.'

William waited for her to continue.

'They did their best to make sure I didn't understand the exact nature of my task. The texts they gave me were fragments of something bigger. I got them out of sequence, a few passages at a time, new pieces at irregular intervals – without ever getting to know how they fitted together. Some of them weren't even genuine.'

The word puzzled him. 'Genuine?'

'They were fakes.' She gave a shrug. 'I've been working with this long enough to know if someone is writing in a language they don't fully command. It isn't any stranger than to hear a foreign accent. You're from Sweden. Franquin is from Belgium, Connors is British. And some of those passages they gave me were written by someone who's alive today.'

'A temporal Professor Higgins,' William said with a smile.

She frowned. Didn't get the reference. And he shook his head, never mind, go on.

'I confronted them.'

'And what happened?'

'From that moment, they changed my tasks. They started to give me phrases in English. Expressions and idioms – some of it pure nonsense. Telling me to translate them in the other direction. *Into* Sumerian cuneiform. As if *that* was what they needed me for all along. To learn the dialect, to imitate it . . .'

No, she told herself. That was speculation. And she changed tack.

'Anyway, most of the texts I got were rubbish. But then there was . . . Some of it said exactly the same thing as the texts I'd picked out as fakes.'

William immediately grasped what she was saying.

'As if somebody had already tried to translate it,' he said. 'But the result hadn't been good enough.'

Janine was taken aback. That had been her thought too, but she was surprised at how quickly he had come to that conclusion.

He saw her reaction, explained himself: 'I'm in the same situation. My job is to find a cipher key. Because the person who tried before me didn't succeed.'

Her turn to be one step behind. 'Didn't succeed with *what*?' she asked.

'With writing an answer.'

She stared at him. 'An answer to *what*?'

He said nothing for a moment. The truth was he didn't know. And that annoyed him, because even if everything seemed to fit, at the same time it didn't fit. How would they be answering a text that was found in their DNA? How do you answer a message if you don't know who wrote it?

There had to be more to this than they were telling him. Every new question he asked himself only reinforced his conviction that the version he'd been given was incomplete.

'AGCT,' he said again. 'Tell me what you know.'

'I don't know any more than what Helena Watkins told me. Strike that: what I gathered from what she said. That the Sumerian texts were embedded in some genetic code, and that somewhere there is a virus, which—'

She stopped mid-sentence. She couldn't decide what marked the end of her actual knowledge and what was mere guesswork. When she started talking again she did it slowly, choosing her words carefully as if evaluating them one by one before saying them loud.

'—which is incredibly contagious, and which is going to be used ... for what? I can only guess.'

The unease in her eyes as she spoke surprised him.

'I don't even know who we're working for. Are we helping them to do good? Or the opposite?'

Surprised him, because he had assumed she knew more.

But the truth was she knew as little as he had known himself until the previous evening. And as that fact dawned on him he realised that his next task would be to tell her the things Connors had told him. It would be down to him to tear her world apart and leave her with an endless series of large and unfathomable questions that he wouldn't be able to answer, the same questions that had been reverberating within him, keeping him awake most of the night.

That was to be his task. And he had to do it now.

He looked her in the eyes, lowered his voice.

And then he apologised for what he was about to tell her.

Janine received the news with considerably more composure than he had. She sat in her pew, her eyes fixed on his, almost letting him read her thoughts, as if he could see them being shunted around and rearranged like crates in a warehouse. And he saw how she waited for them to settle, how she fought against shock and panic and the gamut of emotions William had experienced the night before.

Every now and then she asked a question. Some he could answer, some he couldn't.

'That's everything I know,' he said. 'And the best bit? I don't even know if it's true. All I can say is that this is what they've told me, and on one hand it kind of makes sense, but on the other . . . '

He finished his sentence with a shrug.

On the other, there was something missing.

And they lapsed into silence, minutes melting into one another.

When she eventually spoke, Janine's voice was calm. Verging on formal.

'Helena Watkins' wall,' she said. 'Do you know where it is?'

'I suppose that'd be my wall now.'

She looked him in the eye.

'I need to see it.'

21

There was something about the car parked outside his apartment building that made Albert van Dijk stop on the other side of the street.

He could barely keep his eyes open. His body craved food and sleep, and all he wanted was to get home as soon as possible.

And yet, he'd noticed the car.

Perhaps it was because it was parked a few metres from his door. It was a non-parking zone, as he knew to his cost: the day he moved in, his rental van had been ticketed there, and that very moment he'd resolved never to buy a car as long as he lived and worked in the city.

Perhaps that was the reason it had caught his attention.

Or perhaps it was because the car looked the way it did.

A black Audi. Who in his building would drive a black Audi, or even be visited by one, a visit so pressing that the driver had stopped right outside the door where there was nothing but pavement and a bicycle lane, despite there being plenty of legal parking around the corner?

Albert van Dijk hesitated. The pedestrian crossing light had turned green and around him people began to cross in both directions, a muddle of heads that alternately blocked and revealed the Audi outside his door. Instead of crossing, he stayed where he was. Let the light return to red.

He pulled out his phone, pretending to read his text messages and to look around him for a sign with a street name, as if he didn't have the slightest idea where he was and as if there was nothing odd about remaining there as a second wave of traffic came to a halt and more pedestrians began to cross the road.

Oh, he seemed to be thinking as he peered at the building behind him: *Korte Marnixstraat. I see.* Number *two*.

He played his little charade to himself, and all the while his eyes kept scanning the area for anything else that felt out of place. There was nothing remarkable about the car itself; it was large, possibly a diplomatic vehicle, but it didn't have government plates and the windows weren't tinted.

What did strike him as odd, though, was how it had one wheel up on the pavement, carelessly and clumsily squeezed against the kerb as if it had been parked in a hurry. Who would be in that much of a rush that they couldn't drive to the next street and stop in a legal parking bay? At eleven in the morning?

The crossing was busy with people again, and Albert hoped silently that he wouldn't run in to one of his neighbours. Worst-case scenario, they'd assume he'd finally lost it completely, and they'd talk slowly to him the way people did when dealing with lunatics. '*That's* where you live, sir, see? The big house over there, the one with the white windows? Let's you and me get ourselves safely over the street now.'

But nobody stopped, nobody offered to help him across, and he was just telling himself to stop overreacting and cross the road, when he noticed the four men.

One of them was waiting behind the glass door to his building. Another one was loitering beside the drainpipe where his building adjoined the next, leaning against the dark brickwork with a mobile phone in his hand. And two more men were waiting on the street corners where one block ended and new streets headed off into the maze of streets and canals. As if to stop someone from getting away, he thought. Someone. Him?

All four men were dressed in ties, suits and coats that were too thin for the weather, at least if they were planning on hanging about outside all day. They were middle-aged, or at any rate older than him, but that was about all he could tell. He couldn't make out their faces at this distance, and he didn't want to stare at them in case they sensed that they were being watched and spotted him there.

But once he'd noticed them, there was no doubt about it. All four of them were as busy pretending to do nothing as he was himself, and their nonchalant expressions were as alert and attentive as his own.

He told himself he was being paranoid; what reason could anyone have for following him? The thought embarrassed him, but even so, he couldn't shake it.

He turned, compared the street sign with a text message that didn't exist, acted out a suitably understated gesture of *what the hell,* and started off back down the street as if *clumsy me* he'd gone too far in the wrong direction. He was simply a man looking for an address he didn't know how to find. That was it. And if the four men on the other side of the street had registered him, they'd no doubt dismissed him already and were standing there waiting for the right guy to come along.

Or, so he thought.

He'd walked just a few paces when he heard the steps beside him.

'Albert van Dijk?' said a voice. Suit. Tie. Number five.

Of course they would be watching this side of the street, too.

'Do I know you?' Albert asked, mentally kicking himself. If he hadn't been Albert van Dijk he most probably would have said no.

'We have a couple of questions,' said the man.

'Be my guest,' said Albert.

The man shook his head. 'We have a car waiting.'

∞○○∞

When Janine stepped past William into his office, it felt like unveiling a work of art for the first time.

Not that she ever had, but the feeling, she thought, the feeling had to be the same. The feeling of having stared at a piece of cloth, draped over something and following the contours of the sculpture or the monument or whatever it was hiding, an indistinct hint that there was something there but that you couldn't tell what it looked like.

And now the cloth had been lifted.

And for the first time she saw it in its entirety.

On one wall were the ciphers. They were as unintelligible to her now as when they'd danced around on the walls of the huge room seven months before, that first time the task was presented to her. And just as unintelligible as when Helena Watkins had showed them to her, secretly and in confidence, either to encourage her or to help them find the solution or maybe both.

On the adjoining wall hung the texts.

Her texts. That's how well she knew them. After spending seven months on them they'd become *her* texts; a quick glance at each of the sheets was all she needed to know which of the Sumerian verses she was looking at.

Verses. She called them that for lack of something better. Short, succinct messages that didn't seem to say very much at first glance, but that belonged to a context that she slowly had started to see, a context that had terrified her, and that she finally, finally was about to have confirmed.

And if that context was in fact the human DNA?

Then it terrified her even more.

William watched her as she walked along the wall.

'What do you make of it?' he said. Softly, as if that would distract her any less.

He regretted it as soon as the words were out. *Idiot*, he said to himself inside his head; he knew exactly what she was going through and he had only one responsibility and that was to shut up.

He had been in the same situation often enough to know that at this moment Janine had no time for anything but her own thoughts. And the one thing worse than being interrupted was having someone try to sneak into your consciousness, slowly claiming your attention until you realised you'd lost focus and that you hadn't had it for quite a while.

He didn't say anything more.

And neither did she. Every so often, she'd pause and take a closer look at one of the pages. Then start walking again, keep going between the groups of papers, from verse to verse, on to the next. Minutes passed. And William let them.

'I've been waiting for this,' she said at last.

'For what?'

'The *order*.'

She stepped back. Stood at a distance, studied the rows of Sumerian symbols, took in the entire wall at once. As if finally it spoke to her, as if it was communicating just the way he had tried to make it speak to him for the last couple of days.

He suddenly felt alone. As if the wall was a large piece of sheet music, as if she was the piano teacher and he was the pupil who'd turned up for his first lesson, unable to see anything beyond a series of incomprehensible dots and lines. It seemed overwhelming, hopeless – he would never be able to see it, never be able to read it like her.

But he pushed the thought aside.

'What is it?' he asked.

She ran her eyes over the walls. One more time, just to be sure.

'It's what I was afraid of,' she said. 'It's a timeline.'

22

Albert van Dijk heard the car behind them long before he saw it. It was the whining sound of a turbo kicking in, and subconsciously he registered that it wasn't just going fast, it was accelerating, probably trying to beat the lights at the crossing.

His first instinct was to speed up and try to get across the street before the car hit them. It was pure self-preservation, the very thing the driver expected.

But his second instinct was that this was his one chance.

The man in the suit had a firm grip on his arm, discreet enough not to be noticeable but strong enough to stop Albert from cutting loose and running. The man's other hand rested in his coat pocket, presumably still holding the gun he'd allowed Albert to get a glimpse of, just in case he was thinking of trying anything stupid.

And Albert started to walk faster, exactly as they expected him to.

The suit next to him speeding up as well. The car getting closer. Closer still.

And then he did it.

It wasn't really a push. All he did was take advantage of the man's own kinetic energy and a sizeable chunk of surprise. He stopped dead, leaving the suited man swirling around him in a semicircle. He didn't lose his balance as such; one more second and he would have clutched Albert's arm even harder, steered him across the road, cursing at him never to try that again.

But the man didn't get a second.

The blue Golf didn't come to a stop until well after it had passed the crossing, and by then it was far too late.

By then the windscreen had been smashed by the suited body that materialised in front of the car from out of nowhere, swung into the road against its own will, bounced up over the bonnet and rolled back over the roof with dull thuds against the thin metal until it slumped across the black skid marks the tyres had left behind on the asphalt in their desperate attempt to stop.

The man hadn't stood a chance. The suit that had begun the day newly pressed and elegant was dirty and torn from being dragged on the ground; the arms and legs were spread at angles that nobody would voluntarily spread anything. When pedestrians rushed to his side to help, they were met by a lifeless face, eyes staring blindly into the spreading pool of his own blood.

'He pushed him!' The woman who shouted was in her twenties; she had university books under her arm and horror in her eyes from what she'd witnessed. She searched for confirmation in the eyes of people she didn't know. 'He pushed him in front of the car!'

'Who?' someone said. 'Did you see who?'

'I think it was my archaeology professor.'

∞O∞

'What do you mean *timeline*?' William's eyes stared impatiently at the wall. He turned to her, anxious to catch up, frustrated at being one step behind.

Janine pointed to the Sumerian verses. 'I never got them in this order,' she said. 'But you know how your brain works. You start searching for logic. You automatically start creating a context. Because you think there has to be one, that the pieces you have must be parts of a puzzle, but you don't know how they're supposed to go because you've never seen the lid of the box.'

He nodded for her to go on.

'At first I was just experimenting. What happens if you read this one after that one? Or this after that? Then what will it mean?' She lowered her voice. 'After a while I started to notice that there were too many things that seemed ... familiar. As if I recognised them from somewhere. And the more fragments I managed to combine, the clearer it became. But I kept dismissing it as coincidence, because ... well, it *had* to be.'

She paused, trying to come up with an explanation.

'What you need to know,' she said, 'is that early Sumerian was an ideographic language. There are no sentences, no grammar, it's all symbols stacked together to represent different concepts, and one single symbol can have several meanings. So there's an element of ambiguity. But even if you take that ambiguity into account ...'

Her eyes finished the sentence. No matter how many times she'd tried to interpret the verses differently, she always came up with the same results.

'What did it say?' asked William.

She stared at the rows of symbols, unsure how best to put it. 'Every passage is like a verse.' She rephrased it in her head. 'A summary. No – a description.'

She turned to William, willing him to grasp the significance, but all he could do was stare back at her. So far he couldn't make head nor tail of what she was telling him.

'Of what?' he asked. 'A summary of what?'

'Of the most important events in the history of mankind.'

And she walked up to the wall. Pointed. Stopped alongside select verses, single lines that stood out of their sequence, and told him what the symbols meant and what she had concluded.

The more he saw, the harder it was to deny.

City on river. People who build. Pointed houses, graves of kings.

The pyramids.

Rats. Disease. Contagion, death, an unstoppable plague.

The Black Death.

Moon. Three men, big ship, long journey.

'Don't think I need to explain that one to you, do I?'

William refused to believe her. What she was saying was totally absurd.

He tried to convince her that she was wrong, that no matter how analytical and critical she thought she'd been, she'd hit on a theory and then, unable to let it go, she'd subconsciously imposed a historical significance on to the text. She'd projected her own knowledge on to it, telling herself it was scientific analysis even though it wasn't.

Her response was to snap at him. 'You honestly think I've been sitting here for seven months without questioning my findings?'

For a moment he could see something in her, something that made him lose his balance, something he wasn't prepared for. That flash of temper had reminded him of someone else.

He shook it off, telling himself he was guilty of the very thing he'd just accused her of: framing his current situation with old experiences. There was nothing about Janine that had anything to do with *her*, nothing beyond his longing for there to be a similarity.

He saw her glare at him, and he chose his words carefully. He didn't mean to criticise her; he'd made the same mistake himself several times in the past, stumbling upon a theory and then trying to make the data fit the theory instead of the other way around.

'You're as frustrated as I am,' he said. 'We've been told to solve a problem, and we don't know how or why. So we start looking for patterns. It's not your fault, it's just the way it works.'

'I wasn't looking for a pattern,' she replied. 'I found one.'

He cocked his head to one side. Semantics. And she raised her voice again: 'Do you think I haven't said the same thing to myself? You think I don't find this every bit as inconceivable as you? That I haven't tried to dismiss it as the product of my own, biased logic?' She turned around in a wide arc as if to summon up the energy to explain what she knew but what he refused to accept. 'But then I come in here. And I see them hanging there, in exactly the right order.'

She waited for him to speak. But he just carried on looking at her, that sceptical expression on his face. So she spelled it out for him:

'If I only interpreted these verses as historical events because they happen to match what I know, how come they're hanging here, on your wall, in the *exact order* I imagined? I only got to see them as separate papers, remember? If my deductions are nothing more than biased prejudices, how come this wall shows my disparate fragments arranged and combined exactly the way I calculated?'

He kept looking at her in silence, unconvinced.

And she walked to the far end of the room, started making her way along the wall, firmly tapping various sheets of paper with her palm as she passed them.

'Mesopotamia. The Pyramids. The Rhodes earthquake. Birth of Jesus. Muhammad. The Black Death. The eruption of Mount Tambora . . .'

Between each of these were others she passed without referencing, as if she was running through history and stopping at only the most significant moments, and it strengthened her point, made it impossible not to follow her reasoning.

At regular intervals she turned to William to make sure that he understood.

'First World War. Second. Hiroshima. The Valdavia earthquake.'

This was the proof that she was right, that she'd been right all along, and she saw his face, saw him struggle to remain sceptical, saw him refuse to accept what he heard even though he knew it was futile.

There couldn't be clearer proof than this. If her interpretation of the verses was correct, then this was the order they should be arranged.

And that was exactly what they were.

She walked towards the end of the wall. Slowed down. 'Tangshan. The Armero Tragedy. The Indian Ocean tsunami.'

She fixed her eyes on William. Your turn, her body language seemed to say. Go ahead, tell me I'm wrong. Make me go over it all again, because I will, because we both know I'm right.

They stood there. Seconds that lasted for minutes. Janine with her hand resting on one of the sheets, William across the room from her, their eyes locked.

And the silence lasted so long Janine regained the initiative. 'If all of this is nothing more than supposition on my part—'

William closed his eyes. Knew what she was about to say.

'—why the hell are these events listed in the right order?'

'Do you understand the consequences of this?' William asked.

She nodded. She understood them perfectly. They couldn't be avoided.

'The consequences,' she said, 'are that *if* they've been telling you the truth? *If* these verses come from inside our own human DNA?'

He knew it already. But it had to be said.

So she said it.

'In that case, these events were written in the human genome long before they happened.'

The room was silent for a long time.

They stood there, watching each other, a conversation with no words.

'And yet', she said, finally. 'And yet that isn't what worries me most.'

She felt William's look. Took out a piece of paper, handed it to him.

It was the same paper she'd wanted to show him on the terrace, the one with a series of cuneiform symbols that he hadn't understood and she hadn't had the time to explain.

'It's been worrying me from the moment I saw it.'

He didn't know what to say, gestured for her to go on.

'And now that I've seen your room? With the timeline and the verses and the order? Now it worries me even more.' She swallowed, hard. Steeled herself.

'Tell me,' he said. 'Tell me what it means.'

∞◯◯∞

Albert ran as fast as he could through Amsterdam's Westerpark, his coat billowing in the low afternoon sun and his thoughts racing out of control.

Inspector Neijzen, the son of a bitch. The man he'd trusted, who'd been by his side from the evening Janine first vanished. Who'd sat with him into the small hours, helped him search for answers, looked through databases and kept him updated about every clue or lead or piece of news. It had to be him. Inspector Neijzen had raised the alarm.

There was no other explanation.

Now a man had died. And Albert had caused it. He came to a halt by a large pond, on an open gravelled space crowded with enough pushchairs and elderly people and office workers hurrying between meetings to allow him to melt into the crowd. He had nowhere to go.

He picked up his phone, pulled up his office number – and stopped himself. The paranoia was back, and it was all he could do to make himself think.

Was he overreacting? Or could the police be involved in Janine's disappearance? Did they know who was responsible, had they alerted them about the letter? The same police that he had allowed to search the home they'd shared, inviting them inside the crooked apartment she'd lived in before they met, the same police who'd put comforting arms round his shoulder and sworn they'd done all they could but that everything pointed to her vanishing of her own free will?

The ramifications were almost unthinkable.

If the police knew, then who else? And who was behind her disappearance? How many people were intent on preventing him finding out what happened, and what resources did they have?

His secretary's number was still shining back at him from his phone's display, and he memorised the last few digits of it, once, twice, until he was completely certain he knew it. Paranoid or not, he couldn't use his own phone again. The same went for his credit cards: the moment he made a purchase they would know where he was. He decided to find a cash machine and take out as much money as possible before they blocked his account.

What he would do after that, he had no idea.

The only thing he was sure of was that he had nobody on his side.

And that if he ever wanted to see Janine again he'd have to find her himself.

*

Albert van Dijk stayed in the park for another three, maybe four, minutes.

None of the visitors paid any attention to the man in the coat, skipping stones by the pond.

And none of them guessed that the stone that skipped the most number of times was in fact a mobile phone.

· ∞◯∞

The piece of paper William Sandberg held in his hand still didn't tell him anything. But what Janine was saying didn't leave much room for doubt.

It was the logical conclusion to her deductions, and couldn't be questioned. At least not without going back to her fundamental assumptions and tearing her entire analysis apart. And even if deep down he would have liked to, he wouldn't know where to start.

All he could do was listen.

'No matter how much I studied them,' she said, 'there were sequences I couldn't make sense of.'

William didn't move.

'Sequences that weren't fakes. That much I could tell. They came from the original source, they had the same ancient voice, but I couldn't interpret them to fit any historical event. And at first I tried to explain it away. I'm no historian, that's what I told myself, so obviously there'll be loads of things that took place in between the big occurrences, things that were left out when they taught me history in school. Right?'

But she shook her head. Wrong. That wasn't the reason she didn't recognise them. There was another explanation, and slowly, slowly, the realisation had struggled its way into her mind.

She stopped and looked at William. Waited for him to make the same connection.

'You're not telling me,' he said, 'that some of the verses haven't happened yet?'

She nodded slowly.

'That the human DNA holds information about the future. Things that haven't happened, but that will?'

She nodded again.

'In that case,' said William, 'what do we have to expect?'

There was only one answer.

'Nothing good,' she said. 'Nothing good at all.'

23

Albert van Dijk's office had been empty since the previous after-noon, and then suddenly it was flooded with people.

Some were police, others claimed to be but looked more like bankers, and all of them were rummaging about in the professor's shelves and on his computer and asking questions about where he was. And whether he'd said anything, as in anything at all about anything whatsoever, and whether there were any places he used to go that they didn't know of.

The chubby young assistant answered with shrugs and shakes of his head. He had no idea.

The only thing they would tell him was that Albert van Dijk had vanished. Judging by the commotion, he was probably wanted, and they kept insisting that he should inform them the moment the professor tried to make contact, which he sincerely promised them he would do.

And now he was sitting by his desk. Struggling with his conscience.

In his pocket was the note with the Swedish phone number. Part of him wanted to get up from his chair and show it to the police and tell them, look, I know something that you don't, here you go and good luck. But another part of him felt that he shouldn't. There was something about the cops that didn't ring true; they seemed shifty, evasive. Besides, wasn't it more important to be loyal to one's employer? Wasn't that the point of employing someone in the first place? That they were supposed to help you?

Unless, of course, van Dijk had committed a crime so terrible, so unspeakable, that the police couldn't even begin to tell him what it was.

He sat there. Watching them. And then, he froze.

He had just felt a buzz in his trouser pocket.

He hesitated, realising that this was the moment to pick sides, to decide how much he really doubted the people in the office in front of him.

Or to admit that he'd already picked sides long ago. Why else had he set his phone to silent? Why else was it vibrating inside his pocket, a tickling sensation against his thigh, if it wasn't because he wanted to be able to surreptitiously answer in the event that the professor called him?

It looked as though the decision had been made.

He'd chosen loyalty.

He got up, wandered out into the corridor, gave a convoluted explanation to a dark-suited man who didn't want to listen about how thirsty he was and how he hadn't had enough to drink with his lunch, and that he was going to the cafeteria but they could reach him on his cell if they wanted. And the entire time he was talking he could feel the phone against his leg, and it was all he could do to look the cop in the eye, telling himself that the man couldn't hear the rattling phone because it was muffled by the thick denim of his jeans.

The cop didn't react. Not to the phone, nor to the story about thirst and lunch and lack of hydration. He turned away, leaving the young secretary to make his way to the lift and get inside, even though they were only on the third floor.

The vibrating ceased. His voicemail had taken the call.

He pulled the wooden door closed, felt the lift creak and shift as it started its descent, unstable as a geriatric on an icy pavement, and he thought that one day this lift would be the death of someone, but hopefully not today.

He took out his phone. Missed call. Number withheld. Damn.

But he knew his boss well enough to be certain that, if that had been him, he'd try again. And no sooner had the thought formed than the phone rattled in his hand.

'Hello?' he said.

'Hi. It's Professor van Dijk.'

'Good. I'm in the lift. I'll be down in two seconds, I don't want them to see me on the phone. I'll go to the café, call me back in exactly five.'

And then he ended the call without waiting for an answer. Outside the lift window he could see the ground floor approaching, and stuffed the phone back into his pocket, opened the door and walked out into the foyer. Down the stairs and into the daylight. Turned towards the cafeteria building.

The two police officers waiting outside the main door let him pass, not considering for a moment that the boy who disappeared along the walkway might have sided with their opponent.

∞◯∞

Albert van Dijk stood in the dark corner of a market hall, miles away from the university, trying hard to look as if he had the slightest reason to be there.

Time crawled by. Four minutes. Four and a half.

He squeezed his phone, tightly, as if he was afraid it would tear loose and run off. He'd bought it together with a prepaid card from a small electronics shop a few blocks away; it was used and scratched with sticky buttons and he had to squint in order to read the screen. But it seemed to be working and that was all he needed.

When five minutes had passed, he keyed in his assistant's number.

It rang once. And then, through the familiar hum of the university café at the other end:

'What in heaven's name have you done?'

'What are they saying I've done?' Albert said.

'There've been people here looking for you.'

'Suit and tie?'

'Some of them. And the police. Is it true what they're saying on the news?'

Albert shut his eyes. The news. Of course. The street had been full of people, and there had probably been more calls made to media hotlines than to the emergency service. The news was out, and if somebody had recognised him it would only be a matter of time before his face was on every news site on the Internet. It didn't look good.

'It's about Janine,' he said. 'I understand if you don't believe me. But she was kidnapped, and I don't know why, but now they're after me too.'

The answer wasn't what he expected.

'I know.'

In the café, Albert's secretary checked that he wasn't being watched. Lowered his voice even though the noise around him was loud enough that he had to press a palm to his ear to make out what his boss was saying.

'You never read the note on your desk, did you?'

The note? Albert tried to picture his office, searched his memory for a note he might have missed, but there were infinite numbers of notes and messages about things that needed to be done and it was impossible to know which one he meant.

'What note?' he said.

The boy skipped the answer; the note wasn't interesting now. 'There's a journalist keeps calling, since yesterday afternoon.'

Albert stopped. Held his breath. Journalist? Why?

'From Sweden. Says she needs to see you. Says that what happened to your girlfriend?'

Yes? Albert waited for him to finish.

'The exact same thing happened to her husband.'

∞OOo

Their flight landed in Amsterdam four hours behind schedule, and they were hungry and tired but with no time to eat or rest. They passed through Customs, Christina pulling a light case on wheels behind her and Leo carrying a rucksack that had probably inter-railed its way through half of the world.

They were making their way into the gigantic arrivals hall when they realised someone was talking to them.

The man walked a couple of steps behind them, a newspaper in his hand, pretending to read as he talked without looking at them.

'Just keep looking straight ahead,' he said to his paper.

It was obvious what he meant. But instincts are instincts and before his brain made the connection, Leo had turned towards the voice, staring directly into the man's face.

'*Straight ahead*,' he repeated through clenched teeth. 'I'll be one step behind you, talk to each other, not to me.'

Christina nodded at Leo to confirm that she understood.

Good. At least one of them got it.

'What's going on?' she asked.

'That's what I want to ask you,' he replied. And then: 'How are you getting from the airport?'

'We've a rental car waiting,' she said to Leo, and Leo was about to reply that he knew that already when he caught on and gave a curt nod. Hopefully, that was what he would have done if she'd actually addressed the remark to him. The situation made him feel surprisingly unsure of that. Or of anything, come to think of it.

'Good,' said the man. 'I'm going to follow you out, and when you've reversed out of the parking bay you're going to stop and let me into the back seat.'

They proceeded in silence, followed the signs with the car-rental logos, heading towards the exit.

And then, Christina turned to Leo again. 'Before you do that? Before you get into our car? Would you mind telling us who you are?'

They took a few more steps.

As if he didn't want to say it out loud.

People passed them, heels clicking on the polished floor, and the man waited, keeping pace behind them until there was nobody close enough to hear.

'My name is Albert van Dijk. I understand you've been looking for me.'

24

If Christina and Leo had turned round as they left gate D61 and walked towards Customs and the large arrivals hall at Schiphol airport, they'd have been able to see Captain Adam Riebeeck hurry through security in the other direction.

His flight bag wobbled on rubber wheels behind him, and a group of people in identical uniforms followed close on his heels.

There was a Boeing 747-400 waiting for him at Pier E.

He was going to fly it to Los Angeles with an almost fully booked cabin, and he was irritable and in a bad mood and that was a bad way to start a day.

He hated rental cars.

The one saving grace in the hell that was having to sleep in his own home, with its endless conversations about conflicts that seemed to have materialised in his absence, the compulsory quality time with a horde of children who had somehow been brought into the world even though Adam Riebeeck and his wife spent most of their relationship discussing what was wrong with it, the one saving grace in all that was the fact that he got a chance to drive his own car. He loved his dark blue Mercedes, he loved the sensation of sinking into the leather seats, loved listening to the compressor when all the ridiculously unnecessary horsepower reversed him out of the garage. He'd turn off the radio and the air conditioning, he'd listen to the silence in the front seat, search for the hum of the motor as it rumbled under the bonnet, trying to penetrate the sound insulation without succeeding.

To be honest, it was the only thing he loved about being home.

And now, Adam Riebeeck's Mercedes was at the garage.

It hadn't been his fault. He'd been driving perfectly calmly, always giving his full attention to the traffic around him, when things had suddenly happened out of nowhere. Now, thanks to some lunatic who should never have been allowed behind the wheel of a car he'd had to spend his day off in a fucking Seat that mysteriously reeked of cigars even though the rental company insisted nobody had ever smoked in it. And now he was going back to work and that was probably just as well.

The crew walked on board in silence. The captain's temper hung as a dark cloud over the entire crew, but everyone knew this was how he always behaved when he flew out from Amsterdam, and as soon as they landed somewhere else in the world Adam Riebeeck would be charming and agreeable and a completely different person.

As they settled into the cockpit and strapped their seat belts across their chests, his co-pilot dared to put the question: 'Why the rental car?'

Riebeeck glowered at him. 'You should try reading a newspaper from time to time.'

It took a moment before the co-pilot understood what he meant. 'No way,' he said. 'The pile-up?'

'Some idiot in a Toyota shot off the bridge and landed on the road right in front of me. He said I was lucky to walk away from it.'

'Who did?'

'The doctor. The guy who checked me out. Did you read the paper or not?'

The co-pilot shrugged. And with that, the conversation was over.

When one of the stewardesses stuck her head around the door a few minutes later, putting two cups of coffee down in the holders between their seats, the two pilots were already well into the safety checks.

'Will there be anything more?' she asked.

'Yes,' said Riebeeck. And she looked at him expectantly. 'I really could do with someone to scratch my back.'

The smile she gave him was so dry she might as well have shown him her middle finger. But they had a long flight ahead of them and so she thought better of it.

'I believe that's your co-pilot's task,' she said. 'Union rules, not mine.' And she turned round, exited the cockpit, leaving the two pilots to their routines.

Captain Adam Riebeeck looked after her, amused and disappointed at once. He hadn't been joking. His back itched. In fact, it itched to the point where it was unbearable, and it had been the whole morning.

But he didn't say anything. Merely indicated for his co-pilot to carry on, and as switch after switch was read out and checked and confirmed, Riebeeck let his pen travel down into the gap between his collar and his neck, trying to reach the area that was driving him mad.

His mind was far too busy going through the safety protocols to realise that the soft warmth that spread down his back might be blood.

25

The young guy behind the wheel was such a bad driver that Albert van Dijk asked himself whether his chances of survival wouldn't have been higher if he'd surrendered to the men outside his apartment.

'You need to go right!' he shouted, the desperation in his voice so obvious that Leo looked up and met the man's eyes in the mirror.

'Turn?' he said. 'Now?'

'No. Right side of *the road.*'

Oh. Leo scanned the road ahead of him, saw that he was indeed driving straight towards the oncoming traffic, and swung sharply back to his right. Carried on driving in silence, his hands clutching the wheel and his body awash with adrenalin, wet from sweat even though the heater was struggling to warm the car.

He was a perfectly good driver. He really was. What he wasn't so good at was predicting when a one-way street suddenly and without warning was transformed into a two-way street with oncoming traffic. Leo was positive there must be road signs to relay that kind of information, but here he was behind the wheel trying to drive out of a city that had far too few signs and too many trams. And to top it off, he hadn't a clue where they were going.

Albert's eyes slowly let go of him.

In the passenger seat was the woman who'd called his secretary, and he tried to calm down and concentrate on her instead. Her business card informed him her name was Christina Sandberg and that she was a journalist, but thus far their attempts to start a conversation had been thwarted by the driver's repeated attempts to kill them all.

Christina broke the silence. 'How come you're wanted?'

'They showed up outside my house. I might have killed one of them.'

'They?' she asked. 'Who?'

'I was hoping you would have some thoughts on that.'

Christina shook her head. And the silence returned, broken only by the sounds of sharp turns and a cursing driver.

They had left the city centre behind them. Outside, the late afternoon turned to dusk, light from streetlamps and oncoming cars sweeping over them at regular intervals.

'Why did you come here?'

Christina looked at Albert. 'What do you know?' she said.

'Only what you told my secretary.'

Okay. Christina began at the beginning. William's disappearance, Leo's discovery of the newswire story, the similarities. How both of them worked with codes, albeit from different angles.

Albert listened. Nodded where appropriate, without interrupting.

His feelings were mixed. On the one hand he wanted badly to believe the two abductions were related. That would make everything so much easier; they would be able to compare information and experiences and perhaps reach a conclusion that took them further. But on the other hand it wasn't much to go on. So they were both missing, and they happened to have similar skills, fine. But there had been more than six months between their disappearances and they didn't even happen in the same country.

Christina sensed his scepticism.

'I never got to bed last night,' she said. 'I went through each and every archive I could access, digging out everything I could find. About the investigation. About Janine.'

Leo glanced at her. This was news to him.

'There was one thing in one of the reports. Only a passing reference. To the fact that the police wrote it off as a voluntary disappearance, because ... ' She tried to find the right word, wanted to get as close as possible to what the article had said. '... because, as far as the investigation could ascertain, she had taken all of her personal belongings with her. Something along those lines.'

It was a small detail, but if she was about to say what Albert suspected she was, it was an important one. 'Yes?' he said.

'When my ex-husband vanished?' She turned around in her seat, one leg tucked under the other, facing Albert as much as she could without undoing her seat belt. 'He took everything with him. And when I say everything I don't mean just clothes, toothpaste, you know, the stuff you take when you take everything. But *everything*. Computers, research literature, data on old experiments and notes and stuff he wouldn't be taking anywhere for any reason whatsoever.'

Leo looked at her from the corner of his eye. Waited for the second part, the part about the left-behind photos of their daughter, but it didn't come. She didn't say anything more, just sat there, watching as Albert processed the news.

When someone finally spoke it was from the back seat.

'They kept saying she'd left me,' he said slowly. 'They said she must've planned it, that it wasn't unusual for loved ones to be abandoned without warning and that of course they understood it was hard for me to accept it and the only thing I could think was fuck you right back. But I didn't say it very often.' A pause. 'I just knew.'

'She'd taken too much with her,' said Christina.

He shook his head to say yes. Shook his head at all the questions he'd asked himself, over and over again, and for the first time he said them out loud to someone who seemed to be thinking along the same lines.

'Why would she do that? Clothes she never wore. Notes from old lectures, courses she didn't even care about. Stuff that I had kept from my mother, but that I stored in her wardrobe. *Everything*.'

'And what was your conclusion?'

'That someone did her packing for her.'

Christina nodded in agreement.

Albert hesitated. 'If it is the same people behind both cases,' he said, an emphasis on the *if*, as though he refused to believe it, 'then what does that mean?'

He looked at her, as if negotiating with himself, as if he wanted to say more but wasn't sure whether he should. Then, leaning forward:

'Does your ex-husband have any connection to Switzerland?'

'No,' she said. 'Why do you ask?'

'Because I received this.'

Locking his eyes on hers, he pulled the yellow envelope from his pocket. The one that was addressed to Emanuel Sphynx, that was stamped with a franking machine marked Bern, that he'd shown to the police and that was the reason he couldn't go back home, or to his work, or anywhere else where he was expected to show up.

She took it. Turned it over. Opened it. Three sheets of paper. Written by hand.

A thousand questions. And Christina opened her mouth to ask them.

The moment she did, their car swerved off the road.

Leo's reaction was completely irrational, but may well have been what saved them.

His immediate thought was that they'd been hit, that probably he'd done something wrong, and he veered right, assuming that he must have inexplicably ended up in the wrong lane again without noticing.

But Leo was already driving as far to the right as he could.

And as the rental car heaved itself over the verge to their right there was no more road to find, nothing but grass and terrain and a whole lot of bumps that passed under them as Leo pressed the brake pedal down into the rubber mat with all the force he could muster.

*

It wasn't until the car came to a halt that they realised what had happened.

The noise of their bumping car was gone, but replaced by a growing roar, a vibration that increased in intensity, louder and louder and refusing to end, and above the crest of the ditch the misty afternoon dusk flickered in yellow instead of its usual grey.

They climbed out into a smell of dirt and petrol. Everything dark from smoke. And as they reached the top of the ditch, they stopped.

They'd been lucky.

The airliner had passed directly above their heads, at an altitude just high enough not to take them with it. After hundreds of metres it had finally hit the ground, mowing down everything in its path and with no intention of stopping.

The tree that had made Leo steer off the road lay on the asphalt ahead them, just above the edge of the ditch. It was surrounded by other trees, broken and split and scattered across the road together with TV antennas and telephone poles that the descending jet had brought down, perhaps smashing them with its engines, perhaps with some other part of the fuselage as it came in like a frisbee, sliding flatly through the air, then on through the landscape and through the houses and through the entire suburban sprawl in the distance.

Long before anyone reached for their phones to call for help, the flashing blue lights were already appearing in the distance.

Within minutes the landscape was transformed. From dark and silent to bright and illuminated and teeming with people.

And the calm, chilly night was gone, never to return.

26

Janine led him to the wall, walked to the end of the cuneiform symbols and put her hand flat over one of the pages.

'The paper I gave you,' she said. 'Look at it.'

He did. The last few symbols on his paper were identical to the ones on the paper on the wall. They obviously represented an event that had found its corresponding place on the timeline, and whatever was written there obviously terrified her, but he was still none the wiser.

'I didn't know where they were supposed to go,' she said. 'But it scared me.' And then, after a pause: 'This is the reason we're here.'

He waited for her to continue.

'Everything that's happening. Helena Watkins. The fear about you and I being infected. The virus. It has to be.'

William's eyes told her that he wasn't there yet.

'They knew it would happen. They knew, and now it is.'

'*What* is?'

She hesitated, wondering how to phrase it. She didn't want it to sound naïve or stupid or trite, or like something out of a graphic novel. But she couldn't come up with anything that didn't sound like a combination of all of that.

'I think we're going to die. Correction: I *know*.'

William massaged his temples between thumbs and forefingers, his hand pressed so firmly against his cheek it hurt, as if this would somehow help him to collect his thoughts. It didn't.

'How do you know that?' he said, his voice a whisper. 'Not *how*, I don't care about how, but how the hell can you *know*? How can you stand there looking at those verses, and one second you're telling me it's an ideographic language and can be interpreted in different ways, and then the next you're telling me that you *know? How?*'

'It's language. I can't draw you a diagram. I just know.'

'But why are you so sure you haven't got it wrong? Why can't you have drawn the wrong conclusion? Why can't you be right about *some* of this, about the order, the historical events, about all of that other stuff, but not about what you're saying now?'

Janine wished more than anything that he was right.

The problem was she knew he wasn't. She knew that the texts about the past corroborated the ones about the future, that the wall corroborated her own thoughts, and that no matter how much he tried to shoot them down she'd be able to defend her logic and tell him exactly how she'd reached her conclusion.

As an academic, she ought to be satisfied. Instead, she swung between fear and something else that she couldn't put her finger on.

Sorrow?

She heaved a long sigh, turned back to the wall, worked her way backwards through all the printouts, looking for the right place. There. Stopped beside it, her hand firmly on one of the sheets.

'Here. Fourteenth century. Can we agree on that?'

He cocked his head. And she saw what that meant: Maybe, he meant, maybe, you're right in your assumptions about the timeline and the order and the events. And she threw up her arms in frustration. For Christ's sake! She *knew* that he understood, he just didn't *want* to understand, and they didn't have the time to keep debating the point.

'The rise of the Mongolian empire,' she said, pointing along the rows of sheets to her left. 'The destruction of Samarkand and Bukhara. Go ahead and look it up if you want.'

She kept her hand resting on the fourteenth century. Pointed to the right: 'In that direction: Constantinople. The Shensi earthquake. Novgorod. Objections?'

He had, but held them back.

And she returned to the paper in front of her. 'That makes this the fourteenth century. The outbreak of the Black Death. Again' – she pointed to some of the individual symbols – 'Rats. Disease. Contagion. Death. *An unstoppable plague.*'

She spoke the last words with her eyes fixed on his, as if what she'd just said was something huge and terrifying and as if he already ought to have understood.

'And why,' he said, 'why does that mean we're going to die?'

'Because of this,' she said.

She took the paper in front of her, pulled gently until it came away from the wall, two small tears where the pins had held it in place. She folded it like an accordion, made row after row disappear in crease after crease until only the lowest row of symbols remained visible.

Walked towards William. Walked the length of the wall, past the nineteenth century, the Second World War and the tsunami, all the way to the corner where William was standing next to the sheet whose symbols were the same as those in his hand. Almost as far right as the wall went.

She held up her neatly folded paper immediately below it.
The two rows, perfectly aligned with each other. They matched.
The exact same words. An unstoppable plague.
And she looked at him. Saw that he understood.
'Because of this.'

∞◯∞

Annie Wagner sprinted through the corridors, repeatedly diving out of the way of rattling gurneys and trolleys loaded with equipment, blocking her way in places they shouldn't be.

Confusion reigned, and it was about to get worse.

She'd been working at Dr Joseph Grosse's side all day, had seen the intensity in his eyes as he hurried from one operation to the next, saving patient after patient like a god moving between bodies and breathing life back as it ran out.

He'd been first on the scene; he had tended to the casualties on the motorway, given them first aid and helped prioritise the injuries, making sure casualties were transported to Slotervaart Hospital in the most efficient order. Then, he'd stood in operating room after operating room until his eyes lost the ability to focus, until his exhaustion had made him slow and careless and someone eventually had to order him to get some sleep.

And now this.

When the alarm sounded, everyone's first reaction was disbelief.

It was unthinkable, it couldn't be, not after a day like this, it had to be a hoax, someone's idea of a joke, a cruel, cruel joke. And all the calls that needed to be made, the measures that needed to be implemented, everything had taken far too much time. Everyone was shouting and running about and ambulances were on their way and Dr Grosse wouldn't be getting more than a couple of hours' sleep, at most.

She admired him. No, it was worse than that. She had a crush on him. And if that was a cliché then so be it, if it was corny and immature, then fine, corny and immature was what she was. Perhaps it was the crush that kept her running through the corridors, her posture straight in spite of her exhaustion, her steps springy and rhythmic as she raced along the linoleum floor towards where he slept.

Soon she would lay her hand on his shoulder and wake him with the news that something terrible had happened and hundreds more casualties were on their way in. And he would barely know her name and, if he did, that would be enough to keep her going a few hours more.

Her scream as the fluorescent lights blinked to life was enough to make every staff member on the entire floor stop what they were doing. They came running down the corridors, racing to the door where Annie Wagner stood, gasping for air, her eyes vacant. She'd thrown up on the floor in front of her, and their initial reaction was to make her sit, head between her knees, slow, deep breaths. She'd had a long day. They assumed it must be the fatigue and the drama catching up with her; she needed sleep and water and maybe some sugar, and then she'd be back on her feet again.

Those were everyone's wordless thoughts.

Until they realised why she'd screamed.

One of the male nurses saw it first. His immediate thought was that Joseph Grosse must have been stabbed. Where else would all that blood have come from? The sheets were soaked in it, and it was running in rivulets to the floor, pooling around the drain in the corner under the sink.

The nurse rushed in, turned him over to take his pulse.

But Joseph Grosse had no neck to take a pulse at.

His skin remained stuck to the bed, left behind on the fabric when the nurse turned him over, sticking to the paper cover on the bunk like a half-baked muffin on a badly greased baking tin. Hours earlier Dr Grosse had been a hero in a white coat, running from ward to ward saving lives; now all that remained of him was a hideous flayed corpse, as if his body had been exposed to the elements for weeks instead of left to sleep for a few hours in a dark, cool room in one of Europe's most modern hospitals.

As the young nurse turned to look at his colleagues in the doorway, he could find no words to express himself.

Minutes later the news reached the government.

By then the hospital was already quarantined and in lockdown.

27

Amsterdam was a sea of flashing colours.

There was blue from the emergency vehicles. Fire engines, police cars, ambulances, their deep blue beams sweeping through the air, rotating across the landscape and glinting back off reflective surfaces before disappearing into the afternoon darkness. There was white from the floodlights, some on top of cars and rescue vehicles, others hoisted up on to cranes to illuminate the scene and help rescue workers to see.

But most of all, there was yellow and orange. Fires of every size, from fiercely burning blazes to beds of glowing embers, marking the remains of what had once been a house or a tree or a car or whatever else had been burnt to ashes when the airliner slid through.

Amsterdam was in flames.

The wreckage of Flight 601 to Los Angeles loomed in the darkness, hundreds of metres ahead of them, blackened and glowing and broken into pieces, thick pillars of smoke from under a white blanket of foam.

Everywhere, policemen were telling people to step away, leave the area, even though they had better things to do than deal with ghouls and rubberneckers.

One of the police officers moved along the cordon, came up to Leo, and stopped.

'Are you all right?' he asked.

'I was lucky,' Leo answered.

'You should have someone take a look at that.'

Leo's eyebrow had bumped into the side window; it hurt and it throbbed and he could feel blood smeared over his forehead, but there were others much worse off than him. So he mumbled something non-committal and stepped aside to let the policeman pass. Albert, standing a few paces behind him, did the same, praying that the officer would be too caught up in the situation to remember the description of someone who'd recently pushed a man in front of a car.

'Aren't you freezing?' he heard Leo ask.

He had to think about it. It was cold, yes, but he wasn't freezing, in fact he was too numb to feel anything, even though he was only wearing a blazer and a thin shirt.

'Go and put it on,' said Leo. 'Your coat. Go and get it. It's freezing, trust me.'

And as Albert walked back to their car, Leo turned to survey the devastation in front of him. Watched it all without seeing, was aware of the smell of fuel and dirt but didn't take it in, the same way he heard the engines and the sirens and the screaming without actually hearing a thing.

As Christina Sandberg came wading back through the frost-tinged grass, taking hurried steps along the blue-and-white police tape, it occurred to Leo that he didn't know how long she'd been away.

She had her phone pressed to her ear and was trying to catch Leo's eye, her finger raised in the air as if telling him to stand by. Stay there, the finger said. I'm going to need you.

It was a pointless instruction.

Even if Leo had been capable of a conscious decision, he wouldn't have had the slightest idea where else to go. They were stranded in the dark, in a foreign country on the outskirts of a city they didn't know, where every civilian in sight was as shocked and stupefied and directionless as he was.

She came up to him. Turned off her call, handed him her phone.

'I spoke to the news desk,' she said. 'How do I look?'

Leo had a number of answers to that question, none of them appropriate at the moment. On the one hand, she was frustratingly desirable by default. On the other, she looked very much like someone who'd been in a car crash, seen an airplane decimate a city, and then struggled to bury her emotions behind a press card in the hunt for whoever was in charge of the rescue operations, hoping to transform a catastrophic event into first-rate news material.

Leo chose to tell her none of this.

'You look, what's it called, what are you going to do?'

'We'll be streaming live on the website in five minutes,' she said, as if it was the most natural thing in the world. She smiled without smiling, a face with years of training not to show her actual feelings, her fingers busily plumping up her curls in an unsuccessful effort to give them volume. Then she took her phone back, activated the front camera. Scrutinised the display, her face looking up at her. It wasn't great, but it would have to do. Too polished would give the impression she wasn't actually there. Too scruffy and she wouldn't be taken seriously. She flicked her fingers across the screen again, found what she was looking for, and handed the phone back to him.

'Give me yours.'

Leo tried to pull himself clear of the viscous morass of shock and detachment, and fumbled his phone out of his pocket and held it out to her. He was nervous, nervous to be working with Christina Sandberg, not just *for* but *together with*, and nervous that they were about to broadcast live, everything accessible online the moment they did it. And he knew he was being ridiculous, of course he was, the world had been turned upside down and half of Amsterdam was on fire and no one would give a rat's ass whether he was holding the camera the right way. But it made no difference.

They were the top news site in Sweden. After an incident this big, the number of visitors would be off the chart, and in all likelihood they were the first news channel with a reporter on the scene, and shit, this was huge.

She calmly punched a number on his phone, put his tangled hands-free earpiece into her ear, watched him while she waited for someone to pick up.

'No nerves now. You stand there and I'll stand here, the plane in the background. Okay?'

She didn't wait for an answer, held up her finger, this time as a sign for him to be quiet.

'It's me again. Are we good?'

Sound-wise, she meant. And she started to count into her dangling microphone, giving a voice sample to whoever was sitting at the other end of the line, thick layers of professionalism masking the fact she was feeling the same shock and terror as everyone else.

Leo was already pointing the camera at her.

And the voice in Christina's ear gave her the thumbs up. They had video and audio and it looked fine and everyone was standing by to go as soon as she was ready.

She steadied her breathing, composed herself.

She was good at this. At staying calm when everything around her was reduced to chaos. It was at times like these that she loved her job most, it became a visor of detachment, shielding her, as if she was a parent to the entire world and could make order of chaos by explaining it to them.

Moments like this she knew how to handle.

The personal crises were harder; then there was no shield of objectivity to protect her from the raw emotions. But here and now she was a professional, she was the right person in the right place and she knew that not only was she about to make one of the first eyewitness broadcasts from Europe's worst-ever plane crash, she was also relieved of the need to explain what the hell she was doing in Amsterdam.

Christina Sandberg closed her eyes as she completed her final run-through.

Okay. She was ready.

She stood straight, her demeanour appropriately grave, pulled the headset to get the microphone closer to her mouth, close enough but not in the way. And then she nodded at Leo, looked into the tiny lens in front of her.

'I'm good to go.'

It wasn't until a minute later, as he watched Christina report her findings into his camera, that Leo grasped the magnitude of what had happened.

The green standby symbol in the corner had changed into a red one labelled *live*, and the further she got into her story the more he had to fight to hold the phone steady.

The furrow that the plane had ploughed was over a hundred metres wide, she reported. It started as a crater of soot and soil along the northern edge of the Amstelpark where the plane had hit the ground, and then extended as a vast swathe of levelled rubble and wreckage where the airliner had careered across Euroroute 19 and on through the residential neighbourhood of Scheldebuurt.

Apartment buildings and offices and a school had been razed to the ground in the airliner's wake. The wings had been torn from the fuselage, slid across the ground like giant razors, bounced up and dug themselves back down straight through the flatness of the landscape, until the gigantic pile of steel had eventually come to rest more than a mile from the point of impact.

Schools had still been open. Office hours weren't over. People had sitting in meetings or in classes or crouching over toys; everyone had been full of dreams and plans, and the next moment everything was gone.

'The rescue workers,' Christina said, 'estimate the number of casualties to be several thousand.'

And behind his camera Leo clenched his jaw, let his front teeth dig deep into his lip to stop himself from crying. Not there, not in front of Christina Sandberg, not now.

He shouldn't even have been there.

He should have been at home in his bed on Södermalm, he should have let the phone ring, because who in their right mind calls at five in the morning anyway? But here he was, at the edge of a field on the outskirts of Amsterdam, and everywhere he looked a dreadful reality stared back at him, black and present and full of odours that would stay with him for ever. For the first time in his life he couldn't just take a remote control and change it to something better.

Leo Björk was twenty-four years old.

This was the worst day he'd ever known.

And yet, it paled in comparison to what had already started on the other side of the city.

28

William struggled to pull himself together.

Plague.

He stared at the wall, at the symbols, fought to find the right questions, those that could break her hypothesis. But his thoughts refused to develop beyond half-articulated snatches of ideas, and he couldn't make anything connect. Historical events in the human DNA. A deadly virus that the Organisation had manufactured. A key that would help them encode an answer, but to what? To the predictions?

How the hell could you answer something that wasn't even a question?

And then, from out of nowhere, the answer came to him.

It started as a hunch. But it rapidly grew into a full-blown analysis, watertight and robust, and when the picture became clear the epiphany was so strong it hurt.

I know what the virus is for,' he told her. 'I know why we're here.'

Janine had thousands of questions. But before she could voice them, they heard steps in the corridor.

They immediately stopped talking. Waiting for what was about to happen.

When the door opened, it was Connors.

He cleared his throat and told them to follow him.

∞○∞

Connors marched through the stone corridors, deep furrows of worry etching their way across his forehead.

Behind him he heard the steady echo of Janine's and William's steps, and to a tiny, tiny degree he couldn't help feeling satisfied that they'd finally arrived at the point where they were.

He had been right, Franquin had been wrong. There wasn't any sense in keeping them in the dark – they wouldn't be delivering anything as long as they weren't allowed to know.

Now, they would at last be able to talk.

The only question was whether it mattered.

Because more than anything else, Connors was afraid it was already too late.

∞○∞

Christina Sandberg's phone lay on the table in front of them like an object in a badly arranged still-life, a box of glass and plastic between bottles of water and plates of untouched food.

It was night outside, but nobody was asleep.

Window after window flickered with the gleam of TV sets and computers, everywhere people were trying to grasp what had happened, making phone calls to check if someone they knew had arrived home or still couldn't be reached. And for every time someone sighed with relief in one part of the city, someone's legs collapsed under them in another.

Christina didn't know how long she'd been awake, but she knew she was tired. Every time she moved her eyes the room dragged behind as if it were preserved in a thick liquid, and in front of her sat Leo and Albert, their faces registering the same stunned disbelief as her own – no, as everyone else in the half-empty basement pub.

The bar was dark, hidden away down a flight of stairs in a district full of doll's houses and fairytale castles. Behind the counter at the back of the bar, a flat-screen television was showing footage of the impact site, the same shots over and over, while ticker-tape at the foot of the screen carried the latest updates, the words reflecting and warping through the rows of bottles on the shelves.

And there they sat. Hungry, but unable to eat.

And on the edge of the table lay the yellow envelope.

Albert had taken it out as soon as they'd ordered, told them everything about the contents, the names and the words and the fear hidden inside the letter. And he'd shown them the postmark with the name of the city, and Leo had taken a photo with Christina's phone and sent it to the newsroom in Stockholm hoping the franking machine's identity code might be traceable.

And Christina had called Palmgren, but he hadn't answered.

'Now what do we do?' Albert asked.

'We wait,' Christina said. 'It's all we can do.'

And so the evening passed.

And on the flat screen behind them the jet-crash headlines were replaced by new ones, in a typeface even larger than before. But by then, everybody had stopped watching.

Connors led them along stone corridors and on through metal doors to the newer parts of the complex. They followed a series of sterile neon-lit hallways with cold featureless walls until eventually he came to a halt at the end of a passageway.

A small staircase of ribbed steel led up to the door that marked the corridor's end, and apart from that the only way out was the way they had just come.

It was identical to all the other underground passages they'd passed through. Except for one, crucial difference.

This door was covered in warning signs.

Huge black letters on a yellow background proclaimed the peril beyond, with symbols depicting death and danger and biological hazard.

Authorised personnel only. Risk of infection.

The virus.

William and Janine remained silent, waiting for Connors to explain why they were there, waiting for him to say that he'd been listening in on their conversation, that he knew what they knew and that it wasn't acceptable that they did. Maybe he was going to open that door, push them through and shut it behind them, let them stay in there until no pressure hose on the planet could help them.

But he didn't. Instead his voice softened: 'I'm sorry about this,' he said. 'But I think you've already understood it anyway.'

Janine glanced at William. Saw him nod at Connors.

'I think so,' William said. 'It's the solution itself that's our problem. Am I right?'

'Then you *have* understood,' said Connors.

Janine looked between them. Whatever William had understood, she wasn't there yet.

'What solution?' she said. 'To what problem?'

William turned to her. Said two words: 'Viral vectors.'

He waited for Connors to confirm. But the man stood silent.

'Explain,' said Janine.

William hesitated. Decided that since he had already started, he might as well go on.

'Here's how I think it is,' said William, his eyes locked on Connors, to monitor if he was on the right track. 'The virus is our antidote.'

'Against . . . ?' Janine asked.

'Against ourselves.'

Janine frowned. Ourselves?

'Against the predictions. Against the *plague*. Against our own DNA.'

Janine couldn't decide whether he was talking in riddles or if what he was saying didn't make sense. Either way, it was starting to annoy her.

'What are you saying? That we're the ones killing us?' Her voice was heavy with sarcasm and she knew that it wasn't the most constructive approach. But she was tired and couldn't hold herself back. 'So it was our own DNA that put Helena Watkins in that glass box? It was our own DNA they were washing us clear of in those damned plastic tubes up there? Is that what you're trying to tell me?'

It wasn't called for, she knew that. But she was fed up with information being served piecemeal. She wanted to *know*.

'No,' said William. 'That was the virus.'

'In that case I don't think it sounds like a very good antidote to anything. Do you?'

'No, it doesn't. And that's why we're here now.' He looked to Connors for confirmation.

'Sandberg's right,' he said. A hint of apology in his tone, as if somehow it was his fault that William had understood before her.

'Imagine,' Connors continued. 'Imagine that one day you found a document. And in that document, it set out everything that was going to happen to you for the rest of your life. What would you do?'

'If you'd asked me a year ago, I'd have dismissed it and thrown it away.'

'But what if it turned out that the document was right? What if it turned out that it had been written long before you were born, and that it had been right about absolutely everything that had happened, right up until the present day? And then, what if it said you'd soon be involved in an accident. What would you do?'

She didn't know what to say. Instead, she waited for him to go on.

'You would try to change it,' Connors said. 'Wouldn't you? You'd open the document, and you'd delete the part about the accident, and you'd replace it with something better.'

Janine began to sense where the conversation was going. If she was right, she didn't want to come along.

'In the mid-sixties,' Connors said, 'we discovered that the human DNA was full of predictions. And as we did that? As we slowly started to find out what would happen to us down the road . . . ?'

He looked at her as if that explained everything. But she waited him out, forced him to continue.

'We had to do something. We called out into space, hoping that someone would answer, but nothing happened. We tried to find answers in the writings of ancient civilisations, we turned to every faith and religion on the planet, we did everything we could to make contact, to get to know how those codes had ended up inside our bodies, and why they were there, what we were supposed to do to get them out. But wherever we looked, there weren't any answers. Ultimately, only one thing remained. To change the document.' He paused. And then, to clarify: 'We had to put new predictions into our existing DNA.'

'How?' was all she said.

'A virus,' said William. His voice was low, his gaze distant, almost as if he was talking to himself.

Connors nodded. 'But how could we change the information in the human DNA?' he said. 'Or rather: if this was our shared future, embedded in *everyone's* genes – every person's on the entire planet – how could we access and alter that future? How do you get into every single copy of that document throughout the entire world? How do you make sure that the negative predictions are taken out and replaced?'

He paused before he answered himself:

'Viruses have the ability to enter human cells. A virus can insert copies of its own DNA into the cell, then force the body to manufacture cell with the new code instead of the old. Imagine, then, if you had a virus carrying a genetic code you had designed? A virus that could deliver your code directly into the cells, force them to create new cells that looked the way we wanted them to, with the new genes instead of the old ones?'

He looked from Janine to William. 'Sandberg's right: viral vectors. Modern gene therapy – this is where it was born. But the history books will never get to know that.'

He turned his attention back to Janine.

'Once we'd made the method work, there was only one thing left to do. To make the virus as contagious as possible. As soon as it was, all we had to do was to let it out of the lab and sit back, wait for it to spread across the globe and replace the undesired predictions in the human DNA with – how should I put it? With a more enjoyable alternative.'

'That's what the new verses were for.' Janine held out her hands, struggling to adjust to what she'd just heard. 'The ones you wanted me to translate into Sumerian.'

Connors didn't answer. And that was confirmation enough.

'That's what we're doing here. We're trying to replace humanity's future with one we've made up ourselves!'

'I wouldn't say made up.'

'Then what would you say?'

A pause.

'Developed.'

The room was quiet.

'And now the problem is the virus won't work?' said Janine.

'Something's wrong with it,' admitted Connors. 'Perhaps it's because of the language, the way we've translated the new verses into Sumerian. Or perhaps it's how we've coded it, perhaps the cipher keys we've been using have created sequences that make the virus malign instead of helping us. Perhaps it's both.'

He paused again. Steeling himself for the next step.

'What we do know is we haven't yet found a working virus. Every attempt we've made so far . . .'

For the first time he looked up at the metal door behind them. The yellow warning signs. The flashing electronic lock.

He pulled out his key card. Held it against the sensor.

'It's going to be a bit cold. But other than that, we'll be safe.' He said it over his shoulder, waited for the door to open.

He led the way into the observation room, the same room where he and Franquin had been standing day after day, standing in hope, only to receive the same soul-destroying news. Behind him, he heard them gasp. He didn't turn round, didn't want to look into their faces. He already knew what their reaction would be and that was something he didn't need to see.

The thick pane of space-shuttle glass in front of them. A sea of hospital beds inside.

And they stood there. In silence. Watched the rows of sheet-covered patients, some of them motionless, others with chests moving slowly up and down with laboured breaths, everywhere patches of blood in shades from thickened black to vibrant red.

When Connors finally turned to face them, there was a new look in his eyes. Sorrow. Perhaps something more. Perhaps regret.

'All the viruses we've been able to create so far have caused the infected cells to collapse.'

'Cancer?'

'There's no name for what these people have.'

'And who are they?' Janine asked.

Connors shook his head. It wasn't relevant. Or at least not something he wanted to talk about.

'How did they get here?' she asked again. 'Did they know what their fate would be? Is this where we'll end up, William and me, when we stop producing results?'

The silence around them was complete.

The only thing they could hear were the sounds that should have been there, the hisses and beeps from machines that breathed and monitored pulses, the coughs and the wheezings of bodies that cramped underneath their sheets, all the sounds they should have heard but that stayed on the other side of the glass and left them in a sterile silence. A silence so overpowering that Janine finally had to speak, just to make sure what she heard was noiselessness and not a deafening roar.

'I can't be part of this,' she said, without moving, without taking her eyes off of the room in front of her. 'I can't be part of letting these people die. My god, how many are there? How many have there been? How many people have died in there, all because ... well, all because what? Because we're trying to improve our future?'

'I think you misunderstand,' Connors told her.

'How?'

'This isn't about improving our future. This is about—'

He stopped himself. For the second time, he'd reached a point where he was about to say something he shouldn't. Or, at least, didn't want to.

'About what?' she said.

'It's about doing something before it's too late.'

'What is too late? *What*?'

Connors didn't answer. Just looked at his watch.

When he looked up again, it was clear the decision had been made.

'Right now the council is meeting. You needed to see this first.'

29

Lars-Erik Palmgren drove across the narrow bridge with Neglingeviken's thin ice to his right and Pålnässviken rocking in the darkness to his left.

It represented his own feelings better than he wanted to admit. On the one hand. And on the other.

He tried to think of something else, changed gear to speed up, well aware that the roads were like glass and that he was risking his own life, almost as if trying tell himself that risking your life was unavoidable, and that trying to stay safe was the coward's way.

Christina had asked him for help. And he had said no.

It had been torturing him ever since, and he left the café knowing it was the wrong thing to do – but what choice did he have? The call had made him nervous, the anonymous voice telling him about Sara and then hanging up; he'd known then that whatever was happening was unpleasant and unfathomable and big. And he was insignificant and small.

He glanced at his phone. It lay in the passenger seat, rocking restlessly back and forth as he steered along the road. Restless as his own mind, his own embarrassment over letting fear trump what was right.

Loyalty. Courage. Friendship.

And now she was in Amsterdam.

He'd seen her on his computer, not live when it happened but on a clickable video under thick black headlines. She had been reporting on the plane crash, but what was she doing in Amsterdam in the first place? What could have taken her there, other than the search for William?

On one hand he owed her nothing. He really didn't.

He was retired, a widower, he'd left the military behind and all he did was a bit of consulting here and there and that was all. How could he help her, even if he wanted to? What would he be able to do?

On the other hand, how could he not?

If he didn't, who would he be? *What* would he be? He already knew the answer.

On the seat beside him the phone lay silent, and he knew that behind the black display at least four calls were hiding. Four missed calls from Christina Sandberg.

In a few hundred metres he'd be home. And then he would call her back.

And no matter what she asked him, he would do it for her.

∞◯∞

More than an hour had passed since Leo sent the photo of the envelope to the Stockholm news desk, when at last Christina's phone vibrated on the table in front of them.

'That took a while,' she said when she answered. 'Did you make anything out of it?'

The two men opposite watched her as she spoke. Saw her expression change. First in doubt, then deeply serious. And quiet. For much too long.

'We are . . . ' she began, answering a question from the other end of the line before realising she didn't know. Looked up at Albert: 'Where are we?'

'Haarlem,' he said. 'West of Amsterdam.'

'Did they find—'

Leo broke off as Christina raised her hand, shook her head and splayed her fingers to keep him quiet. This wasn't about the envelope.

'Haarlem,' she relayed into the phone. She was sitting straight in her chair now, turned away from them to avoid any further questions.

Listened. Nodded. Listened.

'When was this?' she asked. And then, without waiting for the answer: 'Can we turn that up, please?'

The last part she directed at the barman, getting to her feet, raising her voice as she repeated: 'Can we turn it up? The television – *now.*'

*

The urgency in her voice made the man behind the bar glance up at the screen behind him. The moment he did, he was jolted wide awake.

He found the remote control beneath a pile of keys and receipts by the till, pointed it at the TV, fumbled for the right button. Turned up the volume, his eyes glued to the screen.

Seconds later, every conversation in the room came to an end.

∞◯∞

William and Janine were escorted into the parliament in silence. They stayed at a distance, taking their places behind the huge, round table and the circle of dark-blue chairs, facing the massive LED display.

Around them various sets of eyes were directed at Connors, and he inclined his head as a silent response: Yes, they're here, and they're here with me.

Nobody spoke, but there was concern in the air, and the uniformed men kept their eyes on him for a few more moments, their gazes lingering until they returned to look at the displays on the wall.

It was against all regulations. Civilians shouldn't be in there. Not now.

But if this was the beginning of what everyone thought it was, it really didn't make any difference.

There was nothing left to protect, nothing to keep secret. It no longer mattered whether William Sandberg and Janine Charlotta Haynes witnessed events as they happened or learned about them in retrospect.

'Do they understand that we have to do this?' Franquin said.

He was standing to one side of the auditorium with Connors, the two of them speaking in low voices while trying to keep their body language as relaxed as the situation allowed. They couldn't afford to show anything but unity, couldn't allow anyone to suspect they had conflicting opinions, not now.

'Nobody can understand,' Connors answered.

And Franquin could only bow his head in agreement.

On the screens in front of them a multitude of TV channels and news websites jostled for attention, side by side. All of them broadcasting the same story:

*Mega-Hospital in Quarantine. Slotervaart Hospital Sealed Off.
Suspected Outbreak Closes Hospital.*

This was the moment they'd known would come. The scenario already existed on paper, even if the hospital didn't have a name and the city been called Medium-sized European City. They'd discussed and debated and made decisions that had been hard to make even when the situation remained hypothetical.

'You know we have to do this,' Franquin said. 'What's the point of resisting?'

Connors wasn't sure that he did know. How could they say that their analysis was correct, that there remained no trace of doubt? Wasn't that why Haynes and Sandberg had been brought there, to help them interpret it one more time, to take one more shot at finding an alternative solution?

Franquin knew what he was thinking. 'We've always known,' he said.

Connors said nothing.

'We didn't know where, didn't know how, didn't know when. Now we do.'

'Yes, we do. Because of *us*,' said Connors.

But Franquin was right. There was no turning back. The decision had been made.

'How many people are going to die?' Connors asked.

'Fewer,' said Franquin. 'What more can we hope for?'

Connors didn't answer.

And Franquin said it again.

'Fewer.'

At the back of the room, William and Janine stood watching Connors and Franquin as they spoke in low voices up front, the rows of chairs next to them, and the uniformed men sitting around, waiting in stillness.

It was obvious what was happening.

The whole room was awaiting instructions, and everyone knew what they would be.

When William turned towards Janine, she had given up trying to fight her tears.

∞◯∞

The moment Lars-Erik Palmgren turned the key in the front door of his suburban house he knew that he wasn't alone, and that it was too late to do anything about it.

Perhaps it was the thin snow that dampened the noise.

Perhaps it was his own failure to be more attentive.

Ten years ago it had been ingrained in his mind; he would have been able to recount every single vehicle he'd passed on the way home, he'd have made unnecessary stops, taken spontaneous detours, all the while looking out for cars that lingered too long in his rearview mirror or that reappeared at regular intervals for no reason.

But that was then. He'd long since lost the habit. And he'd driven straight home, seeing without registering, letting his subconscious take the wheel while his active thoughts remained with Christina in Amsterdam. And eventually, he'd pulled into his driveway and parked the car as if everything was completely normal.

If only he'd allowed himself to think, he'd have realised it wasn't.

Here he stood with his key in the security lock in front of him. And a strange man's black glove resting firmly on his wrist.

'Lars-Erik Palmgren,' said the voice beside him.

It wasn't a question but an observation. And Palmgren didn't answer.

'And you are?' he asked instead.

'Let's talk inside.'

Without another word, Palmgren opened the door, turned off the burglar alarm, and prepared for the worst.

30

Palmgren turned on the integrated ceiling spotlights, first upstairs in the vestibule, then in the staircase down into the basement, all the time expecting the stranger to object.

Sooner or later he would order Palmgren to stop. If nothing else, he should tell him to turn off the lights, to choose a less exposed room, to stand still and shut up and listen very carefully. But it didn't happen, and they continued the last few steps down into the insulated basement, walking across the carpet with their shoes damp from snow, stopping on either side of the low couch and with the vast panoramic window separating them from the bay outside, the faint lights of Saltsjöbaden glowing on the far side.

It was a strange situation. But for a moment Palmgren felt remarkably safe.

If he had to stand eye to eye with someone he didn't know, this was a very good place to do it.

The man was no older than forty, clean-shaven but with a weathered complexion. He was dressed in all black, thin training pants below an equally thin windcheater, its zipper done up all the way to his chin. Black gloves, black sneakers, black knitted cap pulled down to his eyebrows. Dressed so as not to be seen, and to be taken for an evening jogger if he were.

They stood in silence, facing each another across the huge room, the season's first Christmas decorations reflected in the windows together with their mirror images.

They were fully visible from the outside, and they both knew it.

Not that anyone would be on the water right now, it was night and almost winter and freezing cold, but the crucial thing was that someone might see them, and that if the stranger were there to harm Palmgren in any way, he should know there could be witnesses.

The man could see Palmgren's thoughts. 'I'm not here to hurt you,' he said.

'Very well,' said Palmgren. 'I'll hold you to that.'

'And I apologise if you're unable to make any calls on your landline tonight.' He raised his eyes towards the ceiling.

Palmgren understood exactly what he was referring to. The man was familiar with his surveillance system. He knew it was linked to a server via the landline, so he had taken the precaution of disconnecting it at the box out on the street. Considering who had installed the system in the first place, there was only one way he could know.

'Swedish Military?' Palmgren asked, obvious as it was.

'This is not an official visit.'

'But that's where you're from.'

'I have various employers,' he said. 'The army doesn't know about all of them.'

Palmgren studied him. It was a strange answer. 'So why are you here?'

The man paused as if deciding where to begin. Just by coming here he had broken more rules than he could count, so the less said the better. He probably shouldn't have come at all; part of him still wasn't sure it was worth the risk, but when Sandberg's wife had appeared in that newscast it had made him feel uneasy in more ways than one.

And the truth was he didn't know any more. What was right and what was wrong.

'I want you to contact her,' he said. 'You need to get her out of there.'

'Who?'

'It was a mistake to let her go to Amsterdam.'

The room seemed to come to a standstill. Christina?

Palmgren stood frozen in place, but his mind was working over-time, trying to piece the details together. The man opposite let him take the time he needed.

When Palmgren drew breath again, there was a new certainty in his voice. 'You were the one who called me.'

The man said nothing.

'You were the one who called and told me they'd taken Sara.'

Still no answer.

'You didn't *discover* that it was missing, did you? There never was any inventory check. You were the one who took it.'

Again, the man neither confirmed nor denied.

'There comes a point,' he said, instead. 'There comes a point when you're not certain any more.'

'Certain about what?'

'About what you're doing.'

Palmgren peered at him. 'Where is William Sandberg?'

'I don't know.'

'Then what do you know?'

The man paused. He knew far from everything; he was a cog in a wheel and didn't expect anything else. But this was the first time he'd sensed so much fear among the people who employed him.

He'd heard them talk about Amsterdam. About the disaster and about the letter that got away. About their worries that Watkins had the answer.

And whatever it meant, it scared him too.

'Call her,' said the man. 'Call her, right now.'

∞◯∞

Leo Björk was shaking so much that when Christina's phone started vibrating in his hand his first thought was that he was experiencing some sort of collapse.

Leo wasn't afraid. He was terrified.

It was the middle of the night, it was dark and the wind was whipping up. He'd had no idea that he was scared of heights until he opened the door from the stairwell, but the primal fear that had gripped him left no room for doubt. The roof he was standing on was at least ten storeys up, and every time the wind tugged at his clothes his knees seemed to buckle in protest. When he felt the phone buzz, he assumed that was the start of it, and that before he could stop it he'd topple off the ledge and hurtle towards the ground, landing in front of all the police and journalists and crowds· who had gathered behind the security cordons below.

He shut his eyes. Told himself to get a grip. He was just as capable of standing upright here as if he'd been next to Albert down on the street, or next to Christina, wherever the hell she had gone.

He tried to control his breathing again, and looked at the phone in his hand. It was still ringing.

'Christina Sandberg's phone,' he answered.

The voice at the other end didn't introduce itself. 'I need to speak to Christina,' it said.

'I can't, I'm standing on a, she's not here,' Leo replied. He winced in frustration, partly over his own inability to articulate full sentences and partly over the situation and the stress and how the hell did he end up here?

Because he was a journalist, he told himself. He was a journalist, a real bona fide journalist, and here he was on the scene of a breaking story and the irony was that nobody in the world gave a damn if he was wearing a blazer or not.

'My name is Lars-Erik Palmgren,' said the voice, as if this were of crucial importance. 'Where are you?'

Leo looked around. There was only one answer, and it was as absurd to him as he knew it would sound to the man on the phone.

'I'm on a roof,' he said.

'Where? A roof, *where?*'

'Amsterdam. I don't know where. There's a hospital in front of me.'

The other end of the line went quiet. Scarily quiet.

'I want you to get out of there,' said the voice whose name was Palmgren.

'It's sealed off,' said Leo. 'The hospital.'

He was fully aware that the information probably didn't make much sense, but he was confused and bewildered and needed to tell someone about it.

Down on the street, police cars had pulled up with their lights flashing, blocking the approach roads. Vehicles trying to break through the cordon were being turned away; some of them, as far as he could tell from up here, were vans with dishes on their roofs and logos on their sides. News teams.

Christina, being the experienced, resourceful reporter she was, had persuaded someone in the student building across from the hospital to let them up on their roof. And then she'd given Leo her phone and told him to find a good spot.

'I know it's sealed off,' said Palmgren. 'You have to get out of there.'

'What's going on?' said Leo. 'I don't know anything.'

He heard Palmgren hesitate at the other end of the line.

When he spoke again it was even more unsettling than the silence.

'Desperate measures. That's what's going on. Panicky, desperate measures.'

31

Suzanne Ackerman sat behind the wheel of the first ambulance to reach Slotervaart Hospital, utterly convinced that there must be a misunderstanding.

The man in the compartment behind her had survived against all odds. The building he had worked in had been reduced to ruins, split like a breakfast egg by an oncoming aircraft wing; he'd been crushed by debris and had suffered serious burns, but he was alive and she had driven him to the closest hospital. He would be the first patient to arrive, but soon others would follow, god knows how many, a constant stream of casualties that would continue throughout the night.

But in front of her the road to the hospital was sealed off by a man in a military uniform.

She wound down the window. 'It's okay,' she said. 'I'm coming from the crash site.'

She expected him to leap into action, open the barrier, apologise for the delay. Surely the military's purpose was to facilitate rescue efforts, sealing off access to the hospital to prevent staff being bothered by complaints of running noses and splinters, ensuring that medical resources were dedicated to the ones who needed help.

But the soldier shook his head. Pointed in the other direction. Turn around. Find another hospital.

Behind him rows of army trucks were positioned across the road, as if the hospital were a small banana republic and her ambulance an attacking guerrilla troop.

Suzanne Ackerman tried again to explain. But the answer remained the same.

The hospital is closed. It's in quarantine. Turn around.

It wasn't until she was already driving in the other direction, her lights flashing and her speed even greater than before, that the realisation hit her, logical, clearly expressed, and perfectly terrifying.

Terrorists.

First a jet that crashes in the city, then a hospital that shuts down.

Amsterdam was under some sort of attack.

She pushed her fears aside, resolving to focus on doing her job. It was a night of disaster, and the days that followed would be no better, but it was her sworn duty to save and rescue and maintain life as far as she was able, and she would go on doing just that until her legs gave way and she couldn't do it any more.

And as the paramedics fought to keep their patient alive in the back of her ambulance, she pushed the engine a little bit harder, ran red light after red light on her way across the city, not knowing that the man behind her would be dead before they reached their destination.

∞◯∞

If Suzanne Ackermann had been able to follow the news from where she sat, she would have realised she wasn't the only one leaping to conclusions.

The monitors at the front of the dark-blue parliament in the depths of the mountain were all showing news coverage of the sealed-off hospital in Amsterdam, all relaying the same grainy, distant footage from different angles, all of them accompanied by voiceovers reporting the same theory.

Speculation disguised as news rolled across screen after screen, text tickers scrolling sideways at the top or bottom or anywhere a space could be found without covering a journalist's face or the blurry light from the building: *Hospital Still in Quarantine*, they read, or *Suspected Terror Attack Closes Hospital*. Objectivity and panic sat side by side at news desks throughout the world; nobody knew what was happening but everyone wanted to be first.

Police Silent on Threat to Hospital.
No Groups Have Come Forward With Demands.

Franquin stood in the middle of the room, watched the muted reporters on the wall, saw their mouths move and knew what they were saying. Amsterdam was under attack.

'That's good,' he said.

And everyone in the room understood.

It wasn't good as in actually good, but it was good in the sense that, of all the possible explanations they could have settled on, the media had opted to believe that the Netherlands, or possibly the West, or even the civilised world, was under attack from some unidentified terrorist organisation.

In light of what was about to unfold, there could be no more convenient explanation.

∞◯∞

When Christina Sandberg opened the door to the stairwell and stepped out on to the roof, she felt as if she'd just opened the door to her own life.

For the second time in one day reality kicked in and reminded her where she truly belonged. The buzz from the helicopters, the news crews' floodlights, the flashing sirens of emergency vehicles, even the wind that grabbed her and drowned out the noise and made everything sound distant, even that made her come alive, revelling in the surge of adrenalin and energy that rushed through her body and carried her forward.

She didn't know much more than the reporters down on the ground, the ones who stood in front of cameras and microphones and riffed around the theme that something is happening but we're unable to say what as yet. But she had enough to fill a stand-up for as long as they wanted her to. She'd been busy questioning the students in the building below, who'd spent the last couple of hours watching as the cordon went up. One of them even knew of someone who was a patient in the hospital; rumour had it the guy had called his family and told them he was scared, that he wasn't allowed to leave his room and that when he'd pressed the button to call a nurse, no one came. That had been more than three hours ago, and now he'd stopped answering his phone.

She had some good material, and when she crossed the concrete roof to where Leo was gazing across at the façade of the hospital, illuminated by media spotlights, she knew that she'd have a first-class background shot to go with it.

Leo was good. They were a good team. She had to remember to tell him.

She went up to the edge of the roof, turned towards Leo, winked at him. 'You ready?'

She popped the earpiece back in her ear, just as she'd done earlier that day, ignored his attempts to tell her something and prepared mentally for going live.

She was happy. She was actually genuinely happy.

And she didn't know it, but happy was how she would die.

∞◯∞

The thirty-year-old pilot commonly referred to as Jameson, not because that was his name but because of his low tolerance to alcohol, was well out over the sea in the cockpit of his missile-laden F16 when the orders arrived over his radio.

Everything went quiet. So quiet that his commander called him again, checking that Jameson had understood and that the communication equipment was working properly and the pilot hadn't missed what he'd just been told.

Jameson answered that he wasn't sure, and the tower repeated its message, and the same silence returned. The commander didn't have to ask the reason.

When his voice echoed over the radio again, it had a gravity beyond that of protocol. He informed Jameson that he too had hesitated when the time came to issue the order. Sometimes, he said, morality is a complex affair. If killing a few was the price for rescuing many, wouldn't it be a greater sin to refuse?

The pilot in the jet saw Amsterdam come closer, outlined as thousands of white-and-yellow dots in the darkness, and he honestly couldn't answer.

Every fibre of his body told him not to do it.

At the same time, he knew he had to.

And as the landscape grew from dots to houses and buildings and the city he'd grown up in and loved, the arguments for and against raged inside his head.

You can't bomb a hospital with your own civilians inside.

You simply can't.

∞◯∞

William's gaze flitted across the wall of screens, the various news channels and webcasts from across the globe tiled side by side in a giant mosaic. Suddenly, his eyes stopped dead.

His body felt weightless.

From one of the screens across the room, his ex-wife was staring right at him.

Not just at him, she stared into the eyes of hundreds of thousands of people in Sweden and beyond, and at the same time she wasn't staring at anyone in particular, just into a camera somewhere in Amsterdam and what the hell was she doing there? She was standing alone on a roof, lights from helicopters sweeping over the night sky behind her, and right between her and the sky was a metallic cube of ice-blue illuminated windows and there was no doubt what he was looking at.

'Is this *now*?' he asked, straight out, even though he knew.

Nobody answered.

'This. The feeds. All this, is it live?'

Connors was the first to put two and two together. He saw the caption with the woman's name on the Swedish newsfeed, and of course it could just be a coincidence, but the urgency in Sandberg's voice told him that it wasn't. He nodded slowly. His face hard like a general's. And sad like a human being's.

'This is live,' he said.

And William said nothing.

Christina Sandberg was in Amsterdam. She was standing in front of a hospital that was about to be razed to the ground. And he was all too aware and she had no idea.

∞◯∞

Albert van Dijk registered the fighter jet as it passed, and immediately realised what was about to happen.

He was still sitting in Christina Sandberg's rental car, huddled behind the wheel and wearing her assistant's baseball hat, his collar pulled up against his face. Hopefully, it would look as if he was cold and not as if he was worried that one of the hundreds of policemen milling around would pass the car and see who he was. In reality, both were true.

He didn't want to be there.

Christina Sandberg had persuaded the police to allow them inside the cordon, telling them she had come to collect her daughter from the student residence. Sooner or later they were bound to start wondering what was taking so long. And then they would knock on the window, and it would all be over.

But he had nowhere else to go. So here he was, wishing that Christina and her assistant would finish what they were doing and hurry back so they could all get out of there.

He'd been there twenty minutes when the military jet made its first pass.

It shot by at an amazingly high speed, almost frighteningly close above the rooftops, a whizzing silence followed by the roar of the engines as the sound caught up and cut like thunder through the night before it disappeared together with the plane.

Albert stared through the windscreen, trying to assimilate what he'd just seen. There was nothing for a fighter jet to do here. A helicopter could keep the area under surveillance, it could assist police on the ground chasing vehicles or people, perhaps even keep other helicopters at a distance, those from the various newspapers and TV networks that were moving in to cover the breaking story.

But a jet? What purpose could that serve?

And then it occurred to him. There was one task that was perfectly suited to a fighter jet. One single task.

He sat up in his seat, pulled out his pay-as-you-go phone, fumbled around in his pockets for the business card with Christina Sandberg's number. Jumped out of the car, cast his eyes up at the roof above. He didn't care if they recognised him. If he was right, Christina and Leo were in danger. He had to warn them, and if the police took him then so be it.

A fighter jet.

It would be madness. But then, so was everything else that had happened in the last twenty-four hours.

He couldn't find the business card, kept rummaging around, next pocket. Panicking.

If he listened carefully, he could already hear the jet coming in for the second pass.

∞◯∞

Inside the blue parliament, chaos bubbled under the surface.

Glances were exchanged between the uniformed men, phones were pressed against ears to hear better, someone would leave the room and someone enter, everyone chasing the same information.

The jet had passed its target without executing its orders.

The hospital was still standing even though it shouldn't be, and questions bounced around the room without being answered. What had happened? Was it a malfunction? Had the pilot refused orders? What was their next step and how long before they could try again?

William watched it all happen around him.

Until now he hadn't realised how powerful the Organisation

was, how closely linked it must be to the world's governments, or at least to their defence organisations. In a matter of hours they had been able to identify a target, set out a strategy and then obtain the resources to make a move.

A staggering, awe-inspiring move.

He felt himself sweating. He clenched his fists so tightly he could hardly feel his fingers; this was how it must be to sit in the electric chair and watch as someone pulled the lever without anything happening. And now they were going to try again.

On the wall of screens stood his wife, one face among the countless reporters up there.

But her picture was a little clearer, a little closer, a little better.

Christina Sandberg wanted to be the best. Once again, she'd succeeded.

And he was terrified that this time, it would cost her her life.

'Connors?' he said.

Connors looked at him. He hadn't heard Sandberg walk up to his table; he'd been standing with a phone pressed to his ear and his eyes glued to a laptop, and whatever Sandberg wanted, now was not the time.

But Sandberg's gaze was steady, refused to let him go.

'It'll be the last thing I ask of you,' he said. 'But do me this one—'

'Sandberg, this is not the time—'

'That's my wife over there,' he said, pointing at the monitors. 'It's the only time there is.'

'It's too late to stop it,' Connors said.

'She has nothing to do with this. She's what, fifty metres away? Less? A blast wave at that range – for fuck's sake, Connors, let her get out of there first, let her take cover, she's innocent—'

When Connors cut him off, it was with a voice so sharp it sliced through the entire room.

'They're *all* innocent!'

Every set of eyes in the room was watching them, everyone was following their argument as if it were a painful intermission before the real show started again.

Connors lowered his voice, desperation and uncertainty evident in his eyes. This wasn't their plan A, or even plan B; they were so far down the alphabet that he'd lost track of which particular last resort this was. All he knew was that he'd started the game with a stack of chips and reasonable odds and now their money was gone and they were about to go all in with absolutely no chance of winning.

And the scenario was all his. He was the one who'd created it, though it had never occurred to him that one day they'd be standing here for real.

'They're all innocent,' he said. 'Everyone inside that building, everyone aboard flight 601, everyone who was on the ground when it hit. Every single one of the millions of people who are going to be infected by this disease, passing it on like rings on the water until there's no one left to spread it to. Innocent. That's why we have to stop it. No matter how wrong and inhumane and how much of a fucking disgrace it is.'

His calm was back. But it was a sad calm. His eyes pleaded for William's understanding. He didn't want to take command, didn't want to be alone in this. *Understand me.* That was the only thing he wanted to say. *Forgive me, and try to understand.*

'There's nothing I can do, Sandberg,' he said.

'You can give me my phone.'

He thought he'd said it matter-of-factly, calmly, but judging from the silence around them he'd shouted it.

For a moment he sensed a hesitation, and he realised that he had a chance: there was still time, seconds, maybe less, but there was a window and it was closing for every second that passed.

'You have my phone,' he said, each syllable working its way up from his belly, a restrained force vibrating with fear and anger and the threat that there was no telling what he'd do if Connors didn't comply.

And William looked into his eyes.

'Somewhere, you have my phone. You can give it to me. And you can do it *now*.'

∞◯∞

Leo Björk was so intent on his task that he jolted from sheer fright.

One second, he was staring into Christina's composed face, watching her mouth move without hearing her voice above the sounds of wind and helicopters and the traffic in the street below, concentrating on keeping her in the frame with the hospital visible behind.

Then, the next second, he was looking at William Sandberg.

He stood smiling and tanned in a slanted sun, the sky behind him a burning blue, his image filling the screen where Christina had been a second ago. The contrast with the reality around Leo was so striking he didn't understand what he was looking at.

Incoming Call, it said. *William Sandberg.*

And for the first time he heard Christina's voice above the chaos.

'Leo! What's happening?'

He raised his eyes from the screen, saw her pushing her earpiece harder into her ear. Someone from the newsroom was speaking to her.

'They're saying they lost us!'

'It's him! It's William!'

For a moment she didn't understand what he was saying.

She'd been surfing along her own thoughts, she'd heard every one of her sentences lead seamlessly into the next, she'd been on a roll – and the next moment she had an entire newsroom shouting into her ears that she was gone.

It was all extremely frustrating. She'd been right in the middle of a terrific monologue about fear and uncertainty, and now here was Leo, shouting her ex-husband's name and making no sense whatsoever.

He turned the phone around.

And then she got it.

Now he calls me, the bastard. Now.

Part of her wanted to take it. After all, he was the reason she'd come here. But the reporter in her knew that she couldn't, not with a screaming editing room in one ear and the racket of a news inferno going on around her and the wind pulling her hair and drowning her thoughts.

She had to make a decision.

And she already knew what it would be.

'He can call back,' she shouted above the commotion.

'It's *William*,' Leo protested.

'And he's alive. And that's great. And he can call me back!'

She was still shouting as she took the few steps towards Leo, grabbed the phone from his hand and rejected the call.

In less than a second she'd switched it to meeting mode, directing all incoming calls to her voicemail. When she handed the phone to Leo the camera was already running. She returned to her spot, pulled the headset microphone in front of her mouth:

'We were cut off. But we're back. We're ready to go live when you are.'

∞Ｏ∞

Jameson had passed his target, and it hadn't gone unnoticed.

The radio had screamed in his ear.

The commander had raised his voice, launching a tirade about duty and conscience, and eventually Jameson had been worn down.

He had turned his jet 180 degrees in a long, smooth motion and now he was heading back towards the web of highways and suburbs. In the middle of it all lay his target, and he already knew that this time, he'd do it.

Jameson had never said a prayer in his life. But as he flipped up the transparent cover on the firing switch he sent out a plea for forgiveness.

∞Ｏ∞

Christina Sandberg's voice spoke across time. It spoke from back when everything was the way it used to be, from a place where the only background noise came from office machines and phones and journalists, busy at their desks.

It said her name and declared that she couldn't take his call right now, and William let the seconds pass until the tone told him he could leave his message.

'Get down from the roof, you're in danger!' he said. 'Call me. I'm okay, call me now!'

He hung up and tried again. Refused to give up that easily. There had been a number of tones before the voicemail kicked in, which meant the phone was on and she'd presumably rejected him manually.

The green button. A second's silence. Then her voice again.

It was the same formal voice, from the same preserved moment, and then came the same tone and William closed his eyes in frustration and hung up.

This time, no signals.

She'd turned it off.

She was working, and she didn't want to be disturbed. The stubborn woman had turned off her phone. He raised his eyes in exasperation and that was when he saw her again.

He felt Janine touch his arm to get his attention, but he was already watching: on one of the monitors in front of them, where a second ago there had been a black screen and emptiness, the feed was back. And there she was again: Christina, as serious and professional as before, looking straight into his eyes and into everyone else's, as if she hadn't been cut off, as if she hadn't rejected his call, standing in the thick of the action, just as she'd always wanted.

He stood there, watching her.

She stood there, didn't see him.

And there was nothing more he could do.

He didn't even turn around as the uniformed officer stepped in from the lobby, stopped on the other side of all the dark blue chairs, cleared his throat with eyes directed at Franquin.

'He's in the zone,' he said.

'His orders still stand,' said Franquin.

And the officer nodded, made his way back outside, while nobody else moved.

All their eyes glued to the news screens.

Amsterdam in front of them.

There were twenty people in the room and every one of them was holding their breath.

· ∞◯∞

Albert had finally found the business card. He punched the number with shaking fingers, hoping that he was wrong and that the roar of the oncoming jet didn't mean what he feared it would.

As soon as she answered he interrupted her. But her voice carried on, a recorded message in a language he didn't understand, a few short words and then a tone to give him the chance to speak. But he didn't.

Instead, he lowered the phone. Screamed her name straight out into the chaos of the rumbling night. Knew perfectly well that she wouldn't hear, but what else could he do?

It was out of his hands.

And he looked up at the sky and searched for the lights of the jet and waited.

∞○∞

The seconds that ticked by in the parliament couldn't seem to decide whether they were fractions or eternities or both.

There was nothing anyone could do.

Time rushed past.

And yet it lingered long enough for each new moment to pierce everyone's consciousness with an icy clarity.

Connors' eyes on William.

William's on Christina.

Everyone's on the screens.

The seconds came, floated and left, each one perhaps the final one before the inevitable happened, not now, but maybe now, or now, or now—

∞○∞

The light news helicopter hovered around the hospital, the cameraman pressed against the Plexiglas in search of the best angles, his lens chasing across the hospital façade to catch a glimpse of what was going on inside the windows and why.

But there were no signs of movement within, no one looking out, no one walking the corridors, not a single shadow that shifted in any of the windows on any of the floors in any corner of the building.

Perhaps everyone was locked into some other part of the hospital. Either that, or the rumour was true. The rumour on the street, the one saying that everyone inside was dead, that this was the reason nobody was answering their phone, not patients, not staff, not visitors.

The cameraman ordered the pilot to fly as close as possible.

If he could only zoom in on the wards, come up with a shot that would prove or disprove all the speculation, his images would end up being regurgitated on every media outlet worldwide. And so his lens kept hunting while the helicopter slowly, slowly hung in front of the façade like an insect looking for that last, fresh flower.

And then, everything changed.

The moment the windows turned to milk he knew something was wrong.

∞◯∞

William exhaled. Not because the tension was over but because his body needed oxygen. For a moment he allowed himself to believe that the pilot had passed by again, decided to disobey orders. But before he'd finished the thought, it happened.

The blast wave, taking out the windows.

The first thing he noticed was how the huge building behind Christina shuddered, almost imperceptibly, then lit up in purest white for a fraction of a second, and before he could grasp that the white was made up of millions of cracks in the hospital's windows as they shattered everywhere and at the same time, the white was gone, transformed into blackness as the panes collapsed, tumbling down along the façade, leaving the entire building as a black hole behind it.

Christina dived to the ground in front of the camera, instinctively turning to see what was happening. Beyond her, the open floors lit up from inside, a raging glare from a growing flower of fire, starting from somewhere deep inside where the missile had detonated, and swelling, spreading like a concentric cloud, outward and upward and downward through all the storeys until it reached the open windows and the air outside and engulfed the building in a wall of smoking gold.

When Christina turned back to the camera, her eyes fell on Leo.

But on the other side of the European continent, William stood looking deep into the eyes of his own wife, and there were so many things he wanted to say.

∞◯∞

The shockwave pushed the cameraman to the helicopter floor. He scrambled wildly for something to hold, handles and seats and whatever there was, and when he finally managed to stand upright again he realised there was Plexiglas above him and Plexiglas below him and the helicopter was flying on its side and that couldn't be good.

They had flipped over.

The rotor blades continued to turn, cutting vertically through the air, making the helicopter spin sideways around its own axis, and across the seat backs he saw the pilot struggling with his controls, the world passing around them, around and around at terrifying speed, and then he saw the student building come towards them and then he shut his eyes.

His last thought was that if the helicopter didn't stop spinning they would crash right into the woman on the roof.

∞◯∞

If Leo hadn't been so focused on the phone display he might have seen it in time.

The helicopter hit the building, rotors first.

It cut through the masonry taking everything with it.

There was a chaos of smoke and flying debris and then it was all over and Leo knew he should be dead too but he wasn't.

He was standing alone on a rooftop.

He tried to cling to the hope that what he had just seen hadn't happened, that maybe there was an anomaly, an optical illusion that made it look one way on the screen, even though the reality was completely different.

Leo lifted his eyes from his phone. He saw clouds of dust and debris and burning fuel, and the ledge where Christina had been standing. It was no longer a ledge but a hole.

The solid concrete surface was gone. Instead of pipes and antennae and vents he could see straight ahead, straight down, a gaping cavity in the corner of the building as if someone had taken a bite out of it. And just where the bite had been taken was the spot where Christina had stood and talked to the world.

The wind whipped at his clothes and noise thundered around him, but everything seemed remote, at a distance, all the sirens and engines and fire. And here he was in the middle of it all, nobody to see him, nobody who knew that he'd survived, but also nobody who wondered.

He stood there. Didn't move. Impossible to say for how long.

Then, finally, he turned off the phone.

∞◯∞

As the picture from Leo's camera disappeared from the screen in the large auditorium, just as it did from the screens on thousands of desks in Sweden and Scandinavia and probably countless other places, live footage continued to stream from other news networks on the surrounding screens.

The building the helicopter had crashed into had lost a great chunk at one corner. Walls and windows were gone, all the way from the roof and on towards the ground, and where cut-off floors ended in the middle of the air, papers and textiles and building material floated slowly downwards, down towards the flaming wreckage of what had once been a helicopter.

Reporters chattered over each other at the top of their voices, text tickers scrolled across screens, shouting in capitals, screaming that Slotervaart Hospital had been bombed by its own air force, or perhaps the jet had been hijacked and this was the work of terrorists. Everyone was guessing and it was chaos and hands against earphones and journalists panicky telling the world about things they didn't know.

Nobody saw the young man standing alone on the rooftop. Nobody mentioned the woman who'd been standing on the ledge that the helicopter hit.

Only here, in the Parliament with the blue chairs, only here did everyone know what it meant.

And Janine turned to William to see if he was hanging in there.

But William Sandberg was no longer in the room.

32

They found him at his desk.

They'd been through the entire castle, including the chapel and out on the terrace, and they had radioed Evelyn Keyes and got her to search the lists to see where his key card had passed and where he'd gone.

It wouldn't be the first time he'd tried.

The drop from the terrace was at least a hundred metres straight down on to the rocks. And then there were ledges and balconies, and windows in the towers and in front of the chapel. If someone didn't want to go on living, the place was brimming with opportunity.

When Keyes returned with information about his location, everyone's immediate thought was the windows. Janine had sprinted up the staircases, long strides, her feet against the stone floor like so many times before. This time afraid not for her life, but someone else's.

She arrived shortly before Connors.

They threw themselves against the door to his workroom, expecting it to be blocked on the inside, but it swung open and they rushed in and there was nothing there to be late for.

William was standing in the middle of the room. Empty gaze, a notepad resting against his palm and forearm, his eyes going back and forth over the wall. A pen in his other hand, ready to take down his thoughts if only they hadn't been so impalpable and frustrated and full of shock.

He didn't even hear them enter.

It was as if he was looking at the codes through a funnel, as if every new thought in his head made him forget two others, and as if the harder he struggled to understand, the more everything seeped through his fingers.

She was dead.

He'd seen her die.

And he knew that she was merely one of thousands who'd already died, one of the countless millions more who would, but the funnel was there in front of him and no matter how he tried to see the big perspective, all he could see was her.

But inside, he knew. This was only the beginning.

And he wanted desperately to push the panic away, to find the solution – there had to be a key buried in all those numbers in front of him. It was his task to find that key before it was too late, and now he knew what too late really meant, and in his ears his heartbeats pounded like a deafening pulse, drowning out his thoughts and making him shut his eyes.

The context. That was what she had talked about, Janine. The whole picture.

And the fact remined: he didn't have that.

The sequences on the wall had been chosen by others, people who had deemed them central or fundamental or perhaps even just harmless enough for him to see.

But the question was what filled the gaps. The parts of the source material he *didn't* have, the numbers that didn't hang on his walls, that came before and after, all the pieces of DNA that they had concluded weren't part of the code. But how could they know the key wasn't referring to a value in the gaps?

What sequences was he missing? What prophecies were they keeping to themselves? Of the entire human genome, why had he only been given the parts that hung here?

He didn't get any further in his thinking before he felt someone touch his arm.

It was Janine.

'How're you doing?' she said.

It was a stupid question, and they both knew it. But it was code for something else, that she cared about him and understood how he felt. And he appreciated that.

A few paces behind stood Connors.

'My deepest, deepest condolences,' he said.

'For what?' said William. 'For killing my wife? Or for bombing a hospital full of people?'

And Connors could have answered. We only killed your wife, he could have said. The people in the hospital were dead anyway.

But he didn't.

'What's going on?' asked William.

'You know very well what's going on,' Connors said.

'You're right and I'll rephrase. When are you planning on telling us everything?'

'I'm sorry,' Connors replied. 'But you know what we know.'

William turned his head away, not out of weakness but to gather energy, to summon up an even sharper, more commanding voice.

Connors saw it coming, and cut him short: 'This is the moment we were all afraid of. And yes, maybe we could have told you earlier, maybe we should have, but we chose . . . '

He hesitated. It had been Franquin's choice, not his own, but he was equally guilty and there was no point in pretending otherwise.

'For *your* sake, for your own—'

No. He stopped, changed track: 'There is knowledge we're not meant to have. And the fewer of us who need to live with that knowledge—'

The crash as the contents of William's desk were shoved to the floor stopped him mid-sentence, just as effectively as William had hoped.

'For fuck's sake!' he bellowed. 'For fuck's sake!'

Paper, files, pens, everything rolled on to the worn stone floor, and William felt his senses return, as if his anger and adrenalin had found direction instead of purposelessly rushing around in his veins.

'You made this happen! You knew what was coming, and you made it happen! You wanted to play God, you sent that fucking virus out there, you made that prediction come true yourself! *You.*'

The room was silent.

'And now you tell me *I* don't need to know?' He took a deep breath. Fixed Connors with steady eyes. 'You brought me here to help you stop this outbreak. Correct?'

Connors wasn't sure where he was headed. 'We brought you here because we hoped it wouldn't happen in the first place.'

'Tell me then,' William said, his face so close to Connors' that he could feel the other man's breath, 'tell me why I don't need to know.'

Connors stood silent.

'Tell me how I can crack your code. How can I find a cipher key that's based on its own contents, that references itself and points back and forth and fuck knows what else it does, how am I supposed to do that if you don't give me all the material to work with? *How?*'

Still no answer.

'If this is all I get, then how am I supposed to see the structure?'

He walked up to the wall, placed his hand on one of the sheets, the one that Janine had translated into 'plague' and that hung almost as far to the right as he could go. And then he pointed towards the corner. The corner where the wall came to an end.

'What. Happens. Next?' Emphasis on every word.

A second passed. Two.

And William waited, ready for any answer.

Except for one.

When Connors opened his mouth it was as if the words refused to travel all the way, as if William could hear them but didn't understand.

The entire room was silent and he knew he should say something, but everything was empty and chillingly still, and if Connors had said what William thought he just had, nothing mattered anyway.

'I'm sorry,' William said. 'I'm sorry, can you repeat that?'

And Connors did. '*Nothing*,' he said slowly. '*Nothing* happens next. You've been given all the sequences there are.' He locked eyes with William. Waited for him to take it in.

And then he did.

One could tell from his posture, his gaze, his drooping shoulders. He reached out, as if he gasping for air but unable to get any, then he spoke to Connors with a voice that vibrated with fear and mistrust:

'You're lying.'

'I wish I were,' said Connors.

Beside them stood Janine, the same fear in her eyes too, and she took a step forward as if decreasing the distance might make everything easier to grasp.

This was it. This was what the Organisation had been so careful to hide. And now that she'd finally got to know she wished she hadn't.

'We've arrived at the plague,' she said.

That was all. She didn't point at the wall, not at the sheet of paper on the far right of the wall, with one single prediction remaining to the right of it. She didn't need to point, because everyone knew what she meant.

William looked between them both. There was one question left. And he knew they would have the answer, but he still resisted asking it, resisted because he was too afraid of what the answer would be.

'What comes after?' he asked.

And Janine glanced at Connors. Pleading with him to provide a better answer. Hoping she was wrong.

But Connors only closed his eyes. Closed his eyes because his answer was the same.

Janine lowered her gaze. 'After the plague,' she said, 'there's only one prophecy left.'

'What does that say?'

She couldn't bring herself to meet his eyes. She looked up, but past him, through him, tried to find something else to focus on that would release her from having to say what she knew.

But there could be no release. And when she opened her mouth, her voice was barely audible.

'*Fire*,' she said. 'A huge and violent fire that ends it all.'

None of them had said anything more. Minutes of silence had passed, and then Connors had turned and left the room without a word. He couldn't help them deal with what they'd learned – how could he, when he couldn't deal with it himself?

Janine moved closer to William. Didn't say anything, and yet he nodded back.

And he held her, close, for a long, long time.

Held her the way he wished he'd held his daughter.

It hadn't been a week since he'd wanted his life to end.

Now it looked as though everyone's would.

PART 3

Scenario Zero

You can never, ever be ready.
    How could you be?
    When you can never, ever know?

Nobody knows where we're going. Not even time.
    Not even it knows, suddenly the time is now and something just happens, and you can't do anything but to stand there and try to grasp without understanding. Why me. Why now.
    Because how could you understand?
    There are no rules.
    You can't tell what's going to be; if a truck suddenly appears from the left, that's just what happens, and then everything goes black and nobody could know in advance.
    Nobody could ever be ready.

Now they're telling that me I'm wrong.
    That time knows where it's going.
    That there is a set path.
    But even if that's true, it still changes nothing.

Evening, Wednesday 26 November.
    They say the world is coming to an end.
    I'm still not ready.

33

The ceremony didn't take place in the chapel, and it was over in four minutes.

What should have been a coffin was a bag with a zip lock, where should have been flowers were stainless-steel shelves, and what should have been family and friends were Connors, William and a couple of men in uniform, men who probably had names and personalities, it just didn't seem that way when you looked at them.

And Janine.

She stood right up by the window pane, so close she could feel the heat from the fire in spite of the thick glass. Her eyes fixed on the white bag that could well have contained anything at all but that most certainly didn't.

She was the only one in the room who cried.

On the far side of the pane the flames glowed incredibly hot, a private little purgatory inside a hole in the next wall, the blaze casting its light across the small space, out through the glass and landing on the sombre faces that stood there, waiting for it to be over. And all the while, Franquin's voice worked its way through what had to be said, not because he wanted to but because it was his job.

When the words were over, the automatic lift started to rise, slanting the metallic chute at an angle, tilting the bag with Helena Watkins' remains on to the conveyor, allowing it to roll like groceries at a supermarket towards the roaring, steel-blue fire at the other end. When the bag arrived at its final destination, it was engulfed in flames within seconds.

Inside the rectangular opening, the fire danced in whirls of colour. A firework display in thousands of shades, changing as new layers of the bag's chemistry vaporised in the heat and ignited.

And then, the hatch closed behind her.

Inside, the remains of what had been Helena Watkins turned to ash.

And when the chamber was swept out several hours later, both the body and the virus she carried had gone.

The only question being where would it resurface next.

∞○∞

'If we're lucky,' Connors began, and paused.

That's the way he chose to open the meeting.

He stood at the front of the blue parliament, silently surveying the rows of uniforms behind the arched table, pads and pens and mineral water in front of everyone as if this was a regular conference at any hotel in the world.

But it wasn't.

Less than an hour had passed since they'd paid their last respects to Watkins, less than a day since a passenger jet transformed a major city into a muddy, burning wasteland, and the memory of the hospital they had destroyed hung over them like a filter of sorrow obscuring the thoughts they so desperately needed to think now.

Nobody believed him. Nobody believed they'd be lucky.

And he knew it the second he said it, but he went on anyway, stayed with his choice of words and repeated himself. It was his job to be an optimist.

'If we're lucky,' Connors said again, 'we've just witnessed the end of the outbreak.'

No comments. Only a silent scepticism cutting through the room, lingering like an invigilator in an exam hall.

'The man who escaped from us was found in Berlin six days ago, and as far as we've been able to determine there's nothing to suggest he met anyone, except for the owner of the car that gave him a ride. At least not after becoming contagious.'

On the screens behind him the entire world hung as a gigantic map, spread out across the monitors like an electronic mosaic forming a single picture. And Connors moved his fingers across the computer on his desk, soft movements to make the map zoom in on Europe and illustrate his message.

'As for the car owner, he caused a lot more trouble.' He pointed at the map as he spoke. 'Nicolai Richter died in the pile-up in Badhoevedorp, but that didn't stop him from spreading the virus further. We know it appeared again at Slotervaart Hospital, carried there by the doctor who'd declared Richter dead. We also know that the pilot of Flight 601 was involved in the same accident, treated at the scene by the same doctor and then allowed to leave and go about his business.'

He sighed. 'That's where luck comes in. That's where we're going to need it.'

No objections. A room full of quiet.

'If we're lucky,' he repeated, 'this means all outbreaks have come to our knowledge. But what if we're not?'

He looked out at his audience. And for a brief moment, he felt stupid. These were people who knew considerably more than he did, biologists and doctors and medical researchers, and here he stood, relaying their own information back to them. Assembled and combined, true, organised so that everyone could gain insight into areas beyond their own field, but still he couldn't shake the feeling that the collective knowledge in the room was larger than his own. And in that instant he was a child again, for the first time in decades he found himself in an English town that smelled of coal and he was small and everyone else was higher up on the ladder and who the hell did he think he was?

The memory washed over him and vanished as quickly as it came. But it knocked him off balance, made him pause a fraction longer than he'd planned, and he had to force himself back to the present, try to remind himself who he was now and tell himself that in this room, the only one questioning his authority was himself.

He turned to look at the screens behind him, numbers and columns of data appearing as he spoke.

'As we know, there isn't much research on the virus. Primarily because it hasn't existed for very long. And as with previous generations of the virus, this one should have stayed here under laboratory conditions and died with its carriers as soon as we established it didn't work. This time we didn't manage to do that.'

Did. Not. Manage.

Three simple words. Everyone knew what they meant. They had failed, all their routines and protocols hadn't been enough, and now the situation was out of control and they couldn't do anything about it.

And the computer spat out new tables of numbers, and Connors pointed and explained, his voice neutral and matter-of-fact and somehow that made it even worse.

In their two chairs at the rear of the room sat William and Janine. Silent like everyone else in the rows in front of them. Watching the map, listening to Connors, hearing terms they recognised, figures they didn't understand but that scared them all the same, reproduction index and incidence and pathogenicity, and everywhere the numbers were high and made people who understood them shake their heads.

'We call this virus Generation Seven,' he said. 'It spreads through droplets in the exhaled air, which means that it doesn't travel very far from its carrier. That's the good news. The bad news is that there have been no documented cases of people being exposed without developing the symptoms and dying.'

New tables of numbers on the screens.

'The time from infection to the first signs of illness vary from one to four days. Perhaps it differs from person to person. Perhaps there are other parameters – again, we don't know. But what we do know is that when the process has started, things move fast. I don't think I need tell anyone in here what it looks like.'

Nobody interjected. Everybody knew. All too well.

And Connors turned back towards the screen. He had reached the core of his report, the thing that worried him most of all.

With a sweeping gesture over his computer, the tables vanished from the screen, replaced again by the map of Europe. In the centre was Amsterdam and Berlin, framed by the Mediterranean in the south and the polar circle in the north.

'If we're lucky, the outbreak is over. But ...'

His finger on the computer, a movement across the touchpad.

A dot that appeared over Amsterdam.

One small dot, contrasting in a sharp purple against the rest of the map.

'If there's just one single person we don't know about? One person who was present at the crash on the highway, or who met someone at the hospital and walked out of there, or who met Captain Adam Riebeeck at the airport?'

A pause. And then, the words he didn't want to say.

'And if that person infects ten others before he dies? Who, in turn, infect ten more?'

The map. The purple dots. Connors' hand, brushing over the computer, once, twice, three times, making the dots grow and multiply, shining in brighter shades of purple and further and further from Amsterdam. The dots grew into circles, appearing in entirely new places as the computer simulated people travelling and fleeing from the cities, panicking and searching for safety and infecting new people rather than making anything better.

Nothing anyone hadn't contemplated already, and yet it was painful to watch.

What terrified them most of all was how few of Connors' finger sweeps it took. How few steps were needed, how soon the map had to zoom out to accommodate all the circles, how the entire world turned purple within a couple of weeks and how what started as a single dot in Europe spread to encompass the globe.

And still, there was surprise when circles began to shrink.

When the map regained its natural colours, when the purple receded and the circles turned back into dots and the world's countries gradually returned to normal.

For a moment, hope filled the room.

But slowly, slowly, reality caught up.

The circles didn't shrink because the epidemic had stopped spreading, or because somehow its intensity had magically weakened.

The opposite was true.

There wasn't anyone left to spread it.

And eventually, the computer beeped to tell them the simulation had come to an end. There were no more steps, no matter how many times Connors brushed the touchpad.

On the screen in front of them the world shone in luminous detail, countries and cities and places where someone knew someone, where there was a spectacular view or a nice little café.

But in the world that the computer simulated, there weren't any people left. Not at the nice cafés and not by the spectacular views. Everywhere across the globe, life had ceased to be.

And it was no further away than a dozen swipes on a computer.

The meeting finished, but nobody got up.

Papers lay untouched on the tables, bottles of mineral water were left unopened, there was a world to save but nowhere to begin and the feeling of hopelessness hung over them like a dark, heavy blanket.

'If we're lucky,' someone said. Connors words again.

It was the thought on everyone's mind, but the words came from one man and the whole room turned towards him.

'How big is the chance that we are?'

Connors looked back at him. Shook his head.

'In three days we'll know the answer. Until then I want you to give Sandberg and Haynes all the material we've got.'

34

The man who was about to die in the alley had a name, but he hadn't heard it for a very long time. It had faded and been forgotten and lost its meaning through so many years of solitude, that when he heard the military men around him say it he didn't feel as if they were talking to him.

Stefan Kraus had lived on the streets for as long as he could remember. Slept in lifts and tunnels and sometimes not at all, often remaining in constant motion to survive another night in an ice-cold, wintry Berlin. Based on his date of birth, he was just over thirty. But anyone who saw him would guess at fifty, and he floated around in an ageless existence between life and death, and there were days he wasn't sure which was which.

They had come to him in the police station holding cell.

It had been a good morning, he'd slept in a warm room for the first time in ages, he'd eaten food that hadn't been thrown away, and that came to him in sealed packaging and meant he didn't have to worry about being poisoned. And even if he knew it was only a temporary respite, a short break from the reality that was slowly but persistently destroying him, he'd been doing his best to avoid thinking of that and simply enjoy the moment.

He had felt grateful.

Grateful he'd survived another night.

And that was probably one of the reasons he said yes.

They told him he'd be part of a research project. In return he'd get food and accommodation. He'd have the chance of a real life, he'd get exercise and education, at night he'd have his own room where he could read or watch TV and when summer came there was a terrace with a view he'd never grow tired of.

That was what they told him.

But nobody told him what he would witness.

He would see people become sick for no reason. People who were taken to closed-off wards, cared for by staff in hazard suits, and who pined away and never returned. And he wasn't an idiot, he might be homeless but he was not an idiot, he knew his time would come and with every day that passed that time drew closer.

He was going to die, and if he had a choice he would rather freeze to death in freedom, fall asleep to the sound of the subway and never wake up again, rather than become one of the bleeding bodies he'd caught a glimpse of as they brought him downstairs to exercise and breathe in machines and prepare for becoming their next subject.

But he didn't get to choose.

He'd said yes, and now he was doomed.

So when the woman whose name was Helena Watkins had come to him and asked for help, it was as if he'd been given a second chance.

She was a prisoner too, but a prisoner with privileges. She knew things and had a key card, and whatever she'd found out, she was scared and needed him.

She would help him escape. In return, he had to deliver a letter, a thick envelope that was immensely important. Not that he gave a damn what it contained, so long as it got him out of there. She supplied him with names and instructions, and two days later she told him the time had come.

She collected him from his room in the middle of the night. Showed him through corridors that wouldn't end, opened doors and airlocks and guided him to an alcove where he could hide, waiting for the delivery trucks that would arrive at dawn.

That's where she gave him the heavy envelope.

And then she'd hesitated, weighing the pros and cons, trying to decide whether to confide in him or not. And Kraus had waited.

'There's one more thing,' she said, finally.

He remembered her words, remembered how she seemed to be struggling with a decision, as if the envelope was paramount, but that there was something else that she couldn't let go of. Something human and special and personal. And then she made up her mind.

She asked him to deliver a message.

Not for her own sake, but for someone else's, just a couple of words. And she told it to him, made the message up then and there, brief and concise, and yet he understood exactly what it was, it was touching and of course he couldn't say no. And Helena Watkins had thanked him and wished him good luck, and then she'd left him alone.

And Stefan Kraus had hunched in the darkness. Shaking with the fear of being discovered. But the morning had come and with it the deliveries, and where the truck rolled in he made his escape and the air and the chill hit him straight in his face. And for one tiny moment he was happy.

Stefan Kraus was free.

He wandered on foot for hours. The dark of the morning kept him invisible, made him feel safe and calm even though there was nobody to stay invisible from. Behind him, the road led back to the base of the mountain, terminating at the gigantic steel door he'd exited through, and the only vehicle that passed him during his walk was the truck that had brought the deliveries, food or mail or medical supplies or whatever, he didn't care because he was out of there. It passed him on its way back from the castle, just as dawn got under way, and only a couple of metres away but without noticing him by the side of the road.

Gradually, he left the mountains behind him.

He walked along winding, single-track roads, passing a village of Alpine houses that climbed the hills like an illustration on a beer festival poster, only this was the real thing. And after hours of walking, the roads grew larger with separate lanes and traffic that whizzed by in both directions.

And there, at a service station, he stole a truck. Drove it to Innsbruck where he hitched a ride in a red Toyota RAV4. It got him as far as Berlin.

And then everything went wrong.

*

The man he was looking for was called Watkins, the same as her.

His apartment was directly opposite a triangular park in Friedrichshein, one of the parks that had been Stefan Kraus' home for several short periods, and perhaps that was the reason he immediately saw what was right and what wasn't. Along the pavement, two dark cars were parked. Behind the wheel, two men were reading newspapers with feigned nonchalance.

Watkins was under surveillance.

Perhaps they knew that Kraus would come to him; by now they had no doubt discovered that he was missing, perhaps they had made her tell them where he was going, now they were waiting for him here.

And yet it wasn't the cars that made him hesitate. It was the feeling that was growing inside him.

The feeling he'd tried to ignore, the one that had started in the car on the way from Innsbruck, the one he had told himself was just the beginnings of a cold, though he knew deep down that wasn't the case.

So he stayed at a distance. Watched the men that watched the building.

In his hand he held the envelope that would save the world.

That's what she'd called it.

And he was homeless, not an idiot. He knew perfectly well he wouldn't be able to save the world if he infected it at the same time.

∞◯∞

It was morning, but the hour had ceased to matter.

Their TV was on, simply because neither of them could bring themselves to turn it off, it regurgitated the same footage of the hospital and the plane crash and of government officials who wouldn't comment, chewed them over and over like a cow chewing the cud and with less and less substance each time it returned.

'They had slept, but only for short moments, sitting in their armchairs as if lying down would be disrespectful. As if by staying awake they could make a difference, as if everything that had happened could be fixed when the right moment presented itself, and they didn't dare to sleep in case they missed it.

Albert had been waiting in their car when Leo came down from the roof.

Christina was beyond saving. The building had been sealed off and they weren't allowed to get close, but they saw the rescue teams digging and the dogs searching, and she had fallen from a roof and been buried under tons of stone. There wasn't a hope in hell.

And the police had started to ask what they were doing there and Albert had become nervous and finally they'd had to leave.

They'd set off on the A10 and turned east, their only goal being to get out of Amsterdam. And when their eyes started to flicker from exhaustion, the paralysing exhaustion that took over as the adrenalin ran out, when neither of them dared to take the wheel, they'd stopped at a motel and the morning had come and there they sat, exactly as they'd sat down when they came in.

Neither of them had said a word for hours.

And the silence had been replaced by showers starting in the adjacent rooms, feet in the corridors on their way to breakfast, luggage rolling past as people checked out on their journey to new motels on different highways.

Leo was the first to speak. 'I see the Alps.'

Albert looked at him. Knew what he was referring to, said nothing.

Janine's letter. He'd been going over it in his mind, too. The Alps and all the names and find me. And how the hell were they supposed to do that?

'So the one thing we know,' said Leo, 'is that we need to go south.'

'You don't need to do this,' said Albert.

He watched Leo from the side. He was the same young man as yesterday, same hat, same blazer, wrinkled and slightly dated and if you were kind you could say it was a statement, but to be honest it was hideous. But Leo's face had changed. He'd grown. They hadn't known each other for a full day, yet it was as if events had forced him to mature into someone slightly older, slightly more grown-up, slightly more sad.

Either that or he was tired. Which was also a possibility.

'What else would I do?'

Leo's words. Not a complete sentence even now. But it conveyed all that needed to be conveyed, and Albert looked at him, at the weariness in his eyes, his unwashed hair, the curls that might have been styled yesterday but looked as though someone had tossed a toupee on his head and left.

Somehow, it seemed touching in the midst of everything else.

'Did you know her well?' Albert asked.

It was a question Leo hadn't considered. He'd seen her die, he'd been washed out by the shock and all the emotions, and from that moment he'd accepted his role without thinking. No, perhaps he didn't know her. But if he didn't try to finish what she had started, then who would?

No. It was the wrong way to put it. If he didn't do it, then *who* was he?

This was his journey. He was the one who'd found the wire story on Janine, who'd found Albert who in turn was the entire reason they'd travelled to Amsterdam. In a way, that meant that he was the reason that she was dead.

He owed it to her to carry on. To himself *and* to her. And that had nothing to do with how well he'd known her.

'No,' he answered. 'Not knew, not like that, no.'

Albert's turn to talk.

'Let me explain this to you. I've screwed up. I've caused a person's death. The police are after me, they've searched my office, the police and people that I don't know who they are, but who' – and he hesitated for a moment – 'who I think have to do with Janine's disappearance. And if I'm brutally honest, I don't even know what I'm doing.'

Leo nodded. But more to wave it aside than to confirm the truth of what he was hearing; he could tell where Albert was going and that was a place he didn't want to be.

'You're twenty-four,' Albert said. 'You have an internship waiting for you. And you've seen enough in the last twenty-four hours to fill that paper for days on end. And if you're good at it, and I suspect you are, then they will give you a job the moment you ask. Correct me if I'm wrong.'

Leo didn't correct him.

'Of course I'm grateful for what you've done. Without you, without your car, without that I'd never have got out of Amsterdam.

But now you've done your part. I have to go on, I have to find Janine. You don't have to do anything. You can go home.'

Leo may have been exhausted but there was no doubt in his mind as to what he had to do.

He got up. Took out Christina's phone. The one that was his now, after his own disappeared with her. And he turned towards Albert.

'I have a few calls to make. Then we should plan our next move.'

Albert watched Leo open the door to the corridor, leave it ajar, heard the young man's soft steps as he wandered shoeless on the carpet outside. Streams of words in a language Albert couldn't understand.

But whatever he said, his intentions were clear.

Leo Björk wasn't going anywhere.

Albert van Dijk was quite pleased about that.

∞◯∞

The anticipation that Lars-Erik Palmgren felt as Christina Sandberg's name flashed up on his phone was entirely without foundation and he knew it perfectly well.

There was no way she could have survived.

Nevertheless, he felt disappointment hit like a deep hunger below his ribs when the voice at the other end wasn't hers.

'My name is Leo Björk,' said the voice. 'We spoke yesterday.'

'Is she alive?' said Palmgren. It was the only thing he said. It was the only thing he wanted to know.

'No,' said Leo. 'No.'

There could have been better ways to say it. But Leo couldn't think of any. And they both stood silent at their respective ends of the line, a silence that was transformed into ones and zeroes and that streamed in both directions between Stockholm and Amsterdam, filling the air with data that was unpacked at the receiving end and contained nothing.

'I can call back, if, maybe,' said Leo, heard his own words and hoped that logic would fill in the blanks. If this is a bad time.

'I can talk,' said Palmgren.

'I tried to warn her,' Leo said. 'If it helps you to know.'

Palmgren understood. Christina was stubborn, and he doubted she would have listened however much the kid tried to talk her out of it. She'd probably been so intent on the story that she'd have tuned out every word he said.

'Thanks,' he said. For telling me, he meant, and for trying. And maybe he also meant for calling, for not letting him be alone with his feelings, for allowing him to share them over the phone with someone he'd never met but who made things feel a little bit better.

'There's just one question,' said Leo. 'How did you know what was about to happen?'

'I was given the information,' said Palmgren.

'By whom?'

'I don't know. He works in the military. He's high up. Beyond that, I have no idea.'

'And how did *he* know?'

'He works for them.'

'For who?'

'He didn't know,' said Palmgren. Then he corrected himself. 'At least he *said* he didn't know. For what it's worth, I believe him.'

He paused for a moment, wondering how much detail he should go into. It wasn't his job to keep the black-clad man's secrets; if he'd said too much, disclosed confidential information during their conversation in his basement, that was his problem and not Palmgren's. But at the same time he didn't want to put anyone else in danger. He hadn't been able to warn Christina, and that had ended in disaster. He didn't want anyone else to get killed.

On the other hand, if the kid on the phone succeeded in finding William, maybe there was a chance he could work out what was going on, find out what was so unprecedented and terrifying and bad. Should he stand in the way of that?

'What I know is that there is an organisation,' he said. 'He didn't tell me where, because he didn't know, not where or who was behind it or who they reported to. The one thing he was certain of was that he wasn't the only one.'

'The only one who what?'

'Who is *at their disposal*. Those were his precise words. They've got people everywhere. High up. The police. Defence ministries. Probably in governments.'

'And what do they do?'

Palmgren hesitated. 'Leo, right? I want you to listen to me. This man came to me to warn you.'

'But why?' asked Leo. 'Why would he warn us? If he is, you know. One of them?'

Palmgren's answer was simple.

'He was afraid.'

He waited to hear what Leo had to say, but nothing came. What Palmgren said next came out as a plea, which was almost what it was.

'You have to get out of Amsterdam. As far away as possible. Something's happening. That's all I know. Whatever is going on, yesterday was only the beginning.'

'We're already out of Amsterdam,' said Leo.

'I'm not sure that's enough.'

'We'll see.'

It felt like the conversation was over, and it felt like nothing had changed.

The older man had tried to issue a warning but didn't know what he was warning against, the younger man had heard but didn't listen. And if Palmgren were honest with himself he wouldn't have either if their roles had been reversed.

'Can I ask a favour?' he said instead.

Leo waited.

'If you find him. If you find William. Tell him she never gave up on him.' He paused, and then: 'Not because it's what he wants to hear. But because it's true.'

Leo swallowed. 'I know.'

They stood at either end of a telephone line, listening to the breaths of someone they'd never met.

And Palmgren hesitated. There was one more thing. But he'd already said too much.

'The man who visited me,' he said at last. 'He heard them talk about *the disaster.*'

'Amsterdam?' said Leo.

'I don't know. All I know is that they're afraid. Afraid that the solution has gone ... astray.' No. He stopped again. Wanted to relay the man's words as accurately as possible. 'They're afraid that Watkins has the answer.'

It took a moment for Leo to pull the name from the depths of his brain.

It came from the letter. Janine's letter.

'Helena Watkins?' said Leo.

'No,' said Palmgren. 'Saul.'

∞O∞

Someone had seen Stefan Kraus as he exited the station concourse. And the alarm had been raised but it was too late.

His image had been wired out with top priority; nobody knew what he'd done but he must be caught, and his details were forwarded to the right people and the men who were sent out were trained to do as they were told without question.

Stefan Kraus, meanwhile, had carefully avoided human contact.

He knew all the city's alleys and passages, he'd spent most of his life hiding away to protect himself from people. But now the roles were reversed, he was protecting others from himself.

He'd been close to dying before, but this was the first time it scared him. She'd given him two tasks. And he wanted so badly to complete them both.

The heartbreaking message was no longer his problem, he'd given it to the driver of the Toyota and all he could do was to hope the man would keep his promise.

But the yellow envelope remained his responsibility. And nothing was the way it should be; Kraus was back where he'd always been, a man with no options and no future, and someone was chasing him and time was running out faster than ever.

And since he couldn't do what she'd asked him, this was the best alternative.

He ran, empty-handed, zigzagging between the rows of parked cars.

He had left the envelope behind.

It was safe now, perhaps not for ever but at least for the time being, and on his way out of the parking garage he took out the thin, white card he'd stolen from a news stand, dropped it into a mailbox, and when that was done the only thing he could do was to hope. Hope that his shaky writing could be read, that he'd remembered the address correctly, that he hadn't let her down after all and his final act would be something good. That in the end his life would have been meaningful.

The cough and the fever had been possible to explain away.

The itch on his back was maybe just an itch.

But when the blood had come and his skin started to weep as if turning to liquid, he couldn't deny it any longer.

He'd seen them in the long rows of hospital beds. And now he was one of them; he didn't want to die but it wasn't his choice.

That same evening Stefan Kraus was going to be chased into an alley in Berlin, shot by men disguised as paramedics and taken away in an ambulance that wasn't an ambulance.

His body was to be incinerated at an abandoned military firing range at the foot of the Alps.

And the yellow envelope that was supposed to save the world would be locked inside a luggage locker in the basement of Berlin Hauptbahnhof.

And nobody would have a clue.

35

The sounds of the whirring fans echoed with a life past.

That was how it used to sound, every morning when he started up his computers in the imposing stone building in Kungsängen, and here and now the hum from his desk brought everything back.

Sitting down in a battered office chair. Steering its complaining wheels across the plastic floor, taking a careful sip of the white-hot coffee that smelled of morning and possibilities but that only tasted bitter. The sense that he was doing something important, that he was good at what he did, and that even though there was a massive responsibility resting on his shoulders, he was confident he'd be able to do his part.

For a second that's where he was.

And he knew that as soon as he opened his eyes again he'd be far, far away.

William stood in his workroom in the castle. It had only been hours since the last time he was there, but it felt as if he'd just returned from a long trip. He had left the room believing there was a future, and then he'd seen things that rocked the foundations of who he was, now he was back here and he knew that the thing he needed the most was the one thing they didn't have. Time.

He wouldn't be able to work the way he wanted. He would have to cut corners, to push himself through the material, to skip steps in his process and keep his fingers crossed that he would sort it out all the same.

He would have to let the machines do the calculations and it was much too soon for that. He would have wanted to become one with the codes, to spend time with them, working by hand, making them his, getting to know the sequences inside out, and to use the machines as tools instead of unknown black holes that took over and spat out results he couldn't verify.

But there was no time.

In front of him, hard disks whizzed away as the computers started reading, operating systems were loaded and launched and prepared to receive reams of numbers and turn them into something logical.

Last of all, he booted up the heavy, grey-green box at the edge of the table.

Sara.

The familiar crackle from the screen as the cathode-ray tube fired up, shooting its electrons at the curved monitor surface, feeding line after line of text in glowing green as a signal that the machine was gearing up.

It was archaic, to say the least. And yet, this was the machine he was putting most of his trust in. She was old, no doubt, but she was designed for one purpose, and he was the one who'd designed her. If there wasn't time for him to crunch the numbers himself, the next best thing was to give them to her.

It, he corrected himself. It was a computer. And nothing more.

Because if there wasn't time for manual calculations there was even less time to dwell on the past, and he shrugged his thoughts off, stood against the wall, let his eyes wander across the papers one last time.

The codes.

And the verses.

Plague. The end. *A huge and violent fire.*

He tried not to lose his hope, but it wasn't easy.

He'd seen the circles, the circles and the dots on Connors' map, he knew what was written in the predictions and it all made perfect sense. It had begun. And if everything was predetermined, who was he to do anything about it?

There were no answers, all he had was questions, and no matter how many times he asked them he kept coming back to the same conclusion. *It's just the way it is.*

The more he asked, the more childish were the questions, and the more he tried to answer, the clearer it got that it was pointless.

Why? Why were there codes in human DNA?

Who put them there?

Nobody.

It is what it is.

William had seen how it was going to end.

And there was no why.

∞Ọ∞

The cold observation room had become the regular venue for their informal meetings.

Now they found themselves standing there again, Connors and Franquin, staring at the hospital beds on the other side of the glass. Fewer bleeding bodies than yesterday, more than there would be tomorrow. Time was running out in front of their eyes, running in red trickles on to the floor, and there was nothing they could do about it.

There was a question hanging in the air, waiting for an answer, but Connors avoided it, his gaze straight ahead.

'We shouldn't have brought in civilians,' Connors said. 'That was our first mistake.'

Franquin said nothing.

'We should've brought in professionals,' he continued. 'Should have let them work directly *with* us, given them the details, let them know what they were here to do—'

Franquin raised his hand. Five fingers and a palm, telling Connors to shut up.

'Did you just get here?' he asked. 'What would you call Helena Watkins?'

'Helena Watkins was a gamble,' said Connors.

'Quite. And how do you think that went?' He didn't wait for Connors to answer. 'She couldn't handle it. She was a big mistake. If it hadn't been for her—'

He broke off mid-sentence. A moment's insecurity. And Connors pounced.

'Are you sure about that?' he said. 'If it hadn't been for her?'

Franquin turned away. But Connors wouldn't let him go:

'If only it hadn't been for *us!* If it hadn't been for you and for me, then she would never have come here. There wouldn't have been a homeless man to release, and he wouldn't have been infected, because nobody would have manufactured a virus and tested it on him in the hope that the exact thing she started could be stopped.'

His voice had risen, frustrated as much by the reality as the constant need to use it as an argument.

And Franquin shook his head. It was irrelevant.

It was *her* who broke the protocols, predetermined or not. She was the one who'd taken advantage of her freedom, abused her knowledge of routines and schedules and security, and as a result, she had released the virus. Even if that hadn't been her intention, even if she hadn't known that he was sick, she'd still broken every single rule in the book. And that was her doing.

Then she'd given Haynes her key card, enabling her to send a letter to her boyfriend. And who knew what more she could have done if they hadn't stopped her in time.

All this he said to Connors.

'And if that doesn't prove that Watkins was one massive mistake?' Franquin said. 'If that doesn't prove the danger of giving people knowledge and freedom and responsibility? Then I don't know what kind of proof you need.'

Connors gave a deep sigh.

'It doesn't matter now,' he said. 'Because even if she managed to find something out, even if she found a solution, she took it to her grave.'

'*Hopefully,*' said Franquin. And then: 'We'll see about that.'

With that, their discussion ended. They both knew what she had done, and there was little point in arguing about it.

And when Franquin started talking again, he was talking as much to himself as to Connors:

'We're not where we used to be. We're in a hurry. If this had been ten years ago, or twenty, we could have kept going. But we can't. What we need is results. And not a happy workplace.'

Then he turned to Connors. 'So, do I have your approval?'

'Do I have a choice?' said Connors.

'No,' said Franquin. There was sadness in his eyes too. 'No, not any more.'

Connors didn't move. Not a yes, not a no.

And that was enough.

They didn't part as friends, but on the other hand, they'd never been friends. They'd been colleagues, and there'd been times when they'd been colleagues who pulled in the same direction, but they'd always looked at the world through different lenses. And in times of crisis that was clearer than ever.

The message would go out the following night.

Connors had given his unspoken approval. And now he remained in the room, staring at the rows of beds beyond the glass. And he knew.

Knew that none of the people in there had much time left.

Unless William could come up with something, unless they could devise a new virus to test and to place their hope in, unless that happened, everything was lost.

All previous attempts had ended in failure. What Franquin had said before he left was undeniably true.

'In three days we'll know if the virus is still out there.' That's what he'd said. 'And if Sandberg hasn't found a cipher key by then?'

His voice had been dry. Underlining what they both knew already. That the chances of that were slim to none.

'If he hasn't, then stage two is in effect.'

And Franquin had turned and walked out into the corridor. Closed the door behind him.

Connors knew that Franquin was right.

They couldn't wait any longer.

∞◯∞

William spent hours feeding the data into his computers, and then waiting for them to process the sequences he'd been staring at for days.

And nothing changed.

No matter how clever computers might be, they lacked intuition. They chewed on the numbers for hours without finding anything new.

After that, he opened Helena Watkins' files.

He read her notes for the first time from beginning to end, and it was like reading his own mind. Every set-up, every formula and arrow and equation trying to deduce one thing from another, everything that she'd written he had either already thought himself or soon would. She fumbled with the exact same things as him and that could mean only one thing.

He was wasting time.

So long as he was treading the same path as all the people who'd been there before him, he was never going to come up with anything new. And knowing this, William couldn't stand it when anyone asked how things were going.

'You *know* how it's going,' he said.

No, not said, he barked it, and his eyes were dark, not just from rage but from sorrow and sadness and frustration and everything else.

Janine had just come in, and her question had been benign and friendly.

But William snapped.

'You sat right next to me, didn't you? You saw it as clearly as I did. Everything is going to shit, that's how things are going, *full steam ahead* to shit and there's nothing I can do about it.'

He threw out his arms, a gesture so melodramatic he might as well have been a character in an opera, and he felt it himself the moment he did it but couldn't bring himself to care. If his anger seemed comedic, then so be it.

And once the floodgate was opened, there was no turning it off. Everything came out, the frustrations over his own inadequacy, frustrations that turned into accusations, as if it was her fault the code looked the way it did and that everything was too late and that he wouldn't be able to stop it, just as he hadn't been able to stop the things that had happened already, and he counted on his fingers as he spoke: the airliner, the hospital, Christina, and then he became quiet because his voice began to crack.

And Janine stood there. Looked at him.

And got it.

Somehow, she'd let herself believe that she was as upset as him. That they were just as shocked, because they'd seen the same things. And if only she'd allowed herself to think.

If only she had, she would have known.

His grief was immeasurably greater. He was under pressure and it wasn't from her, it was from life. But you can't shout at life, and she happened to be the one who was around.

'You couldn't have known,' she said. 'There was nothing you could have done.'

'It was my *job*!' he shouted. 'My job is to know, my job is to do something, that's the entire reason I'm here! And if I can't do that, then what the hell am I here for?'

She remained silent, there was nothing for her to say.

And his voice dropped a notch.

'Every single time something happens in my life it's not my fault. Every single time, people tell me I have to stop blaming myself, that there wasn't anything I could have done, and there was no way I could have known. Do you have any idea how tired I am of hearing that?'

She didn't move.

'*Every single time*?' She said it softly. 'I didn't know there were more. Talk to me.'

His answer rolled out like a rumbling of thunder. A grown man's sorrows but a five-year-old's dissent. 'Why? So that you can be the caring, listening, human ear who'll offer words of advice and restore me? So you can walk out of this room and feel good about yourself? I've been to see people like that in the past, and it doesn't help.'

'No,' she said. 'Not that. But because I see someone who's carrying a weight. And I'm sorry.' Still calm and steady, soft but sharp and without releasing him from her gaze. 'I'm so terribly sorry, but sometimes when you see someone carrying a burden that's too heavy for them, you can't help asking whether you can help share the load.'

He shook his head.

And it began gently, just as sadly and softly as she had spoken, but his voice grew as he talked and he let it. He let the intensity build until he roared, until something burned behind his eyes, and he didn't know what it was but he didn't intend to stop talking.

Because who the hell was she? Who was she to tell him how he felt? To ask him questions about his wife, about his daughter? What did she know – exactly, *not a fuck* was what she knew – and what help was she, standing there, pretending?

It poured out of him like a torrent, a hurt and offended and infected torrent, and it felt good to let it out, felt good to blame someone else, felt good to roar as if Janine was the author of his misery, as if she had created it retroactively in one single moment. And he knew it wasn't true, knew that he'd regret yelling at her, but here and now it felt unbearably, painfully good and he had no intention of stopping.

'She died,' he bellowed, his voice full of anger and accusation and are you happy now, huh, are you? 'My daughter died, and I didn't see it coming, I should have but I couldn't. I wasn't there when it happened. I couldn't do anything until it was too late. And then I couldn't let it go and that destroyed my life. Mine and Christina's, and now she's gone too and is that a weight you'd like to carry for me? Is that how good you are? That you can just take that weight and carry it for a couple of blocks and then everything will be fine again?'

Nobody can shout for ever. There comes a point when you hear your own voice, when you have to change gears again. And William had reached that point. He clenched his jaw, nothing more to say, and if the outburst was intoxication and regret was hangover, then he was already sobering up.

He didn't want to sober up. Blaming someone else suited him fine. And he threw out his arms again, waved at her to leave, get out of here before everything stops being your fault. Go before it's mine again.

But Janine stayed. Looked at him. No anger. Sadness, yes, but not for herself. She was sad for his sake. For the man who stood in front of her, who'd just yelled at her, thousands of things he really wanted to yell to himself but couldn't. The man she hadn't known for a week but who felt closer to her than people she'd known for years.

The man who'd just told her off, even though she saw he didn't mean it.

And their eyes met. And both of them knew. Knew that he would tell her how sorry he was, not now, but some time, and they both knew that she would understand, that she would have for-given and understood long before he started to explain.

And all of that was said between them without a single word.

Then she turned and left the room, and for the first time in as long as he could remember, William sat in a chair and cried.

36

There wasn't just one message but many.

Written long ago, waiting in sealed envelopes in a safe, and dif-ferent envelopes had different labels and held different scenarios that Connors had devised years before.

It felt like another time.

No, another world, that's what it felt like, a world that was still out there somewhere, where all of this wasn't happening and could be viewed from afar as if it were a game of chess, and then every-one could eat their dinner and perhaps grab a whisky and sleep a good night's sleep.

Yet somehow they had all stepped over into this world. The world that was unthinkable and mustn't happen. This was now their reality, and Franquin thumbed through the envelopes, looking for the right one.

It was large and thick and weighed at least a couple of pounds.

Scenario Zero.

That's what it said on the outside, and they had sealed it and stored it with the others, hoping that they would never have to open any of them again.

Especially not this one.

He placed it on the table, put the others back in the safe and locked it.

Stared at the envelope in front of him, as if it were a time capsule he'd sent to himself. He could still recall the moment when they'd sealed it, him and Connors, in this very office. He remembered the gravity they'd felt, but also the hope. The knowledge that they were discussing a distant future, so distant that it didn't seem to exist. Yet here he stood and the future was unfolding right in front of his eyes. And the now they had been in back then, the one that had been so natural and present and real, that now was suddenly so distant and remote it was as if it had never really happened.

That's how it worked. Time.

It passed.

And there wasn't much to be done about it.

Franquin stayed still for several minutes, looking at the heavy envelope and knowing what had to happen next.

He would break the seal. Tear the protective paper open.

Inside, there'd be neat stacks of smaller envelopes, labelled with names and addresses and each one would contain a set of numbers.

And those numbers would go out to the addressees.

And then there would only be one way forward.

∞◯∞

Connors stepped out through the heavy wooden door, out into the cold of the terrace, wearing only his thin military jacket, even though the air was ice cold and full of crystals that were neither snow nor rain but something in between.

He came and stood next to William, leaned against the banister alongside him, as if he just wanted a breath of air, as if he simply couldn't resist getting out into the biting afternoon wind to gaze at the view for no specific reason.

Of course it was nothing of the sort. He was there because they knew William had yelled at her.

And now they were wondering how he was. Not because they cared but because they were afraid that William was losing his grip.

The two men exchanged glances. A wordless hello, formal and correct. And Connors asked if William needed anything, or if they could help him with anything, or if he'd come up with anything new.

And William replied as Connors expected, which boiled down to no and no thanks and unfortunately not. And that was it. They fell silent, and then it was William's turn to talk.

They both stood for a while, leaning against the stone balustrade, watching the mountains and the lake as the wind kept whipping its nameless crystals in their faces.

'Are you worried about me?' he asked.

'You make it sound like a bad thing.'

'That depends. Whether you're worried about me. Or just worried I won't finish the job.'

Connors cocked his head, the gesture a smile of sorts. 'Couldn't it be both?' he said.

'Thirty years,' William said, avoiding the question. His eyes fixed on the lake and the peaks in the distance.

Connors glanced at him. Didn't know what he was getting at.

'That's how long you've been here. Right? Thirty years.'

Oh. Yes. Connors nodded.

'How do you manage?'

It took a moment for Connors to grasp what he meant. Again, he had to remind himself that William had been there less than a week. Events had unfolded so unbelievably quickly over the last couple of days that it felt as though months had passed rather than days, but William hadn't had time to adjust. And how could he be expected to?

Connors wasn't sure how to answer.

He cast his mind back to his early days there, when the knowledge had overwhelmed him so completely that he couldn't think. When panic took turns with apathy, when everything had lost its meaning and when their work didn't lead them anywhere. And the simple truth was that he hadn't managed. But he'd realised that he would have to manage, and step by step he'd found a way.

And the years had passed.

Years had passed, and now here they were, and even if he'd always known the end was coming he'd clung to the hope that it wouldn't. And he continued to cling to that hope. As hard as it was.

'One gets used to it,' he said.

'You think there'll be time for me to do that?' said William. He smiled a wry smile.

It occurred to Connors he'd never seen William smile, at least like this, for real and without anger and with a sincere, warm irony. He felt a pang in his chest. The man beside him could have been a friend. Someone to share a beer with, or play darts or whatever people in the real world did nowadays, if only things weren't what they were and they hadn't been trapped here.

He wanted to give him a good answer. But there wasn't one.

'I'll let you get back to work,' was all he said. Because what else was there?

And Connors stood up, and moved towards the door.

'You were wrong,' said William behind him.

He'd turned, the clouds and the mountains and the wind in his back now, a sad gaze that met Connors', honest and new and full of pain.

'Wrong?' said Connors.

'Our first meeting. In the big hall, with the table and the chandelier with the projectors. You said that the thing that mattered most to me? The thing that keeps me going? You said it was people.'

Connors raised an eyebrow. 'Yes?' he said.

'You were wrong.'

He, who couldn't stand people. Who would walk in the rain to avoid a crowded bus, who would cross the road to avoid a party of schoolchildren. He who liked it best when he was left to his own company and who was more and more certain every year that other people were a necessary evil, annoying extras in the movie that was his life, obstacles that interfered and got in his way and stopped him on the street to sell him things he didn't need.

And yet. Here he was. Suddenly wanting nothing but to hold them. All of them.

All those people he didn't know, who wouldn't stop annoying him with their existence, who were there only because it would be so much harder to run the world by himself, even if he'd increasingly often found himself thinking he wouldn't mind trying.

All of them.

Suddenly he wanted to do all he could to keep them alive. He wanted to shake them and shout that they were in danger; he wanted to tell them he'd take care of it, that he didn't know how but that he would find a way to stop it, for their sake, for his own, for everybody's sake at once.

He said it with eyes that didn't leave Connors', with a face so void of feelings there was no mistaking how much sorrow it tried to hide.

'Try to make sense of that if you can,' William said.

And Connors smiled at him. A warm smile, a smile between

friends, or at least from a man who could see right through the other and who saw that the inside wasn't as bad as everyone thought.

'It's simple,' said Connors. 'We weren't the ones who were wrong. You were.'

Connors, by the door. William, by the banister.

Two men that could have been friends.

And for a moment he was back again, William, back in his old life, the one with the plastic floors and the same computers as now but considerably worse coffee, the feeling of chatting with a colleague and that his job was important but manageable, and that life as a whole wasn't too bad.

'Even if I do manage to find the perfect cipher key,' William began, 'and even if your friends down there in those steel tunnels use it to make a new virus and spread it throughout the world? How can we be sure that it will help? It's still not a vaccine against the virus that's already out there.'

A moment of silence.

'Isn't it?' Connors said. 'If humanity is carrying a predetermined schedule. And if we manage to change that schedule in time. Wouldn't that, then, be a cure in itself?'

'But how can we know it'll spread fast enough? How do we know the one that's out there won't kill the new, good one? And what if my key isn't any good either, and there are suddenly two viruses out there, turning into purple circles all over the world and killing people? Then what?'

Connors took a deep breath. 'The honest answer,' he said, 'to all your questions.'

'Yes?'

'I don't know.'

His voice was so thin his words blended in with the wind and the snow, and for a moment there was no telling what was Connors and what was air, and somehow that felt perfectly natural.

Then he sighed, broke away from the silence, and summoned his poise and clarity again.

'But I do know what happens if we don't try.'

William nodded. It was that simple.

There were no guarantees, but they had nothing to lose, nothing except time. And he knew he had to keep working until there was nothing left to try.

Connors was about to leave the terrace when he turned in the doorway to answer the question William had forgotten he'd asked.

'I write a diary,' he said.

William peered at him, bemused.

'How I manage. How I've been able to survive all these years. That's the best answer I've got.'

Connors shrugged. It had never been a conscious choice, it had simply happened, one day he'd started to write, and it was nothing but a flow of thoughts, and it shouldn't have made a difference to him and yet somehow it did.

'Why?' asked William.

'I don't know,' said Connors.

Opened the door again, turned for the second time, half of him already well inside and obscured by the darkness of the stairwell.

'It just seemed so much better than doing nothing.'

∞◯∞

William returned to his office, and he sat there as the gloomy daylight rotated across the mountains, grey and shadowless enough to sink into dusk without making any difference. For William, night came before he noticed it, not aware until it was already pitch-dark.

Another day gone.

Another one wasted.

The codes hung on the walls, notepads lay open and computers hummed, sombrely behind screens with rows of numbers but without having come a single step closer to a key or a solution or whatever could help them getting ahead.

He'd wasted a day. And he had a very finite supply of them.

On his desk lay all the books and papers they'd brought from his apartment. And he walked up to it, sifted through them, searching. If they'd brought everything, what he was looking for should be there too. And he rifled through essays and scraps and documents, memories of his own life that hit him one after the other, until at last he found it.

The notebook was black and its pages were white without lines or squares. It had a leather cover and a ribbon for a bookmark, and he knew perfectly well there was nothing special about it.

Or, that it *shouldn't* be anything special.

If only things hadn't been so stubbornly etched into his memory. She.

How she stood by his bed as he pretended to wake up, how she held the parcel out towards him, disproportionately proud and with eyes glowing with anticipation. Glowing because she'd watched him working at his desk, writing notes by hand, and glowing with the pride that she'd come up with the idea herself, and spent her own money on getting to be a part of his life even when he was busy working.

She had been five and William had still been a happy man. And he'd opened the parcel, exchanging hidden glances with Christina, smiles that played in the corner of their eyes but that mustn't be seen. She had stood behind their daughter's back, and of course she'd already told him what Sara had bought, and of course he overacted and was much happier than the situation called for, and of course that was everything a five-year-old girl needed to bubble with joy.

And at the time, that was all it was.

It was a notebook. Nothing more. That, and wrapping paper that rustled between her pyjama-clad legs and the sheets of the double bed as Sara clambered up and hugged him, hugged him clumsily with short arms, wished him a happy birthday and beamed and was happy the way only a child can be.

That was all.

But as time passed and the distance grew it became a moment that he'd never get back.

It became the image of a life he wanted to remember but that didn't exist, a frozen point in time that he wanted to step into and say all the things that he never got to, the things he didn't know then but would experience later. And the image kept dangling in front of his eyes, always close and within sight but always distant and impossible to reach.

And all that in a little black book.

That's what it represented.

Here he stood, holding it in his hand. Felt its structure, the black leather that had dried over the years. Aged. Changed. As one does.

And then, finally, he folded it open. Weighed the pen in his hand, put it to the paper.

Nothing would ever make me keep a diary.

Those were the first words he wrote.

37

The night train from Munich to Berlin left shortly before ten, right on time.

The young family who'd just checked in to their little compartment were tired but happy in spite of everything – their holiday hadn't gone as expected, but eventually they had ended up where they wanted and got to see everyone they'd planned to see. And now they would visit Berlin for a few days before returning home.

Home. The very mention of it made them anxious.

Only three days ago they'd missed their train out of town after being caught up in the crash on the A9.

And that was bad enough for two adults. But when you're four and seven and full of expectations, your cousins are more important than any car crash in the world. And the journey to Munich had had to be by air and it had cost them a fortune but what can you do.

While they were there, all hell broke loose. They sat in the cosy armchairs in their relatives' warm home in front of the TV and saw their hometown reduced to ruins, twice in one day. Amsterdam had experienced the inexplicable, and they had been lucky not to be there, but that didn't help. The knowledge of what awaited them at home, the idea that there'd be people they might never see again, all those thoughts were impossible to shake.

But children are children. And life is what happens here and now. And there was no point in dwelling on what awaited them once they got home.

Everything was an adventure, and sleeping on a train was the biggest adventure of all; with sparkling eyes they charmed their way up and down the aisle, talked to the conductor clipping their tickets, to the lady in the dining car who sold them their sweets, and to all the passengers who simply had to be informed about how exciting this trip was going to be.

Eventually the young parents had led their children back to their compartment, tired but happy and with apologetic smiles on their faces.

In their compartment, the blankets had been cool and the bunks soft.

And there, they had settled down to sleep.

Eleven hours later, at eight minutes to nine in the morning, the train would arrive at Berlin Hauptbahnhof as planned. And nothing would seem out of the ordinary, people would alight and peer into the morning light and wander off, and nobody would stop to think about the compartment where the curtains remained drawn and the door closed.

Not until almost an hour later.

When the cleaners turned their keys in the lock and stepped inside to do their job.

∞◯∞

The operation labelled Scenario Zero had become a running joke.

They called it a staff benefit.

Of course it was merely a way of coping with the terrifying prospect, the doomsday scenario that would make the operation come into effect, the horrifying reality behind their being part of a group to be saved when the rest of humanity died.

There was nothing in the protocols that was the least bit amusing. And consequently, the only way to deal with them was with humour.

Now that the joke was a reality, it wasn't funny any more.

The orders were given at an impromptu meeting. The entire staff was there, from commanders to guards to medical personnel, fifty-four people gathering in the parliament, the air fizzing with nerves.

Everyone knew what the announcement would be.

And even so, the news created stress and confusion and raised hands and thousands of questions. It didn't matter how long anyone had worked for the Organisation, three years or thirty or anything in between, the things that were happening were huge and terrifying and paralysing. Scenario Zero had entered its first phase. And that was the final proof they had lost control.

The orders were tailored to each individual.

And there was no time to waste.

Assets were to be gathered and packed, provisions and medicine and work material.

Personal belongings were to be sorted and selected, their space would be limited but nobody knew what awaited them, and if they were to survive without going crazy they needed some connection to their old lives. Nobody knew how long they'd be away, and *if* they managed to avoid the pandemic it would all be for nothing if they suffered mental collapse in the process.

Connors had written the manual. And in theory, he'd been proud of it. But in reality he stood in the blue parliament in front of everyone else, ran through the orders and wished that he didn't have to.

Around him everyone listened.

Everyone, except for the infected, those who lay in their beds and who'd be left behind when everyone else was gone.

And except for the two civilians.

It was a shame, but that was the way he'd written the protocols.

And as much as he hated it, there was nothing to be done.

Because if reality were logical and obvious one wouldn't need to write scenarios in advance.

When the meeting was over, the work began. The stressful and nervous process of putting the plan into action.

Guards. Medical staff. Researchers and commanders.

They all prepared.

Packed and ran and hurried around.

Fumbled and scurried and followed protocol.

Worked with the knowledge of inescapable terror hanging over them.

And the joke about employee benefits had ceased to be funny.

Saul Watkins was a thin man, but he hadn't always been.

His jacket hung across his chest. Underneath it a shirt was loosely draped over his shoulders, tucked into trousers that had a significantly larger circumference than his waist, everything gathered by a belt until his trousers hung in folds like wrinkled curtains in the home of a deceased relative. He looked as if he'd been washed at the wrong temperature, and that he was the only one who hadn't noticed.

He'd lost weight. A lot, and in a short time. He looked like a man who'd endured something that had taken its toll on his health.

Which was exactly what had happened.

Saul Watkins turned off from the tree-lined avenue and cut across the open area in front of the parliament building, crossed the yellow lawns toward the footbridge and the ultra-modern building across the river.

He was out in the open, and completely visible. Which was intentional.

If he was being followed, they couldn't miss him.

But on the other hand, he would also see them.

It would be virtually impossible to tail him across the open space, in between the buildings and out on to the next, impossible without him noticing.

He stopped on the bridge. Watched the thin ice trying to cover the surface but breaking and cracking open somewhere else as it did. He gazed at the water, his face full of sorrows and pondering, a sad widower taking a walk in search of some new meaning in life.

But on the inside, his mind was on high alert. He searched for faces he recognised, men who stood alone or walked aimlessly or seemed to be waiting for nothing at all. Men like the ones who had appeared outside his home, those who'd watched his front door and who simply had to be connected to everything else that had happened, he just didn't know how and he was afraid to find out.

Her postcards had kept coming for a long time.

They were short and plain, there was no doubt that someone else read them and made sure she only wrote what she was allowed to, but all the same they were from her and that gave him some comfort. He missed her terribly, but she said she was doing well and what more could he ask for.

Then they stopped coming.

And then *they* appeared.

The men. In their cars. They waited outside his house, didn't follow him when he left his home in the morning, but they'd be sitting there when he came home at night. As if they were looking for someone else, but why should they be?

Then, one day, they weren't there. And shortly after, he received the news.

His wife had died in an accident.

And the cars on the street were gone, but it was too implausible to assume they had stopped watching him. They were around somewhere, he refused to believe otherwise, and the thin white envelope that had arrived at his office had left him more convinced than ever that he was a pawn in a game he didn't understand, a game he was desperate to get out of as soon as humanly possible.

He stood on the bridge, watched the ice grow and crack, and eventually he decided that nobody was following him. He straightened up, carried on across the river, over to the glass structure on the other side.

In his pocket he had the note from the thin envelope.

All he wanted was to get rid of it.

Something was happening, and he didn't know what, only that it scared him and that he didn't want any part of it.

He hoped the two men who'd contacted him from their car en route from Amsterdam might be able to help him with that.

38

Night travelled across the globe, just as it always did. But for those who had waited, and who saw what was happening, it was one of the longest nights of their lives.

In different corners of different offices in different countries, men and occasional women paced nervously, alone behind different closed doors but with the same international news on TV screens in front of them. And none of them knew everything, but they were all capable of putting two and two together.

The Organisation that had contacted them.

The obscure instructions they'd received.

The years that had passed, and the task that had almost been forgotten.

And then today.

In different corners of different offices in parliaments and governmental buildings and defence headquarters, men and occasional women paced and didn't know but could perfectly well guess.

They'd received their envelopes with numbers. And they'd opened their old instructions.

And then they had started to understand.

What had happened was just the beginning.

It was time to prepare.

And now they all waited for a phone call none of them wanted to receive.

39

'I think they killed her,' he said.

He looked between Leo and Albert and all the heads that moved around them, his eyes darting as if he was a bird looking for food and Berlin Hauptbahnhof was a buffet table where someone might show up at any moment and shoo him away.

Above them, steel and glass arched into a cathedral of thousands of windows, a gigantic greenhouse where people moved from shop to shop like insects between flowers as they waited for trains to come and go and take them somewhere else.

The clock showed a little after nine.

It was the beginning of the working day, and there were people everywhere.

And Saul Watkins was one of them, invisible in the crowd, one more man who'd run a few errands and decided to break for a coffee; an ordinary, invisible man, nothing to make him stand out from the crowd.

Even so, he was nervous. In fact, he was scared. And he was full of sorrow – on the plate in front of him lay a factory-made sandwich that would go uneaten, the same way every other meal had gone uneaten the past few weeks. It was a prop in a performance, nothing more, the detail that would complete the image and show that this was merely a breakfast, and that would stop him from sticking out.

He didn't want to get involved. But on the other hand, he knew he already was.

'Who are *they*?' Albert asked.

Watkins shook his head. He didn't know. All he could tell them was that *they* had employed his wife, *they* had come to watch his home, *they* had called him on his phone with a short and formal notice that his wife had died in an accident.

His wife. She was fifteen years younger than him, but nobody ever noticed, or at least during all the time they'd been married he'd never heard anyone comment on it. They were both professors, he had a doctor's degree and she had two, they both worked at the University of Potsdam but in different disciplines. He was a scholar of humanities and literature; he knew nothing about numbers but everything about what feelings you get from eating a madeleine cake and how to describe it in as many pages as possible. And she was a theorist. Systematic and logic to the backbone. It had been unthinkable for such disparate characters to come together, and even more unthinkable that they should enjoy each other's company. And yet they had been happily married for twenty years.

'And then,' he concluded. 'Then it happened. *They* happened.'

There was a brief pause.

'Theorist?' said Albert. 'What discipline?'

'Advanced mathematics. Codes, ciphers. She carried on teaching at the university, but in her spare time she developed a new commercial encryption system for transferring data over the web.' An ironic smile played about his lips but died long before it reached his eyes. 'She taught me to say that. The only words I understand in that sentence are the prepositions.'

Albert leaned over. 'Have you heard of a William Sandberg?'

Saul shook his head.

'Do you think your wife could have known him? Do you know if she's ever done any work for any military organisation?'

'What are you saying?' asked Watkins. 'Do *you* know who they are?'

Albert's turn to shake his head. And Watkins peered at him:
'So who is William Sandberg?'

Albert stopped and explained it as economically as he could.
William. Janine. The letter from Janine, the one where she'd mentioned Saul's wife. The disappearances and the dark-suited men in
Amsterdam.

Saul listened and nodded. '*They.*'

And then it went quiet.

'There are differences that puzzle me,' Albert said after a while.

Watkins and Leo both looked at him and waited.

'Your wife was recruited,' he said.

'She went voluntarily. But they kept her there against her will.'

'How do you know that?'

'The advantage of studying literature. You get rather good at
reading between the lines.' Another smile that didn't arrive. And he
clarified himself: 'We had contact. Not every day, but she sent me
postcards. Impersonal, brief postcards talking about the weather.
Literally. And if there's one thing we never talked about, it was
weather. It meant that she was alive, but it also meant that someone
was stopping her from writing what she wanted.

'Postmarked Bern?' said Albert.

Watkins looked up at him. 'Sometimes,' he said. 'Sometimes
Bern, sometimes Innsbruck, sometimes Milan. Never from the
same place twice in a row. If there was a pattern, I never saw it.'

'And everywhere, you see Alps.'

It was Leo speaking. He was already holding Christina's phone,
a map on the screen, and he pinched and dragged and moved it
over the screen to find a centre point between the three locations.

'At least it gives us something to go on. Somewhere here.'

Saul gave an exasperated sigh. 'Which tells us exactly nothing.
There, somewhere. But *where?*'

The moment he saw Leo's eyes, he lowered his voice again.

'I'm sorry. It's just that I've been having those exact same
thoughts for a year now.'

They sat amid the constant buzz of voices, the rattle of trains that
arrived and braked and left, tracks and times that were announced
over speakers and died away in echoes long before anyone heard
what had been said.

Albert leaned forward.

'Could there be anything else you know? Perhaps without being aware of it?'

'Such as?'

'I don't know. But it seems to me that's what they're afraid of.'

'*They*? Afraid?'

'Yes, afraid. They fear a disaster, and they think you might be holding the answer.'

Watkins looked around him in all directions before he spoke. 'Like I said,' he repeated, 'I know nothing.'

Emphasis on *nothing*. His eyes sincere. And yet, something didn't ring true.

'In that case,' said Albert, 'why are you afraid?'

'Because I don't want them to *think* I know something.'

His voice was steady, but his eyes were glued to theirs. He was leaning towards them, his hand halfway across the table.

And there, under his fingers, his thin, skinny fingers where the joints were the only parts that hadn't shrunk, bulging like beads on a string, under those fingers lay a shiny square of paper.

That's right, his eyes said. *Take it.*

He removed his hand, eyes still fixed on Leo and Albert, his face dramatic and serious as if what he had handed over wasn't just a piece of paper but something of major significance.

And Albert placed his hand over it, pulled it towards his side of the table, a brief glance before he slipped it into his inside jacket pocket.

A barcode. That's all he could make out. Small, printed letters, a time and perhaps a price and perhaps something more.

'I got a letter,' Watkins said. His voice a whisper, as if he was about to tell them a secret nobody else could know. 'Two days before they phoned me and told me she'd passed away, perhaps more, I don't know, my days keep floating together. A thin, white envelope, messy handwriting on the outside. As if . . . '

'As if what?' said Albert.

'As if the person who wrote it hadn't written anything for a long, long time.'

He hesitated. Perhaps it was an insignificant detail. But to him it was one of all the things he didn't understand; what he knew for a fact was that someone had tried to communicate with him. And whatever that person had to say, he didn't want to hear.

'No letter. No message. Just that.' He indicated Albert's chest: the piece of paper.

'It's a receipt,' said Albert. 'Isn't it? A receipt from a luggage locker?'

Watkins looked at him. Avoided the question.

And that was an obvious yes.

'I'm almost seventy,' he said. 'My wife is dead. And I'm afraid.'

He indicated Albert's pocket again.

'Whatever it is,' he said, 'it's nothing to do with me now.'

∞○○∞

The man in the black suit hadn't expected to see Saul Watkins. And yet there he was.

Twenty minutes earlier he'd been standing in his spot at the bottom of the escalators, one floor below street level and seemingly fully occupied with the timetables and station maps but in reality scrutinising everyone who descended to his level.

He registered every face, every encounter or change of direction, and yet at first he hadn't noticed. As if his brain had refused to accept what it saw.

Watkins. It really was him.

His head had passed by among all the other heads up there, bobbing past on its way from the entrance and on into the hall, and then it had disappeared back into the crowd. And the dark-suited man had rushed up the stairs, squeezing between suitcases and shopping bags to catch another glimpse of him.

All the time his only thought had been that it couldn't be.

There had to be some other explanation. It had to be a coincidence, because if not he couldn't string it together.

Less than a week ago they'd seen the homeless man leave the Hauptbahnhof. They'd chased him for miles until he ran into that alley they took him down.

But the documents he should've had with him were gone.

The documents that he was supposed to deliver to Saul Watkins, but that for whatever reason he hadn't.

And there was only one logical conclusion.

That this had been the reason Stefan Kraus had gone to the station.

To leave the documents in a luggage locker.

And that left two options, as far as he could tell. The first was that he'd put them there as some sort of life insurance, perhaps intending to retrieve them later or to use them to bargain his way out of being killed. If that had been his plan, it hadn't succeeded.

But it also meant that things would sort themselves out. A week would pass and the locker would automatically alert the lost property department that its time had run out. And in that event the staff had clear instructions: if any locker was found to contain a bundle of documents, perhaps but not necessarily in a thick yellow envelope, and perhaps but not necessarily addressed to a Saul Watkins, there was a number for them to call, whereupon the documents would immediately be collected by himself or one of his colleagues.

The second option was the problematic one. And that was the reason he was standing here, the reason he'd raced up the escalator, the reason he had to find out what in heaven's name Saul Watkins was doing at the Hauptbahnhof.

Stefan Kraus hadn't been carrying a receipt. And that had worried them.

It worried them because on his way from the lockers to the street he'd passed at least three postboxes. It was perfectly possible that he could have mailed the receipt to someone, and that was why they'd been keeping the station under surveillance.

In case that someone would show up.

In case that someone would walk down to the lockers and remove something that looked like a bundle of documents.

It was just so unthinkable that that someone would be Watkins.

They'd been monitoring his mail, both at home and in his department at the university, and there was no way any communication had slipped below their radar. He couldn't have received a receipt. It was utterly inconceivable.

Of course it could all be a coincidence. He might just be here to do some shopping, or to buy a ticket, but coincidences rarely happened by chance, as the man used to say. And whatever the reason, Saul Watkins was at Berlin Hauptbahnhof. That, in itself, was enough.

His instructions were clear and there was only one thing to do.

The man in the suit had taken out his phone. Called the first number on his speed dial.

The others would arrive in a couple of minutes, and then they would take it from there.

40

She expected to find him in his workroom, but not until Janine gave up and knocked on the door to William's bedroom did he open the door and let her in.

Janine was breathless. She closed the door behind her, scanned the area from wall to wall to make sure they were alone.

It took her a moment to notice that William was only half-dressed. Jeans, T-shirt, he'd had a shower but he hadn't shaved, and that was when she knew. Something had happened within him. He was on the verge of giving up, the energy she'd seen in his eyes was fading, and she couldn't allow that to happen, not now.

'Put on a jacket,' she said. 'We need to talk.'

She leaned towards the window, lifted the clasps that held it closed, and the moment the wind grabbed the window and swung it open he realised she was right. It was freezing.

The air was full of tiny crystals that might well have piled up into snow if only the wind hadn't been so strong. They whirled into the room instead, dancing past the windows with a whine that went from toneless rumble to a whistle and back to a toneless rumble again.

'What are you doing?' he said.

'I don't know if they can hear us in here,' she said, gesturing for him to come closer. She kept her voice low enough that the wind would drown her words, so that *if* there was anyone listening they would only hear the sounds of someone being stupid enough to open a window.

'What's happened?' he said, still in his T-shirt.

'Not happened,' she said. 'Happening. It's happening right now.'

∞◯∞

The door had been open for only a couple of seconds, long enough to admit one of the guards. But that was enough for Janine to catch a glimpse of the buzz of activity going on in the high-security corridor.

Crates were being loaded on to carts, uniformed men were taking inventory, checking off lists. The door had closed again before she could see more, but she'd been at the castle long enough to know all the daily routines.

And what she'd seen this morning was entirely new.

She'd run up the stairs to William's room with one thought in her mind.

That this must be exactly what Helena Watkins had warned her about.

Standing in front of the open window, Janine told all this to William, going on to explain what Helena had told her that night when she'd stood outside her room. The night Helena slid her key card under Janine's door. The last time Janine had seen her alive before finding her dying in her glass coffin.

'She said there was a plan B.'

'Explain,' he said.

'I can't. I should have asked, but she was terrified and incoherent and I didn't know what to say. She didn't say plan B, it had a name, I don't remember what. But she said it was just around the corner. I didn't understand a word of it. Until now.'

'What are you talking about?'

'They're not going to fight till the end.'

She paused, looked at William.

'And of course it makes sense. They've had decades to plan for this, so why wouldn't they have a plan B? They anticipated that there might come a point where it had gone too far and they couldn't stop it. I think that's where we are. I think they're about to get themselves to safety.'

He looked at her in disbelief. 'Why would they do that?'

'Does it matter?' she said. 'The point is, they're going to let the virus spread. They don't believe in us any more.'

'And what are we going to do about that?'

'We have to tell them.'

A subconscious gesture at the open window, her hand pointing into the wind to show who she meant by *them*. Everyone. The world. The people on the outside, the ones who were dying without anyone telling them why.

'Perhaps it's too late for you and me to save them. But we have to give them a chance to save themselves.'

'How?' he asked.

'We need to get out.'

'We can't.'

'We have to try.' And then: 'We can't give up.'

And William shrugged. It made him feel like a stubborn child, but he knew he was right, and that what she suggested wouldn't make a difference.

'Why not?' he said. 'Why not just give up, if there's nothing we can do anyway?'

'Because no one else is going to try.'

She looked at him defiantly.

'They are going to stand by and let the world die. We can't let that happen.'

∞◯∞

After she'd gone, William remained standing by the window for a long time. He looked out at the lake, saw it ripple in the wind, saw the ice crystals melt against the window pane and form into tiny rivers, streaming down the panes and meandering around, constantly changing direction in the strong wind. And he didn't move, just stood there looking, wishing that the images would bring him peace.

But there was no peace to be found.

Just uncertainty and sorrow and fear.

Janine was desperate, and he could empathise with that. She had presented a strategy that was surprisingly well thought out and that would definitely buy them some time. But no matter how optimistically he tried to look at it, he couldn't see that they would make it.

He could only see one outcome.

And he stayed in front of the window for ten minutes, without thinking, without seeing.

Then he went into the bathroom to fetch his toilet bag.

41

Everyone assumed that the cleaning lady had to be exaggerating.

The three security guards who made their way on to the platform weren't racing to the scene. They jogged casually with keys and chains rattling against their thighs, not because they didn't believe her but because she was a cleaning lady and chances were she had never seen spilt blood before. When you worked security at a big-city station you got to see a lot; whatever had made the cleaner scream her head off would be nothing to them. Just one more crime scene to be secured until the police arrived.

Then they climbed on board.

And realised the woman was right.

Of the four passengers very little remained. There was blood everywhere, and if this was murder it was on a scale beyond anything they'd encountered. Security guard or not, one of them had to run out on to the platform to bring his breakfast back up, while his colleague stood in a catatonic stupor, unable to think what to do. It was left to the third one to call the police and inform them that they needed backup.

And the police arrived, and forensic teams removed the sheets, and someone decided to call disease control and the snowball began to roll from its own weight.

It was a snowball of fear.

And once it had started to grow there wasn't any stopping it.

∞○○∞

The conversation had ended long before Watkins got to his feet. Several times he'd gathered his gloves and his scarf to leave, but each time he'd spotted something in the sea of people to worry him, an individual loitering or doubling back, and each time he'd changed his mind, put his gloves back on the table and carried on talking to them about nothing at all until he was sure the person was gone.

Albert and Leo had chatted back. Patient and understanding. But Watkins knew scepticism when he saw it.

'I'm not paranoid,' he'd said. 'I understand why you would think I am. But I know what I know.'

They'd offered no argument. All the same, he'd felt the need to explain.

'You can tell when somebody's been through your mail. You can tell when envelopes have been opened and resealed. It's been happening for almost a week, at home as well as at my office. And I've seen them following me.'

Albert had given him a look. 'In that case,' he said, 'how come they let the receipt slip though?'

The question made Watkins smile. It was the first smile to reach his face since the conversation started.

'Because the woman I married was smarter than them.' He nodded behind tense lips. Lips that smiled to hide his emotions, but that still couldn't stop them from seeping through.

There was something heartbreaking about it. Perhaps because in the middle of his emaciated face there were features that hadn't changed: the mouth and teeth and eyes were the same size they'd always been and when he smiled he became a sad caricature of himself, two large eyes smiling gloomily out of thin, wrinkled skin.

Or perhaps it was because he looked at them with such pride, such affection for a woman who no longer existed but whom he wanted to brag about, one last time.

'They forgot that the dead can receive mail, too.'

With that Watkins got up from his chair and disappeared into the crowd. And that was the way he wanted it.

In Albert van Dijk's jacket pocket lay the receipt from a luggage locker. A receipt that had been delivered in a white envelope to Potsdam University. Addressed to the mathematics department in haphazard, clumsy letters.

To a professor named Helena Watkins.

Albert and Leo stayed at the café for another five minutes after Watkins had left, just as he'd asked.

In front of them on the table his coffee sat untouched, like the sandwich next to it, sliced and buttered and wrapped in plastic to no avail.

They didn't speak, but then again they didn't have to. They were both thinking the same thing.

The receipt. The locker. And whatever was waiting there. Was this the answer Palmgren had talked about?

And if it was, then what was the question?

Perhaps it had something to do with the airliner and the hospital, perhaps it would lead them to William and Janine, perhaps it would mean the world – and perhaps it wouldn't help them a bit.

They were soon to find out.

Their car was parked within walking distance of one of the spaces with left-luggage lockers. And from a logistical point of view it couldn't be better; they would leave the café and head for their car, and on the way there they would take a quick detour, checking the lockers adjoining the various stairwells until they found the one they were looking for.

And there was nothing to suggest that anyone was keeping an eye on them.

Whatever Watkins had said.

When five minutes had passed, they stayed seated for another two before finishing their coffees. They got up, merged into the crowd, Watkins nowhere to be seen.

But from one of the walkways several floors up, their every step was watched by a man in a black suit.

∞◯∞

The men who entered the glass-covered main entrance had little to go on. The station was packed with people moving in different directions, stressed faces hurrying to catch trains or dawdling to read timetables or browse shop windows, all of them with bags and backpacks and rolling suitcases and all of them constantly getting in the way. All of them potentially the people they were looking for.

They saw their colleague the same instant they heard him in their headsets. He was standing on the steel bridge with an overview of the entire ground floor, and he instructed them to split up: Watkins had gone in one direction and the two men in another, and there was no way of knowing which, if any, of them, was carrying the receipt.

The suits on the floor acknowledged that they'd received the message and carried on striding through the hordes of people, their heads slightly above everybody else's as if they hoped that their field of vision would bend in a perfect parabola and end in the spot where the two young men would appear.

But the men were nowhere to be found. And the suits continued scanning the staircases and escalators, exchanging looks in the gaps between people, discreet signals to ensure that they had all exits covered.

They couldn't be allowed to escape.

But the time was just after ten in the morning. The station was heaving with people, and it was virtually impossible to move around.

And things were about to get even more chaotic.

∞◯∞

The task force commander's name was Peter Tressing, his rank was lieutenant colonel, and when he climbed out of his large four-wheel-drive LMV outside the main entrance to the Hauptbahnhof he was not a happy man.

His task would be impossible to carry out. In fact, it had failed even before it got underway.

More than an hour had passed since the train arrived at the station, and no matter how many exits they sealed there wasn't a cat in hell's chance that all the passengers from the infected train – if *any* – were still in the terminus.

They were already on their way home to their families or to new destinations or sitting in buses on their way somewhere else, and if any one of them had been in contact with that family yesterday, if anyone had chatted with or been coughed on or whatever it took, if only one or two or three had caught the disease and brought it out into the world, there was only one word for it.

Disaster.

And this he knew, just as he knew that the chance of any other scenario was as good as nil.

Nevertheless, he busied himself giving orders as all around him men in green uniforms climbed out of vehicles identical to his own, and he ordered them to lock down the station and to seal off the area. What would happen next was going to look like civil war and cause nothing but panic.

And Peter Tressing already knew it was going to be in vain.

∞○∞

Like every other terminal building in the world, Berlin Hauptbahnhof was planned with impeccable logic. And in common with every other terminal building, that was something a visitor would never have guessed.

Everything was a mess, and it was a mess full of people.

Leo and Albert had moved between staircases, across walkways that seemed to float in the air between platforms and trains, on between shops and new staircases, and every now and then they passed a nook or a corner where someone had put a bank of lockers. But not one of the numbers on the hatches matched the one on their receipt.

They moved quickly, quickly but not anxiously, careful to look as though they knew exactly where they were going even when they didn't. Watkins' nerves seemed to have rubbed off on them, and at regular intervals they peered over their shoulders to check that they weren't followed, knowing it would be glaringly apparent to anyone following them what they were up to.

They were on the verge of aborting their search and coming back to resume it the following day when they realised that they were standing in front of another row of lockers, and the sequence of numbers was in the same range as the one on the receipt.

And there it was.

The smallest locker size, tucked as far into the corner as possible. And blocked by an elderly man.

He was crouching in front of the locker next to it, carefully depositing his luggage inside. A suitcase and a paper bag and wait, perhaps the paper bag had better go on top of the suitcase, or no, perhaps it was better the way it was.

And they kept their distance. Waited impatiently in the stairwell for him to depart.

Eventually, he closed the door. Fumbled with the lock. And wandered off, leaving the place to them.

The code on the receipt.

They punched it in on the keypad located in the middle of the row of lockers.

And waited.

It felt as if the entire world was holding its breath, as if the number they had punched in was about to change history and cause everything around them to magically transform.

But it didn't.

There was a soft click, and one of the locker doors popped open. Not fully, just a centimetre or two.

They bent down, opened it, and reached in.

It contained a yellow envelope.

And for a second, Albert felt an overwhelming sense of déjà vu. It was the exact same kind of envelope that Janine had sent to him. He stood up, trying to catch Leo's eye. They were getting closer to the answer. From this moment, nothing could go wrong.

It was Leo who saw them first.

They appeared on the other side of the deck.

The dark suits, a man who pointed at them across the walkway, pushed his headset against his ear and set off at a sprint.

And Leo grabbed Albert's arm.

There was only one thing to do.

Run.

$\infty\bigcirc\infty$

They say people are individuals, but when fear strikes the pack mentality sets in and we're really just a mob of running bodies, acting as one.

The main entrance was closed.

People on their way out to Europaplatz were met by revolving doors that didn't revolve, and outside were men in military uniforms with firearms and nobody knew what was happening.

Like a school of fish in the shadow of a shark the mass of people turned and bolted; everyone was afraid and wanted to get out fast. As soon as one started to run, the rest followed.

And Lieutenant Colonel Peter Tressing had time against him, time and geography. There was no way he could seal all exits before anyone got out.

But those were his orders.

He remained in position, outside in the cold winter sun, watching the sea of people moving inside the glass façade. He could see his men spreading further and further away along the exterior towards other doors. And he asked himself how long it would be before panic set in. And what would happen then.

∞◯∞

The black-suited man on the gangway far above the crowd saw everything unfold below him.

It was a bull-run without bulls, a whirling stampede of directionless people, and all he heard was the sound of voices, screaming, shouting, afraid of something they couldn't see but that made them push forward, desperate to get out.

He saw the army trucks outside.

Saw the crowd below discover alternate exits, saw those at the front being trapped against the glass when the new doors wouldn't open, saw the tide of human beings surge and ebb and spill in other directions, spreading through the hall like rills of lava on a horizontal mountain.

The station was in lockdown. And why in heaven's name would it be?

In his ear he heard the shouts from his colleagues. Colleagues who were stuck in the moving crowd, who couldn't change direction for fear of being trampled, who couldn't see Watkins or the two young men and who couldn't understand what the panic was all about.

And then, the voices of his three colleagues on the basement level, the ones who had spotted them.

Two men with a yellow envelope.

They had been so close, just across the floor from them and with a perfectly clear view, and the next moment people had started to stream down the escalators and everybody was screaming and there was panic in the air and then the men were gone.

The suited man stood helpless on his walkway. All he could do was order them to keep trying, to wrestle their way through the crowd and take up the hunt. Their quarry couldn't be allowed to escape, too much was at stake.

And he closed his eyes and hoped that whatever was happening.

Whatever the reason the station was closed off.

Whatever the cause, he hoped it would stop the young men and the envelope from getting out.

∞○○∞

Albert van Dijk crouched in the front seat, hiding his head under his arms as they sped through the underground parking garage.

Not because he didn't want to be seen.

But because he didn't dare look.

He already knew that Leo Björk was a lousy driver, but even so it came as a surprise that he lacked not only good judgement but also survival instincts. The force from the sharp turn pressed Albert into the side of the door, and the only thing drowning his screams was the engine, still accelerating in second gear, squealing as it negotiated the curved ramp that would hopefully bring them out into daylight.

Behind them all hell had broken loose.

It had started with three men chasing them, four at most, but by the time they made it to the car there was a great swarm of people running after them.

Before they sped up the ramp Albert caught a final glimpse of one of their initial pursuers pressing a headset to his ear.

That wasn't a good sign.

There were more of them.

They were almost at the top of the ramp now, Leo steering them round the bend and out towards the street, and Albert was about to warn him that there could be more suits waiting in cars outside, ready to take up the chase, when Leo shouted at him:

'Hold on!'

Albert was already hanging on with both hands, and he opened his mouth to shout that he couldn't hold on any more than he already was, when he suddenly realised what Leo meant.

Outside, there was chaos.

A green military truck was positioned sideways across the road. It was the size of a small bus with massive, rugged tyres, and behind it two more identical trucks were rolling into position and men in camouflage gear were spreading out spike strips and what the hell was this about?

'Careful!' he screamed back.

But judging from the sound of the engine, being careful wasn't on Leo's agenda.

His eyes scanned the car park entrance for an escape route, and spotted a gap to the side of the green truck where there were no spike strips and no other vehicles. On the other hand, there was a kerb and pavement. In theory, it offered just enough room for them to pass, but in practice it wasn't a very attractive option.

Realising what Leo had in mind, Albert did as he'd been told and held on for dear life, pressing his feet so hard to the floor that he wondered if it wouldn't give way. He felt the wheels bounce and the car moan, two tyres on the pavement and two in the street, and he silently prayed the rubber would withstand the pressure.

Men in uniform came running from all directions, but Leo kept his foot on the accelerator and the men disappeared behind them. Albert ducked down again, hoping they wouldn't open fire.

No bullets came. And for a second he let himself exhale. *I'll be damned. We got away.*

Then he realised what was about to happen.

In front of them was a junction: four lanes of fast-moving traffic blocked their path.

And Leo was planning to make them a part of it, without waiting to be let in.

They hurtled past a host of signs telling them not to, and with their engine revving and at high speed, Leo piloted their tormented rental car through a ninety-degree turn, taking them off the end of the ramp and straight into the speeding traffic, swerving into a gap that wasn't there.

For Albert, everything blended together in a concert of horns and screeching wheels, cars flashing past only centimetres away, and he screamed something in Dutch that he knew Leo would neither understand nor care about, and he heard metal crunch against metal and thought that if this car was ever to be returned Leo would have do it himself.

And then, it was over.

He heard Leo change gears. The engine settled down; the vehicle was moving in one direction only, and that direction was forward. And he realised that his eyes were closed and that it was okay to open them now.

Beside him Leo sat behind the wheel, focused to the point of desperation.

'What the hell's going on, Albert? What is this about?' He clenched his teeth, still accelerating.

And Albert tried to assess the situation, the men inside the station, the military personnel outside, the blockade they had somehow managed to slip through.

Nothing made sense. Twenty minutes earlier they'd been drinking coffee in a bistro. Then they'd been chased by men in dark suits, and surrounded by a virtual army—

'They're behind us!'

It was Albert's own voice. It came as a reflex, sudden and panicking and just a bit too loud.

Leo threw a glance in the mirror. It made no sense, but Albert was right.

A black Audi had materialised behind them. It came bolting up from the garage, running through the cordon and forcing soldiers to throw themselves to the ground. But instead of merging into the traffic like Leo, it steered straight across the pavement, taking down a bicycle rack and steadily getting closer until a bus shelter forced it off of the pavement and into the lane of cars behind them.

Leo looked ahead. There had to be a way out.

And then he heard Albert's voice again.

'Red!' it screamed.

In front of them, a line of traffic lights were suspended in the air, with others mounted on poles to the side, shining red at them from every side to stop them proceeding across the intersection. And yet Leo hadn't seen them until it was too late.

But what he lacked in attention he made up for in reflexes.

He slammed on the brakes.

The result, however, wasn't quite what he'd expected. They were travelling too fast, and the car kept sliding forward, straight into the intersection. There were cars coming from the left and cars coming from the right and it couldn't end any other way but badly; everywhere brakes were screaming, and Albert was curled up next to the gear stick, hoping that the car had airbags and that they would save them from being crushed. He couldn't see the road, only Leo's hand shifting. To a lower gear. And his one thought was: *oh my god, what is he doing?*

Leo was speeding up.

Because there was no other choice. There was one way to get out alive and that was to go faster and try to drive through.

The car skated with the automatic brakes rattling under them, the engine howled, and Leo threw the wheel back and forth, whether to save their lives or just out of sheer terror Albert couldn't tell. Because his face was buried in the middle armrest and whatever happened, he didn't want to see.

More screaming brakes around them.

And then that sound, that instantly recognisable sound of cars failing to stop, smashing into each other and pushing each other into a spin.

The sound that should have come from all around them. But it didn't.

It came from behind.

And it stayed there. The distance between them and the sound grew, and for the second time in too short a time Albert forced himself to open his eyes. To sit straight. To look around.

Leo's gaze was fixed in the rear-view mirror.

His hands were clamped to the wheel. The road in front of them was empty.

They'd made it through the intersection.

Far behind them they could make out the black Audi that had followed them up from the garage. It had tried to speed through the crossing just like Leo, but it hadn't succeeded. Everything in front of the windscreen looked like a discarded piece of foil, one of the wheels had collapsed leaving the whole car sloping towards the ground, and seamlessly close to it was a grey taxi with its front embedded so deep in the Audi it was impossible to tell where one car ended and the other one began.

'Well done,' said Albert. And then: 'Never, ever do it again.'

Leo nodded.

And they pushed on.

Didn't speak until they'd driven for a long time.

On the dashboard in front of them lay the yellow envelope.

Vibrating against the windscreen with every bump in the road.

And Albert didn't take his eyes off it once.

42

Connors walked up the narrow, twisting passageway, his head bent to avoid striking the low ceiling, hurried steps along the spiral staircase.

On the open courtyard outside, the helicopter waited, ready for departure, the clatter of rotors between stone walls hitting him like a rumbling echo as he stepped out into the evening air.

The crew-cut pilot sat behind the controls. Drumming his fingers against the levers the way he always did, as if he was the one with the critical mission rather than Connors. He waited impatiently as his superior took a seat, and then they rose into the dark sky, the castle shrinking beneath them, ultimately vanishing behind the mountains as they turned out over the valley and headed west.

The castle.

It had been the topic of more discussions than he wanted to remember.

There were so many reasons for them to stay; the place was hard to reach and few even knew it existed.

It seemed secure. But *seemed* wasn't enough. It was hidden and protected, true, but it wasn't completely impossible to get there. And they would only be getting one chance, and then *seemed* wouldn't cut it.

What they needed was a place where the epidemic couldn't go.

Where no one could come, and that could be moved if somebody tried.

Now that place was ready and waiting. Their cargo bay was loaded with equipment and material to be delivered to the base, and this was just the first trip of many that Connors would have to make over the next couple of days.

He didn't like it. But things were what they were.

From the air, everything looked normal. The landscape lay below them like a billowing model railway, silent and still and secure. And yet, somewhere, in one of those houses, someone would soon start coughing. A soft tickly cough that would feel like the beginnings of a cold, but that would prove to be something much, much worse.

It wasn't right to give up. At least, he ought to try.

But he couldn't.

The decision wasn't Connors' to make. The protocols would dictate what he did next, and it didn't matter who had written them. People would die but there was nothing to do about it, he was part of a process and all he could do were the things that had already been decided.

Or so he kept telling himself.

He watched the buildings whizz by below them.

Knew in every fibre of his being that it was wrong.

And wondered how fate would punish him for it.

43

The alarm came at ten past eight that evening. Feet ran along the stone corridors, people cursed loudly and everybody asked how they'd allowed it to happen.

They knew he'd tried before.

But in spite of that they'd given him all his personal belongings, clothes, shoes, toiletries, everything. Everything had been checked, but apparently not thoroughly enough.

They ran down the stairs carrying William between them, down towards the medical quarters in the depths of the mountain, Franquin on one side and Rodriguez on the other, and behind them the two guards.

A few steps behind ran Janine.

Her face a mask of worry.

Grateful that the two nameless guards had finally heard her.

Janine had found William on the floor of the bathroom, eyes blankly staring at the ceiling, awake but unreachable. Next to him lay an empty paper box and what had once been a sheet of pills, now just an array of plastic bubbles with punctured foil where the tablets should have been.

Twenty of them. For anxiety and insomnia.

It was impossible to tell if he'd taken them all, but things weren't looking good.

Janine had immediately run for help, only to discover that her key card suddenly didn't work. The electronic lock had refused, wasting precious moments, and by the time the guards heard her and followed her back to his quarters, William was beyond contact.

All of this the guards now reported in short bursts of information as the medical team laid him on a table, examined him and checked his vital signs, and then came the tubes and the bottles and the stainless-steel basin and Janine knew all too well what was about to happen and looked away.

She could smell it as the contents of his stomach came back up. And she couldn't help thinking how he must be suffering, how she hoped it was worth it. Then it was all over and they checked his blood again, before one of the nurses came and placed her hand softly on Janine's.

'It's stopped rising,' she said.

'What does that mean?' Janine asked, even though she knew.

'Hopefully, we got most of it out. Before it got into his blood.' She looked at Janine. 'Don't worry, he'll make it.'

Janine gave her a look of gratitude.

It was just as rehearsed as everything else she'd been doing the past hour.

∞◯∞

They got out just before the gates slammed shut.

They steered out of Berlin by the most roundabout route imaginable, not to shake followers but because that was how Leo navigated. Eventually they found their way on to the Autobahn, and once they had they didn't dare stop.

They adjusted their speed to the cars around them, careful not to draw attention, and they kept driving south for hours, nervously keeping an eye in the mirrors and with a jolt of fear every time they were passed by a dark, new-looking car.

There was no doubt they were still being hunted. Either because they'd run through a military cordon and caused an accident, or because of the yellow envelope on the dashboard, or possibly – no, probably – because of both.

Something big was going on.

Something big that had nothing to do with them, but had coincided with their being in Berlin. And whatever it was had probably saved them.

On the radio, it was nothing but voices. Not a single station played music, everything was news and frantic witnesses phoning in or reporters transmitting live with traffic sound in the background. And neither Leo nor Albert spoke enough German to make out more than individual words. Berlin. Hauptbahnhof. And *geschlossen*. They looked at each other and glanced in the mirrors and as long as the news sites hadn't caught up they could only guess what was happening.

They called the paper in Stockholm but nobody answered. They called William's number but his phone was dead, just as it had been since that one call he made to them on the roof.

There was only one thing left.

The envelope.

The envelope that could be an answer – but to what?

It was still lying flat on the dashboard in front of Albert, and eventually, when they were far enough from the city, he reached for the envelope, casting a sideways glance at Leo to check that he agreed. Then he opened it, carefully, slowly, Leo beside him struggling against the urge to take his eyes off the road and see what was hiding inside.

Papers. A huge wad of papers.

Albert flicked through them. Once, and then again. Let his fingertips search through the entire pile, stopping here and there to try to make sense of the contents.

'What is it?' said Leo.

'I don't know,' he said. Because he didn't.

All he could see were numbers. Endless rows of numbers, page after page, and next to them there were symbols, undecipherable Sumerian symbols, the kind that Janine used to work with. But these were blocky from pixels, and if he'd counted them he would have found them to be 23 pixels wide and 73 pixels high, and wedged in between everything else someone had jotted down long, hand-written calculations.

None of it made any sense whatsoever. Albert wasn't a mathematician; all he could see were endless equations with parentheses and arithmetical symbols that he vaguely recognised without understanding in the slightest.

Here and there, the calculations were underlined or emphasised by exclamation marks. Arrows pointed from one expression to the next, trying to communicate exactly how someone had been thinking and why. All of which was totally lost on Albert van Dijk.

'They're codes,' he said. 'Codes and symbols and formulas.'

'What does that tell us?'

'It doesn't tell us anything.'

Silence. Albert, staring out of the passenger window.

'So what do we do?' said Leo.

'I don't know,' said Albert. Then, after a pause: 'Well, yes. One thing. We keep hoping there are two other people who can make more out of it than us.'

∞◯∞

Rodriguez left Sandberg behind in his room, asleep and well, the drama over. Walking back through the corridors he saw her from a distance, but it wasn't until he came close that he could she how sad she looked.

Janine glanced up when she heard his steps. She stood by one of the doors, as if she'd suddenly become paralysed, standing there and waiting for someone to show up.

'I forgot,' she said. 'In all the chaos. I forgot I couldn't get through.'

At first he didn't understand what she meant.

The key card. That's how it had all started. For some reason her card had stopped working, and it didn't surprise him. Not that the cards had a habit of causing them troubles, but computers were computers and sooner or later things happen.

'It's my own corridor,' she said. 'As you know.'

He nodded. It was a part of the castle where she should definitely be allowed to go, and so he took out his own card, walked towards the door to let her through. But instead of opening the door, he stopped.

He saw her tired eyes, and he couldn't help thinking it was all his fault. Not what just happened, with Sandberg trying to end his life, he couldn't help that. But if it hadn't been for him she wouldn't have been there in the first place. He was responsible, and he didn't like it, and here he stood with the key in his hand. And the moment lingered.

'He'll be okay,' he said.

'So I heard,' she replied. Not sounding any happier.

That, somehow, made it worse. He wanted to comfort her but couldn't. *That's not why I'm sad,* she seemed to be saying, which in turn meant only one thing: *It's because I'm here.*

'I'll let you through,' he said.

And yet he didn't move. Hesitated. Didn't open the door, bit his lower lip as if searching for something more to say.

'Here's how it is,' he said. Honesty in his voice. 'You can take this however you want to. And I know it's not going to help.'

Here we go. Too late to turn back. He was heading into an awkward conversation, but so be it, it was the truth and they were probably all about to die and so who cared if he made a fool of himself?

'I wish I hadn't,' he said. He continued, avoiding her eyes: 'When we sat there, in Amsterdam, this spring. When you went from being a mission to actually *being* someone, someone who sat there in front of me and ... who was irritable and snappy and irresistibly funny.' He shrugged. 'Then and there, I wished I wouldn't have to put you through all this. That I could just let it be.' And, after a pause: 'That I could stay and sit there and have a glass of wine and be insulted for a little bit longer.'

That was it. He was done, and he lapsed into silence. Didn't know if he should say anything more, or if he should simply open the door and let her through. Then again, maybe he should have kept his mouth shut and said nothing.

'You were lucky,' she said. 'Ten minutes more and I would have disappeared with your wallet.'

He hadn't expected that.

He looked up to see her smiling. Or rather she was looking at him with an unmoving, blank face, and behind that there was the same suppressed smile that had charmed him at the restaurant in Amsterdam. It was forgiveness transformed into action. And he looked at her with the same stone-faced sincerity, picked up the ball where it had landed.

'You'd be disappointed by the contents,' he said. 'Governmental employee, you know.'

'Oh, of course,' she replied. An over-acted understanding. 'Trial period, is it? Labour market measure? Or did they feel sorry for you and decide to give you something to do?'

'They stopped feeling sorry for me when they saw I was smarter than you.'

You have no idea, she thought. But she didn't say.

Instead, she allowed herself to give him a look, a friendly, sorrowful look between two people who'd met at the same level and who were about to share the same destiny.

She sighed. 'It's fucked up, isn't it?' she said. 'This.'

He couldn't have put it better himself.

'Bottom line,' he said. 'I'm sorry.'

'I'll let you be.'

They stood there, looked at each other, and in another world it would have been the silence before the kiss. But that world was far away, and perhaps none of them would get to see it again, and even if they were two lonely people they weren't lonely enough for it to happen.

She let the silence linger until it became uncomfortable. And then she broke it.

'If we're waiting for me to open that door we'll be standing here for quite some time.'

He smiled apologetically, as if he'd forgotten why she was standing there in the first place. He took out his piece of plastic again, and she moved her hand away from the door to let him past, just as he approached it with his card.

The collision was inevitable.

The key card slid through his fingers, they both backed up instinctively, and there it lay on the floor.

And Janine gave him a look. Bent down, picked it up, handed it to him.

Nothing more than that. Simply and candidly and with the non-smile on her face, the one that told him she was about to say something ambiguous.

'If that was an invitation, I'm going to look like an idiot for giving this back to you.'

He looked at her – was she coming on to him or pulling his leg? It was impossible to tell.

He took the card from her. Looked for an answer.

'I promise to be more obvious next time,' he said. 'I know you can be a bit slow.'

Her face cracked into a half-involuntary smile. And it felt like an acknowledgement: he had just won a victory. He had apologised, and she had accepted.

But the conversation was over. She wanted to leave. And he held up his card against the wall again, as he'd been about to a minute ago, and the door buzzed open exactly as it should.

The card worked perfectly, the diode turned green and the door opened, and there was no reason whatsoever for suspecting he hadn't just opened the door with his own card. Before long, he would hate himself for being stupid enough not to think further. But not now.

'I'll have Keyes talk to you,' he said. 'She must have forgotten to activate it.'

He indicated the key card in her hand.

And she smiled her wry smile.

'I should've known you wouldn't be able to help, yourself.'

'I think I'm more able than you can imagine,' he replied.

'If only you knew what I can imagine.'

And with that, they parted.

Rodriguez stayed on his side of the door as Janine backed into the next corridor. And when the door closed between them they still hadn't let go of each other's eyes.

Seconds later, as she was racing down the hallway towards her room and with only hours to get everything ready, she could hear the sound of her own heart beating.

Seven months ago he'd charmed her and made her drop her guard and then everything had been over. She hated him for what he'd done, and herself for letting him do it.

And now she'd tricked him back.

In his pocket he had Franquin's key card.

With the exact same clearance as the one she'd just taken from him.

Which meant that hopefully he wouldn't be able to tell the difference. Not until it wouldn't matter anyway.

∞◯∞

Thirty minutes earlier, William Sandberg had felt the sour aftertaste of medical tubing lingering in his throat as they carefully placed him on his bed.

His gaze had been distant, but only because he wanted it to be.

Inside, his brain was hard at work, registering all that was happening around him, assessing the situation and deciding that everything seemed to be under control. He had completed his part of the mission. Now he was back in his room, surrounded by three more men – Rodriguez and two others whose names he didn't know – and by one of the walls stood Janine, watching them take his pulse and check that he was okay.

She watched them without talking. Worried but not overwhelmed, a perfectly balanced choice considering that they hadn't known each other for more than a week, and considering how easy it would have been to overact.

The two men had pulled his cover over him, and Rodriguez had combed his bathroom for any pills they might have missed, but they wouldn't find any and eventually they would be satisfied and leave him alone.

Two pills. That's how many he'd taken.

The other eighteen were currently travelling down a sewage pipe, and the stupor he'd been in as he reached the treatment room hadn't been more than a vague tiredness. In fact, it had been rather pleasant. And not in the least life-threatening.

But it had made the illusion complete.

The two tablets had been given enough time to enter his bloodstream, and that had showed up on their tests. And when the treatment-room staff had shoved the tube down his throat to empty him, when the concentration had stopped rising, they had all deduced that they had managed to get to him in time.

And they had sighed with relief, the medical staff and the guards and Franquin, everyone had exchanged exhausted glances, his pulse had been taken and they had monitored him as they waited for the levels to go down. And everyone had kept talking with careful voices and eventually they had turned their backs on him because sooner or later you do.

As soon as the chance came, he had taken it.

Franquin had hung his jacket over a chair, and that in itself was a blessing. It made William's job so much easier; all he had to do was to reach out from his bunk. It was the one moment everything depended on. If anyone turned around, saw him reaching out from his mattress, neither dizzy nor unconscious but with his hand in Franquin's jacket, then his entire adventure would be over and with it their last chance.

But nobody turned around.

Nobody saw him drop his own piece of plastic straight down into the open pocket, nobody saw him take out the other one instead.

Because nobody expects an unconscious man to steal a key card.

Not even Maurice Franquin.

After William had been tucked up under the soft duvet in his own room, Janine had stayed there watching until it was time for her to leave.

Not until she was certain that Rodriguez was about to leave the room as well, and that she would be able to wait for him in the corridor and do her part of the job, not until then did she excuse herself and exit.

It was a fragile plan, but it couldn't have turned out better.

The card in Franquin's pocket was William's.

And Janine had taken over Franquin's card, elegantly and invisibly, when she held William's hand to ask how he was doing.

It had all been her idea, and he had to admit it was a good one.

If she succeeded, it would buy them valuable extra time in case things went awry.

The only obstacle that remained was Rodriguez, and Janine had told him she knew exactly how to deal with that.

William shut his eyes under his duvet and thought he wasn't sure he wanted to know.

Another ten minutes passed before Rodriguez decided that Sandberg was sleeping a calm, healthy sleep and that nothing more was going to happen to him. He got up from his chair, took William's pulse one final time, and left the room.

In the hallway he ran into Janine, and though he obviously didn't know it, she was about to replace his key card with Franquin's.

And in his room, William lay in his bed and knew that this was it.

They would only have one chance to get out.

And that chance had to be taken tonight.

44

It had been dark outside their windows when they left their rooms, and it would stay dark for many hours more.

It was night. And if only they could get down to the entrance, to the areas they had never seen but that they hoped would be there, if only they made it there then perhaps they'd be able to melt into the darkness and escape.

Then all that remained would be everything else.

They sprinted silently through the corridors, Janine in front, at first a dozen steps ahead to show the way, but the distance kept growing and at regular intervals he had to push himself to the brink not to lose her as she rounded the next corner.

It was true that she didn't have his skills and formal training, but then again it was equally true that William lacked hers.

Or to put it another way: she was in good shape and he was not.

His breaths burned through his throat, as if someone was pulling a red-hot grater up and down inside him, but with every rasp came new air and he had no choice, he hadn't run for years and now he was running for his life.

That was exactly it. He was running for his life. His, and maybe everyone else's too.

And he didn't care how much it hurt, the stone tiles against his soft heels, barefoot so as not to be heard, the vibrations that travelled up into his knees and hips and extra pounds, the breaths he had to take even though his lungs screamed at him to stop, as if that would make anything better. He didn't care how much it hurt, because sooner or later someone would discover what they were doing and if they weren't out by then it would be too late.

And they kept running, Janine with well-placed steps, her long hair billowing in the wind and William coming up behind as fast as he could.

They passed door after door.

Pressed Rodriguez's card against lock after lock.

It still worked the way it should.

And they both prayed silently that it would keep doing so for just a little longer.

∞◯∞

It's the small things that cause the biggest changes, and in this case it was a file of instructions.

The file belonged to Maurice Franquin, and it lay on a table in the blue parliament, and it was the middle of the night and nobody usually reads a file of instructions then.

But Franquin was wide awake.

He'd set aside a few hours for sleep, but life had stepped up a gear and his mind was racing and refused to stop no matter how much he tried. Eventually he'd given in, and decided to read the thick dossier once again, the one with all the regulations and routines that he'd already started to set in motion, and that he would follow to the letter over the next couple of days.

That's when he realised it wasn't in his room.

It only took him a second to remember where he had it last, and he stayed under his warm blanket for a few minutes more as he negotiated with himself.

Was it worth it? Would he be able to sleep if he didn't? Or might it be just as well to go down and fetch it?

He already knew the answer.

He got out of his bed, pulled on a pair of trousers and a shirt, felt the cold fabric scrape against his skin the way clothes always do at night, and he reached for his key card and began the long walk down to the underground section of the complex.

The moment he met the hard steel doors, many levels down into the mountain, the forgotten file changed the course of everything.

Suddenly, Franquin's key wouldn't work.

He held it up to the reader by the door, as he'd done day in day out, year after year. But the green diode refused come on. The lock protested with an annoying buzz and flashed its red diode at him and what the hell was this?

He wasn't in the mood. He was too tired to mess around. Okay, he couldn't sleep, but that didn't mean he wasn't tired, and standing around half-dressed in the middle of the night in the depths of a cavernous mountain unable to open a door was the last thing he needed.

He flicked through his phone to find her number.

Knew he'd be waking her up but it couldn't be helped.

It was her job.

∞◯∞

Evelyn Keyes was woken by the sound of her phone, and when she saw Franquin's name flash she answered immediately.

'There's something wrong with the locks,' he said, not bothering with pleasantries.

'Wrong?' she said. Not because she hadn't heard. But because she wasn't fully awake and she needed to buy some time.

Franquin repeated himself, told her how he'd suddenly been locked out of the central part of the complex, and read out the code engraved on a metal plate next to the door, digit by digit to let Keyes know where he was.

And Keyes listened. Peered through eyes that wanted nothing more than to close and go back to sleep. But she did what was required: she started up the handheld terminal by her bed, connected to the security system that let her monitor its status remotely, already aware that if some part of the system had locked up she wouldn't be able to solve it from here but would need to go down to the security centre and please don't make me, she thought, please let it be something trivial and please let me go back to sleep.

She sat on the edge of her bed in the darkness, her face ice blue from the cold glow of the touchscreen.

And then she froze. Midway through sitting up. As if she realised that this was the calm before the storm, and as if she deliberately wanted to hold on to it for as long as she could.

'*Where*, exactly, did you say you were?'

Though she already knew.

And Franquin read the number from the door panel again, and of course it matched the number she'd punched in, as she'd known it would.

There wouldn't be any more sleep for her tonight.

'There's nothing wrong with your key card,' she said, already on her feet, pulling her uniform jacket over the thin top she slept in. 'It's just that you're not really you.'

'What do you mean?' said Franquin.

'It isn't you by that door. It's William Sandberg.'

ooOoo

Rodriguez received the summons from Keyes only seconds after she ended the conversation with Franquin. His immediate thought was that his superiors were idiots.

Of course it had been wrong to give them complete freedom, of course it was stupid to give them key cards, and it had been painfully naïve to believe they'd keep working for them if they weren't forced to.

Perhaps, he thought as he sprinted through the corridors, perhaps it would have worked if that had been the deal from the beginning, if they'd been recruited voluntarily with full knowledge of what they were doing. But once a prisoner, always a prisoner. That's the way it worked. And if you turned confinement into freedom, it shouldn't come as a surprise that sooner or later they would try to escape.

He ran to the hallway leading to William Sandberg's rooms, but he already knew he wouldn't be there.

If he'd managed to switch cards with Franquin – which he obviously had, and which was so painfully stupid that he cringed on his superior's behalf – then he'd hardly be sitting around waiting for someone to discover what had happened. On the contrary, Sandberg would already be on his way out, and Haynes would probably be with him, and all they could do was hope they hadn't managed to leave the castle.

William Sandberg's room was empty, just as Rodriguez expected.

He pulled open the bathroom door and checked the wardrobe to make sure, but there was nothing in there either, and he ran on down the corridor to William's workroom.

As the door flew open he stopped dead.

Stared at the wall in front of him.

Fumbled to put his headset to his ear, hands shaking with concern.

'Sandberg's gone,' he said.

Which was exactly what everyone expected him to say.

What wasn't, were the words he said next.

∞◯∞

Several floors below Rodriguez, Franquin and Keyes ran through the maze of corridors. Rodriguez spoke to them over the radio, and Franquin heard him perfectly clearly, yet he couldn't do anything but ask him to repeat what he'd just said.

It didn't matter how many times he said it. The words were the same.

And it couldn't have happened at a worse time. Half the security detail had already left, and the helicopter was somewhere above central France, on its way back with Connors. The only thing they could do was to make the best of the resources they had.

Keyes didn't take her eyes off Franquin, she'd heard Rodriguez in her own headset and now she awaited his orders, even though she knew exactly what they would be.

Franquin held his microphone tight to his mouth. Breathless, running, agitated. But what he said couldn't have been clearer.

William Sandberg and Janine Charlotta Haynes were not to leave the complex. Not under any circumstances. Whatsoever.

And Rodriguez confirmed that he understood, and signed off.

Keyes and Franquin pushed on, sprinting through the steel-lined corridors of the lower section towards the security centre. And in their heads, Rodriguez's words echoed, over and over again.

'They've taken everything with them.' Those had been his exact words.

'*Everything.*'

∞◯∞

Rodriguez received Franquin's orders over the radio and turned it off.

He had a security team to wake up. Reduced, but a team nonetheless.

And when that was done they would have two fugitives to catch, and this time they wouldn't fail.

Nevertheless, he lingered for a second, one more second of silence before everything kicked off.

He stood there, in the middle of the stone floor of William Sandberg's workroom.

Along one of the walls was the table with the computers.

And along the others there was nothing.

All the rows of code, of cuneiform script, everything that had hung on the walls, printed out in red and black so that William could pace up and down trying to make sense of it. All of it gone.

William and Janine were making their way out.

And with them they were carrying the information that had been kept confidential for more than fifty years.

∞◯∞

For every metre William and Janine put behind them the complex seemed to become larger and larger.

They ran through hallways they'd never seen, far beyond the parliament and the server rooms and the medical observation section where infected people lay waiting to die in hospital beds. They opened new doors and descended new staircases, constantly moving deeper into the mountain and hopefully closer to freedom.

With each step they took, new chapters of the Organisation's past opened up and revealed themselves. Telling them about the people who'd once worked here, researching and struggling with the task, the countless people who'd been eradicated when the first virus spread inside the complex in the eighties.

They passed offices and halls and meeting rooms, spaces designed to accommodate hundreds of people; worn office chairs at empty desks beneath the cold glow of fluorescent lights, relics of another era.

They passed rooms that were storage chambers, and William noted them without stopping, surprised by what he saw even though he knew he shouldn't be.

Stacked in room after room were crates.

Some were wooden, some were metal. Some were grey and some were painted olive green or different shades of green and brown. And on all of them, there was writing. Some of them in white and some of them in yellow, numbers showing quantities and weight and dimensions, sometimes in Russian and sometimes in English, and Arabic and Japanese too.

Guns. Ammunition. Grenades. What else? Endless reserves of firepower. And of course it shouldn't come as a surprise.

After all, this was an international organisation. Set up to protect the world.

And nobody knew against what.

There would be thousands of scenarios, thousands of imagined enemies, they had shouted into space and what if someone had answered by coming here, of course there had to be a defence and if you don't keep weapons in a military base then where would you keep them?

Because that's just what it was: a military base, command central, research station, all rolled into one. And it was vast.

Vast and deserted.

There was no way to ignore what it was telling them about the personnel who'd been exposed and died, and what they could expect to happen next.

And every time the thought of the virus crossed William's mind he did the same thing:

He pulled his T-shirt a little tighter.

Not the one he was wearing, but the one he'd fashioned into a bag, put his arms through like rucksack, and where stacks of paper and files were pressed together, thudding against his back as he ran.

The material. The codes and the numbers.

Everything that had hung on his wall and that now hung behind his back and that hopefully would make sense to someone else.

That was their plan, to get it out in the world and into the right hands, hoping that many brains would do a better job than just his own and Helena Watkins' and Janine's and whoever had tried before them. And hoping that someone out there, or many people together, would find a solution while there was still hope.

Before the purple circles became a reality.

And they kept running through the mountain, stopping only to hold their card against lock after lock, ran and ran and didn't know where they were going, but hoping.

Hoping that they were running in the right direction.

Evelyn Keyes used the last few steps to her office to plan her next move.

She wasn't tired any more, instead her mind was racing through all the controls that would be waiting for her, which monitors she'd start first and which menu and which commands.

First, she'd find the unique code assigned to Franquin's card. It was long and complex but that's how the system was designed, she'd find it and feed it into the system and when that was done she'd be able to block his card.

Her next step would be to check where it had last been used. Then she'd know where they were and it would only be a matter of dispatching the security team. And then her work would be done.

Those were her first thoughts. And then she had another thought. And once it had occurred to her she couldn't shake it off.

What if that *wasn't* what she should be doing?

Deactivating Franquin's card would be the obvious thing to do.

But perhaps it was so obvious that it was precisely what they wanted.

Because there was an alternative.

It was a definite possibility, she thought, that the card they were using wasn't Franquin's.

If they'd managed to switch cards once they might well have managed it twice. And yes, that meant putting yourself at unnecessary risk, but it also meant they'd have two clear strategic advantages in the event they were discovered.

The first would come when Franquin realised he had William's card instead of his.

If Keyes did as they were anticipating, if she went ahead and deactivated his card, everyone would feel confident and secure that the fugitives couldn't pass any more doors. And that would be advantage number one.

Then the guards would be sent out to fetch them. And that would be advantage number two.

Because the person waiting there wouldn't be the fugitives.

If Franquin's card had been switched, if it had ended up with a third person, then someone else would be left standing with a blocked card and guards running towards him with weapons drawn.

And meanwhile doors would continue to open for Haynes and Sandberg, and before everyone realised they were chasing the wrong person the two of them would get further, and, worst-case scenario, even exit the building.

It wasn't likely, she thought.

But possible.

It was devious and clever, and wasn't that why they'd been chosen in the first place, because they were clever people?

The only thing she could do now, the only thing to do before she knew who was where and carrying which of all the issued key cards, was to block *all* the doors for *all* the cards in one single blow.

That was the ideal solution. It would be a whole lot quicker than punching in codes one by one. And most of all, it would stop Haynes and Sandberg, no matter what card they were using.

Those were her thoughts as she rounded the corner to her office.

There wasn't anything left of her tiredness.

She saw the door ahead of her, and she knew exactly what to do and in what order.

∞○∞

It was the smell that told them they were heading in the right direction, and as soon as they felt it they picked up speed. They were so near now that they simply couldn't fail; it would be unforgivable and disastrous and mustn't be allowed to happen.

It smelled of air.

There was a gentle draught coming from somewhere, and it could only mean that not too far away there was a way out.

They moved faster, down the sloping passage, feeling the temperature drop. It filled with them with hope but also with anxiety.

And they almost missed it.

The small corridor that opened up in one of the walls.

It was dark and innocuous and looked like another dead end, and why would they make a turn when the corridor they were running in was steadily sloping downwards? But after a couple of steps the chill suddenly faded, and they realised what it meant.

They turned back.

Fumbled along the wall for a light switch.

The passage was long, straight and ice cold. The ceiling was lined with fluorescent tubes that blinked into life; the floors were worn, with black scuff marks trailing off into the distance.

Rubber wheels. Trolleys.

Janine and William exchanged glances; one said 'Deliveries!' and the other nodded in agreement. This was where supplies came into the castle, computers and food and mail and yellow envelopes. They were on the right track. If this was where things came in, it was also where they would find a way out.

At the end of the corridor was a metal door.

And when the diode turned green and the door swung open, the cold air hit them as if someone had just opened a window.

On the far side was a cavern, natural or perhaps blasted out, it was hard to tell which, but it formed a vast hangar and the door opened directly on to a loading platform.

It smelled of oil and rubber and exhaust fumes.

There were no vehicles, but the smell told them there usually were; perhaps it was just luck that the hangar was empty now.

Or, more likely, they had already started evacuating the castle and the cars and the trucks were already on their way somewhere else.

Whatever the reason, they were now just one door away from freedom.

Below the platform, the ground was covered with asphalt. Painted lines marked zones for loading and unloading and parking, arrows showed where to drive and stop and give way. And at the far end of the hangar, a huge archway ended in a tall, rusty, rolling gate.

A gate to freedom.

Folded sheets of metal, a massive chain linking them together, rusty rails stretching up towards the ceiling and bending in where the door would rattle its way up and let them out.

And Janine ran across the loading platform. Down the steel stairs. Sprinted over the asphalt.

And, for the last time, pulled the blue key card from her pocket.

∞○○∞

Franquin realised he hadn't let himself breathe for several minutes.

He stood behind Keyes, watching as her hands danced over the grey-green plastic keyboard, switching between screens and monitors and working methodically without a word.

It took it time. Everything that should have been easy required a number of steps and several pushes of buttons in the right order. But neither of them said anything, neither of them complained about equipment or its state or its age, they both knew it too well and things were already too critical to waste time talking about it.

Because critical they were.

The bank of monitors above them showed slanted images from surveillance cameras dotted about the complex. But there was no trace of Sandberg, no trace of Haynes, and while the monitors kept flicking from camera to camera, Franquin kept repeating the same mantra to himself.

They *must* still be around.

They *must* be between cameras.

They must be. But he couldn't stop worrying that they weren't.

Eventually, Keyes leaned over towards the microphone on the control desk.

'This is Keyes,' she announced. 'I'm disabling your key cards starting now.'

She didn't do anything.

Which meant she already had.

All the cards were blocked and no door would open for anyone, not without her explicitly unlocking their card first.

'Everyone report to me from your nearest door,' she said, 'and I'll reactive you one by one. Over and out.'

She leaned back in her chair. No tapping of keys, just silence, accompanied by the emptiness on display in the monitors.

Neither of them spoke. Both too intent on watching as the screens jumped from image to image.

The corridors. The meeting rooms. The offices.

The transit passage. The loading bay. The hangar.

And outside, barely visible in the darkness of the night:

The rolling gate. The turning area. The steep mountainside.

Images everywhere, light blue and flickering and low definition.

All of them empty. No signs of life, no glimpses of movement.

They kept their eyes on the monitors, waiting. And then Keyes turned to him.

'There are two possibilities,' she said. 'Either they're somewhere inside the complex where there's no camera. In which case, we'll get them sooner or later.'

He didn't answer. That was the either. The problem was the or.

'Or,' she said, 'they're out. And if they are, we don't have much time.'

Franquin had already come to a decision. 'How many men do we have?'

'Six. Plus Rodriguez.'

'Good,' Franquin said. 'Tell them to report immediately.'

She transmitted the orders over the radio.

One by one they heard the guards report their positions, and one by one they held up their cards at a door somewhere, and when they appeared on her screen as a new red line, Keyes could confirm who was who.

One by one she unlocked their cards, and the guards ran into the next section and the next, down towards the cargo hall and the only way out, and all the time Franquin stood motionless with his eyes glued to the screens.

Now and then one of the guards would pass a camera, sprinting downward according to orders.

But still no Sandberg. Still no Haynes.

And this just weeks after the incident with Kraus.

It couldn't happen again. They couldn't be allowed out.

It simply wasn't an option.

45

William ran barefoot across the freezing asphalt, but even so he couldn't stop laughing.

He was free.

They were free.

Janine sprinted ahead, steady strides along the painted lines on the side of the road, straight posture and fit as a middle-distance runner, not a hint of fatigue after their race through the complex.

Not that there was much evidence of his exhaustion either. He was only twenty, maybe thirty metres behind her, but he was going at full speed and all the pain and stress he'd had to fight through, all the thoughts and doubts he'd had to push aside, all of that was gone now. She could keep up that speed for hours without him falling behind, that's how good he felt. He could run for the rest of his life, they were out and they were free and everything was intoxicating and marvellous.

They'd done it.

Janine's plan had worked. Switching the key cards and taking the documents had been crazy, it shouldn't have worked. But that was life: nothing went the way it should.

Gradually the night blindness from the corridor lights started to fade, and the landscape around them came into focus in all its icy clarity. The single-track road they were running on, short dashes painted down its sides and no streetlights above. A thin veil of freezing mist sparkling under the star-filled sky. The mountains behind them sloping downward, together with the road, carrying them down towards the low-hanging plain that was the rest of the world.

And freedom.

Far in the distance they could make out the lights of what must be a main road.

There, they would find people. There, they would find cars.

And sooner or later, someone would either lend them one or give them a ride, and then they'd be on their way out of there.

Then they'd save the world.

They'd get to a city, go public with the codes and the verses, copy them and send them to universities and to hospitals and to governments and companies all over the world, to anyone who could possibly help. And then they couldn't possibly fail.

Someone somewhere would find the key, and labs across the globe would manufacture a virus that worked, because if humanity was given the chance to save itself that's what it would do.

Anything else was unthinkable.

And Janine and William would make it happen.

Behind them the sheer cliffs receded, and they ducked away from the road where someone might see them, cut across the upland meadows, and the ground was uneven and cold and hurt under their soles.

Soon enough their absence would be noted. The alarm would be raised.

But by then, they'd be far away from here.

That's how it was going to be, simply because it had to.

*

They'd been running for fifteen minutes when Janine noticed the shrubbery as a black silhouette against the night sky.

They were still barefoot, scared to stop and put their shoes on, not because they believed anyone was chasing them, but because they wanted to make sure no one would be able to catch up.

Hopefully, they didn't have anything to worry about.

Hopefully, nobody had discovered that they were gone, and hopefully they wouldn't be missed until tomorrow morning when breakfast was delivered and neither of them could be found. First they'd check their beds, the bathrooms, then their workrooms. Only then would the guards raise the alarm, but by then they'd be long gone. And with a little luck they'd be impossible to find.

It wasn't tomorrow morning that was the problem, though. It was now.

Now they were running across grassy meadows, two adults on flat, open ground, and even in the dark it wouldn't be too hard to pick them out.

Janine peered at the bushes, wondering if they were thick enough to shield them. Whether it would be possible to disappear among the branches. Perhaps they could hide there, *if* someone turned up and *if* they hadn't come any further than this.

Behind her, she heard William. Still tight on her heels. But the question was how long he'd be able to keep up.

And she had to make a decision. Either to veer into the cover of the bushes and risk tearing up their naked feet on branches and roots, or to carry on in the open and risk being seen.

She slowed down. About to call out to him, to ask what he thought.

Then she heard.

Footsteps. From several directions.

William wasn't the only one behind her.

And she stopped breathing, spun around as silently as she could, scanned the darkness trying to see.

As she did, she saw William Sandberg's face.

Illuminated in white against the black night sky.

And that couldn't be a good thing.

*

The moment the first flashlight hit him right in the eyes, William realised what was happening.

He reacted without thinking: he threw himself to the side, a gigantic leap mid-stride that almost cost him his balance, but he regained it and carried on, running faster and darting from side to side to prevent the light beams from locking on him again.

They'd been found.

And the flashlight was accompanied by more. One after the other they lit up and he had four beams to avoid now, no, five, they swept through the night like stray lighthouses over a black sea, and that was all he could make out, which obviously didn't help.

The light had hit him right in the eyes, and the night blindness that had finally disappeared was back with full force.

And he ran, ran as fast as he could, bare feet on the frozen soil. It was uneven and it hurt and every time his foot hit the ground sooner or later than he'd expected, the blow travelled like a stab of pain through his body. And all he could think about was Janine.

He strained his eyes.

Somewhere in front of him was a row of bushes.

It wasn't far away; he'd seen it as a dark outline before the flashlights came. Janine had steered them towards it, probably because she was thinking the same as him, that with a bit of luck they could melt into them and hide, and perhaps the bushes were still their only way out.

In the corner of his eye the light beams kept moving, sweeping over the landscape, and he saw the bushes getting closer and closer, just another couple of metres. It was going to be his only chance. He picked up speed in a final spurt, now or never, and at that moment he heard the voice from behind.

'There!'

It took him a split second to see what it meant.

Janine.

She was trapped in one of the lights.

She was already halfway into the bushes, but the branches were tired and sparse and it was like hiding in an open square.

The beams were gathering on her, following her every step.

And eventually she realised everything was lost. And stopped.

Waited.

In the darkness William watched it happen.

Saw the guards rush up to her, two, three, four of them, pushing her down on the ground and screaming things in French that he didn't understand yet knew full well what they meant.

He stood there, breathless, looking at the bushes that were supposed to save them but that weren't going to help at all.

And sooner or later the flashlights would find him too, and then it would be over.

The first thing he saw was his own breath.

How it suddenly became visible in the dark, revealing itself in front of his eyes, seal-grey clouds against the black sky.

And for a second he didn't understand why, as if his eyes saw it first and forgot to ask his brain, and a second later came the realisation and by then it was too late.

Someone's light had hit his breath.

His own lungs had betrayed him.

He stood still in the middle of a field, illuminated from all sides and impossible to miss, and the next moment he was bundled to the ground with knees in his back and voices in French.

William Sandberg had failed.

It had been up to him, and now it was over.

He hated himself so deeply that when the syringe was shoved into his neck, robbing him of consciousness, it almost came as a relief.

46

They met at dawn, as the protocol dictated.

It ought to have been emotional. And it should have given them hope.

And yet they felt neither.

The cars had returned from the night's business and were waiting on the turning area outside the gate, crates were loaded into trunks and cargo spaces, and people climbed into their allocated seats and waited to depart.

Nobody asked questions, because there were none to ask.

Everyone had their instructions, everyone checked what they were supposed to, nothing was left to chance. Behind them the huge metal door rolled shut and Keyes confirmed that the mountain was sealed.

They were moving on to a new chapter.

And all they could feel was fear.

∞◯∞

Deep inside the mountain, in the server room, Connors stood listening to the fans and the computers and felt the mountain sigh with emptiness.

He was the only one left.

They'd followed the protocols to the letter, they'd made four trips to prepare for the others' arrival, now one task remained and it fell to him. The computers hummed around him, hummed as if nothing had changed, and without a clue that the things they were doing they were doing for the very last time.

One last dump of the data was all that remained. Everything was to be stored on portable devices, and then he'd take it with him: the codes, the cipher keys to read them, the cuneiform symbols that hid inside.

The verses. The predictions. Everything would be saved for posterity. They were to keep them safe until it was all over. And *if* they survived, *if* they came out on the other side, then the knowledge would be carried on into the new age.

It mustn't be lost. That was how he'd written the scenario. It was his job to make sure.

And one more thing.

He wished he could avoid it, but things were what they were.

Responsibility. An overrated thing to have.

On the helicopter pad, the pilot was waiting to take off.

But before it could carry them both to their final destination, they had an engagement at an abandoned military firing range.

∞◯∞

By the time the convoy of black vehicles arrived at the airfield it was full daylight. The Organisation's private jet stood waiting on the apron, and the cars drove out on to the tarmac and parked alongside it.

Rodriguez stayed in his passenger seat, watching his colleagues as they climbed the shaky metal steps up into the plane. Rolled his blue key card between his fingers, a card he'd never need to use again, but that he'd taken anyway as a memento.

Assuming there was a future. Assuming there would ever be a chance to remember this as a past.

'By the way . . .'

A voice, next to him. It was Keyes. She'd returned to the vehicle to collect her belongings, and now she leaned in through the door, gave him a dry look.

'. . . you know that isn't your key card?'

Rodriguez looked back at her.

'It's Franquin's. The card they used to get out was yours. I'm going to leave it to you to work out how that happened.'

Her smile grated like sandpaper on bare skin. It was snide, revelling in his discomfort. Then she turned and walked to the jet.

Rodriguez remained in his seat.

She'd set him up, charmed him the same way he'd charmed her. And he'd said that he was smarter than her, and she must've been laughing inside as he said it; he could see her face and couldn't stop himself from smiling at the thought.

Haynes. Janine Charlotta Haynes.

She was a worthy adversary.

It didn't make him any happier about what awaited her.

47

The run-down motel on the country road was none too impressive, but there were people inside and everything seemed open and that was all that mattered.

They were unbelievably tired.

Leo had driven the entire night and seen the dawn come, they'd passed signs that said Leipzig and Kulmbach and Nuremberg and they hadn't eaten or slept, and sooner or later you have to.

Even so, they drove by the motel with its flagpoles and neon logos and signs with rates, and Albert pushed the car even harder, onward and southbound, passing a couple of exits before he finally swung off on to a side road that took them to a small, sleepy village.

They had no choice.

As much as they would have like to park in front of the motel and check in and collapse into bed, they knew there was no way they could risk keeping the car.

They'd been lucky not be discovered already. And they had to act before their luck changed.

They parked outside a supermarket. Bought a parking ticket from the machine and stuck it on the dashboard, one more innocent car waiting for its owner among the other cars. But instead of going inside they turned north and walked back up the road they'd just driven down. What had taken them ten minutes in the car took them an hour on foot.

They got a room on the ground floor. The view consisted of a melting pile of ploughed snow, the minibar was an empty refrigerator that refused to stay closed, and the twin beds were covered by bedspreads adorned with a pattern that Albert and Leo could only hope was intentional and not the result of years of complicity in guests' private lives.

They lay on their beds with their ankles crossed, the TV in front of them, too tired to talk, too tired to eat and too tired to feel.

No doubt, they were wanted. Perhaps by the police, maybe by someone else, they didn't know.

What they needed was rest.

As soon as they woke up they'd rent a new car using Leo's credit card.

And then they'd continue south, and with a little luck they'd find William and Janine, and with a little luck they could help them prevent the big disaster that nobody knew was coming.

Leo was finishing that very thought when Albert sat up, extended his arm, palm raised.

Hush, said the palm. As if Leo had said anything.

And he looked at Albert, saw his face and followed his gaze to the TV. And realised that Albert hadn't been hushing him.

Wait. That's what the hand had meant to say. Stop.

And it hadn't been directed at Leo, it was directed at the entire world, at time and reality and everything else: Wait, this can't be happening, it can't be true.

But the world didn't wait.

And true it was.

Albert too sat straight up in his bed, stared at the TV screen and at the news streaming in front of them.

This was what everyone had been so afraid of.

This was the disaster.

And now they realised it had already begun.

48

Behind every purple dot on Connors' map there would be a person.

A person who was sitting at their desk.

Who was shopping at a local market, coaxing an infant into its Babygro, drinking coffee with milk and two sugars. Who was busy in a meeting or having sex in a hotel or gulping down an extra glass of wine at an airport to overcome their fear of flying.

Who was going about their normal, everyday life when the itch began.

They were scattered all over the globe, some had been travelling and were now coming home, others were going away with freshly packed bags, and the itching grew and became unbearable and it kept travelling across borders. And people who were a purple dot appeared in country after country.

The authorities saw it happen.

And everywhere their orders were clear.

And that was how it had to be.

And it couldn't be anything but chaos.

Not just here or there, in single places. But all over the world.

Feet marched across railway platforms, bags rolled behind their owners through departure halls, frightened people waved their tickets in the air and demanded to know what was happening. Everywhere the air was thick with questions, groups of people crowded around gate personnel and railway conductors and policemen and soldiers, and everybody wanted answers but nobody had any to give.

In airports and train stations and bus terminals and ports, displays were showing destinations and cities and venues. But on each and every one the departure times had been replaced by a single word: Cancelled.

And everyone had someone waiting, everyone was in a hurry and had to be allowed on board. And nobody wanted to give in.

As the news started to spread, so did the panic.

In country after country there were new suspected cases of a terrifying illness the like of which nobody had ever seen. With every report the desperation and terror got worse, and nobody wanted to be left behind, wherever behind was.

People fled. Nobody knew where they were running to. Just what they were running from.

The highways were solid with cars, people desperately trying to get away, only to find themselves stranded with thousands of people they didn't want to be near. And everything was someone else's fault and can't you see I've got kids and for fuck's sake let me through.

Fights broke out. Helicopters hovered over the traffic jams. Cities echoed with sirens, and hospitals released their patients to get ready for the storm.

Everything happened in no time. It happened all over the world, quickly and relentlessly and everywhere at once. And for every new case that was verified, more and more people panicked and their actions became less and less rational.

The rumours spread faster than the virus.

People burned their neighbours' homes because what if they're sick.

Shops were looted because what if we run out of food.

On TV the newsreaders appealed for calm; the same men and

women who'd been shouting at the tops of their voices about the horrible things that were happening now adopted sober tones and pleaded with people to stay calm and stay at home. And of course it was too late.

Far, far too late.

ꝏꝏ

Franquin turned away from the screen.

He didn't want to see anything else.

He knew that this was only the beginning. That things would get worse and that over the coming days, weeks, months there'd be more of the same, only worse, more desperate, sadder.

He screwed his eyes shut.

The others would soon be here.

And there was still much that needed to be done.

He opened the heavy steel door and stepped through it, out across the high threshold, a clang as his foot landed on the metal floor.

The thrum of the engines, the smell of oil and metal.

He hated boats.

And no, this wasn't technically a boat, it was a ship, and no, it was much too large to get seasick on it, and shut up, he thought, he knew perfectly well what he felt, he hated boats and he hated them with a vengeance. All the more frustratingly ironic, then, that he must rely on a boat to save his life.

He picked up his phone as he hurried along the narrow gangways of grey metal, passing rounded cabin doors on either side, climbing the clattering metal stairs to the deck above.

Connors' number was at the top of the call history.

Down the list it appeared again and again.

Franquin had called and called and Connors hadn't answered and something wasn't right.

He should've been done by now.

He should already be on board.

Franquin pressed the button to call him again.

And felt his anxiety grow.

49

William Sandberg woke up to the sound of helicopter engines.

They were nearby, that much he could tell, but the sounds were muffled. Softer than if he'd been outside, but louder than if he'd heard them through solid walls, and his first instinct was to sit up but he couldn't.

It was dark. Pitch-dark and impossible to see.

A couple of centimetres above his head there was a roof, and in his effort to sit up he'd hit his head against it. It hurt, but not as much as it hurt a moment later as he fell back on to the surface under him.

His arms were tied behind his back. The angle was tight and uncomfortable, and whatever it was that held them together, it was thin and rigid and hurt.

'William?' It was Janine.

And she was close.

'William, what's happening?'

He heard her breaths. They were short, irregular breaths, as if she'd been crying or was in pain or both. He felt her body against his as she breathed, and he realised they were lying next to each other in a confined space, her legs bent in front of his own, her back against his chest. And every time their bodies touched he felt her shake.

It wasn't pain. It was restrained panic.

'I can't move,' she said. 'I can't breathe.'

Her voice was composed, but she was talking fast, every word reeking with fear.

'You're breathing all the time,' he said. Calm and steady. 'Can you see anything?'

She didn't reply. She didn't know. Didn't want to.

'Janine? Janine, where are your hands? Can you feel anything around you?'

She listened to him, wanting to be calmed down but at the same time unable to let go of her panic, as if the panic was her friend, the one thing that might be able to get her out of there, and if she let go of it she'd be stuck for ever.

She could take a lot. She had no fear of heights, she could endure physical pain, but this ... small spaces, the feeling of not being able to breathe even though she was, as if someone was holding a pillow over her mouth and pressing and pressing, creating that pre-emptive panic of running out of air long before it actually happened.

'My hands are tied behind my back,' she said. 'I think I'm bleeding.'

'Okay,' he told her. 'We'll get through this.'

'How?' she said. The same, panicked voice.

He didn't answer.

And neither did she.

He'd hit his head against a roof of metal. It smelled of oil and synthetic carpeting. There wasn't much doubt where they were.

And above them, a helicopter hovered in circles.

Janine's voice again.

'What are we doing here? William? What are they going to do to us?'

William didn't answer.

Didn't answer, because he was afraid he knew.

∞O∞

The young crew-cut pilot gritted his teeth to keep his mind clear, steered the helicopter in another large circle around the mangled landscape below. The metal skeletons littering the ground. The withered bushes and yellowing grass, trying in vain to cover all the craters and old tracks.

Nothing was right. Nothing.

He'd known it the moment he got out of bed: it was going to be a terrible day. It had shaped his entire awakening, a strange air of discontent that covered everything like an impenetrable layer, and here he was and the discomfort was only growing and no matter how he tried he couldn't shake it off.

There it was. Right below him.

One of their own black Audis.

One squeeze of the trigger, one single squeeze and then the car would disappear in a blanket of fire and he knew he shouldn't care, by then he'd only be a tiny dot on the horizon, far away before he'd get to see what was left of it.

No. Not it. *Them.*

And even if he couldn't see, he'd still *know*.

So what difference would it make whether he saw it or not?

She, who'd been with them for months, who couldn't be much older than himself and who he'd never got the chance to talk to even if he'd wanted, and he, the older one, who'd shown up a few days ago and who turned out to be too old to be kept in line the way they'd planned.

There they were. He couldn't see them, but there they were all the same. Locked inside the boot, tied up and with no hope of getting out, and it made him so uneasy that it was almost physical, an anxiety so heavy that he shifted in his seat, a decision he had to make even though it wasn't his, and he felt himself sweating but what else was there to do?

His orders were perfectly clear.

And he was alone now, alone with his orders, and that was wrong too. Connors should have been by his side, but he hadn't showed up and eventually Franquin had told him over the radio to take off and carry out the damn order anyway. And of course it shouldn't make any difference, Connors would have nodded at him and he would have squeezed the trigger exactly as he was about to, but at least he wouldn't have been alone with it.

There they were, inside the car.

No hope of escape.

And here he sat with his thumb hovering over the trigger and an anguish so intense it hurt.

The only thing he wanted was to get out of there.

He kept hovering in circles over the Audi, knowing what he had to do, but unable to do it.

∞◯∞

The communication centre was located several decks up, and Evelyn Keyes was sitting in front of the bank of screens. She glanced briefly at Franquin as he came in.

'The helicopter on its way yet?' he asked.

Keyes turned to a young man further inside the room. He was dressed in a uniform Franquin hadn't seen before, possibly Greek or Italian, he didn't know where they'd requisitioned the ship from and it didn't really matter.

All he saw was the man shaking his head. And Keyes relaying the gesture, as if he hadn't seen it already.

'Get the pilot on the radio,' he said. 'Where can I stand?'

Keyes pointed to a headset hanging between lights and buttons and more of that ubiquitous grey metal, and Franquin pushed the cushioned headphones down over his ears and heard the world outside go silent.

Just the static from the radio. And the answer that should have come but didn't.

He called out again. Then, more static.

'When did we last hear from him?' Franquin asked, and when the man in the unknown uniform responded from the other end of the room, the answer came in a screeching treble straight into his brain. It took a moment for him to remember they were still talking over the headphones.

'Not since you gave him his orders,' the voice said.

Franquin shut his eyes. That wasn't good. There was no reason for him to be taking so long.

'Call again,' he said.

And he listened, heard the static, and still no answer.

Not again, he thought. It had almost happened in Amsterdam, the jet pilot who'd got cold feet and almost failed in his mission to destroy the hospital, and now his own pilot was hovering above the shooting range where Stefan Kraus had been blown up in an ambulance. Could it be that this pilot, too, was starting to feel remorse?

Then there was the issue with Connors. Who should have been in the helicopter, too. Who should have been there to supervise, but who hadn't shown up.

Everything was taking too long.

It had to be done, and it had to be done now.

Not that he bore any personal grudge against them, it was simply that the clock was ticking and they couldn't afford emotions at this stage. This was just one in a long series of rational decisions they had made and must stick to.

William Sandberg and Janine Charlotta Haynes had jeopardised the entire mission. They had no value now. They were ballast.

And as little as he knew about ships, he knew that ballast was the first thing that got thrown overboard.

He ordered the nameless man at the radio to open his microphone too. And then he started to talk.

∞◯∞

It was Janine's terrified breathing that made him decide to do something long before he decided what. His first objective was to distract her, try to release her from the grip of her fear. His second was to escape, if that was even possible.

'Try to roll over,' he said. 'Keep your back up.'

It wasn't easy. But they braced themselves against each other, and eventually she confirmed that she was lying as he wanted, telling him through her clenched jaws that this wasn't making her any less frightened so whatever you're going to do, make it quick.

'Can you reach up?' he asked.

'Are you kidding?'

'Try. Try to reach the roof, feel your way to the edge.'

And she did.

She stretched out, her wrists exploding in pain where the thin, rigid strips bound her hands together, and when her shoulders wouldn't bend any further she kept pushing through the pain anyway, and she felt how it drowned out the panic and to be honest this was much better.

Her fingers touched the roof. Metal. Sharp edges, like thin beams crossing each other right above her. She could barely scrape it with her fingertips, but it was enough to confirm what she suspected.

'We're in the boot of a car,' she said.

'I know,' William answered. 'Try to find the edge.'

She understood what he wanted. He wanted her to reach the lock. And then they would both say a silent prayer that she'd be able to release it from inside, and it would probably hurt like hell but she wouldn't give up.

She let her fingers walk along the bonnet, her arms following at a more and more unnatural angle, and it pressed her down into the floor and diagonally into William, every ligament in her body screaming in pain but she wouldn't listen.

And finally, she found the lock.

It couldn't be anything else.

A thin slit between two pieces of plastic, and inside she could feel metal, perhaps it was the bolt or the clasp that secured it, or maybe it was simply her brain trying to remember what the lock of a trunk looked like and recreating an image that fit what her fingers felt.

Whichever it was, it wasn't helping.

She could barely touch it with the tip of her finger. The opening was too small.

'I can't!' she said.

'Try!' he said again.

And she shook her head, her pain and panic replaced by strength and adrenalin, and she screamed back at him, not in anger but because there wasn't any point debating:

'It's a tiny crack. I can't reach inside. We need a plan B.'

He said nothing. There was no plan B.

'I'm not a fucking contortionist,' she yelled.

He couldn't see her, but understood perfectly.

He'd heard her groan from the pain as she bent backward and could only imagine how much it had to hurt.

'Okay,' he said. 'You can relax.'

'Then what?'

She stayed in her unnatural position. Didn't want to let go of it, knew that it would be impossible to put her body through the same thing again, didn't want to relax until she was certain he wouldn't ask her to repeat the exercise.

'I don't know,' said William.

Silence.

Just the helicopter hovering above.

Waiting for what? Why couldn't it put them out of their misery, do what it was supposed to do, instead of leaving them lying there with no way out?

So he thought. But didn't say it.

Instead, again:

'I don't know, Janine.'

Eventually, she let her fingers fall away from the bonnet.

And without that support, her body collapsed on to the floor mat, her arms behind her back, and she screamed with pain as her limbs tried to stretch out into their normal position.

There had to be another way.

And she let her thoughts wander through the inside of every car boot she'd ever seen, tried to remember the details, the constructions and angles, but no matter how hard she tried she couldn't think of a single way out.

Until she realised out wasn't where they should be getting.

∞◯∞

Franquin had no way of knowing whether the helicopter pilot could hear him.

But it felt as if he could, and he convinced himself that what he was about to say would make a difference. He stared out across the water, his headset clamped to his ears and the thin microphone a shadow on the edge of his vision. And he started to talk.

It wouldn't help to be bombastic. He needed to be honest. And steer clear of talk about duty or loyalty or saving the world.

Instead he spoke of understanding.

His own understanding for the young pilot.

Understanding for his fears, his reluctance, and the impossibility of comprehending the incomprehensible.

He stood there, speaking into the ether, voicing what they all felt.

How nobody had dreamt it would go this far.

How he too knew what it was to lie awake at night, and how that was something he didn't let people know but that didn't make it any less true.

And he said that he'd known for more than thirty years that this was what it would come to, for thirty years he'd known and yet even he had hesitated when the time came.

And he talked about how there had been nobody to turn to.

No one to confide in when he had doubts, because he was the one who roared and stood firm and gave orders and couldn't flinch simply because things had become difficult.

And his nights had been sleepless.

He'd killed people in the hunt to create a virus. Innocent people who had served as guinea pigs and who he'd seen die and who stayed as images that refused to go away no matter how hard he closed his eyes.

He'd killed civilians. He had personally authorised a strike to destroy a hospital in Amsterdam, and even though that had been laid down in the plans that had been stored in files and binders for thirty years, that hadn't made it any easier to live with.

And now. Now there was an Audi on a field and he understood what he was asking and how hard it was.

But he asked anyway.

No, he didn't ask, he pleaded.

He pleaded with a helicopter pilot who maybe heard what he said, maybe not, begged him to do what he had to do, not because it was the right thing — because who knows what's right or wrong — but because this was the best plan they had and even if the easiest thing to do would be to bail out, their survival depended on nobody doing that.

All of that he said, all the time with his gaze locked on the horizon.

And he felt his colleagues' eyes behind him but didn't turn around. He'd exposed his innermost self. But they didn't know if he had, or if it had merely been a speech to persuade the pilot to comply. And he had no intention of telling them.

When eventually he removed his headset, he could only hope his words would make the same impression on the pilot as the people in the room.

∞◯∞

Janine was smaller than he was. Smaller, thinner, more supple. And that meant the task had to be hers. It would probably hurt like hell but she didn't have much choice.

Janine had taken command. She'd ordered William to lie as flat on the floor as he could, and then she'd pressed against him, told him that they needed to switch places and that he had to help her over.

He couldn't quite grasp what she was trying to do, but he clumsily turned on to his other shoulder, Janine's body heavy on top of his, making it hard to breathe, and their bodies scraping against steel and bolts and hurting more with every moment. But their hands were tied and they had to find something to brace themselves against in order to get the leverage they needed.

And finally she landed on his other side.

He heard her wriggle around, felt her breath against the side of his head as she positioned herself with her back towards the cabin of the car.

'What are you doing?' he said.

'The back seat.'

He understood immediately.

They would never be able to open the boot. But with a little luck, perhaps they could go the other way. Perhaps there was a crack between the boot and the back seat, a crack into the car itself, and perhaps it was impossible but what else was there to do but try?

She pushed her arms behind her again. Forced them to crawl up the back of the seats, pushing the pain away as she let her fingers explore the surface, up towards the handles that would hopefully be located on top of the seat. The ones that would release the seat-back and allow it to fold forward. The ones that maybe, maybe she could reach, if there was a crack to push her hands through.

She searched with her eyes without seeing, let them flicker from side to side as if that would help her hands to see, tried to picture every car she'd ever seen in order to work out where her fingers needed to be going.

And there it was. The tiny hole where the seat was attached to the chassis. And she pushed, bent, forced her hands to wander inside, her nails clawing their way up the upholstery to drag her fingers forward, millimetre by millimetre, closer to the lever she hoped would be there.

And she screamed.

Screamed in pain and with all the air in her lungs, screamed to increase the flow of adrenalin, screamed to make herself bend just a little bit more, and then she screamed for joy: 'There!' she screamed, the feeling of hard plastic between her fingertips. She'd found it.

A tiny lever.

'Can you move it?' William asked.

She didn't answer.

Braced herself, closed her eyes, let her fingers keep searching. This was definitely it, a curved plastic surface in a cavity, the lever she needed to pull, yet she realised it was impossible, how could she transmit any strength to her hands when her entire body was twisted into unnatural angles? But it was the only chance they had, and she fought to reach around the handle, fought because she had to.

Almost. Almost. One centimetre more.

She had the clasp in a weak, feeble grip, just the friction of her skin against the plastic. And she tried to pull it, maybe it moved a fraction of a centimetre, maybe she only wished it did, and the next moment her fingers slipped off of the surface and the grip was lost.

It was no use. Her arms were on fire. She couldn't take it much longer. And her mind flooded with desperate thoughts.

Thoughts of Albert, of the world outside, of everyone who would die and what if they still could stop it. What if they actually still could?

'Push me!' she screamed.

He hesitated.

'Push me against the seat, push as hard as you can!'

He got what she was trying to do. And it would no doubt cause her a lot of pain, but she was obviously aware of that. So instead of debating, he did as she asked.

He braced himself against the other side of the boot. And Janine held her breath, made herself as big as possible, tensed every muscle as William pushed his legs against the chassis, full force, squeezed her harder and harder against the seat-back. The seat kept refusing to budge, she couldn't breathe and the pain was unbearable and even so she screamed at him to keep pushing.

And William pushed. Harder and harder and harder. Her arm twisted more and more behind her back. And she tried not to think about which would break first, the seat or her bones, instead she struggled to make the handle move, straining to make contact between the plastic and her skin in the hope that the friction would dislodge the catch. Perhaps William's pressure could help, perhaps it would make the clasp slide up or the seat give way and maybe, just maybe they'd finally make it.

If they didn't she'd die in the boot of a car. And then what would it matter if her arms were broken.

'Come on!' she screamed.

Her tone was higher the harder he pushed, and she willed him to keep pushing because she could feel the seat bow under the pressure and—

—and then, it happened.

The clasp slid off its hook.

The seat folded into the back seat, and they both gasped for air, as if they'd just surfaced from a long, dangerous dive. And at that moment—

The moment the car opened up before them.

The moment daylight poured into their wide-open eyes.

In that moment, they saw the helicopter through the windows. A shadow against the blinding sky. But that was enough.

In that moment, they knew.

Then came the explosion.

It was the fuel that made it happen so quickly.

It was the fuel that made the flames spread in a fraction of a second, evaporating in the sudden heat and blending with the oxygen in the air, igniting in a single blast of red and yellow and black and starting a whirl of dancing fire that never seemed to end.

The heat warped the metal out of shape, glass was shattered and turned to dust, melting into soft clumps that fell to the ground and would lie there forever, sparkling in the sunlight for no one to see.

All that had lived was suddenly gone and wouldn't return.

Where grass had grown a new crater gaped, glowing red-hot and covered in flames, and a new steel skeleton had been added to the field's collection of worn-out tanks, once targets for shooting exercises but now nothing more than forgotten wrecks; of debris from armour-piercing shells and grenades, and of an ambulance that wasn't an ambulance and that had been blown to pieces in the hope of stopping a future that was already coming.

And with time the crater would cool. New plants would take root, cover the ground, and everything would start anew in the perpetual ring dance that is life.

For the plants on the abandoned firing range at the foot of the Alps it didn't make much difference.

For William Sandberg and Janine Charlotta Haynes it was the difference between life and death.

PART 4

Fire

I don't know who you are.

The truth is I don't even know if you exist.

The only thing I know is that I hope. And that is what keeps me going.

Maybe that's the reason I'm writing.

Because as long as there's someone shouting, there has to be someone who hears. Because maybe you can create a future by mooring to it, by throwing out an anchor and holding on, by planting a flag on a mountain and saying, this is mine, this place exists and no one can take it away.

Like planning an event in a calendar to make sure that day will arrive, so even if the world is going to end then at least it can't happen until then.

Midnight. Thursday 27 November.

Tonight we're going to escape.

One last attempt to stop what's happening.

And whoever you are, I want to believe you exist.

I want to believe you're reading this.

I want to believe that means it went well.

50

They awoke with a feeling of emptiness.

And their thoughts ran in circles the way thoughts do.

First the anxiety that something had happened. Then the realisation that it was only a lingering dream, because it had to be, because it always is. Then the struggle to recall what kind of dream it had been, where it took place and who was in it, and why the feeling stayed and wouldn't let go.

But there was no dream.

And the search went full circle.

They'd fallen asleep to footage of chaos and rioting, theories and experts and here's what you should do to protect yourself. And maps showing where the virus had reached and how it was spreading.

And their TV showed the same images over and over, the same ones it had shown before they fell asleep, only more desperate, more terrified, more panicked.

Albert and Leo sat on their beds in silence, watching the images without turning up the volume.

The empty feeling was gone.

Replaced by the feeling that everything was coming to an end.

The world had closed.

Schools and libraries and supermarkets were locked and boarded up, as were the railway stations and airports and every other place where people might meet and breathe the same air and spread the virus.

Armoured vehicles ordered people to stay inside, hospitals would only admit the infected, and men and women in rustling hazard suits desperately tried to treat them but didn't know how. The course of the illness was terrifyingly quick, and in labs all over the world researchers and experts were running between tests and machines, and nobody had any idea what it was they were seeing.

In city after city, the authorities commandeered ice rinks. The same rinks where ten-year-old children had chased pucks or practised pirouettes only days before, and where parents had stood cheering and freezing and drinking hot chocolate while they waited to drive their children home. Now the rinks had been turned into cold-storage facilities and the ice was covered with black plastic bags laid in rows, and in some of the body-bags lay the very people who days earlier had been performing pirouettes and drinking hot chocolate.

And where the ice wasn't enough, fires were lit.

Body after body was fed into the flames, incinerated to destroy the virus, and when the black smoke rose towards the sky one source of infection was neutralised, but everywhere across the planet new ones kept appearing.

Everything was moving in one direction.

And the only thing anyone could do was to try to slow it down.

In the hope that if they slowed it down long enough, maybe someone would find a cure.

Someone didn't have much time.

∞○∞

There was no reason to suppose the police had discovered Leo's identity, much less blocked his credit card. Even so, his hands fidgeted from the tension as he checked out of the motel.

The car they'd left behind had been rented in Christina's name. And even if anyone was searching for it, there wouldn't be any way to link it to him. They would be looking for Albert, of course, but everything that could reveal Leo's identity had been carefully disposed of.

Leo was simply a young man checking out of a motel. An extremely nervous young man, it had to be said, but since when was that illegal?

'Trying to escape?' the man at the reception asked him.

Leo looked up, panic in his eyes.

How did he know? Had the card triggered some warning?

'We've been talking about it,too,' the man continued. 'My wife and I. But what is there to escape to?'

It was a rhetorical question. And Leo got it. There was only one thought on everyone's mind: the disease.

And a deadly virus was obviously of far greater concern than the fear of being caught by the police for running a red light in Berlin. Even so, Leo couldn't help but breathe a sigh of relief when he realised the man was only talking about the disease.

Only.

And he smiled at the receptionist, mumbled something that didn't make sense even to himself and that the man was too polite to ask him to repeat, and they both bade each other farewell with a feeling of sympathy.

The sincere feeling of sympathy that only exists in the shadow of a disaster.

∞◯∞

Chiefs of staffs and political aides worldwide picked up their phones to receive the same message.

Scenario Zero was underway.

And everywhere the message was passed onward and upward to the highest authorities, cars were readied and families woken and driven through deserted cities to planes standing by for take-off.

There hadn't been much time.

Less than forty-eight hours had elapsed since the first envelope was delivered. It contained a short code, and that had been used to retrieve the orders, those that had lain in wait for decades, and after that the wheels had started to turn.

Presidents and prime ministers had been allowed to assemble a group of family and staff, and those who were included were winners and those who weren't were losers and would never know. In silence the important documents were assembled, those that would be needed to run the country from afar, and were packed together with toys and family photos and whatever seemed necessary, stowed in trunks and cargo compartments before setting off at high speed in vehicles where nobody spoke a word.

On the horizon, smoke rose from fires.

All over the world, leaders abandoned their homes and their friends and their countrymen and a disease that refused to die.

Heading for a future on a ship.

Alone and isolated from the rest of the world.

And everyone was scared and frightened and full of grief.

It was a small price to pay for surviving the end of the world.

∞○∞

Albert was already outside waiting in the car when Leo got the call from the newspaper.

He'd been trying to reach them since he woke up, but nobody had answered. He'd left messages but no one had called him back and at least two hours had passed. And he couldn't blame them.

He could picture the scene in the newsroom, the whirl of activity, frenetic phone conversations and improvised meetings and newsfeeds and information streaming in, all of it needing to be converted into headlines on the web before the competition got there first. They were doing the most important job in the world, at least in their own mind, and that notion kept fear at a distance and made them invulnerable, as if they weren't part of the world but reported from the sidelines and couldn't die – the same way Christina had believed she couldn't die until she did.

And he knew he wasn't their priority. A stranded intern paled into insignificance compared with a global epidemic and the collapse of civilisation.

So when they finally called him back, he was concise.

He jammed the phone between his ear and his shoulder, one hand on the card machine to pay for their new car, and the other gripping a bag of breakfast that would probably only make them high on sugar but sometimes you have no options.

He started talking as soon as the editor on the other end of the line said his name.

'The franking machine,' he asked. 'Have you traced it?'

He heard a no.

And more words followed it, but Leo interrupted him without listening; there was no time for excuses or explanations and the person he was speaking to would surely agree.

'I sent you a picture,' he said. 'Someone there must have it, check with Christina's people, we found an envelope, another one, or never mind. But I think the things that are happening are connected to William. We're being chased. And I think because of the envelope, someone is after us—'

The voice at the other end, irritated, cutting him off.

'Leo? Please?'

He stopped talking. Replayed what he'd just said, and realised that he'd been babbling incoherently. Not a good quality for a journalist.

'Let me speak,' said the voice.

'Sorry, I'm – go ahead.'

And at the other end the voice began to speak.

From that moment, Leo lost all interest in the franking machine.

∞◯∞

Seconds later, Leo yanked open the passenger door, jumped in beside Albert, dumped the paper bag on the back seat and clipped his seat belt in one single movement.

'Drive,' he said.

Albert, sitting behind the wheel, reacted immediately.

Exhausted after only a few hours' sleep, he'd allowed himself to relax, and now he realised what a fool he'd been to think he could. Someone had tracked them down, or Leo's card had triggered an alarm – whatever it was, he wasn't about to hang around. He started the engine and reversed out of their spot with screaming wheels, bracing himself for bad news.

'What's happened?'

'Nothing,' said Leo. 'Or, rather, it has. We're going to head south.'

Albert looked at him. Now what?

Leo buzzed with an energy that had surfaced out of nowhere and that he didn't know how to channel, tried to organise his thoughts into something that resembled a logical flow before letting them out of his mouth.

'The call,' he said. 'William's call. When Christina and I were on the roof, when he called and interrupted the transmission?'

'Yes?' said Albert.

'They traced it. I know where to find them.'

∞◯∞

The young crew-cut pilot had been sitting in his helicopter with the black Audi below.

He'd circled around it, pass after pass. He'd fought against his feelings, on the one hand the duty to follow orders and do his job, and on the other that tormenting restlessness that refused to stop vibrating within him, as if trying to remind him what was right and what was wrong.

And he couldn't stop thinking about the pilot in Amsterdam.

The one who'd disobeyed orders and flown past his target, only to reconsider and return to and finish the job.

Then he'd heard Franquin's voice in his headset.

It was as if the man could read his thoughts, as if Franquin knew exactly what was going on in his mind; this was just like Amsterdam, he thought, smaller in scale but exactly the same situation, and if a fighter pilot could listen to his conscience, shouldn't he too?

In his ears, Franquin kept talking.

Talking about how hard it was for them all.

And the pilot hesitated, he wanted to object and tell Franquin that there had to be a better way, but he knew he could never do that, knew that the moment he allowed it to become a conversation he would lose. Franquin would tell him it was too late to duck out. He'd remind him that he'd squeezed the trigger before and it was his duty to do it again.

And he knew it was a lie.

Blowing up the ambulance was not the same thing, the man inside was already dead, but in the Audi there were two living people, and they weren't even infected but simply in their way, and that tore him up inside, literally tore him up all the way from the marrow and out, it was a feeling he'd never experienced before but that couldn't be misinterpreted, and how could he ignore that?

And he fought to keep Franquin's words away, he circled the Audi one last time, and then he straightened on his course, steered away from the firing range, away from the valley and the mountains and the castle, didn't know where, but away.

He was many miles away from his target when Franquin finally breached his defence.

His orders might be wrong but what he was doing was worse.

He heard Franquin over the radio and he still didn't answer but deep within him, he knew.

He had no choice.

He couldn't hold out.

And eventually, he did the only thing there was to do.

He turned the helicopter around.

He saw the test range come back into view, and the black Audi, and he pinched his skin to drown out the painful feeling, the sweat that soaked the back of his shirt, the stinging sensation of anxiety that wouldn't stop growing but that made him rub his forehead to think, rub his back against his seat, rub his skin and inside his shirt and everywhere, literally everywhere, a restlessness that ached, that stung, no, that itched and that wouldn't stop and that drove him to insanity—

It wasn't until he saw the blood soaking his uniform that he knew.

The discomfort he'd been feeling all morning.

What he'd thought was anxiety.

It wasn't.

And once he'd started to scratch he couldn't stop, his body screamed and burned and fell apart and he needed both his hands to stop it. Outside the air howled around his compartment and reality spun faster, circling as a ring-dance of hazy streaks past the windows and eventually there was nothing left to do.

He had long since let go of the trigger when the helicopter hit the ground, exploding into a fireball of burning fuel and melting glass.

A few hundred metres away stood the black Audi.

Waiting for the inevitable fate that never came.

For William and Janine it was the difference between life and death.

51

William and Janine clambered out of the black Audi and left it behind, left it with the explosives inside and the black smoke billowing from the wrecked helicopter next to it.

They helped each other to cut through the cable ties that bound their wrists, and they walked through the landscape without uttering a word. They needed food. Food, warmth, sleep.

It took them an hour to reach the village. It looked like a page out of a travel brochure, if people made travel brochures about places where there wasn't anyone left.

Everyone had fled, the same way people all over the world had packed up and climbed into their cars and thought that we can't be safe here, not *here*, but somewhere else.

The name of the village was the German word for hills, and that was very much what it looked like. A handful of houses with weathered wooden cladding were scattered on either side of a winding street, the asphalt a mass of cracks and potholes where it had lost a life-long war against the annual thaw.

In the background, the Alps stood in stark relief against the sky. And beyond one of those distant ridges, somewhere on the other side of all the clefts and gullies, somewhere over there was the castle and the lake and everything else they'd fought so hard to escape from.

There wasn't a car in sight. Every gate and door was closed. Windows had been boarded up. All that remained was a village full of memories but devoid of people.

They made their way between the houses, weathered signs telling them what sort of business had been going on inside. They passed the convenience store and the hairdressers and the shop that used to sell clothes and shoes and outdoor equipment. And they knocked on doors and rang bells, but everything was locked and no one answered.

It was beginning to get dark.

The evening was clear and crisply cold, and the ground that had thawed in the sun began to turn hard and icy, crunching under their naked feet as they walked.

The temperature was dropping. They needed somewhere to spend the night.

And eventually they chose a house with old, rickety doors where they wouldn't have to do too much damage to get in.

They washed in someone's bathroom. Scraped gravel out of their wounds with towels smelling of someone else's detergent, towels that had been folded and stacked neatly in a cupboard, waiting not for them but for someone who might never return.

In the kitchen they found coffee and canned food. And they ate in silence, William on the living-room couch and Janine in the armchair next to him, their plates as protection against whatever they might drop, as if they were polite guests careful not to leave stains, as if they wanted to be able to look their hosts in the eye and apologise for breaking in but assure them that they'd done their best not to leave a mess.

Food that presumably had flavour even if neither of them could taste anything.

On a shelf in front of them the TV showed the same looped footage.

Cities. Villages. Countryside.

People in hazard suits, bodies being dumped in fields and burned on pyres, desperate attempts to stop the disease.

'Fire,' she said.

And he said nothing.

'That will end it all.'

The last part didn't reach him, that's how thin her voice was, little more than an exhalation.

But he didn't need to hear her. He already knew what she meant.

This was it.

A huge and violent fire.

This was the final verse.

∞◯∞

The first helicopter arrived later that same evening, and more would come throughout the night. Franquin would shake hands with presidents and prime ministers and their partners and their families. And even if he knew that from time to time he'd wonder, he knew he'd never ask.

Why these people, he wouldn't ask.

Because this was simply the way it was decided. It was impossible to save everyone. And someone had to choose who got to live, and he was relieved that choice had fallen to someone else.

There was no point debating whether it was right or wrong.

Nobody deserved what was happening, and no one could determine who was worth saving and who was not. It was a desperate attempt to save a species. The individuals didn't matter.

The huge carrier ship could stay at sea as long as it had to. Eventually the disease would subside, and then, only then, would the ship return to land.

Perhaps they'd succeed. The odds were no better than that. Perhaps.

But something had to be done, and this was the plan they'd devised. Franquin had already heard the crew referring to the ship as *The Ark*. Behind his back, he knew they were calling him Noah and he didn't like it.

Not because the comparison was unwarranted.

But because it was terrifyingly accurate.

And the hours passed. On board, the mood was heavy and all the new faces that kept arriving were red from crying and stiff and scared, and nobody questioned anything but they weren't grateful either.

When night fell and the first twenty-four hours were done, everything had been checked off against the plan.

With two exceptions.

Their own helicopter was missing from the radar.

And Connors still wasn't answering his calls.

∞◯∞

Every place on earth has its own unique silence.

And when night fell and the news became unbearable a new type of stillness came to replace the old.

William lit a fire in the grate, not that he was cold, but he needed to hear the crackle of the flames. There was comfort in seeing that some things kept working as they should, that if nothing else, at least fire and air and gravity would keep cooperating, and that even if humanity died out there would be other things that stayed.

There they sat. Listened to the fire.

Life about to end. And the only thing they could do was wait.

*

'We were going to celebrate our first anniversary,' she said, apropos of nothing.

She wasn't trying to start a conversation, that simply happened to be where her thoughts had ended up, and she rested her gaze in the fire, hoping that the loneliness would be easier to endure if they shared it with each other.

William didn't reply.

She told him all about it, about Albert, about the life they'd had together, about that evening in the restaurant, how angry she'd been that he was late and how pointless that anger felt now. About the plans they'd made for the future. The places they'd wanted to live, the jobs they'd wanted to have, the vacations they'd intended to take.

The future. It was all they'd ever talked about. So sure had they been that there would be a future for them.

'And then we'd be parents.'

She said it plainly, no emotion. No hint of self-pity. One more of the thousand things she needed to get out, as if saying them aloud would give them a chance to survive, rather than just dying as silent thoughts buried inside her.

And William looked at her across the polished wooden table. The table and the cloth that was draped on top of it, knitted or crocheted or whatever method kept the mustard-brown threads together, a project that had been important to someone once but that had lost its meaning and been left behind when reality fell apart.

'We'd name him after one of the great scientists,' she said. 'It was always a he when we talked about it.'

She shrugged apologetically as if that were something that needed to be excused.

'Alexander, after Bell. Or Isaac, like Newton. Christopher after Columbus, you know, those kinds of names. We wanted to name him after someone who'd changed the world.'

William sat silent. The air full of the words he ought to say.

Words that were created for moments like this, words that perhaps were clichés but so what, provided they did their job? Words that had become clichés because they were comforting, because who didn't want to be comforted when everything around them was fear and uncertainty and chaos?

But he didn't say them.

If that's what you want, then one day you'll get it.

That's what he ought to have said.

You still have all the chances in the world.

But he knew it would be a lie.

And he was certain she wouldn't want to hear lies.

Instead, he let his eyes linger on the fire, staring off into eternity until everything became a unity of colour, contourless fields that floated into each other and flickered in time with the flames.

'What did they want to make of it?' he said finally.

She looked at him, bemused. 'Who?'

'The Organisation. Of the future. The new predictions you translated into Sumerian, what were they?'

She thought about it for a moment.

'What you'd think. Prosperous harvests. Finding oil.' She gave him a sad smile. 'Who cares, really. It's not our future, and it never was.'

He nodded. And they sat like that.

The silence warmed them as much as the fire, wrapped itself around them, brought stillness to the whole room.

And it filled him.

With peace.

And he realised it was the same feeling he'd experienced that night: peace, stillness, calm. He just hadn't understood that's what he felt.

That night, it had came from the warmth of the water, the water that slowly filled the bathtub around him, that spilled over the top and made him weightless right there in his own bathroom. The water that freed him from all the thoughts that had kept refusing to be silenced.

This time it wasn't the water. It was the warmth of the room. And this time he wouldn't die.

Or then again, maybe he would.

But not by choice.

And he sat in silence.

And felt that if ever there had been a moment to talk, this was it.

'We adopted her,' he began.

They hadn't spoken for so long his voice came almost like a

shockwave, even though it was barely more than a whisper. Janine looked at him. Saw the outline of his face, a thin edge of light where the glow from the flames hit him in the darkness.

She knew instantly what he meant. The sorrow he didn't want to talk about. The one that everyone had told him wasn't his fault either, the one that he couldn't do anything about and shouldn't blame himself for. That he hated everyone's opinions about, and that he'd refused to tell her about.

But now he did.

Low voice, slowly, and with his eyes staring into distance.

'To us, she was always our daughter,' he said. 'But to her . . . '

He paused for a moment, and the moment grew into seconds, and the silence lasted for god knows how long and Janine let it.

'She thought we let her down. As if one day we were her parents, and the next we'd suddenly decided to renounce it. And we couldn't understand her. For us, nothing had changed. For us, she was a part of us and there was no before and no after. But for her . . . '

He gave a small shrug.

'I think that was the beginning of the end.'

Janine said nothing.

'And then she died.'

Just like that. And that was all.

And the fire kept crackling and it's never quite as silent as when there is a sound to show how silent it is.

'How?' she said.

'I didn't see the signs,' he said.

All the things he'd never told anyone before, that were too painful to confront, all those things were waiting. Waiting, only an exhalation away.

And he held his breath. Until, eventually, he let it out.

'She stopped talking to us. She moved out, she'd barely turned sixteen, but she emptied her room and told us she wouldn't be coming back. And then she stopped seeing us. Not just us, gradually she stopped seeing her friends too, and they'd call and be worried and what can I say? We were, too, naturally. But were we worried enough?'

He shook his head.

'We told ourselves it was something she needed to do. That she was developing as a person. Finding herself, creating her own future. We all have a right to do that, don't we?'

He paused.

'All the signs were there. And we didn't see them.'

'Signs of what?'

'Of what was coming.'

He told her in short sentences, single words, as if he was writing a telegram and every unnecessary letter would cost him.

The thefts. The things that disappeared: money, mementoes. Minor things to start with and then bigger, more expensive things that couldn't be explained away, and they knew she'd been there, but how could they forbid her to when all they wanted was for her to come home?

She'd come when they were out. She'd sleep in the guest room, or in her old bed, she'd eat at their table, and every time it made them feel a ray of hope, as if deep down inside she wanted to be there, with them, as if all the other stuff was just a phase she was going through and that would pass.

But it didn't.

The things that went missing grew larger and larger and there was no pretending any longer.

Then one day she'd left it behind.

The equipment.

They'd been abroad over the weekend, and she'd returned to their apartment, just as they'd hoped she would. She'd slept in her old bed and eaten sandwiches with fillings they'd bought just for her. And even if she wasn't there when they got home, they thought that next time, maybe next time she might stay for good. The same thing they always wished for.

And then they'd found it.

It was clean and neatly arranged and lying next to her bed. A case; a small black case that could have been a purse or a toilet bag, but instead it held needles and syringes. And when they understood, they stood motionless and didn't know what to do.

Their daughter.

Why?

The details that meant the most to him were least important to Janine, so he skipped over how they'd waited in the darkness.

Waited for her to come home, double-locked the door and turned off the lights and moved the car to make her believe they were out.

And like the expression in her eyes when she found them sitting there. The look of disdain and sadness and a will to be forgiven all at once. And like everything she'd threatened them with, all the things he'd said to her, all the doors that had been slammed shut and how he hadn't realised that when she rushed down the stairs that night, when her steps faded out downstairs and the street door closed behind her, how he hadn't realised that that was the moment when everything changed for the last time and would never return to the way it had been.

They'd put up a security door to their apartment. A security door to protect them from their own daughter, and that was a terrible thing to do and it hurt and yet they believed it was right.

But they wouldn't ever need it.

She wouldn't ever come back.

They found her locked in the toilet on a train, his daughter on the floor of a toilet, and of course it was a first-class coach and she couldn't have said it any clearer. The lies behind the surface, she said, right across time and space and life, *this* is what they look like. The darkness and the loneliness and the ugly, right in the middle of the polished veneer and the free coffee and newspapers. That's what she told him, but without any words. This is what my life became.

She was lying on the floor in a foetal position. Her hands under her head, her hair flopped over her shoulders, both knees squeezed up tightly against her stomach just as she always used to sleep. And in his dreams that was all she did, she slept right there on that filthy floor among the footprints and the damp, rested and waited for him to wake her up, waited for him to hug her, hard and long and not letting go, just the way they used to hug when he woke her up before he set off for work, when she would lie newly awake in flower-patterned pyjamas and beam at him from under her sheets.

But in reality she wasn't asleep. She couldn't be woken, couldn't be saved, she was lying in a foetal position because that's how she'd ended her life, there were drugs in her blood and her body had given up and that didn't stop him from hugging her, desperately and hard and now he was the one who wouldn't let go, and the police had stood behind him watching and she hadn't hugged him back and there and then his life had ended.

He didn't tell her everything, far from everything, but he told her that, and he did it objectively and matter-of-factly, as if he wanted to stay detached from it, and then he was done and nothing more was said for several minutes.

'I didn't see the signs,' he repeated after a while.

'And you think you should have?'

He shrugged.

'Because that's your job?'

'No. Because she was my daughter.'

Simple as that.

'And I failed to see it, failed to read her, I didn't see the signs and that was my job. Because if I don't then who does? If the future is there and I have everything in front of me, everything I need to stop it, and I can't see? Then who will?'

Janine gazed at him. Knew what he meant, and at the same time not.

It was as if he'd merged the tasks into one, as if he punished himself for Sara and for the codes at once, as if somehow one could have stopped the other, as if Sara's death and Christina's death wouldn't have happened if only he'd found the cipher key. The one that nobody had found in fifty years. And that was the only thing that had to do with what was happening now.

She told him as much, and he didn't reply.

'She wasn't your task to solve. You mustn't think that.'

The faintest of shrugs.

'You can't know what will happen. Not then. Not now. One thing leads to another and everything's connected. And nothing begins and ends with you alone.'

Maybe so. But William didn't answer. He'd said all he wanted to and his eyes had returned to the fire.

And the silence came back, and stayed.

'What about your plans?' she asked him.

He turned to look at her.

'If you weren't here? If the virus had never gotten out? What would you have done with your life?'

He waited. Chewed the inside of his lip, as if the gums were words and he wanted them to taste just right.

'I never thought of the future as something I was a part of.'

He closed his eyes. Lowered his voice.

'And I regret thinking that.'

They didn't speak for hours. Janine stayed in her chair, watching William stare into the fire as it turned into embers, staring and breathing and stroking the leather of the black book without knowing he was.

The black book that had meant so much. That had been in his pocket when they got out of the Audi, the only thing the guards had left with them when they took their key cards and all the pages of codes and signs. She saw him sitting there, holding it like a parent holding his child, and when she couldn't bear watching it any more she got up and moved over to the couch.

She leaned against him, William with his arm behind her back and her resting her hands in his lap.

They fell asleep right where they sat, huddled together on a couch that smelled of someone else's home. And with no other comfort to find, it was the best option there was.

52

They woke up to the sound of a car engine.

They had just about got used to the silence, to the thin layer of gentle wind and the occasional chatter of birds as they searched for something to eat, unaware of the horrors taking place around them.

And then, in the midst of that stillness, there was a hum. The muffled hum of an engine shifting gears. Revving to make it up a slope. It woke them both at the same time, and they sat motionless, close together the way they'd fallen asleep, looking at each other and hearing the sound grow.

There was someone coming. In a village that had been empty the day before, abandoned and evacuated, now someone was coming and perhaps they were looking for them.

They had no guns.

Nothing that could help them defend themselves.

And they moved in silence, took cover next to the windows, prepared for the worst.

There would only be a handful of houses to search. And the embers were warm in the fireplace; perhaps the smoke would even now be visible from outside.

They'd escaped more times than they would have believed possible. But this time they wouldn't stand a chance.

And they saw the car's headlights, saw them come closer, the beam of light growing along the village street.

Janine was the one who saw it first.

The sound of her scream surprised even her.

ထⓄၺ

They'd had direction but no destination.

And their thought had been that as long as we get there, as long as we do, we'll know where to look. But they never really got there, they got as far as they could, but if you don't know where *there* is, then you can't make it all the way.

Liechtenstein.

That was all they knew.

And now that they were there, what next?

William Sandberg had tried to call Christina twice from his own phone, the first time she had rejected it and the second he'd gone directly to her voicemail. After that, his phone had been on for almost an hour, before somebody turned it off, which was how it had stayed since.

During that hour, three mobile masts had made contact with his phone.

All three masts were in Liechtenstein.

Miles away from each other.

And now that they were here, Albert and Leo realised that while it was indeed a contained area, it was still impossible to search. They were looking for part of a needle in a land full of haystacks, and neither of them wanted to say it out loud but they had both stopped hoping.

That's when Leo had seen the sign.

And it was a long shot, but at least it was something.

The name was the same. So why not.

And they had left the main road in the early dawn, kept driving upwards through winding hill roads, scarred by years of erosion, and at the end of the road was a cluster of houses with wooden panels and steep roofs.

The name on the sign.

It had been part of the designation for one of William's masts.

It was the German word for a hill.

The first thing they heard was the scream.

It terrified them, but not as much as the woman who ran straight into the light of their car, waving her hands wildly above her head.

Their immediate thought was that she'd called for help. That she was infected and wanted to be saved. And Albert stepped on the brakes, looked around as he threw the car into reverse. If she was sick there was nothing they could do, nothing other than to avoid contact, and he scanned for a space to turn the car around, scanned for other people, terrified that they would be surrounded before they could turn the car and drive away.

That's when he heard her call his name.

And he turned to look straight ahead.

And then he saw.

Albert van Dijk didn't even stop the engine.

He opened the door.

Climbed out.

As impossible as it seemed, finally, they were there.

53

There were only two things to do, and still they couldn't decide which order to do them in.

The envelope had to be passed on.

And seven months of lost love had to be made up for.

And they held each other, Janine and Albert. She was alive and

he had found her, her letter had found him and he had understood – those were the only thoughts they wanted to think and
nobody expected more from them.

They stood in the morning light in front of the car.

The street was empty and they were the only ones there and
when they cried they didn't know why, perhaps they cried retroactively, cried over all the anxiety and loss they'd been pushing aside
for more than six months.

They cried with relief and they cried with happiness, and it was
beautiful and genuine and it had to take its time.

And it was impossible to watch.

That's how badly it hurt.

Hurt not to be a part of it.

Hurt because there could have been another person in that car,
should have been, but now there wasn't and that hurt.

And it hurt Leo, too. Hurt to see the man up on the front porch,
the same man who'd appeared on that phone in front of him just
days before, but older than in the picture, more worn and more
tired and sadder. Hurt to stand there and watch a reunion that
should have been his.

And Leo knew it was his job to interrupt them.

'Albert?' he said.

Albert pulled Janine tighter, inhaling her scent as if that would
give him the strength to talk about something else. Then slowly he
released her from the embrace, glancing over her shoulder at Leo to
let him know he understood.

'Sorry,' said Leo.

But there was nothing to apologise for.

Albert cleared his throat.

'We've got an envelope.'

He said it softly, like a declaration of love to the woman in his
arms, but he was speaking to both William and her. And she heard
him but didn't understand.

'You've got a what?' she asked.

'We don't know what it is,' said Albert. 'But they were prepared
to kill us to get it.'

When that was said the stillness was over.

Love would have to wait, there were other things to be said first, and William walked down the wooden steps, out to the couple on the street, and everything that had to be told came out in streams of explanations from everyone at once.

How Leo had travelled to Amsterdam with Christina. How he was there when she disappeared. Janine and William who saw the same things but on monitors in a castle. Who'd been taken there by an organisation and who were supposed to interpret texts and stop a disease and now everything was too late.

And Albert and Leo both said the same thing.

'Maybe not.'

Albert went on to tell them about the heartbroken man in Berlin, about the people who'd watched him in case he had the solution, *the answer,* and when that word was said everyone's pulses raced and William interrupted them with questions they were about to answer anyway but that he wanted to know *now*:

What solution? Why did they believe that? And why did anyone believe the solution would be in Berlin?

Leo's answer meant more than anything.

'All we know is it came from a Helena Watkins.'

∞◯∞

William's heart was beating so fast he couldn't help but worry that he'd die from a heart attack before he got the envelope open.

He rushed up into the windowless drawing room, cleared the dining table of candles and cloths and ornaments, and set down the yellow envelope in front of him.

Janine by his side. Leo and Albert a step behind.

The solution. It could only mean one thing.

It meant Helena Watkins had succeeded where William hadn't, and for some reason she'd sent her results out into the world, perhaps because she didn't trust the Organisation.

She had sent it out, so that the world would get to know.

But her messenger had died, and her husband had been too afraid, and now the material had gone full circle and ended up in William's hands, hands that shook as he folded open the edge of the envelope, and of course it would have been better if the solution had made it to the media or even been put online, but at least it was with them and that was probably the next best thing.

He spilled the sheets of paper on to the table.

Spread them across the worn surface where dinners used to be eaten and wine used to be drunk. Now it became a large desk, and he leaned over it all and let his eyes dance from page to page.

This was the solution.

He thumbed through it, felt the excitement grow in his chest, ached to find out what it was he'd been missing, thumbed through pages and looked and ached again.

Page after page of codes.

Their codes. The same codes he'd worked on.

The verses, Janine's verses, all the same.

There were pages with calculations, set-ups and variables, and his eyes darted from side to side like a skier on a slalom, zigzagging past every number, every mathematical sign, everything there was until he reached the final page.

Breathless.

The feeling he'd missed something.

The feeling that there was something he should have seen, something that was hidden in all he'd read but that he'd been too excited to notice. And he thumbed through it all again, searching for that crucial detail he'd missed at first glance.

Once more.

Then again, to be absolutely certain.

And once more, again, page by page, desperation in his hands as he shifted the papers around, turned to the next one, held them up to read. His breath erratic as he studied the papers, examined the numbers, tried to find one value, perhaps a single figure, a scribble in the margin he didn't recognise, or perhaps the other way around, a detail that should be there but that was missing.

Read and read and read.

Fuck.

Read it again.

And slowly, it dawned on him.

'What are you looking for?' It was Janine's voice.

'*Something,*' he said. Frustrated and with a tone that meant only one thing.

He kept looking and looking, but no matter how hard he looked he couldn't find it.

He turned towards Janine.

Only then did she see his face.

His eyes, energetic and focused only minutes ago, so eager they could hardly wait to get the envelope open and study the material.

Those eyes were now dull with despair. All the hope and drive and desire and spark had gone, and the others looked at him, saw him sigh, saw his hands fall to his sides, and as they did some of the papers fell on to the floor and he didn't even care.

He shook his head.

'It's exactly the same.'

William had remained standing with the papers spread out in front of him. All hope had run out, all that was left of him was an empty, silent shell, standing there, trying to find the words to explain what he'd found.

It was the same material.

The documents in the envelope were identical to the papers that had covered his wall in the castle, identical to the numbers and figures he'd paced up and down in front of day after day, that he'd studied and tracked and tried to understand without success. These were the same calculations he'd read in her binders. The same arrows and the same assumptions and the same extrapolations he'd already seen. And that he already knew were wrong.

There was nothing new. And the solution that Albert and Leo thought they were carrying. The answer they thought they had found.

It was nothing more than a copy of the question.

Nothing more.

'Why?' she asked.

Janine's voice was so weak that she barely heard herself.

'Why on earth would she send out something like that?'

William shrugged. How could he know?

Perhaps she *thought* she'd got it right, perhaps she believed this was the answer and her calculations would solve all their problems if only they were made public. Maybe that was it, and perhaps it was just another dark paradox that she would die too, that she had died from a virus she had helped to develop herself and that she had believed would work.

Or maybe she'd come to the same decision they had. Maybe she'd seen the end was drawing closer and felt she had to act. Maybe she'd realised she couldn't make it on her own, and decided that the only way to succeed was to spread the secret to people on the outside.

It was exactly what they had been trying to do.

So why wouldn't she?

And her papers had travelled in a circle, out from the castle and to Berlin, and there they'd been collected and brought back and here they were again. People had died along the way, fought to bring the secret into new hands as the Organisation did everything in its power to stop them. And now the envelope was back at the foot of the mountain where it started.

It was one terrible irony after another.

As if life had decided to laugh in William Sandberg's face one final time, as if it wanted to tell him that it wouldn't stop laughing at him until everything was over.

The irony that the solution was no solution.

The irony that, in her anxiety to stop the virus, Helena Watkins dispatched the courier who spread it beyond the castle.

The irony that all of this was predicted in everyone's DNA.

And the irony that what finally made everything happen were the decisions made by the people who'd made it their mission to stop the prediction being fulfilled.

Nobody spoke for a long time.

But then again, William had said all there was to say.

They were all thinking the same thoughts, they all saw how the last glow of hope had faded out, if it had ever been there to begin with, if it hadn't just been their own wishes that had made it seem so.

All hope was lost.

Nobody said it, but everyone knew.

And with that, William turned and walked away.

∞◯∞

Helena Watkins had been aware that she was dying.

She'd been lying in a coffin of glass, feeling her time run out, and in a way what she felt had been gratitude.

They'd given her her own room, far away from the sad rows of beds where men and women slowly bled to death.

They'd given her the best treatment there was, lessened her suffering far more than with any of the others, and slowed down the development as much as it could be slowed down. But she knew it wouldn't change the outcome. Knew that all they were doing was to delay the inevitable.

And she knew it was her own fault.

She had believed he was healthy. He hadn't shown any symptoms. And if he was well, that was proof that she'd finally succeeded.

Nevertheless, they wanted to wait. But Helena couldn't wait: she had found the solution, a solution that needed to get out there *now*, out to molecular biologists and researchers and institutions all over the world. Out to everyone who might understand it so they could start manufacturing a working virus before the predictions came true.

There was a world out there that had to be rescued.

And there was a man who thought he'd lost his fiancé.

And Helena Watkins had taken upon herself the task of putting everything right, that was how she'd seen it. And when the homeless man disappeared with the formulas and the envelope and her brief message of comfort to a professor she didn't know but whose name she believed was Albert, just a few words to tell him his girlfriend was alive and well, when she knew he was on his way she could feel how everything would at last be put right.

Instead, that had been exactly how it had started.

And she had been the one who started it.

She woke to the sound of someone coming into her room. On the other side of the acrylic glass that marked the edge of her universe stood the woman they'd kidnapped, she who'd been brought to translate the cuneiform signs and who'd had a boyfriend and who they should've known would become depressed in captivity.

Janine. Only centimetres away, but out of reach all the same, and next to her was a strange man who couldn't be anything but her own successor.

And she had a thousand things to say and no energy to say them.

She had already tried once, but didn't know what she'd managed to say, she was scared then and even more scared now and all she wanted was to warn them.

About the virus, about the codes, about time running out for all of them.

About the project that nobody called Noah's Ark, about how they'd ceased trying to save the world, and started to choose the people to build a new one.

All of that, she wanted to tell them.

But her mouth had already given up, her tongue was swollen and tasted of blood, and as much as she wanted to, she couldn't speak.

The word she whispered was *run*.

And behind Janine she saw the door being blown from its frame, guards in hazard suits pointing guns at them, and perhaps they'd been trying to run and what she was witnessing was their failure.

And Helena Watkins knew what that meant.

It meant that hope was lost.

And with that thought, she'd stopped breathing.

54

The first time Franquin summoned Rodriguez, twelve hours had passed since Connors' last contact. He informed Rodriguez of the situation, because protocol dictated that he must and there was no reason not to comply.

After twenty-four hours they had a second meeting. And so when Franquin heard the knock on his cabin door again, he knew what it meant.

'Thirty-six hours,' said Rodriguez. 'You want me to do it?'

The question drew a shake of the head. This was Franquin's responsibility.

It concerned him that he didn't have full control of the situation. Connors didn't seem to have made it on board the helicopter. The pilot had refused to follow his orders – either that, or he'd experienced communication problems, there was no way of knowing – and then they'd lost all contact and it had accident written all over it, even if there was no telling there either.

If Connors had been on board, there were two possibilities.

Either they'd gone down together or the two of them had made the decision to leave the Organisation and fly out of there.

But that hadn't been the case. Connors hadn't come to the helipad. So regardless of whether the pilot had died in a crash or chosen to run away and die of the pandemic instead, Connors' whereabouts remained a mystery.

And it was Connors' task to ensure that the data was delivered, that it remained secure.

And if he failed there were protocols for that, too.

'Give me three men,' Franquin said. 'We leave as soon as we can.'

Rodriguez turned on his heel, leaving Franquin standing at the steel table in his cabin.

He'd thought he wouldn't ever see the castle again.

Now he would, after less than two days.

∞◯∞

William had stopped at the end of the village street.

He was looking down the slope, past the mounds of frozen grass stretching into the valley, to the hills that he and Janine had climbed the day before.

Leo had spotted him from a distance. He'd followed him outside, felt he had to keep an eye on him. No, not had to, but wanted to. He wanted to see how William was doing, if there was anything to say, anything that he could do to help.

After all, William was the entire reason why he was there. This was the man Christina had been so determined to find. And now he was standing in the middle of the street, shoulders hanging and a body that had given up on the future.

Leo walked up to him. Slow steps on the frozen ground. Stopped abreast of him, not close but at the edge of the road, half a street between them to show he wasn't trying to intrude.

'I know I don't know you,' he said eventually.

William looked up at him. A sharp glance to interrupt whatever was about to be said.

'I don't know what you're planning to say to me,' he said. 'But don't.'

It came out of the depths of his lungs and through gritted teeth, as if the muscles in his jaws were the only things stopping him from grabbing Leo and doing something stupid.

'I just wanted to say,' Leo began. And then he ran out of words and ground to a halt and realised he didn't know where he'd been going to begin with.

A pause before he started over.

'I know I haven't gone through all the things you have. I know I can't, what's it called? Imagine. What you two have been through, here.'

He spoke to William's profile. Hoped he was listening.

'And of course I'm not the right person to tell you who you are. But if I could, all the same?' A pause. And then he did: 'You're not the type of person who quits.'

That drew William's reaction. The sound he made through his nose was not a breath by any stretch of the imagination, William snorted at him, and he made no attempt to hide it.

'What would you know about that?'

'It's the information I've gathered.'

What?

Oh. It took a second for William to understand what he meant, and when he did it stung him, hard and unexpectedly and much more brutally than he deserved. Christina had talked about him, she must have, and now the little brat was standing across the road thinking he had William all sussed out.

'In that case I think you need to double check your sources,' William said, his lips tightening over his teeth to keep his emotions at bay. 'I'm the best quitter there is.'

He paused before concluding.

'And if she told you something else it's because that's how she wanted me to be.'

He turned to look over the valley again.

Cursed to himself. It wasn't the kid's fault that he was standing here, the boy had the best intentions; he wanted to make contact, and of course he couldn't help it if William's own feelings were trying to pull him back down into the abyss again.

He'd allowed himself to hope. And that had been his big mistake.

'We've reached the end of the road,' he said. 'We're not getting any further. And that's not going to change just because you come running with a bunch of notes that don't mean anything.'

He sighed. That was the reality. He was back to square one.

No, square one had come to *him*, square one had travelled in a yellow envelope out of here and to Berlin and all the way back.

'Stop trying, Leo. It's over. It's pointless.'

There was a second of silence.

'I don't believe that,' said Leo.

William looked at him from so far out of the corner of his eye that all that showed was a pupil and a whole lot of contempt.

'What is it you don't believe?'

'That it's pointless.'

William said nothing.

'I think it's the opposite. I think this *is* the point. I think we were meant to give you that envelope. I think we were meant to, so that you wouldn't give up, so that you could get another try. This isn't life being ironic, William, it's the other way around. It's a chance. Life gave you a chance, because you were *meant* to have it.'

The corner of the eye.

The same amount of contempt.

'*Meant* to?'

'Yes.'

'Nothing is meant to happen, Leo.'

He spat out the words. As if *meant* was a vulgarity, as if the mere word made him want to give Leo a slap, as if it were an insult that mustn't be spoken again.

'My wife died, and you saw it happen. Was that meant to be? I was half a continent away and saw it happen in widescreen. Meant to be, was it? People are dying all over the world, nobody knows how to stop it, are you trying to tell me that's meant to be, too? *Meant*?'

His voice was a roar now.

And that was unfair, nothing was Leo's fault, but William was past being fair. He couldn't take any more well-intentioned, empty words of support, he couldn't take all the people who wanted to comfort him and who thought that everything would feel better simply because things maybe, perhaps, potentially, had a higher meaning.

Life was too short for bullshit.

Life was too short to say everything was mapped out and steered by someone who knew better and that when life got tough it was because you didn't understand that the problems were actually teaching you a valuable lesson. You can't change fate. What happens, happens. If something is meant to be then that is what will happen and there's nothing to be done about it.

Bullshit, that's what it was. And he said as much to Leo.

'What happens to you is your own decision,' he said. 'And what happens to me is mine. And if we happen to be fortunate then something good may come of it, and if we're not then everything turns to crap. But if you come to me and surrender your responsibility by saying the future is what it is ... No, if you try to take *my* responsibility away ...'

He stopped, let the sentence trail off into silence. Started over. Calmer now.

'Christina didn't die because it was meant to happen. She died because a whole lot of people made a whole lot of decisions that led up to it.'

A pause.

'And you didn't turn up here with that envelope because someone or something meant it. There is no meaning. And if you want to believe the future is predetermined, then be my guest. But it isn't. The future is what you make of it.'

There had been a long silence. And Leo had watched him intently.

Inside, he was picking his words, one by one, stacking them together. He wanted them to come in the right order, no stumbling, no hesitation or starting over. He meant every word he was going to say, and he wanted them to carry weight.

'In that case,' he said. Paused for effect. For precisely as long as he'd planned. His eyes on William's, sincere and steady. 'In that case I don't understand why you're standing here.'

William looked at him.

And Leo didn't move.

And then came the rest of it. Clearly. Calmly.

'Because if we create our future ourselves, I think you should pick up those codes and do something about it.'

55

William stormed back into the house, half angry as hell and half full of admiration. As a motivator it was one of the best combinations.

He was a sucker for logic. Simple as that.

Nothing impressed him more than a well-constructed argument, and the brat had stood there in his stupid baseball hat and hit him square in the face with his own argument, reversed and used against him.

He didn't believe in fate. Nothing was predetermined.

Ergo the prophecies couldn't be impossible to crack, and ergo the only one who shaped the future now was he who didn't try to.

Quod erat fucking demonstrandum.

He'd asked Janine to follow him into the dining room, recreate the room the way it was laid out at the castle, and this time they would begin at the beginning and do it the right way and on his terms.

There were no computers. No software. And that was exactly how he wanted it.

In one of the bedrooms they found a desk, and in the drawers were pens in different sizes, rulers and a calculator, and an unopened, shrink-wrapped pack of notepads.

It was going to be a gargantuan task. In front of them lay endless amounts of numbers and they had very little time, but the only thing they could do was to start afresh.

William browsed the pens until he settled for one with enough weight and a nice, gliding ballpoint, took out two of the notepads from the plastic and placed them next to him on the table. And then he asked Janine to start reading.

And so she did.

Digit by digit she read the first of the sheets: one, three, zero, two, three, long lines of code that seemed to mean nothing but that still held all those verses of Sumerian signs. And she saw William write them down into the first pad, number by number until the first page was full and he tore it out from the pad and pinned it to the wall.

Next page.

And so it went on. And for every new sequence he wrote, for every new page he pinned up and the more the material grew in front of him, the more he became a part of the codes. He could find his way back and forth along the walls, see the connections, feel the rhythm.

This was what he should have done from the start.

He should have gone back to the source, he should have torn everything down from his stone walls and started from scratch, what he and Janine did now he should have forced himself to do back then.

And he had known it too. He just hadn't had the time. But in reality the opposite was true, he'd wasted valuable time by not doing it, he'd stood there before all the printouts and told himself that it would work all the same, but deep down he'd known.

His pen danced across the pages, and every time he felt a similarity or recurrence he stopped and moved back to an earlier sheet, compared and checked and made intuitive calculations in his head, calculations that weren't really that but rather images in his mind.

Behind him stood Janine.

Listened, read, waited as William walked around, sometimes around the room and sometimes inside himself, waited while he did whatever it was he was doing until he asked her to read the next sequence.

Leo and Albert watched from the lounge.

They sat in the armchairs without speaking, fascinated by the process but not understanding what he did, what patterns he seemed to be seeing and how he could possibly hold it all inside his head.

Page after page were torn from the pad, filled with new rows of numbers, and he pinned them up one after the other and went on to the next as Janine continued to read.

The pad got thinner and thinner.

And when he ran out of pages he took the second pad from the table, and the process went on and numbers were read and William wrote and drew lines and wandered around the room.

And then the time came to switch pads again.

And he fumbled with his hand on the table.

There was nothing there.

'Pad,' he said. Not demandingly, not stressed, just anxious to go on and with thousands of thoughts that he didn't want to lose track of.

Janine looked around. Couldn't see them.

'Pad,' he said again. 'Please. Give me another one.'

His drummed with his fingers in the air, as if that would magically make a notepad materialise out of nothing. He didn't want to risk taking his eyes off the wall.

Somewhere up there the answer was hiding, he knew it. Somewhere between all the rows and sequences that meant nothing to him, not *yet*, but that might just as easily transform right in front of him, take a sudden step right out of the chaos and become clear. It had happened before. And he hoped that it would happen again.

He couldn't afford to lose his flow. Not now. He hesitated, but only for a second; he still had the black book in his pocket, Sara's black book.

And he took it out. Flipped past his diary entries. And told Janine to continue the process where they'd left off.

Again, numbers were read. Pages torn out and pinned to the wall. And he was several pages into the dry, leathery notebook when he realised everything was exactly the way it should be.

Here he was, working, his daughter a part of his life even though he was busy. Just as she had planned, only several years too late.

And he was right where he loved to be, surrounded by a chaos he couldn't understand but that he knew how to attack, where he could use his logic, provoke himself to disregard any preconceived notions, force himself to search for something even though he didn't know what it looked like and to trust that he would know it when he saw it.

The one tiny detail that would turn everything on its head.

The one that would be there, somewhere deep inside the sea of numbers, the one that he'd missed but that he mustn't search for, because it was hiding in the whole picture; it was that whole picture he needed to find, and he forced himself to take a step back and look at it all from a distance—

And then he stopped dead.

The detail. In the whole picture.

The tiny, insignificant thing you didn't see for all the big ones.

I'll be damned.

It was just a thought, a vague and abstract thought, and he shook his head. No, it couldn't be.

Or could it?

He was still a moment. Then took a step back.

Looked at the wall from a distance.

Looked at the book in his hands, Sara's beloved black notebook with its unwritten pages, and that was it, of course it was, this was what it had been about from the beginning. To see the context. How many times had he said so himself? Or heard it said? *The whole picture?*

When he looked at Janine again he realised he couldn't hold back his laughter. He laughed, loud and uncontrollably, and it was the first time in as long as he could remember.

It was as if he'd been trying to open a jar for weeks and now he suddenly turned the jar over, looked at it from the other direction and saw that the label said *open here*, and now that he'd seen it, it was obvious, *of course* it was supposed to be opened there.

It was the very feeling he'd been yearning for, the one he'd tried to find in front of his wall at the castle, and now that it came to him it filled him with emotions he'd almost forgotten. Relief. Excitement. And hell if it didn't fill him with happiness, too.

And all of that came to him in one single blow.

Janine stared at him.

'What is it?' she said.

He was still facing the wall, but his eyes were closed, he breathed with long, deep breaths as if he'd suddenly come to some deeper insight, as if he'd suddenly found inner peace.

She'd never seen him behave this way. And it scared her.

He looked as if he'd come to understand what was happening, and as if he accepted it, as if the fight was over because he'd seen the logic and realised it couldn't be escaped.

As if he was ready.

No, as if he enjoyed it.

'William?' she asked. There was fear in her voice, but she did her best to mask it. Tried to collect herself. Again: 'William?'

He turned towards her. Opened his eyes.

'It's over?' she said. 'Is that it?'

She felt as if she already knew the answer, but she asked him all the same, just for an extra second of hope that he'd say no.

'It really is over, isn't it?'

He looked at her. Wanted to explain, but didn't know how.

Instead what he heard himself say was:

'Call me vain if you want to. But I'll be really disappointed if you don't name him William.'

He was already out of the room when Janine got what he meant.

56

Janine caught up with him on the street.

It was blisteringly cold, snowflakes had started to fall, thin and white and floating silently in the windless afternoon air, settling like icing sugar over the landscape as if the village was a wedding cake and they were two figurines standing between the houses.

William was still holding the notepad. He'd stepped straight out from the dining room where they'd stood with the papers and numbers, he was only in his shirts and his sweater but his thoughts were too many to let him feel the cold.

His breath played in front of him. Swirling clouds, suspended for a moment before breaking up and fading away. One moment he stood there, motionless and with his gaze towards the mountain behind the houses. And the next he hurried down the village street, as if to get a better view, a different angle, as if he was looking for something.

'Where do you think it is?' he said.

He paused again. Looked. Kept walking down the street, his eyes fixed on the peaks in the distance.

Janine walked after him, long strides, trying to keep up.

'The castle?' she asked. 'I don't know. What difference does it make?'

She wanted to brush aside the irrelevant question, get back on to the subject of whatever it was he'd discovered.

'The road has to be over there. Right?'

He pointed towards the valley, past the houses, past the slopes, and Janine nodded, somewhere over there it had to be. The single-track asphalt road, the one that had led them away from the large gate in the mountain, the one they had run along in the middle of the night, when they still believed their escape had gone well.

'What are you thinking?' she asked.

'We need to get in.'

'So you know how to stop it?'

She was almost side by side with him now, walking with quick steps, staring at his profile and not taking her eyes off him for a minute.

Waiting for him to nod in reply.

Waiting for him to put an end to her fear, waiting for him to explain what they'd been missing. Whatever it was he'd discovered, whether it was the key or some other detail they'd overlooked, she wanted him to tell her.

But he just shook his head.

'No,' he said. 'What happens, happens. There's nothing we can do about it.'

Disappointment sapped the energy from her. She slowed down. Watched him walk on in front of her.

And William sensed it, slowed down too, turned around.

Still walking, but backwards, down the street away from her.

Still throwing glances up at the mountains.

The distance growing between them, growing until he had to shout:

'We have other things to do.'

And then he came to a halt and shouted:

'I think they're going to prove much more important.'

∞◯∞

They sat around the large wooden table in the kitchen of their adopted home.

Dinner consisted of dried and canned foods, a fire burned in the grate, a slice of everyday in the midst of everything, weird and strange and wrong but also just the way things were.

A strange calm had settled over them.

Albert and Leo sat across from each other. Sitting in silence, like spectators, listening to a conversation they didn't understand but dearly wanted to. Listening to Janine and to William. To the questions and the answers. To fear and to confidence, sitting on opposite sides of the table.

She couldn't understand. Wouldn't understand his calm, his pride, his happiness. There he sat, telling her again that he hadn't found a key. Not only that, but the key wasn't the point, they had been looking for the wrong things, staring at details and missing the context.

'Then how are we going to survive?' she asked. 'If we don't have a key, if we can't change the future. How are we supposed to stop it?'

'We don't need to stop it,' he told her, his voice serene, untroubled.

She started to protest, but he cut her off before she could get a word out:

'The Black Death.'

This drew a blank look. She shrugged, urged him to continue.

'The prophecy you showed me. The one from the fourteenth century. The one you compared to what's happening now.'

She didn't need him to remind her, she knew perfectly well what she'd said.

'You compared it to the verse on the end, and they both had the same word, the word that once described the Black Death.'

'Yes?' she said. More and more restless. *Plague.* That was the word. So what?

William leaned towards her.

'We didn't die, did we?' He gave her a faint smile. 'Many did,' he said. 'But the human race didn't die. We didn't die *out.*'

She was about to protest when her brain caught up. Suddenly she got it too.

It was as obvious as it was surprising.

It was a thought she'd forgotten to think.

'We've survived epidemics before,' he continued. 'And we will do it again. And a lot of people will die but not everyone. Eventually the virus will become weaker and enough people will develop resistance or perhaps someone will come up with a vaccine. And until that happens, it's going to be brutal and tragic and horrible. But it's not going to be the end. Not the end of everything.'

She stared back at him. Stared for a long, long time.

Hoped that he was right but couldn't be sure. What if he was only saying what she wanted to hear – no, what they all wanted to hear? What if he was clutching at straws and making it sound believable enough to comfort her?

'How?' she asked him. 'How could it be anything else? How could it be anything but the end, if there is no future left?'

'I think there is,' he said.

'The codes!' she said. 'The texts! We've seen it ourselves.'

'We've seen *what*, exactly?'

'We've seen them end.'

'No,' he said.

He felt the calm of his own thoughts, felt the comforting warmth as he chose the right words to explain. Warmth that could only mean one thing. That he knew he was right.

'We've done a whole lot of things,' he said after a while. 'But we didn't *see.*'

57

Franquin could still taste the Atlantic as he climbed the metal steps past the whining jet engines, walked down the aisle between the light-brown leather armchairs and sat down in one of them.

It was far from ideal. What he was undertaking could endanger the whole project.

One of the carrier's helicopters had flown them from the ship to the Portuguese NATO base where their jet temporarily resided, and with each journey they made, with each new landing and each person they introduced themselves to, they risked exposure to the disease.

But it was almost worth it just to have a few hours away from the boat.

The plane taxied on to the runway and he closed his eyes, trying to anticipate what he would find.

He couldn't rest until he knew where Connors had gone.

And the helicopter.

And whether it had followed his orders.

He leaned back in his seat and counted in his head.

In a few hours they'd be back at the castle.

Then he'd know.

58

'The context,' said William.

He said it as an answer to the question that lingered, the question in all their minds and that Janine had asked aloud, and that still didn't seem to have a plausible answer.

How could there be a future when everything was about to end.

That little question.

'The whole picture,' he said again. 'We always knew we needed the whole picture.'

They were still sitting at the kitchen table. And he turned to Janine as he spoke:

'You kept telling them we needed context, and then I said the same thing. And it turns out we had it all along. We had the whole picture right there in front of us, we just didn't see it. Because we were too busy looking at ourselves.'

Her impatience bordered on anger.

'*What* whole picture?' she said.

And then he told her.

He'd been up in the drawing room when everything fell into place. Janine was reading from Watkins' papers, reciting the numbers and the codes, and he was writing them down and pinning them up, thinking and looking for patterns just the way he thought that he should.

And when the second pad ran out, it dawned on him.

When he pinned the paper on to the wall, when he didn't have anything to write on, when he took out Sara's notebook and carried on working.

That's what he told her across the empty plates and the saucepans with pasta and with Leo and Albert observing him from the side.

'I needed another pad,' he said.

Janine peered back at him. So?

'Page up and page down, you read the numbers and I wrote them down, and then I suddenly had nowhere to write – and then what do you do?' He answered his own question. 'You get yourself another pad. You go get something else to write on, and keep writing there.'

She hesitated.

And he saw that she did. Nodded in encouragement, willing her to keep thinking the thoughts she was thinking. And the moment she threw a glance out the window, he knew she'd understood.

There. Outside.

'You can't be serious,' she said.

William nodded. He was.

And next to them sat Albert and Leo and they didn't understand a thing.

William gave them an apologetic smile, turned towards them and tried to formulate an explanation that wouldn't sound corny and naïve. Having found the solution that had confounded experts for the last fifty years, he didn't want to sound banal.

But the truth was simple.

So he told it like it was.

Humanity was just a pad.

And all around us there were other pads, countless species with endless reams of DNA, billions upon billions of lines of junk DNA that wasn't really junk and that ran from species to species, making our genome one single chapter in an infinite book.

The context.

It really was that simple.

The history in humanity's DNA didn't just belong to humans. It never had. It belonged to the world. Mankind wasn't the whole picture: she was a *part* of it. She carried one single episode in a shared, eternal story, and the whole picture started before us and went on after us and if the world's future was indeed already chronicled that didn't mean it would end because one of the notepads ran out of pages.

And that was all we were.

'A notepad on a shelf,' he said. 'Or a page in a pad. A fraction of a whole that we had around us the whole time but that we forgot, that Franquin and Connors forgot and an entire Organisation before them, all because we were so terribly busy staring at our navels, *so* damned short-sighted that we forgot that nothing begins or ends with us. Nothing.'

And they all looked at him.

Knew what he meant but needed to make the words their own.

'It wasn't the future that ended,' said Janine. 'It was the paper.'

She said it with a smile; it sounded as ridiculous as it was, and yet it made perfect sense.

And William looked back. And smiled, too.

They stayed at the table for a while, deep in a silence that none of them tried to break. Each of them too busy trying to absorb it all.

And time passed, but time wasn't their responsibility any more. There was nothing they could do to change the course of events. And nothing could be more of a relief.

The first person to speak was Janine.

'Does that mean, then, that what we're seeing now ... that all the things that are happening, that unstoppable plague out there? It only happened because they *read* that it would?'

He didn't answer. Rested his eyes on hers, but silently and perfectly calm.

'So if nobody had found the predictions in the first place,' she said. 'None of this would ever have taken place?'

Silence returned. And William nodded.

That was the reason he'd rushed out into the street. The reason he'd looked at the mountains.

'Can we get back into the castle?' he asked.

'Why?' said Janine.

'Because I think what we're meant to do is to make sure nobody ever makes the same mistake again.'

59

The first impact made the window crack into a huge white spider web.

It hung in place before them, millions of tiny fragments clinging together, a multitude of cracks as if the window was a city map where all roads led downtown, and the centre was where the spade had hit.

William still had it in his hand.

And he lifted it to take a second swing.

None of them liked breaking in, nobody wanted to destroy other people's property, but there was no better way and besides, if they succeeded, wouldn't it be worth it?

The glass was covered by safety film, and it took blow after blow to get through, but eventually there was a hole in the pane and they could hack it open enough to get in.

Inside, there was skiing equipment and running shoes, and even if the village was small and the sports store's supply limited, Janine knew exactly what they needed.

They packed the rental car that Albert and Leo had arrived in.

And now all they had to do was to wait for it to get dark.

∞◯∞

William sat on the porch next to the house, his legs stretched over the stairs down on to the ground, a pleasing kind of restlessness while the hours counted down.

In front of him the village carried on downhill like a retreating set in a theatre, the street vanishing amid the houses, fresh snow falling to rest untouched by feet or wheels.

In the lounge just inside the door Albert and Janine had fallen asleep on the couch. They lay tight together, Albert behind with his arms around her and Janine in front with hers as an extra layer of arms on top of his. As if they wanted to make sure not to lose each other again, not ever, whatever might happen next.

And slowly, slowly the light turned blue.

The day turned into afternoon.

And in the windows around them no lights were turned on, nobody came home to prepare dinner; nothing happened but for the darkness settling and the temperature dropping. And William pulled the thick jacket from the store even tighter around himself.

When dusk started to fall, Leo came out and sat next to William. It was genuinely cold now, cold and quiet, and the only thing that could be heard was the sound of the ice crystals sliding with the wind across the ground, that and the rustle of their down jackets whenever one of them moved.

A flock of birds passed high above the houses, distant wingbeats in the winter twilight, and Leo followed them with his eyes, watched them disappear above the rooftops and down into the valley.

And once the thought had been uttered there was no escaping it.

The birds. Everything else. Everything that was alive, everywhere around them.

All of them carried a chapter.

A single chapter of the story, not humanity's, and not their own, but everyone's, together. The world's.

As William had said, no matter how you put it, it sounded banal. But that didn't stop it from being true. And it didn't stop Leo from feeling it.

'It's this kind of thing that makes you a vegetarian,' he said.

William gave him a huge smile.

'There's DNA in plants too, you know.'

Idiot, he added. But just inside his head. And with love.

Leo shrugged. 'Then I guess breakfast is a no-go tomorrow morning.'

The silence returned, and they stared at the setting sun, saw it disappear and take the last of the light with it.

'Who?' Leo asked after a while.

One single word, but William didn't need more. It was the same question that he himself had asked when he first learned about it, the same that Connors and Janine and everyone else who knew had asked at one time or another. The one that kept recurring, no matter how dearly one wanted it not to.

Who put the codes there?

'Does it matter?' William said. 'Who or what or nothing at all or coincidence. Whatever the reason, things are what they are.'

He felt a deep calm. He didn't know who. Or why. He didn't know anything, except that he didn't need to know.

They didn't know too little. They knew too much.

And he said as much, and then he listened to the silence again.

He looked up to see Leo smiling. 'I still think it was meant to be,' he said.

William gave him a bemused look. What was?

'Us coming here with Watkins' notes. I think it was supposed to happen.'

'You know what?' said William. 'I don't really give a damn what you believe.'

And then he leaned over to put an arm around the young man's shoulder.

They sat for a while, not father and son but as close as they could come, and Leo realised that this was him. This was the man Christina went looking for, this was William the way he'd been, the William who'd made her call Leo in the middle of the night and go to Amsterdam on a whim to track him down. And now that he saw him, he understood.

They sat there, next to each other in the icy wind.

One single thought in Leo's mind. To say it or not?

Maybe this was as good as things could get, maybe he would just be stepping in things that were no business of his and ruining the moment. But at the same time, he felt that he should. For her sake, if nothing else.

And eventually, he made the decision.

'She was wearing her ring,' he said.

William glanced at him. Didn't quite follow.

'When we went looking for you. She'd put it on.'

Oh.

William turned his face away. Said nothing.

'I wanted you to know.'

Still no answer.

And the silence refused to move, it lingered and was compact and impenetrable, and Leo could only think that he'd blown it, that he shouldn't have said mentioned it. He should have let it lie, but instead he'd scratched a wound he shouldn't have touched, and now he was sitting in the evening darkness with a stranger's arm around his shoulders and no idea what would happen next.

He felt William's arm slide off of him.

Heard him stand.

And walk away.

No. He stopped.

'Thank you,' said William.

Nothing more. 'Thank you.'

Then he turned and walked back into the house.

And his voice was thick and low and on the porch sat Leo. And he couldn't help smiling, happy to have let him know.

∞○○∞

They drove for much longer than they'd expected to before they found the single-track road.

It branched out from another road several miles from the village, and instead of being blocked with barriers or gates it had been made to look like an insignificant gravel track, either temporary or perhaps private, and it modestly wound off away from the main road.

Not until it was out of sight did the asphalt return and the road lines begin, and after another half-hour ride they could make out the weak contours of the gate at the foot of the mountain.

Progress was slow. They waited until darkness fell before leaving the village, then drove with the engine kept low and the headlights off. The only light they had to guide them was the moonlight through the thin clouds, that and the white edges of the snow-powdered hillside, and they leaned forward in the freezing car, straining their eyes to see. To see where the road turned beyond the next bend. To see if anything moved. *Anyone.*

But nobody seemed to have noticed them coming, and eventually they decided to stop while they were still a fair distance from the base of the cliffs. Janine and William got out, went to the trunk and collected the equipment Janine had borrowed from the store.

Ropes. Crampons. Gloves.

William took his share. He attached it according to its instructions, fighting not to acknowledge his apprehension; he didn't like what he was about to do but he knew he had no choice. Indeed, he'd been the one who'd suggested it. And if heights scared him that much, so be it. It was the price he had to pay.

As Leo and Albert turned the car back towards the village, Janine and William set off on foot.

Walked beside the road, tramped across the meadows.

The same meadows they'd run across two nights ago.

But this time not to flee from the castle.

This time to break in.

60

The landscape transformed into mountains as imperceptibly as one season moves into the next, and they found themselves climbing rather than walking, unaware of when one turned into the other.

In the distance they could see the gate they'd escaped through, far away along the mountainside and tens of metres below, and William forced himself not to think about the drop, forced himself to register the things he saw without thinking of where he saw them from.

The turning area by the door was empty.

No vehicles, no movement, nothing.

No tracks in the shallow snow.

Perhaps it meant they'd all left the castle already, or maybe it just meant that there never had been much traffic, and that this was the way it always looked.

From above Janine waved him on. And he did as she'd instructed him, he watched her moves and tried to copy them, put his hands and his feet where she had put hers, and slowly, slowly they climbed higher and higher.

Janine, moving and fastening her hooks and her clips.

Trying routes, advancing upward.

Stopping to wait for William.

And all the time, the abyss under them grew deeper and deeper. And William came after, trying to think about anything at all. Except what would happen if he fell.

When William and Janine finally rounded the ridge, they saw for the first time just how huge the castle really was.

The building swelled out of the mountain like a mushroom on a tree trunk. It crept out from below with walls that seemed to have been blasted into the cliff, following the rock upwards before taking a new turn and surging outwards, forming turrets and towers and terraces and banisters, growing along the mountain in all directions and constantly branching out into new sections. In this manner it continued to rise, with rows of windows and alcoves and ledges and walls that led on to more of the same, like an entire city of stairs and pavilions and gates and towers, topped off by an array of little roofs.

It was a castle that a child could have made from unlimited amounts of Lego. But this was for real, and just as absurd as the thought that someone had once decided to build it, just as absurd was the thought that now it was the base of a military organisation, and that underneath it there was an even larger complex, hidden in the modern zones under the rock.

Janine peered into the darkness, barely able to make out what she was seeing, trying to decide how to reach their target.

The huge, stained-glass windows to the chapel.

From there, they'd get to the stairwells.

Then on to the metal doors where the new section started.

That was the extent of their plan.

After that, they were relying on a whole lot of luck.

∞◯∞

The car Franquin saw coming at them on the single-track road didn't have any lights, and shouldn't have been there to begin with.

There were two men in the front seat, that much he was able to make out, one of them young and the other one slightly older. He couldn't remember seeing either of them before and there was no telling what they were doing there.

They might be terrified civilians, trying to escape the disease, hunting for a place to sleep.

But his instincts told him it wasn't that simple. And he ordered the other men in his car to keep their eyes open for any sign of a movement, either on the road or out on the meadow.

The gate at the foot of the mountain was still just a shadow when the man behind the wheel nodded at the asphalt ahead of them.

'There,' he said. 'That's where they turned around.'

He was perfectly right. There were tracks in the snow, tyres that had tried to do a U-turn but had been forced to stop on the narrow road, reverse to get space to turn, and then driven off.

But beside the tyres there were other traces.

'Engine trouble?' someone asked.

Nobody answered. But everyone saw. Footprints at the side of the road and out in the ditch, traces of someone who had got out of the car and walked around.

And it might be nothing to worry about, merely proof that their car had run into trouble and that the driver and his friend had tried to fix it. Perhaps that's why the lights were out, because of problems with the battery or the generator or whatever else could malfunction in modern cars.

No one spoke but they all knew there was another possibility. This was the perfect place to get out and continue on foot if you didn't want to be seen from the gate.

Franquin told the driver to turn off their headlights, too.

And they crept the final stretch in darkness.

Without talking, and with their eyes scanning the meadows.

61

William had promised himself that he'd never do it again.

He had sworn, piously and solemnly, vowed that if he survived the last time he'd never risk his life again, ever. And yet, he was back. And fatalist or not, he couldn't help wondering if Fate would keep its side of the bargain given that he'd failed to keep his.

Those were his thoughts as he threw himself out into the air.

The fall came like a punch to his stomach.

There wasn't a single cell in his body that didn't scream in panic, his vision blurred as he felt the icy wind rush past, felt his body become weightless and lose control, and the ground coming at him from below.

Then the sharp tug as the rope took him. The vertical fall levelled out and became a pendulum motion, and as he swung forward he knew that his entire life depended on a pin in a cleft somewhere above, knew that if it gave way then he and the pin and the rope would plummet to the frost-covered rocks and certain death.

His head counted the microseconds. That's how long they seemed to be, that he could count them one by one as he floated through the air, every fraction of every second lasting an eternity, full of opportunities for things to go wrong. He refused to look, his eyes wide open so as not to miss her, but his brain determined not to see a thing until everything was over.

Janine reached her hand out to him.

She stood on the sill where the window had been, the gigantic arched window of coloured pieces of glass that had been assembled hundreds of years ago, carefully joined into a display of men with mantels and halos and beards, but that was now gone. She'd hit it feet first, shattering the entire mosaic into a multi-coloured, razor-sharp rain, and now the chapel lay open and waiting for them inside.

The same chapel where she and William had sat and talked only days before. When all they wanted was to get out.

As William's feet landed next to hers, he clutched her hand, trembling with fear and adrenalin and his eyes had only one thing to say: Let's never do this again.

∞◯∞

William and Janine moved across the screen like dark blue silhouettes against the noisy background. Behind them gaped the ruined window as a black hole of nothingness, just where the monitor had always shown a mosaic of nuances, subtly ranging from thousands of monochrome shades to shining, bright fields of white, depending on the time of the day and the sun's position outside.

Now the window was gone, and the two bodies that moved past the rows of pews were consumed by the darkness, merging with the camera grain. And when their silhouettes disappeared out of frame there was no knowing where they'd be showing up again.

The cameras were too few and too far apart.

It had never been resolved, and never would be.

Right now, that was a problem.

Not just to him, but to them.

They sped along in silence, walked with purposeful strides along routes they already knew they would be taking. Routes that Janine knew by heart, that she had memorised and that were etched like a map in her head and that they hoped would take them straight to where they needed to go.

Ropes and hooks swung from their backs and harnesses clinked in time with their steps, and William forced himself not to look at them, not to think about what they meant: that they were going to need them to move between storeys, that they didn't have any key cards and that their only way down would be on the outside.

It scared him, but he had no time to be scared.

Instead, he pushed on, his teeth gritted and his eyes alert, just as Janine's were in front of him.

It was night and it was dark and they didn't know how many people were still in the complex.

And they didn't care very much for suddenly finding out.

∞◯∞

William and Janine never reappeared on the screen, and that made it easier to deduce their position.

They didn't have key cards. Those had been taken from them together with the codes and the papers and everything else they were carrying, and then brought back into safety here at the complex.

And that meant there was a limited number of routes at their disposal.

He stood there, watching the monitors.

Whatever they were planning to do, he had to make a move.

Janine had taken the lead and he followed tightly on her heels. He tailed her through staircases and passageways, she'd passed them all before and knew exactly how far they would take them, where the next door would block their way and how far they'd be able to get without keys.

They headed downwards, because down was where they needed to go. There they would find windows where they could exit and carry on descending until they reached the server room. And then they would make sure the material would never be read again.

They had just emerged on to a landing. A large, open hallway, linking the stairs they'd come down to the next set of stairs. In one direction, a long corridor extended into the distance, and on the other side of it shimmered the cold blue light of the night sky.

A window.

Janine signalled to William, that's where we're going, and he was right behind and ready to go, and just as they were about to, they saw the silhouette.

At first, they couldn't make out who it was. All they could see were the dark contours of a man at the other end of the hallway, his features invisible in the darkness beyond the window.

He stood with his legs apart. But this wasn't the posture of a guard; his gait was unstable, as if his legs were spread to help him stay on his feet, and his arms were extended in front of him, one hand on the grip of a black handgun.

Aimed straight at them, ready to fire.

'Connors?'

Janine's voice. Half-question, half-exclamation.

It *was* Connors, but he'd changed: he was sweating, his eyes strained to look at them, pain radiating from every part of his body.

'Stay where you are,' he said.

William put up his hands, palms flat in front of him: Wait, I've got something to say. Take it easy.

He took a step forward, a single step, but that was enough to make Connors back up, tense his arms, his right forefinger so tight on the trigger he could feel the resistance from the spring.

'Do not come over here. And listen.'

'I want you to listen to me,' said William. 'We're going to be all right. If you trust me, Connors, we're going to get through this.'

Connors shook his head.

'*I'm* not.'

That was all he had to say.

'You're infected,' William said.

'Don't come any closer,' said Connors.

And that was a yes.

William could have asked him how and when and why. And Connors could have told them. Not that he knew for sure, but he could guess; in all likelihood it was someone he'd met when they prepared the evacuation – perhaps he'd shaken someone's hands, or maybe the pilot had and then they'd infected each other. It was the way it was. There was no one to blame but himself. He had written the protocol, and it had become his own death warrant.

'You shouldn't have come back,' he said.

'We wouldn't have. If we'd had a choice.'

It was Janine again. And Connors looked directly at her, his eyes begging for forgiveness, knowing what she'd been through the last couple of months, knowing how much she'd suffered and all to no avail.

'There's no saving us,' said Connors.

'We think there is.'

'It can't be stopped.'

'We know that.'

Silence returned. And when William broke it, his voice was calm, a stillness settling in the corridor, the feeling of a hostile situation that was slowly becoming a conversation.

'We're not here to stop the virus.'

Connors. Confusion in his eyes.

'Then why?' he said.

'We're here to stop ourselves.'

∞○∞

The cold moonlight grew across the tarmac floor. It started as a slither, spreading into a sheet of blackish blue across the painted lines and arrows and all the way up to the loading dock at the far end of the chamber, before the rolling door clicked into its housing in the roof.

Outside stood Franquin. His three men. Flashlights playing across the hangar. Scanning for movement, for shadows that didn't belong, for anything that might constitute a threat.

But there was nobody there. And Franquin left two of the men outside to watch the entrance, set the door to close again and signalled to the third guard to follow him.

He placed his key card on the reader by the interior door, continued through the long neon-lit passage with its scuff marks, and on to the steel corridors that waited on the other side.

∞○∞

Connors looked straight across the corridor, his features twisted in a sceptical frown.

What Sandberg had said was breathtakingly simple.

And yet he couldn't believe it.

For thirty years they'd been working here. And for thirty years before that, hundreds of other men and women had searched for answers, deciphering codes and making calculations and trying to stop the human race from coming to an end, and none of them had thought what William had thought and he couldn't take that.

Not one of them had looked up and taken that one step back and widened their perspective.

It tortured him to think of it, but he said nothing, he just stood there with his eyes smouldering with resistance while the seconds passed in silence.

It occurred to William their roles had been reversed. Suddenly he was the one opening doors inside Connors, doors that Connors hadn't seen before, and now he was the one stepping over the threshold and finding himself in free fall, exactly as William had done.

A page in a book. A book on a shelf.

And William spoke slowly and carefully and kept his voice low. He used the same words Janine had said at the kitchen table.

'If we'd never discovered what we have inside us,' he began. 'If we had never been paranoid enough to find sequences in our own DNA, if we hadn't interpreted them and read about our own demise? Then, would we still have created this virus?'

His voice was soft and to the point, as if he already had the answer but wanted Connors to get there by himself.

'I have been asking myself that question,' said Connors. 'More times than you can imagine.'

'And what did you conclude?'

Connors glared up from under his eyebrows, as if William was being sarcastic, as if the whole conversation was beneath him and he didn't want to answer.

But the truth was that he had never concluded anything. Every new answer had turned into its own question and he'd stopped asking a long time ago. Once the virus became a reality there was no alternative but to focus on the problem at hand, dedicate every resource to finding a solution, and that's what they had done.

'When I demanded access to all information you had,' William said, 'remember what you told me? You said that the fewer who knew, the better. You said there's knowledge we're not meant to have.'

He said it with emphasis, to make Connors see where he was heading. As the echo of his voice died away, the corridor was enveloped in silence.

'You're saying I was more right than I knew,' Connors said eventually.

'Than any of us knew,' added William.

Then it went quiet again. And slowly Connors lowered his weapon.

He looked William in the eye, then Janine. His gaze was clear now, he knew what they were trying to say, knew what had to be done, no matter how much it pained him.

'You're going to destroy the material, aren't you?'

'What happens, happens,' said William. Which was a yes.

'And the only thing we can do is to make sure it never happens again,' said Connors. He had understood. And either he could choose to trust William or he could stick to his protocol, the one that he'd written himself and claimed was the only possible way out. If he chose William's path it meant everything he'd done for the last thirty years, all his thoughts and plans and conclusions, all of that had been wrong and pointless and not worth a thing, and it wasn't easy focusing on thoughts like that with an itch spreading through his body, telling him he was about to die.

He shook his head, as if in answer to a question he hadn't said out loud.

He'd planned it all. He'd drawn up the guidelines for how they'd survive, how to get to safety, how to cheat death when nobody else would. And how well did that go?

Then along comes someone with a totally different plan.

Perhaps it was time to let someone else take the helm. Perhaps.

Eventually, he reached a decision.

'I can make it to the security centre. I'll unlock the complex for you.'

ooOoo

When every lock in the complex switched from red to green, Franquin's attention was elsewhere.

He was on familiar ground. The tracks on the road still had him worried, but there had been nothing to suggest that anyone had tried to tamper with the hangar gate, and there was no other way in, unless they came by air.

He'd come as far as the long, cool corridor, the one that sloped down and where there was a draught from outside, momentarily hesitating over whether to go on alone or bring the guard with him.

And the moment the locks switched to green, his gaze was directed down the passage he'd just come through. He'd left his last guard behind to watch the hangar as the protocol instructed, but now he was debating whether it would be better to ditch the routine, settle for two men on the outside to guard the entrance and bring the third along for protection.

But he had everything he needed to access the computer, log in to the system and retrieve all the sequences and codes. It was a one-man task, and it wouldn't take him more than a minute to accomplish his mission.

Telling himself that the protocol was there to be followed, he left the smell of fresh air behind and set off along the corridor. Key card in his hand. Never thinking for a second that the locks might already be open.

∞○∞

The strategy Connors presented was far better than their own, and would put a definite stop to the risk that anyone would read the codes again.

Janine and William raced through corridor after corridor, passing doors that stood unlocked and with diodes in shiny green, moving through the network of concrete and metal passageways without having to change floors.

And finally they stood before the room they'd passed only two nights before.

Everything was heavier than they imagined. But there were carts for the purpose and they lifted and struggled and loaded them up, as efficiently as possible, working as fast as they could, knowing that time was running out.

Connors didn't have too long.

And for what they were about to do, they needed him to be alive.

∞○∞

The distance shrunk by the minute and none of them knew.

Not Janine, who worked in silence, dragging crate after crate across the floor and placing them firmly in front of William.

Not William, who stacked them at right angles on top of each other, praying under his breath that the thin cart underneath would hold.

Not Franquin, who hurried up through the complex, staircase after staircase, his heels clicking like gunshots on the hard floors.

And not Connors. He stood in front of the monitors; he'd only seen them pass in one direction, which meant they must still be busy in the storage area.

He closed his eyes and tried to shut out the itch, the knowledge of what was happening to his body, but most of all he tried to shut out the feeling that this was what they had all experienced. All the men and women he didn't know, those whose names he'd been careful not to learn, those who'd lain in their beds behind the glass and felt their bodies decay without knowing why. It had been his fault that they went through this agony. His and everyone else's, and it had been completely in vain, and that was the feeling he tried to shut out, that was what he couldn't bear thinking of now.

His skin was itching, his back was itching, his arms too, and the more he thought about it the worse it got. And even if he didn't scratch, he knew that his skin would soon start to disintegrate.

He stood there, watching the monitors.

He wanted to see Janine and William return, wanted to be allowed to stop fighting, wanted to let the end come and set him free.

And next to him was the computer that controlled the locks. That monitored the doors and showed what cards were swiped and where.

And he didn't give it as much as a glance, because why should he?

The doors were open. And William and Janine had run straight through them all; he knew which room they were in, and there was no reason whatsoever why he should be watching that monitor.

But if . . . If indeed he had.

Then he would have seen Franquin's card being logged at door after door. He would have seen line after line pop up on the screen every time he passed a door, from the corridor with the rubber marks, through the abandoned passages, away from the level with the draught and on and upwards. And habit is hard to break, all the locks along his way were already shining in green, but Franquin was hurrying and had his key card ready, marching through door after door without a clue that he wasn't the one unlocking them.

And if Connors had looked at the screen he would have seen.

And if he'd seen, he would have acted.

But he didn't.

And Franquin carried on making his way up.

∞◯∞

They could only fill two carts, but that was also as much as they could move. And when the carts were loaded to the brink, William took one and Janine the other, and they pushed them out into the corridor. It was hard going, but they had no one to complain to, and slowly they started following the route that Connors had directed them to.

The power of their load was more than enough.

And once the process started, nothing would be able to stop it.

∞◯∞

At last, the moment came that Connors had been waiting for. William and Janine passed the camera on their way back after an eternity that probably hadn't lasted more than fifteen minutes. And he gave a sigh of relief, turned to exit the control room.

That's when his eyes fell on the monitor.

And the lines from Franquin's key card, travelling up the screen as he used it again and again and again.

Connors hesitated for exactly two seconds.

He didn't have more time than that. When the seconds had passed, he did the only thing he could.

∞◯∞

The timing was perfect and the irony complete and none of it was intentional.

Franquin had just reached another door and pushed his card against the reader when he realised that everything was wrong. He realised it because the box switched from green to red.

His body went stone cold. The door had been open and suddenly it wasn't. And there was no reason in hell why that should be.

He held up his card again, tried over and over, but the box buzzed and shone red and the lock refused to open.

He felt a sudden anxiety in the pit of his stomach, and he turned, ran back along the corridor to the door he'd just come in through. To his frustration, it wasn't open, either.

He was stuck in an underground passageway beneath a castle with no way out.

o○○∞

Connors called out to them down the corridor. Called to them to stay where they were.

'Franquin,' he shouted. 'Franquin is back.'

Three simple words. In a tone that said it all.

'Where is he?'

'Right now,' said Connors, 'he's trapped between two doors. One storey down. He can't go anywhere. But the problem is, neither can you.'

He could have explained. But his strength was running out. He was sweating and exhausted and it was getting worse by the minute, and somewhere below them was Franquin with a key card whose code he didn't know. He wasn't Keyes. And if only he'd known how to block it, just that one card, so that Janine and William could run away while Franquin remained trapped, then there wouldn't have been a problem. Aside from his itching back and stinging eyes, but that was something no one could fix, not even Keyes.

He closed his eyes for a second. Somewhere in the distance he'd heard William's voice, he'd heard it asking what to do, and he couldn't tell if it was one second ago or ten.

He summoned his energy, forced himself to come back. Looked at them, down the hall.

'There's only one way,' he said. 'How long will it take you to unload the carts?'

William looked into the room next to him. It had taken them fifteen minutes to load up; unloading shouldn't take more than five.

'I don't have a choice,' Connors said. 'For you to get out, the doors have to be unlocked. And the moment I open them for you . . .'

The rest of the sentence didn't need to be said.

If Franquin caught up with them, he wouldn't be as forgiving as Connors.

'I'll give you exactly five minutes. After that the doors will open. When they do, I want you to get back up into the castle and out of here.'

William nodded, but nobody moved.

'What about you?' asked Janine.

There was concern in her voice. A sincere and heartfelt concern that made the question real, and for a moment Connors seemed stunned, almost as if it was the first time he'd allowed himself to consider it.

'I think we know what happens to me,' was all he said.

He said it with a smile, but it was a smile devoid of joy.

And they watched him where he stood across the hallway, alive but sentenced to death, watched him without knowing what to say. There was nothing evil about Connors. He was a good man in a strange place, and everything he'd done had been well intentioned.

He deserved a better fate. He deserved to come with them, to get out of there and see the world recover, to sit in a pub some day in the future and drink a beer and know that life went on.

'How're you doing?' asked William through the silence.

'We've got pills,' Connors replied. As plainly as he possibly could. 'I'll be okay.'

Nobody spoke. But their eyes showed that they didn't believe him.

'It's the truth,' he said. 'I feel okay, we can ease the symptoms, it will be bearable. I promise.'

Bearable. The word alone hurt them.

'I took half a box this morning, I can hardly feel the itch. That's a good sign, don't you think?'

William paused for a second. Two seconds. Then:

'It's a very good sign.'

Connors gave new smile. *Thank you*, it said.

And he looked at Janine, looked at William, and they stood at opposite ends of a corridor, a goodbye without handshakes because that's how it had to be.

They lingered as long as they could over their silent parting; they knew it would be the last.

∞〇∞

Franquin was standing with his head against the wall when the diode suddenly turned green for no reason at all.

Exactly five minutes had passed, and he'd gone from anger to panic and then he'd pulled himself together and tried to come up with a solution. He'd failed and lapsed into resignation. And then he heard it. The lock, clicking behind him.

At first he could only look at the green diode in disbelief, as if it was toying with him. And then he'd raised his gun, left hand cradling his right, ready for anything.

In theory it could have been nothing more sinister than a technical malfunction. But that wasn't a theory he favoured. There shouldn't be anyone else still here. *Shouldn't.* But Connors had to be somewhere. And whatever was happening with the locks, it had to be because of him.

He pushed open the door with his shoulder.

Nobody there. Just metal and concrete. At the end of the corridor ahead of him was the next door, and behind that were the stairs to the next floor, and he ran sideways through the hallway, back against the wall and both hands on the weapon, ready to respond if anything happened.

Next door.

Already green.

There was no doubt. Someone was there.

Again he pushed it open with his shoulder, advanced up the stairs in quick, quiet steps, into the hallway at the top.

It was silent. Sterile. But he moved along it, gun in hand, ready for danger.

∞◯∞

The doors stood open, but even running takes time.

Janine and William sped through the castle, running without stopping and without looking back, their feet pounding across the smooth floor slabs, knowing that they were running for their lives.

They passed stairwells and corridors and the room where Janine hid William from the guards, archways and passages and the huge room with the chandelier and the projectors – places that they would never see again.

And every one of the thick security doors along the way stood unlocked, and they took them at full speed, breathless and scared but full of hope, and their mouths tasted of blood and their lungs hurt with the effort, but they kept running because it was the only thing they could do.

They ran and breathed and hoped and ran.

Behind them time ran at their heels.

And it was catching up fast.

∞◯∞

By the time Franquin sensed movement it was too late.

It was the light he noted first, the light that flickered, not the shadow behind it. Then suddenly a figure detached itself from the darkness and there he was, standing in the middle of the hallway, his gun raised at Franquin, just as he'd pointed it at William and Janine only minutes earlier.

But this time there was confidence in his stance. He was still shaking, but it was caused by the fever and not nerves. He knew he was doing the right thing and his body could itch all it wanted, because soon it would be over no matter what.

'I'd stay there if I were you,' said Connors.

The light danced across him from the side, and in the dark corridor it gave his contours a white glow, almost as if he was separated from the castle and floating mid-air, floating but with his feet wide apart on the floor and a gun in front of him.

Franquin raised his own weapon, his right hand firm on the grip, measuring the distance to his target, taking aim.

Of course he'd suspected. But he was disappointed all the same.

'Why are you doing this?' he asked.

Stopping me, he meant. Stopping me and violating protocol, staying in the castle instead of coming to the ship – and what the hell happened to the helicopter?

He was about to ask, but he stopped himself.

He already knew the answer. He could see it in Connors' eyes. No, not his eyes, he saw it in his entire face. There was a sheen of sweat on his skin and his features were etched with stress and pain. Franquin had seen others who looked that way.

'You're ill.'

He said it without lowering his gun.

And their eyes locked across the floor.

'So many scenarios,' said Connors. 'And yet I didn't come close to predicting this.'

He tilted his head to show what he meant. This. Here and now and the castle and you and me. This is where it will end, and how could we have known.

'You know why I'm here,' Franquin said.

And Connors shook his head. Not because he didn't know, of course he did, but because he couldn't allow it to happen.

'You know how we always used to say that it's better to save a few than let everyone go down together?'

Franquin didn't answer. Whatever Connors was about to say, he suspected he wouldn't like it.

'We were right,' Connors said. 'But we're not going to be among the saved.'

They stayed frozen, guns pointing at each other, both aware that they were caught up in a situation for which the protocol had made no provision. There were no rules to cover this, it was a chess composition that couldn't be solved: Connors was a larger threat to Franquin than his gun could ever be, and Franquin's gun was no more lethal than the illness Connors already had.

'Let me pass,' Franquin said. 'I have a job to do.'

Connors mutely shook his head.

'I don't want to shoot you.'

'You won't,' Connors replied.

And there was something in his voice. Something that made Franquin register the light that kept flickering from the side.

It was only then that he realised they were standing outside the crematorium. And that he understood the significance of the flickering light. Fuck Connors, he thought, fuck everything, and he ran up to the door to look into the room.

And Connors let him past. Backed away, without lowering his gun, let him stop at the doorway and take it all in.

'You can't!'

Franquin turned back to him, anguish in his voice. His gun was still raised, but it was a stand-off that meant nothing. Soon it would be over for both of them and nothing anyone did could stop it.

The crematorium fire roared inside a hatch in the wall. Heat radiated through the thick layers of security glass.

And on a slightly tilted conveyor lay a single crate.

The flames swirled hungrily inside the opening, the same flames that had once consumed Helena Watkins; they would now consume the olive-green crate, and when that happened everything would be over.

Around the conveyor lay more boxes of the same kind, waiting on top of the carts that had brought them there.

Grey, green, shades of brown. Labels in white and yellow, in English and Russian and other languages.

'This,' said Connors. 'This is how it's going to be.'

∞◯∞

They had just reached the wooden door in the low, narrow passageway, the one that led to the winding staircase which in turn led to the terrace where they'd hurl themselves over the edge to escape.

She was a dozen steps up when she heard her feet against the steps and realised there should have been another set of footsteps behind her.

She turned.

Crouched to get a better view of the door below.

'I can't,' William said behind her.

He stood at the bottom of the steps, wouldn't move, hadn't even started to climb the staircase. And she stepped down towards him, one step, one more, knew that they didn't have much time and definitely not for this.

'What're you doing?' she said, bewildered and frustrated and scared in a combination that probably just seemed angry.

'Give me five minutes,' he said. 'If I'm not back by then, go without me.'

She barked a reply, but he had already disappeared, his footsteps ringing out on the stone floors.

Part of her was prepared to leave him to it. After all, if the stupid old bastard wanted so badly to die then let him get on with it.

But she knew that she couldn't.

∞◯∞

Franquin had been the first to lower his gun.

And Connors had followed.

And there they stood.

Connors smiled.

Smiled through eyes full of tears, not from sorrow but because they had finally reached the end, smiled with a warmth and a confidence that surprised Franquin, no, it made him sad, sad and uncomfortable and overwhelmed by the knowledge that it was really over.

Connors had told him.

Told him what William had said, told him that all their theories had been wrong. That many would die, many but not all, and the tears had come when he said it, tears even though he smiled: the purple circles would grow and grow, but then they would start to shrink, and not everyone would be gone.

He had told him about the one thing they never considered.

That the codes didn't end where they thought, but went on and on and on. Who knew, maybe humanity would see more disasters, or maybe successes, or more likely the same old mixture of both, and somewhere, that was written too. Even though no one had read it yet.

They had spent their lives looking for the answer.

But the question was badly phrased.

That's what Connors had said, and that was all that Franquin had needed.

'You said the worst thing that could happen would be if they found out,' Connors said. 'Turns out you were wrong after all.'

But he said it as a friend, smiled as he said it.

It was a smile that said thank you. Thank you for the time we got. Thank you for everything.

'I think both of us were wrong,' said Franquin.

They stood there, looking at each other. Two men in uniform. It was all they had left, the pride and the posture and the knowledge that they'd spent their lives trying to do good.

'I can live with that,' said Connors.

∞◯∞

Janine caught up with William in his workroom. The one where all the pages had hung on the walls and where everything else had been left on his desk: all his books, all his computers, everything.

She stopped in the doorway, didn't speak.

Didn't know, but understood all the same.

All she could see was his back, but she didn't have to see his face to know.

He was biting his lip. Not crying, he was biting his lip, his eyes empty and his tongue pressed hard against his teeth to keep his emotions at bay.

Finally, he crouched down next to the table.

His face level with the computers.

The heavy green machine on the far right was the one he called Sara, and he rested his hand on it, gently and carefully, he let it lie there and didn't say a word, and yet it felt as if he was talking.

And one second passed and two seconds passed and then he stood again.

He hadn't heard that she came in after him.

He saw her standing in the doorway, he met her eyes with his, saw her wonder without asking.

And he shrugged. Smiled without smiling.

Nodded to her that they'd better be going.

And answered the question she hadn't asked.

'This time, I wanted to say goodbye.'

62

Sooner or later it had to happen, and so it did.

The green crate was made of wood, and the heat from the hole in the wall was so great that it couldn't resist.

Though it was still a metre away from the fire, the side started to turn black and the heat began to spread through its fibres in glowing red. After that it took only a matter of seconds for the flames to reach the heavy ammunition inside.

And there was no way to stop it.

All around stood other crates, stacked in line, and the fireball surged through them like a vibrating chain reaction that grew and burst and broke through the impenetrable safety glass and went on.

For the two men in the corridor outside, everything ended in one devastating wave of air.

63

They ran for their lives.

They left William's room and emerged out on to the terrace, and once there Janine didn't allow him time to hesitate. She lowered herself down into the darkness and he followed right behind; it was as death-defyingly dangerous as before, but staying behind didn't feel like an alternative. There simply were no options: if they stayed they would die and if they fell they would die too, and the only thing he could do was to hope the ropes would hold and that he could do what she had done before him, and if so then maybe they would survive after all.

They lowered themselves, gradually and with bouncing kicks against the vertical mountain, until finally they reached the ground. William was soaking with sweat. It was night and below zero and he was freezing, but his fear came out through his pores and the only thing he wanted was to lie down but there wasn't any time.

They kept running downhill. Left the castle behind, the terrace far above, kept running down the slope towards the lake. And then they circled around it to get as far away as possible before it happened.

There couldn't be much time left.

And they were halfway up the opposite hillside when time ran out.

William fell first.

The vibrations threw them both to the ground, face first into the sharp rocks, and they tried to hold on but couldn't. Next to him Janine lay clutching the surface, the same panicky grip as him but to no avail, both of them with eyes closed and tucking their heads into their chests to protect their faces from stones and pebbles that kept shaking past them down the slope.

Once the tremors began it felt as if they would never end. The steep slope and the shaking ground beneath them made it impossible to get a grip, and they slid down, skidding over gravel and scree, trying to ignore the stinging pain, the ground scraping against their skin, scrabbling to find things to hold on to. But neither of them managed to stop, and below them were the drops they'd avoided on their way up. The last thing they wanted was to pass them on their way down again.

Janine was about to give up when she managed to catch hold. She felt the flat stone as it passed underneath her, and she was prepared with both hands, grabbed it with a climbing grip around its edge and managed to stop. And she reached out to William, and their hands locked at the same time, held on to each other with cramping grips as the tremors continued, the shaking and the roar and the rocks that rumbled by on their way down.

Somewhere underground it had already begun. And nobody knew how long it would last.

And William opened his eyes. Carefully, slowly, his head close to the ground and his face covered. He let his gaze continue under his arm, across the alpine lake below, across the concentric waves whipped up by the shaking ground, and over to the castle on the other side.

It stood there.

Stood the way it had for hundreds of years.

They had done all they could. There was nothing more they could do except to hold on, waiting for the earth to stop trembling and for an end to the increasing subterranean roar. The process had started.

And no one could stop it.

The explosives had done their job.

They had rolled along the same conveyor belt as Helena Watkins, into the same flaming furnace, and like her body they had caught fire.

The resulting shockwave ripped through the maze of tunnels like a speeding subway train made up of heat and fire, finding its way through the corridors in a cloud of smoke, splitting up where passages peeled off in different directions and joining again where staircases and hallways met.

Like liquid in a network of pipes the fire surged through the underground maze, grew in size and strength and heat and disintegrated everything in its path.

The parliament. The blue rigid chairs in front of the rows of thin monitors. Nobody was there to see them ignite the moment before the fire train rushed in, nobody saw them char in the oncoming wind, but that was what happened. And the train went on and on, seemingly endless, filling room after room with clouds that bloomed in red and yellow and made everything melt and evaporate, and nowhere did it stop, it just travelled on.

The treatment room with its rows of bodies.

The corridors of steel and concrete and aluminium.

The storage rooms with other crates that boarded the train and made everything bigger and larger and stronger and hotter.

And the computer hall, the rows of rolling storage tape, the working consoles with controls and lamps and panels that had blinked the same way for fifty years. Everything was engulfed by the flames, and nobody would ever get to learn their secrets.

Where the corridors ended the thick security doors proved no defence. Without a crumb of resistance they folded to the pressure, allowing fire and heat to stream past, surging onward into more and more passages, obliterating walls and the load-bearing beams that had been put there to prevent it all from collapsing.

And above it rested the mountain.

And on that, all the stones that formed the castle.

And eventually, it became too much.

On the outside, it started gently.

Fragments breaking off and tumbling down the façades, falling like a powder at first, pieces so small and fine as to be almost invisible, and then bigger and bigger as the cracks spread and the debris increased in size.

Once the first stone had left its spot it was as if the floodgates opened. Every new hole created another, stones that had rested on their neighbours had nothing to rest on, and with a roar everything started to crumble, whole sections toppling out of place, twisting as they fell and causing new holes until the entire the structure began to disintegrate, teetering as if fighting to stay intact but unable to resist the reverberations within.

It went on for longer than William and Janine had expected.

The mountains echoed to the thunder and roar and clatter of stones striking stones against even more stones. Bit by bit the castle seemed to pull itself apart and one section after another fell down into the cloud and disappeared.

The building that had started the day as a medieval castle, almost a city of masonry that sprang from the mountain and reflected in the lake with a beauty that was only known to a few, that building was reduced to a thick curtain of dust, hovering over a crater of fire and heat as if the mountain had opened a door to the centre of the planet.

And all that time, they lay there. Shielded their faces from dust and rocks, watched and didn't watch and wondered when it was going to end.

And then, finally, it did.

No walls were left to crumble, no towers to collapse, and the huge cloud of smoke was slowly starting to drift to the ground again, settling like a thick, transparent soufflé in the pot that were the mountains.

And then came the silence.

The rumble had stopped, and no one had noticed.

It had faded out into a crackling hiss, the rumble lingering as an echo across the lake, like waves after a storm that had passed. And in the midst of the silence the mountain seemed to sigh. One last, suffering breath that swallowed everything, and when the castle was gone the flames reached the surface.

And they danced towards the sky as if celebrating a victory.

It was supposed to end in a fire.

That was how it was written.

It would be large and violent and end it all.

And perhaps this was it.

Perhaps it was some other fire, somewhere else.

Whichever it was, it didn't matter any more. Whichever fire it meant, it wasn't the last thing to happen.

64

The season seemed to have been waiting for the news.

Now that it had arrived, it was as if the snow dared to melt, the earth dared to begin smelling of spring, grass that had been glued to the ground dared to stand up, slowly like after a fight, ducking yellow straws in a wind that dared to be warm.

The danger was over.

No new cases had been reported in the amount of time that the authorities had specified and around the world health organisations cautiously lifted their restrictions. No new bodies were lined up in overcrowded ice rinks, no new homes were sealed off and people moved freely outside without being stopped.

It had been a war with no victor. In the cities there were no parades and no confetti, everyone had lost and the only thing that remained was to piece the world back together.

The main thing was, the danger was over.

Four months had passed, and it was over.

And reality didn't mind clichés.

The new season arrived with a vitality that belonged on a choco-late box, fluffy clouds hung above the mountains, layer upon layer of distant alps in increasing shades of blue the further away they were.

It was spring.

And just like every other year it brought with it a sense of wonder that life could begin again.

∞◯∞

She found him out on the hillside.

William sat gazing over the landscape, the plains and the meadows and the firing range that they couldn't see but that lay there, somewhere beyond the hills and the roads that swirled like ribbons over soft parcels, down into the valley and vanishing in the sunny haze.

Janine sat down next to him.

Laid down, her back in the cool grass.

And they lay there, side by side, two copies of the same page in one eternal book, surrounded by other pages all around them on the ground and in the air and watching them from the distant cliffs.

They lay there until the sun moved on and settled behind the mountains.

Until the sounds of cars began to hum in the distance.

Neither of them had to say it.

They knew. Like migratory birds, they knew.

The time had come to leave.

∞○∞

The people who returned to the alpine village were few in number, but nobody could know whether more would come or if this was all.

The reunions were fond but sad, and in the streets there were cars with open trunks, bags in rows between trickles of snowmelt, people of every age hugging and opening doors and removing protective boards from their windows.

And all of this they saw from their car.

They saw them pass outside their windows, the people who'd been their involuntary hosts, the people who'd fled and come back, and with tyres crunching against gravel Leo steered them out of the village, left it like a shrinking Tyrolean scene behind them.

They had been on the road for hours, taking shifts to drive and taking turns to sleep, when Janine leaned over towards the front seat.

William sat in the passenger seat, watching as the road lines kept disappearing under their car, his mind empty of thoughts.

He sensed Janine's head next to his.

Didn't say anything, and neither did she. Perhaps she had nothing to say, perhaps there was nothing more to talk about, and they sat with their heads close, mile after mile, and there was nothing strange about that.

'If they'd never found the texts,' she said at last.

Her voice was relaxed, it was calm and silent, as if it was the most natural way in the world to start a conversation.

And he nodded, still watching the lines.

He already knew what she would say, it was the same question again, but she was about to turn it around and ask it backwards.

He knew, because it was the question he asked himself. Over and over again.

'If they hadn't read them,' she continued, 'and hadn't made a virus, and never caused all this to happen. Would the predictions still have said the same thing?'

William raised his eyes, watched the landscape billow past. Felt his thoughts walk in circles around the question. Would it somehow have happened anyway, just because that's what was written? Or would the predictions have read differently, because the disease would never occur?

If a tree falls in the forest, he thought. Who the hell cares.

But he didn't say that.

'No matter how much we ask ourselves that question,' he said, 'we'll never ever get to know.'

She nodded.

And then he turned in his seat. And looked at her.

'I think that is for the better.'

Neither of them spoke again for hours.

It was a warm and peaceful silence that nobody had to talk to fill.

They travelled north along empty highways, passing town after town, some were empty and would stay that way, others were alive with people who'd returned and were cautiously trying to start afresh.

The future had begun.

And nobody knew what it held.

After all, that was how the future worked best.

∞O∞

They parted ways in Amsterdam.

They did it without ceremony, quietly nodding their good-byes.

There were bigger things to mourn, they were the ones who

were left and there was no reason to waste sorrow on someone you could see again, probably wouldn't, but *could*; they knew how to get in touch if they wanted, but nobody knew if they should. They had survived together. And maybe that was enough. When everyday life returned and things went back to normal, who knew if they would have anything left in common?

William stood up too, got out of the car in a wordless goodbye, and now he stood behind the car and watched Janine and her fiancé disappear down the street.

Past the crossing where Albert had seen Neijzen's men.

Down the street where the blue Golf ran down one of their pursuers.

Memories that ran through Albert's head, but that William couldn't imagine; all he saw was a street that was empty and starting to bloom and that waited for everyone who was still alive to return to their homes.

Only once they'd gone inside did William get back into the car.

Leo sat behind the wheel. Looked at William, said nothing.

They were parked up against the kerb, a drain cover half-hidden under the car on William's side. And for a moment William sat there, staring at the asphalt through the open door.

He pressed himself back into the seat. Reached into the inside pocket of his jacket. There.

The black notebook.

And before closing the door, he leaned back out of the car, felt his way with the edge of the book along the ground until its spine slotted between the bars of the drain cover. Let it go, watched it drop into the darkness.

Because who the hell reads a diary.

When you're gone, who wants to know what you did some Monday in March?

Leo remained silent.

And William looked straight ahead.

'Mind if I sleep for a while?' he said.

Leo nodded.

Started the car.

If he drove without stopping they'd make Stockholm by sunrise.

65

The apartment on Kaptensgatan had had a sheet of plywood nailed to the doors where his shattered windows had been, and he paused in the stairwell with the key in his hand before finally summoning the courage to unlock them.

Inside, the security door stood open. Unlocked and sawn to pieces and impossible to close. And behind it hung the smell that always came when the apartment was left for long enough. The smell of reality, the one that took over when nobody was there to create the illusion that the world had a natural scent of lemon and was a neat and tidy place, and that there was nothing strange about that, in spite of the chaos and hell that was life.

On his doormat the newspapers had grown into piles. Their headlines larger and larger as things had evolved, their pictures darker and sadder.

The last one dated January.

Then they'd stopped coming.

They lay on his floor, like a record of the last months' events. Like a timeline, not in code, but in black and white. Written after they happened, and not the opposite.

It had only just blown over.

And yet it seemed distant.

Nothing had happened.

And everything had changed.

He remained standing inside his door for minutes.

Didn't breathe. Didn't know what to do.

Looked into the apartment. Into his place. His life.

Finally, he took off his coat, hung it over a chair by the door.

Continued down the hallway.

He was home.

William Sandberg walked into the bathroom and turned on the taps.

Acknowledgments

They say writing books is a lonely job. Truth to be told, it isn't. It's just what people around me gradually start wishing it were.

As always, the more important the text, the smaller the type. So here's my warmest gratitude, expressed in the most illegible of fonts.

Wilhelm Behrman for telling me to write this book.

Bettina Bruun for standing the fact that I did.

Skelle, My and *Nevas* just because.

Mum and *dad* and *sister* for never asking when I'm going to get a real job. I guess by now that ship has sailed for good.

Calle Marthin for an enthusiasm I hadn't expected.

Jonas and *Agnes* and *Céline* and *Julie* at Partners in Stories for an adventure I hadn't been able to come up with myself.

Helene and *Katarina* and *Klara* and *Isabella* and everyone else at Wahlström & Widstrand for warm guidance in a new landscape.

And not least *Mats Almegård* for the Christmas buffet. You're next, goddammit.

Finally, my warmest thanks to everyone who read and asked me clever questions. *Bettina*, of course. *Wille*, incessantly. *Kerstin Almegård, Birgitta Wännström, Jerk Malmsten, Fredrick Tallroth*.

Without the lot of you this hadn't been half as much fun.
Which is true about many other things as well.

About the Author

Born in 1969 outside Göteborg on the Swedish west coast, Fredrik T. Olsson spent most of his childhood writing, acting and producing plays. Refusing to grow up, this is pretty much what he has kept doing since. A full-time screenwriter for film and television since 1995, Fredrik has written scripts in genres ranging from comedy to thrillers, as well as developing, showrunning and head-writing original material for various Swedish networks. He is also a standup comedian and makes occasional contributions as a director.